BLOOD AND FROST

The door was open; he was enveloped in warmth, the cottony drumming of the jukebox, the smell of food—but it was different now. One color washed over it all.

White. The bone-white color of death, of frost, of the full moon. Bleached and frozen faces looked back at him.

Marla. But he hadn't come for Marla, not this time.

Wendy. He saw her standing there, Ben Taylor beside her, towering over her.

Ransom felt the contractions of laughter in his throat, but there was no sound.

Then: amazement.

He moved with such grace, with such speed, with such power. He felt himself in motion, as if he were watching from the window of a machine, in awe of what it could do.

Talons flashing, the machine swung at Taylor. Bone exploded against flesh, and Taylor's face jerked out of Ransom's line of sight. Taylor staggered backward, one hand covering his face, blood running between the fingers. Ransom lunged into him. Blood and frost. Blood and moonlight. The machine of his body raged out of control. He felt terror, he felt joy, and they were the same . . .

FULL MOON
MICK WINTERS

BERKLEY BOOKS, NEW YORK

FULL MOON

A Berkley Book/published by arrangement with
the authors

PRINTING HISTORY
Berkley edition/May 1989

ISBN: 0-425-11472-4

A BERKLEY BOOK ® TM 757,375
Berkley Books are published by the Berkley Publishing Group,
200 Madison Avenue, New York, NY 10016
The name ''BERKLEY'' and the ''B'' logo
are trademarks belonging to the Berkley Publishing Corporation.

PRINTED IN THE UNITED STATES OF AMERICA

10 9 8 7 6 5 4 3 2 1

*To Ron Wolfe and John Wooley
who showed me the way
out of the cellar.*

—M.W.

PROLOGUE

And the moon rose. . . .

The full moon ascended into the night sky over Lookout Mountain with a brightness that smothered the rows of candle-lit party lanterns on the McGivern's back lawn. Kate McGivern, as always, was playing the perfect hostess, her smile worn as stylishly as the white silk with lace medallion gown she had "discovered" for the occasion on a rushed shopping flight to Memphis.

Not one of the local shops has been able to show her an "entirely suitable" choice, but that was Chattanooga for you, Kate thought: a place content with being old and picturesque. The big houses on Lookout Mountain sat as if in judgement of the city, and the mountain itself seemed less imposing than the McGivern estate—especially tonight, the night of Kate and Chester McGivern's annual Fall Fete.

Kate was a whirl of motion, of greetings, of introductions, of discreet but inviolable instructions to the serving staff.

By Kate's order, the buffet table was never to appear "picked over." It was bountifully stocked and replenished with sliced smoked turkey, fruits, cheeses, wines, and a chocolate dessert fondue. The white wine was Antinori Galestro, and the finest cheese a French Camembert encrusted with grape seeds.

"The best for the best," Kate liked to say.

She managed it all with a practiced grace as flawless as the waves of her silver-blue hair. Nothing put her off-stride that night, not even the questions about her husband—the awkwardness, the embarrassment of those questions about Chester.

1

"Where *is* Chet?"

"What's become of ol' Chester, Kate?"

"Chester is all right, isn't he?"

He was called to the phone, she said once. And won't you try the Virginia baked ham? He had gone to meet friends at the airport, she said. And here—you simply don't dare miss the Waldorf salad.

He had gone to search for something "entirely special" in the wine cellar, she said, or—to Judge Winegar, who expected a joke—gone to hide the good Scotch.

The truth was, she didn't know. But only Kate's closest friends might have noticed the slightly flat tone of her voice, the surreptitious darting of her eyes.

Now she scanned the crowd of suits and black ties, satins and pleats, all belonging to bankers and chairmen of the board, state and national officeholders, a former governor, a symphony conductor. *They* were there, the *creme de la creme*, many of them from out of town and even from out of state, from Georgia and even farther. And Chester—darling husband Chester.

Where was he?

The musicians assembled again, striking up "Tennessee Waltz." With the first bars of the song she slipped away, as unobtrusively as possible, through the crowd, making her way toward the house. She slipped through the back door, looking around stealthily to see if anyone had noticed her departure. Satisfied that they hadn't, she turned, her eyes scanning the room.

"Chet?" she called. The sound of her own voice echoed harshly from the high ceiling of the foyer, and her image, reflected in the mirror beside the entranceway, showed something more than irritation, something less than concern. She paused before the mirror, brushing at the waist folds of her gown out of habit, but she needn't have bothered. It was flawless, the lines displaying that smoothness, that *rightness*, that came only in a designer original, right down to the ruffled sleeves, as white and as sinfully soft as whipped cream. The effect, she decided, was marred only by the shadow-etched scowl on her face, and that was Chester's fault.

With a deep, quivering outrush of breath she took the curving stairway up to the second-floor bedroom level.

Chester had made no secret of dreading her parties. He never spoke much about the investments and tax shelters that bulwarked the estate, and outside of business he scarcely talked at all. He was certainly no good at lawn-party chitchat. But he knew there was no way of getting out of it—Kate made sure of that.

"Chet . . . ?" she called again.

A cold slap of moonlight crossed the floor from the window facing the second-floor landing. The hallways were dark.

Suddenly Kate's foot struck something on the floor. Kneeling, she picked it up. A man's shoe. She looked down the hallway, and there was the second shoe, just out of her reach. As she stared, her eyes seemed to burn into the darkness, adjusting, and soon she could see that the hallway was littered with clothes, littered all the way to the door of Chet's bedroom. It was closed.

Her face flushed as her mind raced back to the last time she had seen him that night, standing perfectly alone beside the punch bowl, his hands in his pockets. She clicked off the names, the dress styles, the jewelry of the women who might have found Chester appealing, double chin and all. She looked again at the randomly scattered clothes. They were all his.

Creeping to the door, she leaned carefully over and pressed her ear to it. From within she heard a scraping noise, a kind of scuffling. And sobbing.

Kate pushed open the door.

The room was a shambles. Every drawer had been pulled from every dresser, the cedar chest lay upset and spilled, and the closet doors had been thrown open. Throughout the room Kate made out the images of laundry-wrapped shirts, ties, dress coats, pants, underwear, pajamas—all scattered as if a burglar had rooted through them, all tossed ragtag across the floor and draped randomly over the four-poster bed.

"Ches-*ter*!"

He stepped naked out of the closet, looking through her. At his back, the drapes to the window were open, moonlight flooding in around him. His face looked slack and white in the half darkness.

Kate suddenly laughed without knowing why. She started to turn on the lamp beside the bed, stopped, and stood looking at him, her hand dangling in midair near the switch. He didn't move. Beyond him, through the window, she saw the couples dancing to "Greensleeves" on the lawn, and muted strains of the music came to her ears. It all seemed impossibly far away.

After a moment her husband's mouth began to move. Tentatively, as if it were trying to form words, as if it were groping. And then, "I . . ."

"You can explain?" Kate suddenly felt dreadfully sick.

He swallowed. "I . . . I never thought of it before," he said slowly. "I don't know where . . . it came from."

"It?" Still looking at him, she felt herself backing away.

"The *question*. The damned *question*, Kate. It won't go away. It came in my head like a whisper, and now it's *screaming* at me. It hurts, Kate." With a quick movement that surprised her, he clapped his hands against his ears. "It *hurts*!"

She straightened. A deep breath gave her the resolve that in other circumstances she would have sought with a stiff brandy and a Dvořák recording. "Get dressed and come down," she said firmly, her gaze unwavering. "We will talk of this later."

He looked at her helplessly, his hands sliding down the side of his face. "But . . . the *question*, Kate."

"*Later.*" Her voice bore the anger that she had wanted to load into it the moment she had seen him there like that. His mind had been slipping; she knew that. The sale of his company had changed him. But he could wait, damn him. He could hold on. Whatever was wrong with him, he could last the night.

She turned from him, realizing that the music from outside had stopped, replaced with polite, faraway applause.

He called to her. "Which are the clothes that I'll wear when I die, Kate?" His voice was querulous, pleading. "Do I already have what I'll wear when I die?"

Dizziness clung to her as she stepped into the hallway, her mind trying to block out his words, refusing to believe what it was hearing.

From behind her: "Will I die wearing . . . *this*, maybe? This coat, these pants? This shirt? Is *this* the shirt? It feels cold, it feels . . . *dead*, Kate. You hear me? I can't put *this* on. Tell me. You always tell me what to wear, Kate. Which . . . ?"

Insane. The man had snapped, and she wanted to run now, but she knew she couldn't in the high heels. She crossed the hallway as rapidly as she could, her skirt swishing against the polished oak floor, her heels clicking. She grasped the banister, started down the staircase toward the sound of barely audible conversation and the three-four rhythm of ''The Waltz You Saved for Me.''

''*Which*, Kate?'' And now he was bellowing, and his voice went through her, around her, seemed to fill the air and carry to the party outdoors.

She whirled around as if to face him, but all she saw was the moon looming through the landing window, the pits and craters in vivid detail against the glowing white, so close that it suddenly looked as if it might fall through the glass and crush her.

She backed up a step, felt her foot slide past the edge of a carpeted stair, the heel of her shoe snapping. Her knee buckled, twisted, and then she was sailing backward, screaming, arms outstretched as if to clutch at the moon.

She hit, and something tore loose at the small of her back. Rolled and hit again, her legs numbed.

She knew then, with freezing clarity, that she was in the air, that either time had stopped or she had gone through the banister, that she was dying or had died or would die, and it didn't matter which.

Which? Which, Kate? Which?

A white silk with lace medallion gown, and a special trip to buy it, and she thought of how it had stood out, had practically called to her from the store window.

Nothing else would have fit the occasion.

And the moon rose. . . .

It rose, spilling a flat light the color of frost over the highway.

''Two nights now, an' no sign of th' flong-donger,'' Busted Tom was muttering. He talked in a closemouthed way that scarcely twitched the stub of a cigarette between his lips. ''I'd say th' man ain't gonna show.''

''Can it!'' Rooster made the order stick with a sharp backhanded slap to Busted Tom's dead right arm. ''An' that goes down th' line, hear me? All of you. Just shut up an' watch.''

A beer can hit the pavement with a hollow clang that was louder than it would have been anywhere else but out there, out where the silence was trapped like a fog between the night glow of Phoenix and the dark wall of the Superstition Mountains.

Rooster eyed left and right for any show of a hassle. The bikes were aligned on either side of him in a blockade across the two-lane. The riders—Busted Tom and Stoney, Kite, Joseph, Booger, Slug, Randy, Shovelhead—knew better than to give him any shit; they sat and watched, and the road stretched like a long, pale blade stabbed into the mountains ahead.

Rooster spat. Chewed the ends of his moustache. Spat again.

He felt the warmth of his lady's breath against the back of his neck, but he didn't respond when she held him.

She called herself Freedom. She had blond hair that streamed in the wind when she rode behind Rooster. Her arms barely reached far enough to wrap around the barrel-shaped expanse of Rooster's chest: the muscled shape of a weight-lifter with a taste for pain.

". . . you still think he's for real, babe?" Freedom said. "For real, not a ghost? . . ."

Rooster knew the game she had going. She wanted the rest of the Satyrs to know she could question him, and she could get away with it. He liked the feel of her: the way she fit against him.

"Yeah, he's real." Rooster clasped both of Freedom's interlocked hands in one of his; he squeezed until he knew it must have hurt. "He's too much for real."

"Yeah," he said quietly. "He's too much for real."

Slug set fire to the end of a marijuana cigarette, the lighter flame illuminating the huge tattoos of green dragons and black panthers along the insides of his pasty forearms. Rooster turned toward him, saw what he was doing.

"Toss it, brother," Rooster ordered. "You've had enough. I want you straight tonight."

Slug looked up, the flame reflected in his deep-set eyes. "Man . . . !" he began petulantly. He had a woman's thin, high-pitched voice.

"Rooster's right," said Joseph, his three hundred pounds giving his Harley the look of a polished toy gleaming beneath him. Even on a ride he kept the bike sparkle-dusted like a show machine. "We come halfway 'cross th' country, man. We don't get shitfaced and screw it up now."

Slug looked from Joseph to Rooster, then sent the roach spinning to the road, showering orange sparks.

"We'll set the man's heart right, Rooster," Kite said. "That's for sure. We'll get 'im for Tony."

Rooster's fists tightened to white knuckles against the handle grips. "He's mine," Rooster said. "Remember that."

They sat in silence then, looking toward the black mass of the mountain range, the highest peaks outlined in moonlight against the night sky. After a moment Rooster blinked, then jammed shut his eyes with a quick, violent shake of his head, but the smell—friggin' hospital smell—stayed with him. Every time he thought of Tony he could still taste the stink of the place, feel it sinking into him. It went with the image of Tony lying there, and the pieces of Tony's face showing through the bandages, purple and green and white, as white as the bed sheets.

Tony. Little brother Tony. But, Rooster remembered, between the two of them it seemed like Tony was always the big one. The bitchin'est chicks, the fastest bikes, the meanest fights—Tony got the first and best of everything, and Rooster loved him for it. Just about nobody got the high hand on Rooster, but nobody, flat *nobody*, took a ride over Tony. Not until . . .

It all went together. That sick smell, the bandages, Tony rolling around burning up with fever, babbling garbage. And the two words that came at last: Moon Rider. Tony's voice, dry and low and cracked; the blood at the corners of his mouth. And him saying, "Moon Rider."

Stoney straightened, his boots scraping against the road. "Rooster," he said, "I been thinkin'."

"You scared, man?"

"Nah." Stoney swiped at the spill of white-blond hair across his face. The scar over his left eye looked lightning-white in the moonlight. "Thinkin' is all." His eyes locked straight on the highway.

Rooster knew what he meant. Even in L.A., the stories got around about the Moon Rider, about how you don't want to head east out of Phoenix anytime near the night of the full moon, and not on *that* night, not ever. Booze stories. But, all the same, a lot of the bros took a wide sweep around Phoenix when the moon was ripe.

Tony must have heard the same crap, too, Rooster thought. Moon Rider comes out of nowhere, wheels on fire, and watch out, brother. He'll kill you for the shine in your eye.

Tony, though—he was the kind to hear a buzz like that, to aim his knees to the breeze and go on out looking for trouble. Tony would've taken it as a dare. Maybe that was the way it happened, Rooster thought.

And the truth was, Rooster hadn't asked the rest of the Satyrs to ride out with him. But he was damn glad they had.

Booger slouched forward across his bike, snapping open the blade of a fold-up buck knife with a practiced flick of his thumb. Practice had paid off for Booger; he could work the thing as fast as a switchblade. Randy was fooling with a length of chain draped over the tank in front of him. The moon climbed to the center of the sky.

Busted Tom broke the silence. "Maybe this ain't always th' road he cruises," he said.

"Told ya to can it." Rooster's voice was a leathery hiss. Sure, he thought, it might've made better sense to stay on the move. But this was the place—*the* place—where Tony got scraped off the roadside, where they had picked him up and hauled him down the road to the hospital in Phoenix. In a station wagon, a fuggin' station wagon with mom 'n' pop and the back end full of rug rats; a pisser of a last ride for him.

Something startled Rooster from his thoughts. He peered up ahead, squinting his eyes, and saw a flicker of light playing against the dark rise of the mountains, in line with the highway.

Freedom suddenly pointed in the direction of the light. "Rooster—" she began, but he silenced her, nodding. His pulse thudded.

Across the line of bikes, the riders straightened. The light sharpened as they watched, sharpened to the white bead of a headlight, and then they heard it: the unmistakable, angry thundering of a Harley. Wide open and coming at them.

"Let 'im get up on us," Rooster directed in a voice that was half whisper, half growl. Behind him, Freedom slid from the bike seat, taking to the safe side without being told for a change. She peeled out of her tube top, knotted it onto the handlebar of Rooster's bike, and then she was gone into the shadows, just as the sound of the oncoming bike turned to a dragon's roar.

"Now!" Rooster shouted. "Kick 'em!"

The bikes screamed to life, a wall of noise, their headlights flaring on and sweeping the road, bathing it.

Rooster watched, waited for the Moon Rider's bike to cut a *U*, the scene to come playing in his mind. The motha would turn and run, and they would chase him down, and Rooster would be leading the pack. He'd get to him *first*.

"What's *wrong* with 'im, man?" Slug whined through the noise.

"The fugger's insane," returned Joseph. With a grunt he bent forward, pulling the .38 snub-nose out of the stash pocket strapped to his ankle.

"Rooster," Busted Tom shouted, "maybe we got the wrong man here. You think of that, Rooster?"

The oncoming bike reared onto its back wheel, up and up, the headlight piercing the sky, like a screaming beast erect on its hind legs.

"We got the right man," Rooster said. He felt ice in his throat.

Ghost stories, beer stories, didn't scare him. Insanity did. The cold, moon-white spectre of insanity scared the hell out of him.

Moon Rider!

The bike seemed to be coming in slow motion toward him. It was madness on wheels; it was coming straight on.

Rooster took count of the odds. There was going to be blood spilled. And death—he could sense it.

He felt a flash of anger at Tony. If Tony had just hauled his tail out of here—a small show of brains, man—then Rooster and the Satyrs wouldn't be out on this road now.

They wouldn't be about to get themselves broken up.

But Tony wouldn't have known how to run, Rooster thought. If he had known, then he wouldn't have been the Tony that Rooster loved. And maybe this was the best thing of all that Tony could have left to him: the chance to finish the fight.

Rooster spoke to the thing on the road in a voice so low, it might have been only a thought.

"You could be the devil himself for all I care, you son of a bitch. You're dead."

Tears of rage slashed at Rooster's cheeks. He geared his bike into a lunge toward the Moon Rider, even as the Rider tore into the bleached sweep of the Satyr's headlights.

Rooster caught only a fragmented glimpse of man and bike, chrome and black leather, red mouth wide and laughing, wind-shipped mane of dark hair, huge hands gloved in black, the knuckles spike-studded.

Busted Tom, then Stoney, got knocked aside. Stoney's bike hit the road surface spinning, throwing sparks and metal, grinding Stoney beneath it.

Rooster saw Joseph's pistol flash then, but the flash was a ragged splinter fired high into the air, and another bike—Kite's—went crashing. Rooster twisted out of the way, and Booger, pitched backward, cracked headfirst onto the concrete in front of Rooster's bike, his mouth spilling scarlet.

With an oath Rooster gunned into the middle of the thrashing, shadowed bodies—into roaring, screaming, the whistling swing of Randy's chain and Shovelhead's bellowing. He was aware of a pale thing, writhing and twisting on the pavement beside him in a pool of glistening darkness. Slug's dragon-and-panther tattooed arm—*and hell, where was the rest of him?*

Then nothing made sense, nothing came into focus but the hand thrust against his neck, locking around his throat, so close to his face that Rooster could smell the leather.

Rooster suddenly felt himself being lifted, his legs flailing like a hanged man's. And he was amazed at the feeling of his eyes bulging, swelling out of their sockets like a pair of boiled eggs. He hung there a moment, and then he was suddenly falling, and still falling, and he knew he had been thrown, tossed like a piece of scrap meat.

When the impact came, it was as soft as a pillow slap. He didn't feel hurt at all, and he lay there, marveling, wondering why he couldn't move, couldn't so much as turn his head.

The Moon Rider. His face filled Rooster's vision, the mouth grinning above him, opened black as death, the teeth smeared red. And then the Moon Rider's bike yanked, back end toward him in a half-circle turn, the Rider's laugh rising above the exhaust blast. The taillight was blindingly crimson. Rooster saw the Rider's arm shoot out, clubbing Randy to the pavement, and then he was gone in a shower of road gravel.

The image was replaced by Freedom's face peering into Rooster's, her hot tears falling onto his cheeks. "Babe, babe," she cried, and the curls of her blond hair fell against his face, stirring the wetness of her tears.

Rooster's eyes flickered, first to one side and then to the other. There was Randy, bent to his knees and spitting blood. Over there, Shovelhead, standing crookedly, grabbing at his knee. He could hear Joseph moaning softly, somewhere nearby.

Rooster swallowed, and Freedom's eyes swam before him. "Get 'im," he said, his voice rasping. "We'll . . . get 'im. I . . . want . . . his eyes."

"Sure, babe, sure." She ran a hand over his forehead. It felt cool.

"Get me . . . up."

The sound of the Moon Rider's bike came to him out of the darkness, taunting him. Rooster felt Freedom's hands, trembling, under his shoulders.

Suddenly she jerked back. Rooster's eyes flashed again, and he saw Randy's head snap toward the road, Shovelhead's lurching step backward.

The bike sound roared louder, louder. And there again— the piercing star of the headlight.

Rooster knew before she said it.

"Oh, Lord, Rooster," Freedom said. "He's coming back."

And the moon rose. . . .

Splinters of moonlight slid through the window blinds into the darkness of Petey's apartment. He rose, trembling, out of his bed, with its stiffly ironed sheets—Petey's mother ironed *everything*—and crossed the creaking hardwood floor, looking out toward Iowa's Capitol building.

There was no chance of sleep for him. Upstairs, the people were having a party again, and the stereo bass made it sound like they were dropping rocks on the floor in time to the music. They had a lot of parties up there. Sometimes he would pound on the ceiling with the back of a kitchen chair,

but they would just pound back and laugh at him. One girl—
Linda, he knew somehow that her name was Linda and that
she had long hair as fine and straight as corn silk—had a voice
like a bell chime, so clear that she might as well have been
standing beside him, laughing at him, saying "Farm boy . . .
farm boy . . ."

The window, five floors up, gave him a view over the rooftops and store tops of Des Moines like he imagined it would
look from an airplane. If he thought about that hard enough,
he could even feel the shake of the engines, and the ground
would move under him.

Moonlight ran, glinting, over the golden dome of the distant state Capitol building. Petey didn't like to look at it, but
he only had one window, and therefore little choice. So he
gazed out at the dome, and he thought about how it had
seemed to him the first time he ever saw it, about how it had
felt to be five years old and rattling into Des Moines in the
back end of his dad's rust-red old Ford pickup and suddenly
catching sight of that dome. Gods and dragons lived there;
he had been sure of it. And afterward he hadn't cared anymore for playing hide-and-seek in the rows of corn, or even
watching when the vet came at midnight for a calving. He
had begun to dream of gold and magic.

Upstairs they had Motley Crue and "Girls, Girls, Girls"
on the stereo—he knew because he had heard the song on his
radio a couple of times, but he bet they didn't know he knew.
Would they ever be surprised if he told them. Suddenly one
of the girls whooped, and a bottle or something else made of
glass broke against the floor, and somebody moved the furniture around for a minute. Linda called, "Sooorrry, farm
boy." He tried to ignore them.

Petey shuffled around the apartment, picking up clothes
and paperback books, rinsing off the dishes in the sink because his mother would be coming again tomorrow to check
on him. He dreaded that. It meant that he would have to
spend the day walking around town or at the library, so she
wouldn't come early and find him at home and know that he
had lost his job. She would talk about how he ought to be in
college, how his dad would be willing to sell off some of the
land for tuition money, even though Petey knew that the farm
was barely a paying operation as it was. She would coax him,

trying to get him to come back, even though the work was not enough to justify a part-time hand. She would leave, and he would ache with guilt at the thought of her driving so far and so often to see him.

Some of the books he shoved under the bed—*Conan the Barbarian*, *John Carter, Warlord of Mars*, and *The Hobbit* and the Lord of the Rings trilogy. A few he stacked in a row on the window ledge so she wouldn't be suspicious but at the same time wouldn't start in again about his spending so much time reading "all that tomfoolery."

"Hey, farm boy . . ." It was Linda again. "Come on up, farm boy. Come up with us. You'll have a *real good* time." Her voice choked with laughter.

Petey stared through the window blinds. The dome seemed to shimmer; it did that when he looked at it hard enough, long enough, but only under a full moon. It radiated gold. He could stand on top of that dome, he thought, clad in gleaming gold armor, and call down a dragon out of the moon.

Of course, he knew better. Many times he had walked across town to the Capitol building and had found it to be just another office building full of dull-faced men carrying briefcases and newspapers. There were guards there to tell him, in bored tones, that the dome rose to 275 feet above the ground floor of the building, which was of modified Renaissance architecture, and that no, he could not climb to the top of it.

They didn't know the magic. But he did.

The trick was, he would have to fly. And now the light seemed to whisper to him: *Fly, Petey. Fly.*

He backed away from the window.

Upstairs, the record changer clicked, and a new record dropped, scratched, and started again. David Lee Roth.

"Faaarm boy. Oh, faaarm boy. We're waiting for you." Linda's voice started high then went low, like nobody else was supposed to hear. "Please, farm boy," she said.

Sometimes, when she called that way, he really wanted to be with her. He wanted to be all alone with her, and he would tell her all about the magic dome and the gold and the dragons, and she would nod to him. Yes . . . *yes* . . .

Moonlight. He looked out of the window, thinking that her hair was the color of moonlight. Odd.

"Faaaarm boy!"

Petey turned his back to the window, trying to shut out her voice. He didn't like looking at the Capitol anymore, didn't like hearing the noises coming from over his head. Most of all he didn't like the sound of Linda calling to him. Her voice made him feel sick and lonely and scared, all at once, and the more he thought about it, the worse he felt.

The fifth floor was the top. There was no one above him.

And the moon . . .

The moon rose like a stage prop over the wooded hills outside of Branson, Missouri. It was almost corny, Marla thought, looking through the window of the cabin. Almost too perfect. A lover's moon, hanging like a mirrored ball over a dance floor.

"Pawn takes bishop," her husband said, and she turned from the window to answer him.

He winked, pointing to the chessboard, his face agleam with the same look of schoolboy deviltry that kept people up nights watching Johnny Carson. She marveled at Keith's range of expressions. Broodingly handsome sometimes, with his dark eyes and the wave of blue-highlighted dark hair that swept across his forehead; tousled and with a look of sleepy-eyed bemusement other times; given to quick grins and looks of glowering intensity . . . she wondered how long they would be together before she knew all the configurations of his face.

"Pawn," he stressed, "takes bishop."

"So?" She reached to the board and made her move. "Knight takes castle, and so there." She could just as well have captured the black queen, but she wanted the game to last.

"Oh, no, you don't," he said. "First things first."

"Hm. Well." She felt herself smile coquettishly, pleased with how effectively she seemed to be teasing him. The first time she had seen him—up there at the front of the class, smooth and assured—he had seemed as untouchable as an actor on stage, and she just a part of the crowd beyond the footlights.

"Okay, then, this bracelet," she said.

"Jewelry doesn't count."

"A shoe."

He frowned. "Shoes go in pairs."

She shrugged, still smiling, and slipped off both of her canvas deck shoes, dropping them over the side of the bed, alongside his boots and checkered shirt.

"Your turn," she said.

"A sock."

"Socks go in pairs."

Watching him, Marla thought of how she had arrived early at the admissions office and stood in line for almost an hour, just to be sure of getting into his Contemporary Poetry class, even though it wouldn't really help toward her degree. She had simply wanted to find out why there was so much talk about Keith Ransom in the coffee shop and dorms and sorority houses of Reinholdt College. That had been—was it possible?—almost a year ago.

"Knight takes pawn," he said. He shrugged to tell her he knew it was a dumb move; it left his knight in the line of her queen.

She made a show of yawning, sliding her thumbs around the waistband of her jeans and tossing back her hair before finally sliding off her jade-colored pullover top. She sat then, naked from the waist up, and as she leaned toward the board she felt suddenly sexual and embarrassed at the same time, like a schoolgirl.

Her hand caressed the playing piece. "Queen takes—"

"Wait," Keith said threateningly, laying on a bogus Teutonic accent. "You do *that*, my dear, and I vill haf your king in the next two moofs."

She smiled, studying the board. She couldn't see his plan. It might have been a bluff, but she knew that if he was playing even halfway seriously, he could make good on a call like that. She didn't like to play serious chess with him.

Completing her play, she said, "Maybe. But I've got your pants right now, and a bird in the hand . . ."

"Not only bad moves but clichés as well. Both Bobby Fischer *and* John Simon would be ashamed of you."

"Off."

He complied, yanking down his jeans from a sitting position and kicking them to one side. She peered over the table.

"This is so disappointing," she said. "I thought, now that we're married and all, I'd be seeing boxer shorts with little pink hearts or something."

"Grounds for divorce," he returned, "and I'm not through with you yet, thank you. Bishop takes castle."

Standing, she unsnapped the jeans and inched them down to the floor. Clad only in her cotton briefs now, she again felt that curious, excited embarrassment, and a quick flush crept across her when she met her husband's eyes, glimpsed his crooked, appreciative smile. She looked away from his face, her eyes tracing the muscled lines of his arms, the flat plane of his stomach. Not Superman perhaps, she thought, but he'd do. Yes, he'd certainly do.

At first Marla had thought Keith to be one of those lucky types who could stay fit without ever working at it, but that had been before she had caught him doing arm isometrics at the movies, making the seat next to her quiver until she jabbed him to make him stop. He went on binges of exercise sometimes, she found out later, days of swimming and tennis and vegetarian cooking, and just when it was getting to be genuinely irritating, he would quit the whole regimen and there would be Twinkie wrappers and Slim Jim packages scattered again on the bedside table.

"Look," he said now, "you're a good kid, essentially. What you need is a break. Here. Have a pawn." And he advanced one on the board.

She closed toward his king with a knight, acutely aware of her near nakedness, trying to seem casual and not awkward.

"Hah!" He surprised her with the sweep of his remaining bishop from across the board, taking her knight away. "Now"—he smiled—"the moment of truth."

"It's nothing you haven't seen before."

His smile grew wider. "Like I say in class: Works of quality are worth going back to again and again."

"Give me a break." Was she actually *blushing*? She certainly felt like it, a sudden heat lightly warming her face. She thought of herself as cute maybe, even pretty, given the right time and effort and some help from the Revlon company, even though nothing could keep her nose from being too small. But the way that Keith watched her made her feel beautiful.

Almost too beautiful. Involuntarily she crossed her arms over her breasts.

The time, the place, the moon, the newly born fact of being *Mrs.* Marla Ransom—all of it was so unreal, it didn't make sense, but the senselessness, the foreign feeling everything had was at the same time comforting and thrilling to Marla. It was something she hadn't planned. She hadn't gone after Keith Ransom feeling anything deeper than curiosity. That, and maybe the undeniable fact that her relationship with Ben wasn't going anywhere and that she had already begun loosening up *those* particular ties.

But then, there was the coffee they had had together after class, the first time. Not intimate, of course, not with Keith Ransom, superprofessor. There had been four or five other students, and the talk had been of John Steinbeck and Joseph Conrad and Thomas Mann, and Keith, damn him, had sat there wearing the de rigueur corduroy jacket with leather elbow patches, smoking a bent-stem briar pipe, and he should have looked silly and fatuous, but he hadn't. Then, coffee again, this time just with her. And a movie one night, *Grapes of Wrath* at a revival theater, and another movie whose title she couldn't remember. And that first Friday night she had turned down several other offers, including Ben's, and stayed in her dorm, just in case he might call, and he had.

"Do you need some help?" His voice shocked her back to the present.

"I believe not, thank you."

"Well, I don't want to rush you, but we have to be back at school within, oh, say, the next day and a half."

She scowled at him, suddenly remembering another intimacy, the first time she had ever seen the inside of his house. Now she realized that she had felt momentarily uncomfortable because stepping into that house had been a little like stepping into his mind; then she hadn't known whether to gasp or to laugh or simply to stand in stunned silence. The walls were covered with framed movie posters, comic books, jigsaw puzzles, neatly squared collections of baseball cards, mixed randomly with watercolors and letters and autographed photos of old-time cowboy actors and people whose faces she vaguely recognized from television late shows but whose names she couldn't place; and books on shelves, books in stacks on the floor, books everywhere, and records; and the back kitchen wall jangling with coffee mugs hung in rows on little hooks; and a Christmas tree sagging with antique ornaments; and a model steam train running on a ledge around the living room.

"I sort of . . . collect," he had said then.

"Is something the matter, Marla?" he asked now.

"No." She squeezed her arms tighter around her. "I was just thinking."

"Fine time for it. What were you thinking about?"

"About when we met. Getting to know you. The things you're supposed to think about on your honeymoon."

"How about getting around to thinking about taking off what clothes still remain on your body? Scant though they may be, a game is a game, and I remind you that the game is still in progress."

She looked at the board but couldn't concentrate. Quickly sliding off her panties, she said, "What else have I got to lose?"

"Maybe we'll think of something. I might make you stand on the bed and cluck like a chicken."

"You wouldn't dare." She cast a glance toward the window. "But I think maybe we should close the curtains."

"There's no one around, Marla. When you ask for out-of-the-way around here, you get out-of-the-way. C'mon, quit stalling. It's your move."

She pretended to study the board, thinking that someday, sometime, the things that used to seem important to her would probably matter again. The senior art show was coming up; she would have to get to work on that, and she still held that goal of a gallery show in New York before she was twenty-five, and maybe she could talk Keith into living in Paris for a while so she could study there, as she had always planned. And sometime, after things settled down a bit, she would have to make things up with her family for getting married— and sometime, maybe sometime, she would be able to sit down and analytically figure out how he had done it, how he had made the whole world shimmer and shift and change around her, and so fast.

"My move, huh?" she said. "Okay." And she reached up and snapped off the light over the bed.

"What kind of move do you call that?" he asked out of the sudden darkness.

"Surrendering."

Above her, the moon framed his face. A smoky haze of moonlight played around him, and his face was dark and blank in silhouette, except for the glinting of his eyes.

"Keith, is that you?"

The voice came, low and forced. "Naw. He had to go to town, but he asked me to kinda take care of things while he was away."

She reached up, touched his bare shoulder. "Quit it, Keith."

"I'm sorry." His voice was normal again now, his hand squeezing hers.

"Sometimes I just . . . In the dark, sometimes I get a weird feeling, like you're not you. You know? And that I'm not me, that you change in the dark."

"Sounds to me like you need a little proof."

Marla tingled a little at the soft, sliding touch of his hands on her, the almost tickling sensation of his lips against her skin, all over, and the feel of her legs moving against him on the cool, rustling surface of the bed. She closed her eyes to the moonlight. And soon he was a part of her; he was a soft, rhythmic pulsing inside of her. He was the beat of her heart, going faster, faster, so fast, and she clutched at his shoulders, thinking what it would be like if she reached for him now, *now*!—and he wasn't there anymore and would never be there again. She clutched him more tightly then, pulling at him, wanting the warmth and the rush of his breath, and her mind flickered images: Keith in class, the way he had of rocking back and forth on his heels; Keith playing his terrible old Spike Jones records and laughing like a child; Keith and the darkness that crossed over his face sometimes when he thought she wasn't looking—what darkness inside him could cause such a change? And her body arched to meet him, to dance with him, fly with him, away and away and away.

She lay nestled in a cloudy warmth, packed into sleep like a small china dish packed in cotton. How long she lay there she didn't know, but she stirred suddenly into consciousness.

The bed was cold to her touch, and that was what had awakened her. Keith . . . gone. Keith? The thought was glass-edged and brittle; it had no place in the blur of her sleep.

Her eyes flickered open.

The room was dark and soft-focused, and for a moment she could not remember where she was. A strange bed. Suitcases on a squatty little rack against the wall. A plastic ice bucket on the desk across the room, and . . . Keith?

The red glow of a cigarette betrayed him. Marla saw him silhouetted, standing silently, motionlessly, inside the little screened-in porch in front of the cabin door, just standing there, his face upturned toward the moon.

She started to call to him. He should be with her, should be . . . What was *wrong* with him? But the thick dream-fog closed in around her, folded over her, packing her away again, making her last waking question soft, dim, and finally shapeless. Her last waking question.

What in hell was he thinking about?

CHAPTER ONE

Outside the isolated cabin, down the sloping piece of dark land dotted with trees to the lake's edge, the iridescent light of the full moon shivered down on the water's surface and whispered with the lapping of the water.

Keith Ransom lit another cigarette and watched the light through the screened-in porch, listened to it whisper.

"Where'd you *get* it? C'mon, lemme—"

"No." The boy had been holding the piece of colored cardboard up in front of ten-year-old Keith Ransom, but he suddenly whisked it behind his back, leering at Keith.

"Bobby, c'mon. I just wanna *look* at it."

"Sure. Sure, you wanna *look* at it."

The two of them stood on the playground near the bike rack at McIntosh Elementary. Their classmates, freed another day by the sound of the bell and anticipating summer vacation, were pulling Schwinns and Western Flyers out, mounting up, and taking off for home, the sound of unsuppressed laughter trailing behind them like streamers. Keith hardly noticed the activity around him; he had noticed almost nothing since the middle of fifth hour, when Bobby Hall had passed him the note during Mrs. King's spelling class, the note that read: *I got Terwilliger.*

Bobby was Keith's best friend. And because of that Bobby knew better than anyone how much Keith wanted that card. Bobby knew it because Keith had told him one day, their bikes parked under the big elm tree in Bobby's backyard, that this year he was going to get them all. The first packs had just hit the shelves at Huffman's dime store then, in a big red-and-blue carton set up between the malted milk balls and Flavor-Aid, and Keith had begun immediately, laboriously making penciled X's on the checklist cards, seeing what gaps he needed to fill, and going back, again and again, with money made from selling pop bottles and mowing lawns, until he had them all. Except one.

Wayne Terwilliger.

The dust kicked up by bicycle tires, and children's feet swathed the playground like gauze as Keith stared at Bobby, feeling a tightness in his muscles, a dizzy soaring in his head. *That card!*

"I won't do anything, Bobby," he said. "I promise I won't. I just wanna look at it, like I said."

"You promise?"

"Yeah. Sure."

There were a couple of holes in Bobby's grin, where his baby teeth had fallen out and his permanent teeth hadn't come in yet. He cocked his head. "I don't know," he said broadly, the grin splitting wider. "I don't know if I can trust you."

"Bobby!" A spring breeze blew up between them, and Keith began to tremble inside as he stared at Bobby's grin. He couldn't control it. He wanted that card. He *had* to have that card. Something inside of him said: *Get it! Get it now! Don't take this anymore!* And the trembling increased.

Jump him!

There was nothing in the world, in the *universe*, he wanted more than that card. He started for Bobby, his fists clenched and rigid at his sides.

Something flashed in Bobby's eyes. He blinked once, then brought his hand out from behind his back, handing the card to Keith. "Okay," he said. "Okay. Gaw. Don't get *mad*. It's just a dumb—"

Keith took it from him, forcing his hand to be slow, hoping Bobby didn't see it shaking, because if he did, then he'd know how much he wanted that card.

The back of it was still dusted with sugar from the gum, and Keith brushed the powder away; the rows of statistics and cartoon on the back blurred as he looked, his chest tight, almost bursting, and the voice inside him saying, *Take it! Take it and run!*

It was like someone else talking, whispering in his ear, like those pictures of the devil tempting kids in his Sunday School quarterly.

"How'd you get it?" he asked, his voice harsh and whispery. The voice inside him began to shout: *Go!*

"At lunch. In a penny pack. Give it back now."

"What'll you take for it?"

Run! You've got it! Run!

"Don't wanna trade it. Give it—"

"I'll let you have every double I got, Bobby. I swear. Every one. You're not trying to get 'em all, you told me, you just want all the Cardinals, and some of the good Yankees, and I've got—"

"Give it—"

Bobby lunged. He sprung at Keith, his head hitting Keith's chest where the card had been, his hand cuffing Keith on the side of the head, and Keith held the card up high, higher, as Bobby's arms reached around him.

"Look out!" Keith shouted. "The card—" And then he was falling, Bobby upending him and shoving, Keith still trying to hold the card out of Bobby's reach as he slammed, shoulders and head, fingertips losing contact with the card, and the voice yelling and rolling and jarring around inside him, jumbled now, confused. On the ground, pain lancing through him, Keith twisted his head around, trying to see the card. Bobby hugged him, his face in his chest, slugging at his sides, and then Keith saw the card, blown up against the inside of the bicycle rack, and began to shove at Bobby, trying to push him off.

Get that card!

They fought silently, straining against each other, and Keith was dimly aware of the feet of kids gathering around, and then those feet were gone, and as Keith dodged one of Bobby's elbows and pushed and rolled to his side, he saw one pair of shoes—only one—but a big pair, and a sick feeling skittered through him.

"I said, stop this!" Large hands pushed them apart, brought them to their feet, and they were looking up into the face of the principal, into his angry eyes.

The man looked from one boy to the other, finally settling on Bobby. "What started this?" he demanded.

And Keith was scared, scared because he'd never been in trouble before, scared and shaking, and the voice came back inside him and said: *Get that card!* It hissed at him. It was a command.

Keith leaned down, watching Bobby and the principal, and his hand skimmed across the grass under the bike rack, and like magic the card almost jumped into his palm without him even looking. Quick as light, he slid it into the back pocket of his jeans and straightened. No one had seen him.

"You mean to tell me you boys fought over a baseball card?" The man turned from Bobby to Keith, his eyes glinting.

"Yes . . ." said Keith. "Yes, sir." Now that he had the card, he felt bad again, bad and scared and wrong.

"Don't you think that's a pretty silly thing for two friends to fight over?"

Keith nodded, glancing at Bobby. "Yes, sir," he muttered, Bobby echoing him.

"I should think so. Where is this card?"

A sudden sick thrill ran through Keith, and he answered before he knew he was even saying anything. "I—I don't know, sir. I guess it blew away when we started fighting." As if to lend credulity to the statement, a south wind came up from nowhere, whistling across the playground and whipping at the principal's tie.

For an awful moment Keith thought that the principal wasn't going to believe him, that the man had somehow seen him reach down and get it, that he was going to go through his pockets and know that he had lied, like his dad had done once when Keith had taken a dollar off the dining-room table.

"All right," said the man. "I'll tell you both something right now. If I ever see you two fighting again, I'm not going to ask any questions. I'm going to paddle you, and then I'm going to tell your folks and you'll get paddled again when you get home. Understand?"

"Yes, sir," they said.

"You two are supposed to be friends. Let's see you act like it."

Keith looked at Bobby, then wiped his hand on his pants

and stuck it out. "I'm sorry, Bobby," he said. "It was dumb. I'll help you look for the card if you want."

Bobby took his hand limply, without looking at him. "Naw," he mumbled.

"Really. I will."

Bobby dropped his hand and shrugged. "Naw. I don't care. It wasn't even a Cardinal."

"That's better," came the man's voice. "You boys need to learn that friendship is a lot more important—a lot more—than some . . . baseball card."

Keith suddenly looked up at the principal, something singing inside of him, a pressure behind his eyes, and he couldn't help but smile.

"Yes, sir," he said. "It sure is."

Funny thing, thought Keith Ransom. *I wanted that card more than anything, and I was so damn afraid that Bobby would find out I had it, I hid it under the mattress in my bedroom, scared to death. But then, after about a week of worrying and sweating, after I was sure Bobby didn't know I had it, I put it in the box with the rest, and then the glow faded and I shoved the box up in the closet. . . .*

And that was the last year I really collected baseball cards. The year I got them all.

The cigarette sizzled, a brief, glowing redness in the dark.

The car, then. The first car he had ever owned. He had been sixteen then, and it had been a 1956 Buick Roadmaster belonging to old Mr. Farley, a neighbor, until old Mr. Farley had gotten too old to drive it anymore and had put it up for sale. Keith had been the first one to find out about it because he mowed Mr. Farley's lawn, and the man had taken him aside and told him about it and said, "Since it's you, boy, I'd let you have it for a hundred dollars," and the grass was deep green, the mimosa trees in bloom, and Keith felt the electric touch of the old man's hand on his shoulder when he told him, and the voice inside was awakened again.

So he mowed more lawns that summer, took a part-time job at the drugstore, and at night, sitting at the desk in his bedroom, he took pieces of notebook paper left over from school and drew the car, making sure to get the fins just right, putting in the line of holes along the side in front, the voice inside him singing as he worked.

And he got it, finally. And it burned oil, and swallowed gas endlessly, and had no compression, and before the winter came, the seat covers were unraveling and the floor was grimy, and Keith didn't even much want to drive it to school anymore.

The voice always went from one thing to another, pushing Keith relentlessly toward a certain goal, and once that goal was attained, popping up again, driving him in a new direction. He had heard the voice many times between the spring of his youth and his autumn, but never had it been more insistent, more powerful, than a couple of years ago, when it came to the job at the college. He had a B.A. from one college and an M.A. from another, but everyone—his classmates, his instructors, his graduate adviser—told him to forget about Reinholdt College. Not with just a master's degree, they said. Not with your grades, they said (he had started strong but lost interest as he went). And, besides, they said, you're a white male.

The voice told him: *Get it*.

He got it. He got it by weaseling his way in as a part-time instructor of classes that were too late or too early for the regular faculty to want, by showing up ahead of time with elaborate lesson plans, by waiting around and getting to know the people in charge and ingratiating himself with them.

He got it. And two months later the voice dead and cold in him; he hated the job. He was bored with it, with the faces that looked up at him, and the dull time-killing chatter of the faculty members, and the endless meetings. And lately he was beginning to suspect that his administrators realized his boredom, and he couldn't even work up enough enthusiasm to try to make them think differently.

He didn't have tenure. He hadn't been there long enough. They could dump him out on his butt and he'd have no recourse, and the way they had been riding him lately, it seemed likely that the ax was ready to fall.

Especially now. Now that he had Marla.

The hell with it, he thought. The hell with them all—the chalk-dusted men, the pursed-lipped women, old before their time, drinking endless cups of thick coffee in the cafeteria, watching the coeds go by, and the men winking and muttering under their breath.

The hell with them.

That's right, I married a student. So what, Dr. Thurman? In his mind he saw the stern, horn-rimmed face of the English Department chairman, looking constipated as usual, tapping the tip of a pen on his glass-topped desk, chewing on his lower lip.

She's the best-looking one at this whole damn school, you know. I'll bet you've sat on your bony ass and watched her walk across the cafeteria floor and thought about how much you'd like to sleep with her, but now you can't. She's mine now. You want to get rid of me? Fine. But don't do any of your insufferable pontificating around me. She's mine.

The thought of his department head and his imagined scene had caused a surge of adrenaline in Keith Ransom, but now that faded, and with it, the image, diffusing into tiny dots and receding into the darkness around him.

And the voice within him was cold and still.

He turned to look at Marla, asleep in the room, moonlight dappling the sheets, and the voice was still silent. Standing there in the dark, he suddenly felt as if some celestial object had fallen through the ceiling of the cabin and landed in the dark bed, with no relation to him except that of chance.

Not Marla, he thought. It's different with Marla. But the inner voice was unconvincing and hollow, and the deeper voice was silent, and in his mind he saw baseball cards, the car, college, Marla, on a straight line that started when he was a child and ribboned off into infinite darkness.

He had pursued her for months, driven to her, obsessed with her, her hair and her eyes and her nose and the way she rubbed her neck when she was weary, her tapering fingers, her short nails. He had pursued her for months, months of competition with football players and fraternity studs and guys from out of town she had known in high school, and the more she tried to leave him, the more he pushed, and finally she had loved him.

He stepped into the doorway now, looking at her, following the dark curvature of her flesh where she had kicked the sheet off.

And now?

And now . . . what? Ransom pulled at his mustache, feeling suddenly anxious and afraid and out of place. The silence, without and within, was damning. He glanced around the honeymoon cabin, at the shadowed corners, the faint outline of the kerosene lamp. Alone. Alone and empty.

Walking slowly to the bed, he reached down and drew the sheet up over her leg, her back, her body, as one would do to a dead person. He lit another cigarette, exhaled slowly, and turned away from her, and in the distance the midnight moonlit lake shimmered out in front of him like something unattainable, something always and forever just out of his reach.

CHAPTER TWO

The moon was a pale white, frosty shape, a ghost somehow trapped in the daylight. It was no more than a milky wisp against the cold blue of the October sky, and it hung in the air like a whisper. He kept turning toward it.

"Keith . . . ?" Marla reached to him, not so much needing his help up the hillside as just wanting the touch of his hand. He stood there, one arm tightened by the weight of the ice chest he carried, the other slack. He stood watching the moon in the same intense way he had the night before, when she had glimpsed him standing on the porch before sleep overtook her again.

"What does it mean when the moon shows up in the daytime?" she asked, using the question as a way to get through to him. "Good sign or bad sign?"

She smiled as she asked him, her best smile, but his lapse in answering lasted just long enough to hurt her feelings a little. "I don't think it means anything," he said.

"Then let's make it a good sign," she returned, jiggling her hand as if she were waving a scarf to catch his attention.

A quick tug and the laugh that went with it brought her toppling toward him, past him. They landed together, plopping into the high grass and dry, crackling leaves. Marla breathed in the morning air. It was clear and crisp and tasted like cider. With Keith she looked across the gray waves of Lake Taneycomo, across to the wooded hillsides beyond—a mad but pleasant artist's canvas of reds, oranges, and yellows.

She turned at the sound of Keith cracking into the ice chest, laughing as she watched him peering into it, like a pirate looking into a chest full of gold. She had been laughing a lot lately, she thought. And why not?

"A loaf of bread," he said, producing a long French loaf. "A jug of wine," which was cherry-flavored apple juice bought from a roadside stand. "And"—he reached dramatically into the chest—"a chunk of good, hard-smoked cheddar, no knife. Who packed this fiasco?"

"You did."

"Right. And that's what you get for marrying a bachelor."

They traded kisses and sips of apple juice from paper cups, Marla feeling giddy and free and almost newborn. They talked nonsense. They had a leaf fight, and Marla stuffed a handful down the back of Keith's shirt, and they tossed bits of bread to a squirrel and a blue jay. And Keith muttered threats at the low clouds that had begun to line up across the horizon, rumbling of rain; but Marla was glad, in a way, to see the clouds. They made the moon dim away.

"I hate to break this up, but we really ought to be getting back home," Keith told her finally.

"So soon?" Marla picked a dandelion ball and blew the feathery seeds toward him. "I was just beginning to have a good time."

"Yeah? Well, tomorrow's a long day for me, the night class and all, and you, my dear, have got the dreaded midterms coming up."

"So?"

"So it's a long drive back."

The subject of going back to the college was like a lump in a soft pillow. Marla didn't want to think about it, let alone do it. She dreaded the gap that their positions—he the teacher, she the student—might pry between them, the division of *his* friends from *her* friends, Keith in his cubbyhole office (but an office all the same) and Marla in the hallway with an armload of books, and what if they met between classes? She would almost feel like she ought to call him Mr. Ransom, just like before.

"I don't plan on having more than one honeymoon," she said. "And when it's just Friday and the weekend, I want every last minute of it."

So they drove into Branson and bought chocolate-covered strawberries at the candy store downtown, and to Mountain Home, Arkansas, for an arts-and-crafts show, and Marla found a homemade crazy quilt for sale there that she thought would be a perfect match with the framed Marx Brothers *Duck Soup* poster and shelf of first-edition Oz books that Keith had assembled in his—*their*—bedroom. And for supper they stopped at a mom-and-pop steak house off the highway outside of Harrison, where Pop grilled the steaks and Mom set the table and played "Amazing Grace" on a dulcimer.

And the moon rose.

The rolling Ozark countryside had become no more than a shadow show, the tops of the tallest trees stippled with moonlight. Marla sat on the far side of the passenger's seat, one arm braced against the dashboard. The car swooped into a turn.

"You playing Burt Reynolds or what?" asked Marla.

He felt a sudden irritation at her words. "I just want to get there." The road bent under them in a U-shaped curve, plunging downward. He tapped at the brakes as the back tires slipped and squealed. "Look," he said. "It's late and we're nowhere near home. Why don't you try to get some sleep?"

"You're kidding, right?"

"No."

"I'd have better luck sleeping on a roller coaster."

"Well, then, just try to relax. It's a long way home, but I'll get us there."

"Promise?"

"I promise."

The road bent again, and a Coke bottle clanked and rattled under the seat. The floor of the little Datsun was scattered with film wrappers and hamburger sacks, the back end a jumble of suitcases and packages that squeaked and tilted, threatening an avalanche. They wouldn't have had room for a fourth day on the road, Keith thought. It felt suddenly good to him to have things in the car that weren't his.

But then that feeling was gone, like the now-and-away flutter of a moth in the headlights, gone almost before he could recognize it. Something within him rejected that feeling; caught it, killed it, and threw back in its place an aching loneliness, the feeling of being with a stranger who somehow reminded him of the yearning he had felt for Marla. It was like being somewhere and hearing a song that he had loved when he was a kid—happy at first, in remembrance, and then ineffably sad, with the realization that his youth was gone.

Again the question jabbed at him: *Now what?*

He knew that his rush to get back to the college had nothing to do with his job; it was simply the answer to *"Now what?"* And not a good answer at all.

He meant to slow down, to take it a bit easier over those treacherous curves, but despite what he meant to do, his foot was pressing against the accelerator pedal, and the speedometer needle was climbing again. The cold wind, whipping at him from the slightly opened driver's-side window, felt pleasant and almost hurt at the same time. Or felt good *because* it hurt, he thought.

Odd. It was an odd thought and he didn't like it. He cranked the window tightly shut, keeping his other hand tight against the wheel.

Marla's voice startled him. "I'm keeping a list—did you know?—of all the new things I learn about you." He glanced over to see her writing in the air, her finger tracing elaborate sweeps and spirals. ". . . runs bats out of hell off the road."

"Give it a rest, *okay*?"

He turned his eyes back toward the road as her face began misting with hurt. Wanting to say something, he held back, not trusting himself, thinking that whatever he said might make it worse. Conversation between them was headache talking to blearliness after a long day, with hours of driving still ahead. That was it, that was the trouble, Keith Ransom tried to tell himself as he fixed his attention on the centerline of the twisting highway, on the wavering path of the headlights. They rode in a silence that settled between them like a third passenger, one that didn't want to be disturbed.

Vampire Night, Ransom thought. He could still hear the dark, brooding chords of the opening rift, just the same as when he had written the song the summer between his sophomore and junior years of college.

It was the best and last of the hundred-some songs he wrote that strange summer, songs that burst into his mind like fireworks, even though he'd never studied music. He bought

a tape recorder that he carried with him, heedless of the pe-
culiar looks people gave him when he sang into the micro-
phone. He learned to play the guitar; learned to read and
write music. He entered songwriting contests at ten and
twenty dollars a throw, and won enough to break even.
And he wrote *Vampire Night*—the one that edged into Billboard's top 40 list for a few weeks.

The royalties from *Vampire Night* cleaned up his student
loans and paid for his last year of college. But the fireworks
dimmed to sparks, and the sparks burned out. He never again
experienced the sort of flash of inspiration that resulted in
Vampire Night; and in time, the tape recorder jammed, and
the guitar, long out of tune, wound up in the back of the
closet. Ransom only tried to care.

But now, he thought suddenly of how nice it would be to
get out his guitar sometime again soon and maybe finish some
of those songs he had left hanging years ago, with only a
verse, perhaps, or a verse and a bridge. And the song began
playing in his mind: *"Used up and gone, but the silence lives
on, in the heart of the vampire night."*

The dream, the fantasy, of being a singer/songwriter. Days
on the road, motel rooms, the entourage ready to supply him
with anything he needed or wanted, the wonderfully infinite
variety of women. . . .

"It's a pretty long list, you know," Marla said, and a quick
irritation flitted through Ransom. He glanced over at her.

"The list. What I've learned. Today I added a new one.
He likes to sneak around and buy me things he knows I'd like
to have. Arkansas diamonds, for instance." She held her arm
close to the speedometer light, tiny highlights sparkling from
the bracelet on her wrist.

Ransom forced a smile, then noticed that the speedometer
was reading close to seventy. He dropped it to fifty-five with
a conscious effort, as if he were trying to slow down his
breathing, and the engine seemed to sigh with relief.

That song. Ransom wondered why it had come to mind
here, tonight. And he couldn't remember the verses, just the
ends of them, and they had all ended the same way: *"in the
heart of the vampire night."*

Twin stripes of no-passing yellow flanked the centerline as
the highway rose sharply. On the hilltop a sign proclaimed

WONDERLAND CAVE in letters that glittered against the head-lights. Ransom heard a shuffling sound from Marla's side, heard her say "Got it," and turned to see her holding up a color-printed brochure.

It was a safe subject; something soft and light he could toss back and forth with her with no chance of injury. He welcomed the opportunity and dreaded it at the same time; he didn't want to talk anymore, wanted to be lost in his thoughts, but at the same time another part of him wanted her to be happy and in love with him.

"You get on me for what I collect," he said as gently as he could, "and look what you bring home. Pictures of all the places you didn't get to see."

"I guess we'll just have to come back. These are to remind you."

He had known she was going to say something like that. "I guess we will."

"I'm not doing anything next weekend," she said.

"Oh, but you are."

She seemed surprised. "What?"

"Next weekend is *Dr.* Thurman's dreaded—and not to be missed—Halloween party." Ransom said the *Dr.* as if it were a joke, or an obscenity. "It's a laugh riot, I'll guarantee that. You come dressed as a character out of Shakespeare and watch all conversation in the room stop when you take over two glasses of wine." He glanced at her again. "Welcome to the wonderful world of the Reinholdt English faculty; this'll be your initiation, and any resemblance to Hell Week on fraternity row is purely coincidental. Just think of it as a rite of passage—painful but unfortunately necessary."

"C'mon. It sounds like fun."

"Don't count on it."

"Sure. All those costumes and everything." He heard her giggle. "It'll be fun seeing all those instructors dressed up."

"And less fun to listen to them." He veered into a turn, both hands tight on the wheel. "Thurman's idea of a big time is to stand around dissecting the faults and failures of those who didn't show up, and then a second round for those who leave early. We'll have to stick around to the bitter end just in self-defense."

There was silence for a moment as the car whizzed through

the night, and then Marla said, "I guess it's going to take practice, isn't it?"

"What is?"

"Being a . . . faculty wife."

She said it with just the proper amount of light sarcasm, but the term drilled into Keith with sharp edges. *Faculty wife.* It was the blandest description of a woman he could imagine, calling up images of silver-haired matrons in wool suits drinking coffee out of china cups, the smell of boredom all around them. As if to reassure himself, he looked at Marla, and even in the darkness he could see the old plaid shirt draped around her, collar opened to reveal the gold chain and sapphire charm centered between her breasts. She looked like a high-school prom queen out slumming, and he suddenly felt like a thirty-four-year-old schoolyard flasher. Faculty wife . . . a flitting insanity. But a faculty wife was what she was— or would be, as soon as they got back to the college.

Ransom imagined the talk, or rather the *sounds* of the talk, that would have been going around Reinholdt College ever since the wedding: giggles and whispers in the hallways between classes; low, stern tones behind closed doors in the inner sanctum of offices. And it all seemed so foolish and at the same time . . . oddly useless.

"So how do we go?" she asked, stirring him once again from his thoughts.

"How about under assumed names?"

"I'm serious." Then: "I know. I'll go as Juliet, and you—"

"Nope," Ransom said quickly, anticipating her.

"I can't be Juliet?"

"Sure. But you were going to hand me the Romeo part, right? I'm afraid I'm a little long in the tooth for that one."

Her voice bubbled. "That's how much *you* know. I was thinking Francis Bacon for you. He was the one—wasn't he? —some people say wrote all of Shakespeare's plays—"

"If he didn't, he certainly missed a wonderful opportunity."

"—and was a little bit of a troublemaker, besides. It's perfect."

Perfect. Even as Ransom smiled, his mind was locking on an image of the department chairman—the gray-suited, gray-

haired, and gray-minded *Dr.* Thurman—searching through the
college's policy papers to verify *what to be done* about a
faculty member with the temerity to marry one of his students. *What to be done*, taking into account the sizable annual donation made to the college by the father of that student.
What to be done, given that Marla's father had refused to
provide a full church wedding, had in fact refused even to
attend the ceremony.

Ransom rubbed at the ache in his temple. He fought to
calm the spreading tension, the push-pull, yank-shove of fear-
ing to lose a job he no longer wanted.

The vampire night . . . the line played in his head, stuck
there, over and over.

"Where are we, anyway?" Marla asked.

The countryside was a blur of shadows, of dark tree shapes
and a distant, lighted window now and then, the glow as
remote as starlight. A cloying scent of apples came to Ransom's nostrils, from a box of Arkansas Jonathans Marla had
packed in the back. He wanted to open the window then but
didn't.

"Eureka Springs is next, as nearly as I can tell," he said
finally. The light of the full moon cut down through the tree-
tops with startling clarity, the moon itself unnaturally bright
and perfectly flat, oddly white, a smokelike mist surrounding
it.

"Eureka Sp—" Again Ransom heard the rustling and knew
she was reaching into her purse. "Oh, Keith! I read about
that. It's supposed to be just like a little village in Switzerland." The sound of a brochure unfolding. "Look, Keith.
Look at these pictures." The dome light flicked on then, and
Keith looked over.

"See?" she continued, her finger stabbing at the pictures.
"Beautiful old gingerbread houses built right up the hillside.
I could make some sketches for a painting, and we could
always have that to save."

A tired bitterness began to creep through Ransom, bitterness at the impossibility of stopping, bitterness at having to
go back, bitterness at disappointing Marla, and at her putting
herself in a position to *be* disappointed. His eyes went back
to the road, and when the dome light snapped off, he strained

to focus them through the sudden haze of white. Moonlight chilled the highway.

"Just one more night, all right?" she asked. "Car trouble. We had car trouble; that's what you could tell them."

"They'd never buy it."

"Then the truth." Her hand went to his thigh, squeezing it. "Tell them that your wife felt the need to reconsummate the marriage, perhaps repeatedly, because she is in love. How about that?"

The road warned of an *S* curve and made good on it. Her hand tensed against him as they banked into the first turn. Ransom almost had to pry his foot off the gas; the rumble and shake of the speeding car felt good to him, like something he could lose himself in and not have to think or feel.

Her voice, beside him: "Along about now, shouldn't you be telling me something along the lines of 'I love you too'?"

The bitterness grew inside him, a living thing. It was loathing and self-disgust, and it threatened to take him over. He reached for the radio and switched it on, playing through the channels, the crackle and hiss of static and broken voices, hymns and promises of damnation, looking for noise, for something to dam the rising, formless feelings.

"Keith?"

He found a rock song, a hypnotic female chant that sounded wavering and tinny through the speaker. He wished it would drown out everything, would—

"Keith, did you *hear* me?"

—drown out the sound of her voice, drown out *her*.

He forced pleasantness he hoped would pass for sincerity in his voice. "I'll do better than that. Anyone can say 'I love you,' but you're different. You're a *gotta*."

"A what?"

"That's what my grandmother used to say when I was a kid and I wanted something so much that it was all I could think about. She'd say, 'He's got the *gottas*.' Gotta have a slingshot, gotta have a new bike or a BB gun or some prize in a box of cereal. . . ." He turned to her. "Gotta have *you*."

She smiled. "That's not romance, that's compulsion." Her hand touched his cheek, and he almost recoiled from her. Shrugging, he turned back to the road, the bitterness inside him a heavy, fluid thing, held back by the flimsiest of barriers. For no reason he could find, he wanted to pound the steering wheel, to scream. Damn! *Damn!* The nerves in his body were alive and raw.

"I guess I'll take what I can get," she said, and gave his leg a squeeze.

The car crested another hill, took a spiraling descent, and the darkened trees seemed to close overhead like long-fingered hands—claws, Ransom thought—folded over the highway. He turned the radio up.

Souvenir shops, restaurants, and more and more motels, mostly darkened, began crowding the roadside. The Grape Mountain Inn, the Swiss Alpine Lodge ("World Famous Biscuits 'n' Gravy")—Ransom's mind noted them as he passed, orderly and friendly images that might fill his head, leaving no room for dark thoughts and feelings.

"Well, look at that," Marla said coyly. "Are we in Switzerland or what?" Her voice was sawblade-jagged against his nerves.

"You don't really want to stop."

"Try me just once. Like over there where it says 'Vacancy.' "

Ransom looked at the blinking red sign, half meaning at that moment to just turn in and be done with it. Almost with surprise he watched the motel sign slide past the window, the red neon glow mingling with the red of the taillight that showed in the rearview mirror. *I should have*, he thought, *should have* . . . and he thought of the warm scene, the reassuring scene under the motel lights, Marla hugging him for stopping, making little noises of delight, the two of them symbolically thumbing their noses at Dr. Thurman and walking into the little office.

And it made him angry, the anger and bitterness swirling around inside him, tilting as he took the curve that put the sign out of sight forever. He suddenly wanted to get past the town, away from the lights. There was a straight stretch, and he whipped around a station wagon with suitcases in the back and a couple of bleary-eyed kids between them returning his gaze. He stayed on Route 62 as it bent past a sign that pointed toward the Eureka Springs business district.

Again Marla's voice: "I think it's up there where they have all the little shops and things. . . ."

He almost snapped then, but forced himself to look away from her, toward a Texaco station that was still open, with a uniformed man in front locking up the pumps. *I should stop*, he thought. The gauge read half empty. *I should stop. Get out, walk around a little, breathe some fresh air.* The air in the car seemed stifling to him, thick like a blanket thrown over his face.

He didn't stop. The gas station, floating in a pool of brightness from its platform lights, fell into the background. The lights of the town dimmed behind them.

"*Dumb.* This is so *dumb*, Keith," Marla said. "To come up here, and everything so pretty, and then to end up driving through in the dark."

His own voice surprised him. "I want the dark."

"What?"

The bitterness, the anger, rolled and boiled inside him, spilling up into his throat.

"What are you telling me, Keith?"

"Just . . . *shut the hell up*!" His voice echoed inside him, lancing through the bubbling of emotions like laughter. He didn't look at her, and the laughter became a ringing in his ears, in his head. It was the sound of the music on the radio and the engine noise, and the silence between them rushed through him like a vacuum, like the darkness. He felt enveloped by a dark void, that only the moon played through. His rational voice from the back of his mind was tiny, and he couldn't get it to make any sense.

Dimly he heard her. "Keith, can't you even *talk* to me anymore?" Dimly it registered: the hurt in the voice, the quavering. He could not call forth the power to answer her.

And—that was strange. Frost. Frost on the windshield. It wasn't that cold out, but there it was on the glass: frost, the color of moonlight.

Perhaps he could outrun the frost, he thought, and the car picked up speed underneath him. He liked the speed. Ever since his twelfth birthday and the English racer bicycle he had wanted so much that he stayed awake nights thinking about it, pumping his legs under the bed covers, making the wheels sing; ever since then he had liked going fast, so fast that no one could follow him, no one could stop him.

"Keith!"

His head cleared a little at the shock of her voice, enough so he could see that he had taken a curve without slowing, hear the gravel of the shoulder spraying against the underside of the car. He cut the wheel back hard, the car shuddering and bouncing back onto the road. Out of nowhere a semi shot past them in the oncoming lane.

He started to talk, but his mind faded, contracted, frosted over, struggling with half-formed connections. Something about . . . speed, the exhilaration of it, and the songs, how he had felt writing them, what he had dreamed about, and *the vampire, the vampire, the vampire*—and Marla. Especially Marla.

He wanted her *so much*. That was it. Damn the college, damn them all if they didn't like it. *And damn me, damn me for thinking I didn't—WANT HER!*

Ransom marveled at the frost that glazed the windshield. White frost, and it was shifting, stirring, forming vague pictures, constantly moving, and there were eyes in the frost.

Look, Marla, he thought. He couldn't tell if he was speaking or not. *Isn't that funny? Eyes, and I want you so badly.*

The voice screamed in his mind—*"Keith!"*—and he felt the steering wheel being wrested from his grip. But didn't she see? The face, forming in the frost shapes, a face . . . his own face. But no, it wasn't really; there was something wrong with it. Except for the eyes. The eyes were his, and he was looking straight at Marla, and then he knew he was on her, on top of her, and she was powerless against him. So he let her go, let her run, gagging and crying, until she thought she might get away, and then he bore down on her again. Out of the shadows of moonlight he came for her, giving her time to turn, to know him, to scream—and he was on her again, ripping at her, ramming hard into her. When her eyes went wide, they gleamed of moonlight, and his teeth sank into her throat then, softness giving way to a hot spurting of blood, and still he thrust into her, and the blood rushed, tasting of the night. He thrust and she fed him, again and again, until he was spent. Against his face, her face, the lips trying to form words, trying to gasp out "I . . . love . . . you" beneath him, and only for a moment he drew back to watch her before his hands—*claws*—covered her face, her cheeks cupped in his palms, the nails raking into the soft spots under her eyes, and then digging and squeezing, twisting her head around slowly until her neck wrenched wetly and the moon died in her eyes—

Ransom's head snapped forward. Apples rolled and thudded in the back, and the box with Marla's quilt in it half spilled into the front seat. He looked, saw her foot slammed against the brake pedal, both of her hands gripping the wheel.

The slam of a car door and she was no longer beside him. Ransom's head reeled. He peered out the windshield and saw that the car had stopped on the highway shoulder at an angle that would have taken it off the road and down a dark, steep embankment. Weak with nausea, he pulled himself out of the car, looking for her, trying to make some sort of sense out of everything that had happened.

She stood nearby, crying, with her back to him, a figure all moonlight and shadow against the empty highway. The chilled air was a knife in his lungs, but he drew it in deeply. It seemed to pump into his head. As he walked, he became aware of his feet scuffling against the pebbled surface of the road. "Marla . . . ?" he called.

When she turned toward him, he was suddenly struck by the miracle of her. Every breath, every blink, every second of life in her—a miracle.

"Leave me alone, Keith," she said, turning away, her voice a choked whisper. "I think I'm going to be sick."

He approached her tentatively. "I don't blame you. Me too. I . . . I don't know what happened to me."

"You were *gone! Spaced!*" She whirled around almost savagely, to face him again. "I couldn't even *reach* you!"

A deep sadness began welling up in him as he stood, looking at her. "I . . . don't know what *happened*, Marla."

"Are you all right?"

He looked at his hands. They weren't taloned, were not wet and clotted red, *not at all*; they were pale and trembling. He almost laughed at the sight of them. "I think so," he said.

Marla tried to hold back a choking sob, hands pressed tightly against her mouth.

He wanted to hold her then; never before in his life had he wanted so much to hold another person. He wanted to feel the living warmth that pulsed through her. But even as he reached in her direction the vision rammed into his mind, not cloudy and dreamlike but—vivid. He turned away, reeling at the thought of what he had . . . *done* to her.

Her hands were on his shoulders. "Come on, Keith," she said. "The first thing we need to do is get ourselves off the road." Allowing himself to be directed, he walked beside her, trying not to lean against her, trying not to let her know how suddenly close he was to breaking down and crying like a helpless child.

He cleared his throat. "Who's driving?" he asked, looking at her. It made her smile a little, and she said something in answer that might have been soft and forgiving, but the vision jammed his mind again, blocking out her face, her voice. A part of his mind tried to grope for answers in the clarity of that vision, but the vision was all, locked in his head like wasps in a jar, and he saw again what he had done . . . to her face. . . .

He forced himself to speak, to communicate with another living human being, to drive away the vision and come back into the world. "We—let's go back, Marla. Like you wanted. We can go back and stay as long as you want to, wherever you want to."

She kept guiding him on, and he was aware of the pressure at his elbow, the soft touch of her fingers on his shoulder, and then her voice. "I think what we'd better do is go home, Keith, and get you to a doctor."

The vision was receding from his mind, but it was still cloudy and heavy and threatening, its residue thick and sickening. He would not accept it. He had to know *why*.

Marla. Something about Marla.

They neared the car. He set the car as a deadline. *I will know what's gone wrong with me by the time we get to the car.*

"That's not romance, that's compulsion," Marla had said to him, and perhaps she had been joking—he hoped she had—but also she had perhaps gotten closer to him than she thought. A compulsion. He thought back to the night before, about standing on the porch of the little cabin looking up at the moon, his mind wandering back to his other . . . his other *compulsions*, his *gottas*, from the time he had been a child, and then turning to look at Marla and feeling as if she were something alien.

But the vision—how did it connect? Quickly his mind flipped through possibilities. Acid flashback? He had only done LSD once, years and years ago, an unpleasant enough experience—but no, that was too easy, a myth perpetrated by people who wrote for *Reader's Digest* and gave lectures to junior high schools. Fatigue? Dread of returning? A quick, comatose doze at the wheel?

All explanations were too easy, too simple, to contain the magnitude of what he had seen, what he had felt. Pat, insufficient answers to a huge and horrible question.

Why?

And the word kept coming back, circling through his mind. Marla's word.

Compulsion.

The passenger-side door clicked open in front of him, the sound breaking into his thoughts, and he knew there would be no explaining. Not tonight. There would be no answers for him or for Marla, just one last and lingering question: Why did he suddenly feel sure that a wreck would have killed her but not him?

"Are you sure you're okay?" she asked.

He eased down into the seat, squeezing her hand. She stood in the open door, concern masking her face.

"Yeah. I just need some . . . rest." Behind her Ransom saw the moonlight, sifting frost white over her shoulders, the trees bent and stirring as if from the weight of it. "Let's get the hell out of here," he said.

She leaned down and kissed him on the forehead, and then he felt her hand leave his, and his eyes tracked her as she walked to the front of the car where the headlight beams played into the moonlight, the light a faint blue-white outline around her, seeming to cling to her—

And there in the front light—*there!*—he saw it move. It was light against light, soft-edged, as silent as smoke. The light moved, glinting and shifting, now a man shape, a swirl, a mist, come and gone and back again, looming over her, watching her with eyes of frost, eyes that flashed the white of the moon.

Keith's heart slammed against his rib cage. The nightmare—it was starting again, but this time he was outside of it. A noise tore away from his throat.

In front, Marla, looking at him. "Keith? Keith, *now* what's the matter?"

Behind her the light took on a translucent hardness. It was ice come to life. Arms reached. Taloned hands closed toward her neck, the nails hooked to pierce her throat. And the eyes lifted toward Ransom—beckoning. Inviting.

Time slowed as if to taunt him. Ransom felt his insides knotting like the slow twists of a rubber band, ever tighter. His legs moved in aching, dreamlike slow motion, drifting him out of the car and toward her. By degrees in front of him, her face melded into a dumbfounded look.

No! His mind screamed. *Not again! NOT AGAIN!*

He grabbed at the hand closest to him, fastened his fingers around it. The hand shimmered frost white, crystalline stars glimmering inside of it, and even as he clutched it, he knew it could be of no more substance than moonlight.

He *knew* that—but the hand slipped out of his grasp and caught his arm, and it was suddenly burning cold. He saw the fingers tighten, the claws begin cutting into his wrist—cruelly precise, it seemed—just slowly enough to let him hear the tearing of his skin, just deep enough to let him know how bad it could have been.

And grinning teeth in the light, the teeth the last of it Keith saw, his head craned back and looking up, his eyes burning and blurred from the light. Off-balance, he staggered and then sprawled onto the road's surface, clenching at his wrist. As he struggled to his feet he saw the blood welling up between his fingers.

Marla was next to him, her hands on his arm. He licked his lips. "Fell . . . on . . . a piece of glass," he said.

Her expression was blank. Not disbelieving, not scared, not angry. He could have accepted any one of those.

Just blank.

"I believe I'll drive," she said, and got in.

CHAPTER THREE

"Tonight we're going to study cinematic lycanthropy," said Keith Ransom, looking down from behind the sixteen-milli-meter projector at the auditorium half full of students, all in their seats, all waiting for the show to begin.

From the middle a girl twisted around and peered up at him, brushing her raven-black hair back from her shoulders. "Dammit, Keith," she said, "I thought we were going to watch a horror movie." Her eyes met his, briefly and mock-ingly, and then she turned back around, basking in the laugh-ter of her classmates.

Ransom grinned back, although he didn't feel like it. *All right, Wendy,* he thought. And then, *Just get through the class. Forget it.*

"If we had popcorn, it would be a horror movie," he said. "If we had beer, it would be a drive-in movie. But when you take notes, that makes it cinematic lycanthropy. Write that down, okay?"

The class buzzed with laughter. They would have laughed at just about anything he might have said then, Ransom knew. But this was one time he could have done without it.

Damn bunch of smart asses. The innumerable cups of cof-fee he had thrown down, just trying to get himself to and through this last class, washed back through his system as he stood, the acid burning thickly at the base of his tongue. His forehead tightened, throbbed.

Just get through it. Forget her. You've got—

Marla? His only chance was not to think of her, not now,

not here. A pain lanced through his stomach, and he fought back the now familiar images, a preliminary wave of revulsion sweeping over him. There would be time, he told himself, but not now. Please, not now.

"This is a film called *Curse of the Werewolf*." He managed to sound authoritative, and the murmuring of voices stopped, replaced by the scraping of notebooks, the flipping of pages. "You need to know that it was made by Hammer Films of England in 1961, directed by Terence Fisher, who was pretty famous for these sort of films, and scripted by Anthony Hinds, using the pseudonym of John Elder. Also, even though it's set in Spain, Hinds based his script on a book called *The Werewolf of Paris*, by Guy Endore. That's E-n-d-o-r-e."

He took a breath and continued. "As for the players, there are a lot of Hammer stock company people, guys that look convincing in period costumes, but the only actor you'll probably recognize is Oliver Reed. He shed the facial hair and jumped to 'A'-budget features." Most of the students were writing furiously, the scratching of their pens and pencils a kind of background music in the hollowness of the auditorium. His eyes settled on Wendy. As nearly as he could tell, she wasn't taking down a word.

Fighting back a sudden, irrational anger, he asked, "Any questions?" There were none, and the noise of note taking died away.

"Keep in mind that the werewolf, or lycanthropy, idea has been with just about every culture at one time or another. Think about Romulus and Remus, for instance. That goes back a ways." His throat felt thick, clogged. "At its most basic, lycanthropy is rooted in the idea that people can be raised by animals and take on the characteristics of those animals. It's also a valid psychological term—there have been cases of people thinking they were wolves, and therefore behaving like them. In a broader sense, though, we might say that any story that involves a man, or woman, changing into something else is—" Suddenly an image flashed into his mind, the image of him, over Marla, reaching for her. His voice went rough, and he swallowed once, twice. "Excuse me," he muttered.

Someone said, "Late night, huh?" and that set the class off again.

Ransom coughed, driving the image from his mind, concentrating on the class, a class peppered with sophomoric smart alecks who knew—or thought they knew—all about him and Marla. "Yeah," he said. "Too late. So, anyway, any story we hear about a human being changing into something else, some other form, is a lycanthrope story. *Dr. Jekyll and Mr. Hyde*. There's one."

A boy twisted around in his seat. "Clark Kent and Superman?"

"No, not really."

Someone else: "The Incredible Hulk?"

A few members of the class started to chuckle, but Ransom stopped it. "Yeah, that's it. And the difference is that the Hulk is . . . well, more bestial, more animalistic. Not"—he paused, the images flitting darkly on the edge of his mind— "not given to, shall we say, moral considerations. Not human. Or as human, anyway." *Like me*, thought Ransom. *Like what I saw . . . what I was!* His mouth formed words. "This idea of going from humanity to bestiality is an important archetypal myth, and this film illustrates it about as well as any. We'll talk more about the ramifications next week."

Before anyone else could interject a question or observation, Ransom switched off the lights and turned on the projector. Sinking back into his chair, he realized with relief that the images were gone from his mind, and he knew the words had done it: *archetypal myth, ramifications*. Nice big professorial terms, safe and dusty and removed from humanity and reality. The countdown numbers popped on and off the screen, and up came the music and picture, the sound track muddied a little. Ransom hit the loop restorer on the projector, once, twice, and the music smoothed out.

What a laugh, this class, he thought, grateful to have something else to think about. What a pompous, pedantic, high-toned laugh.

The class was officially listed in the school catalog as English 4223: Film as Literature, an upper-division elective for Arts and Sciences majors. Ransom had fought for that class, fought against a group of calcified old men who viewed Ransom as representing some sort of sixties atavism, and he had worked on them, arguing eloquently and at great length, making them at least tentatively swallow the idea that film was

an art form, deserving of study at institutions of higher learn-
ing. He had pointed out the prestigious schools all over the
country that had extensive film courses in their curricula, had
had for years, and didn't they want Reinholdt College to be
right up there with the big guys? And the faculty members
had cleared their throats, and scratched at the elbows of their
serge suits, and looked at each other as if to say, "Do we let
this damn, impertinent fool put one over on us or not?" Ransom knew the look. He had seen it often enough at Reinholdt
to have a firm idea of what the founding Presbyterian fathers
must've looked like most of the time, and it wasn't pleasant.

Finally he had worn them down by presenting the curriculum committee with several copies of a detailed syllabus
containing intricate and arcane cross-references between literature and the cinema, notes on myth and symbolism and
metaphor in film, and they finally got around to letting him
run a trial class in the fall semester. Ransom had figured
since then that the only reason they let him have the class
was that they didn't know half the time what the hell he was
talking about in the syllabus and were afraid to admit their
ignorance. And why not? He had planned it that way, using
the knowledge he had gleaned through years of being a film
fan to snow them under with minutiae.

So he got it. And finding students was no trouble. When
word got out that Keith Ransom was teaching a class on film
and that you could take that instead of a Thomas Hardy or
Chaucer course, they practically knocked each other down
getting in. The swelling enrollment of Film as Literature
didn't do Ransom any good with his peers; the rest of the
English faculty grumbled and complained because their own
classes weren't filling up, and it didn't take Dr. Thurman long
to clamp a lid on the number of students who could take the
course, even though it was being held in the auditorium and
easily could have accommodated four times the enrollment
allowed by the department head.

Now Ransom's eyes swept the room in the dark, barely able
to make out the backs of the lucky ones' heads. Thurman had
limited the class size to thirty, and for every occupied seat
three or four were vacant.

So what? thought Ransom. What the hell difference does it
make?

He wondered now why he had even come up with the idea, much less spent time and energy working up a syllabus and overcoming the hostility of the faculty committee long enough to punch it through. What difference *did* a silly and not particularly well-taught little class on the movies—large or small—make, anyway, in the overall scheme of things?

He had thought it would be great. To get paid, and to help students along like a hip older brother, his arm laid familiarly across their shoulders, easing them along toward graduation and life, a light, knowingly bemused smile always playing faintly on his lips. The guru. Besides, he had been a movie buff a long time, and this class seemed the logical culmination of what he had learned, a way of making some money without having to do any unpleasant boning up. He had wanted the class dearly. He had been . . .

Obsessed. Again?

"That's not romance, that's compulsion." Marla's words singed his mind, and he forced them away, forced himself to think again of the class. *So look at me now*, he thought. *I'm not even watching the damn film. I looked forward to it so much a few months ago when I booked it from the rental agency, and now I'm not even looking at it.*

A coldness began working up his spine. His mind burned, popped, connections like sparks along a fuse, hissing, out of control.

Not watching—too tired—drive back last night—
Marla!

It exploded in his head, and suddenly it was a movie. A two-dimensional unnaturally lit, garish, dark movie. Something he had watched a long time ago, maybe, or late at night by himself, drunk or stoned so that time was stretched all out of perspective. A bad movie with graphic killing and blood spurting and no moral underpinnings, just blood and violence and sex and shock slamming into one another, just perverse thrills. A movie to feel sickeningly guilty about having watched, about watching, the kind of movie one would see in a sleazy theater with sleazy, bloodthirsty people all around, laughing and screaming for more. And you could walk out on it all and leave it behind forever.

He tried to walk out on it then, to put it out of his mind. He told himself that Marla—the real Marla, not the Marla being attacked by shadows with claws in the recesses of his brain—was home now, in his—their—apartment, sleeping probably, or waiting for him with some wine, and once this last class was over, her husband, Keith Ransom—the real Keith Ransom—would go back and join her, and everything in his apartment would be where it should be, and there would be nothing wrong, nothing out of place, in his life.

He would not think about that night on the highway, would banish the demons from his mind by making everything into a movie, something seen and not experienced, something that happened to a couple of actors who just happened to look something like him and Marla, something that he and Marla had watched together. And he was sorry he had made her watch it, because it had sickened and disgusted her, and he would promise never to take her to *that* kind of a movie again. He imagined himself explaining to Marla that well, yes, he did like those kinds of movies, but that one went too far, even for him. He saw her concerned eyes—concerned for *him*—gradually soften around the edges as he reassured her he was no maniac, no dark creature of the night, that he just liked bad films. He would call them his "guilty pleasures" —he had read that term somewhere, being used by other-wise normal people, respected people, who liked to watch lowest-common-denominator movies—and they would smile together and everything would be all right.

Still, the demons fought in his mind. Not clearly but threat-eningly, mockingly.

Ransom glanced over at the projector, studying the reel. Experience had taught him how to gauge the amount of film left on it. It was a sixteen-hundred-foot reel, one of two, and as it fed the film into the projector he saw that it was still roughly two-thirds full.

So, about fifteen minutes had elapsed. Fifteen lousy min-utes of a ninety-minute film. One sixth.

He wanted to be anywhere else. He wanted to be home, where he could hold Marla tight, could close his eyes in the womb of his bedroom with her beside him, her leg curled over his, and let sleep erase his mind.

The projector whirred beside him, louder almost than the sound track, and he reached over and boosted the sound, forcing himself to concentrate on *this* movie, to get into it and off on it so the time would pass. And, after all, it was only a movie.

He had missed a little, but he knew the story. A baby was now being taken into an old English church for the baptismal rites, and that was the baby who would grow into a werewolf. Ransom settled back in his chair. There was the priest, making ready for the ceremony. The baby, offered up in front of him. And—

What was *that*?

Ransom stiffened. Superimposed over the screen, in one corner, there and yet not there, like a failed special effect—

A piece of lint, Ransom thought. Something caught in the lens. He leaned over, blew into the film gate.

It was still there. It was growing larger, undulating, spreading over the filmed image of the priest like . . . like *frost*.

No! Ransom's mind shouted. *That's not in the film.*

It shifted again, became vapor and smoke and ice.

And now it had eyes, and the eyes looked at Ransom, and the sound track shrieked as a vial of holy water on-screen began to bubble, smoke, boil over—and hands came up, hands with claws, dead white, nails clicking—

Ransom slammed his hand against the light switch behind him and, with the same motion, stopped the projector. The sound died—and with it the shape.

"Hey, what the hell?"

"Awwwww."

"Kill the projectionist."

The student's faces turned toward Ransom as he watched the now blank screen for any sign of life. There was none. It was gone.

Ransom closed his eyes, his heart slamming in his chest. He heard the clicking of a pair of shoes coming toward him, and he slowly opened his eyes.

Wendy reached out, put a hand on his shoulder. "Anything wrong?"

Ransom straightened, took a deep breath. Everywhere, there were eyes on him. He turned away from Wendy. "Sorry," he said to the faces. "Looks like the projector."

The crowd began to murmur, turning from him to each other.

"We'll have to call it off for tonight. I'll reschedule for

next week, and maybe we'll have to run a little over for the discussion, but we'll get it done." He forced a smile. "Equipment malfunction. What can I say?"

The class fell quiet. Wendy's hand dropped from his shoulder, and still he didn't look at her. He watched as the class prepared to leave, an enormous sense of relief washing over him.

"Wait a minute, Mr. Ransom."

The voice scraped his nerves raw.

"Can I take a look at it?"

Walking toward him was a young man, not one of the regulars, not one of the students who hung out with him. Ransom didn't even remember his name. He let the boy get within a few feet of him before saying, "No use."

The boy grinned. "I work for AV. Know these things front and back, inside and out." He reached toward the projector.

"No!" Ransom said with sudden fierceness, his body crawling. The eyes, all the eyes in the room, fixed on him again.

The boy jerked as if he had been stung, his mouth dropping, the faces of the students behind him a staring, accusing still life.

"I mean," Ransom said quickly, "that . . . well, I know something about projectors myself, and if anything more happens to it than what already has, they're going to have my ass." He wasn't making sense and he knew it.

"Sure. I just thought . . ."

"I appreciate it. But I'd better take it on back now."

The kid shrugged. "Sure. Whatever." He turned awkwardly to go, and as if on signal, the rest of the class stirred themselves and headed for the exits, sneaking an occasional glance at Ransom.

"Keith?"

He looked around. He had forgotten about Wendy, had subconsciously wished her away, out the door with the other students, but now they were gone and she was still there beside him, looking for all the world as she had the first day she had breezed into his last semester's Utopian Literature class wearing jeans as tight as flesh, her breasts jiggling under a half-unbuttoned blouse.

"Yeah?" For a moment, just a moment, he wanted to reach

out to her, to smooth his fingertips along her neck and slide them down, feeling the weight of the silver chains along the backs of his fingers, and down.

"Trouble?" she asked.

"With the projector, yeah."

"Are you sure?"

"I'm sure."

There was a pause then, and a sudden, tired chill zigzagged through Ransom. You couldn't ignore Wendy Layton. The only thing you could do was try to stare her down, and he concentrated on that, forcing away all other thoughts. Their eyes locked.

"Then," she said, "how come you turned the lights on before you shut it off?"

Keith started to lie, but the words wouldn't come. "Look," he said. "What do you *want* from me, Wendy?"

"You have to ask?" She smiled then, one finger playing at the chains at her throat.

Ransom exhaled. It was an effort. "Wendy, I'm very tired. I've got to go home now, and I haven't got the energy—"

"Ohhhh. That's right." Sarcasm drenched her voice, but still she smiled. "Big honeymoon weekend, huh?"

"Right."

"How is old Marla in the sack? Does she moan well or—"

"That's about enough, Wendy."

"Excuse me. I thought I was among friends here." She shook her head. "How soon they forget."

"Wendy, I—"

"Just forget it, Keith. I don't want to hear it."

Anger built in him then, and he turned away from her and began unthreading the projector. There wasn't enough left in him for a fight. He didn't need it, couldn't take it, not her, not on top of everything else, not tonight. Taking the film out of the gate, he lined it up and punched the rewind button, and the reel caught and began taking up.

"Funny," came Wendy's voice from over his shoulder. "It seems to be working fine now."

Ransom's head whipped around, but she was already moving past him toward the door, grinning to herself, the top of her blouse laid open under the silver chains just like always, and like always the swell of tanned breast above the cloth, and the scent of musk in the air.

He raised a hand toward her, started to say something, and then froze as she whispered out the door, closing it behind her. A singing began in his temples, the sound of screaming and pounding and high, shrill music, and the writhing phantoms swooped in his mind. With one hand he felt for the chair, eased down into it, his other hand still raised in front of him.

The cut on the wrist. ("Fell . . . on . . . a piece of glass.")

He reached over with his other hand, slid back the cuff of his shirt, and touched the wound tentatively, as if he were stroking some small animal.

It smeared.

CHAPTER FOUR

Friday. Wasn't it?

Three weeks since her wedding day. Friday, and just three weeks.

Marla thought of herself as she had been, as she had felt, on the day of her wedding to Keith. She thought of herself then as some other person entirely, a radiant, smiling stranger. And she asked of the stranger, "How do you think you'll feel in just three weeks from now?"

"Wonderful," the stranger replied.

"What do you think could go wrong?"

"Nothing."

The stranger who looked like her turned and was gone, clasped in the arms of another stranger who looked just like Keith. For them life was a smooth path to happily ever after.

For Marla it was waiting alone in the hallway outside the Reinholdt College cafeteria.

Again she shifted the weight of her books from one arm to the other, watching the glassed front doors. A moment later she straightened and smiled, but it wasn't him, just a man wearing a corduroy jacket that looked like one of Keith's.

The line of students going into the cafeteria had dwindled to only a few. It would be closing soon, and even if she left right now, she would still be late for the start of her life-drawing class, where the assignment was going to be a finished pencil study. Keith knew she'd be late. He *knew* that.

The smell of fish wafted into the hallway—fish sticks and

frozen French fries, euphemistically termed "Fish 'n' Chips"
on the menu board. The last thing she wanted was fish sticks.

Go, then, she thought. Go. Why not go?

She leaned against the tiled wall, watching the doorway.
She'd leave right now, and that'd teach him to be on time for
a change. And that would . . .

That would ruin the day for her, would torment her with
guilty visions of Keith waiting and looking for her, maybe
missing a class of his own. And oh, but wouldn't the slightest
trouble between her and Keith make for talk-talk-talk around
the campus.

Taped to the wall across from her was a poster proclaiming
a dance in the gym after the night's football game. Marla
tried to ignore it. She could almost imagine, slapped in black
letters over the poster, the edict "No Marrieds Allowed."

Marrieds. She had never thought much about marrieds before, except that they didn't quite belong, that they seemed
to occupy a different space and social order. They lived in
marrieds housing, and they went to marrieds parties, bringing the kids. It was another universe, parallel to but removed
from the rest of the students, one that had seemed a little
dull, a little stultifying to Marla as an unmarried student when
she had thought about it, which wasn't often.

And now she was part of it.

Marla glanced down the hallway, through the window of
the campus bookstore with its paper Thanksgiving turkeys,
past the rows of textbooks, to the back of the store's wall,
where the clock was. *I'll give him ten more minutes*, she
thought. *Just ten more minutes, and then I'm leaving*.

Other students passed her, coming and going in the hallway. A few spoke to her, but most of them seemed awkward
about it. She was a married, a curiosity in a bottle labeled
"Wife of Keith Ransom."

Five more minutes . . .

Keith probably expected her to wait around forever, but he
was going to find out differently, Marla told herself, feeling
suddenly vengeful. She'd go on to class, and maybe afterward
she'd gather up a few of her old friends and go out for a good
time to the Keg 'n' Pizza like before, and he could just sit
around the house and wonder what had become of her.

He certainly wouldn't be lonely. Not with his closets full

of comic books sealed in plastic bags, his baseball cards, mechanical banks, coffee cups, music boxes, movie posters . . .

It was like a kid's playhouse there, Marla thought, except that there didn't seem to be much joy in it. Each of Keith's collections must have been of great interest to him at some point—why else would he have spent all the time and money required?—but the interest was gone now, even though the stuff was still there, important to him only because it belonged to him. She tried to be interested, or amused, or at least not bothered by it all; but somehow she felt threatened. Maybe it was because of the nagging fear that she was just one more thing to be kept but eventually forgotten, a living version of the autographed pictures stacked in a box in the closet.

Keith was so *hard* to figure. Marla's art classes had made her keenly aware of gestures and body language, and she had tried to use this awareness to understand her husband. She took note of the way he kept his arms folded when he talked to her, of the way that he crossed his legs away from her when they sat together watching television on the sagging sofa. If they held hands at all, it was because she reached to him; then, very often, he flinched, and his hand was stiff and cold.

He was pointedly nice to her, cracked jokes with her, seemed to enjoy cooking supper for her now and then, making a production out of it. *But he doesn't want to touch me. He doesn't want to be close to me.*

Sometimes he would look at her with what seemed to be undisguised longing, but nothing ever came of it unless she took the lead and practically hauled him to bed, which made her feel cheap. And while he went unhurriedly through the motions of lovemaking with a textbook kind of care, she could sense that he wanted nothing so much as to be done with it. *To get away from me.*

And the drinking. She had known he liked to drink, but lately he had been increasing the amount and frequency, had changed from beer to Scotch. Too many times she had come home in the middle of the day to find him sitting alone amid his collections, a drink in his hand, his eyes already glassy and faraway.

Marla wondered often if it was her, but he had loved her when they were dating, loved her with a passion she could see burning in his eyes. Had something about her changed? Could anything about her have changed in just *three weeks*?

No, she knew, nothing could have. Her confidence in that kept her much more bewildered than hurt, more worried for Keith than for herself. She wanted him to see a doctor, wished he would go. But when she had called for the appointment, just to make it easy for him, he had "forgotten" to go. She hadn't pushed. She didn't want any more tension.

Over and over again she had replayed that night in the Ozarks. Sometimes the memory of it was so vivid that her stomach lurched when she remembered the car veering off the road and the ground beneath it disappearing. And Keith's face—*that* was the part that still gave her bad dreams, the way he had stared at the windshield, his eyes blank.

In those dreams she saw his eyes frosted white and glowing, as if the reality of it hadn't been bad enough.

Keith had never been the same with her after that night, but he still liked to drive. If the trouble was still that he was afraid of hurting her, then it seemed to her that he shouldn't want to drive with her in the car.

"Hey, there she is."

"The old married lady."

Marla turned at the sound of the voices, the residue of her thoughts still clinging to her, and spotted her friends, Brenda and Staci, coming toward her with broad smiles. She suddenly remembered that she hadn't seen them, hadn't even talked with them, since the day of the wedding. The two of them had been witnesses to the civil ceremony and later had been the only two people to see them off. She had intended to drop each of them a card from the Ozarks, but she somehow hadn't gotten around to it.

Now, as she watched them approach, it was as if they were figures out of the distant past, as if all the running around and late-night sharing of dorm-room secrets belonged to another time, a time already only dimly remembered.

Three weeks, Marla reminded herself again.

"We thought you'd dropped off the planet," said Staci, a statuesque, opal-eyed brunette. "How's it been?"

Marla fidgeted a little, glad to see them but feeling a little guilty too. "It's been fine. I meant to send you a card while I was on my honeymoon, but—"

"*But* you had other things to do, right?" said Brenda. She was the smallest of the three, a blond PE major who could drink more beer than any woman Marla had ever seen. "Look, Staci, she's blushing."

"Quit that." Marla turned away, smiling.

"Hey, it's okay," Brenda said. "We know how it is, don't we, Stace? A woman in love." She stretched out the last word.

"I've been meaning to call you," Marla said. "I want you to come over soon."

The silence that followed was short but uncomfortable. Staci answered, "Sure. Sure we will, Marla." She shook her head. "I don't believe it. Married. Remember how we used to wonder who'd get married first out of the three of us?"

Marla chuckled. "I always figured it'd be you."

"Wish I'd've put some money on that," Brenda said. She checked her watch. "Hey, I've got to get to class."

"You've got time," said Marla.

"Not much. I have to meet Hardage before class starts to find out why the old fart gave me a *D* on my last paper."

"Still giving you trouble, huh?" Marla asked.

Brenda smiled. "What do you mean, *still*? It's the same trouble he was giving me a month ago, when you lived in the dorm with us. There hasn't been *that* much water under the bridge."

"I guess you're right."

"Look, Marla," Brenda said. "I'll see you, okay?"

"Right."

"See you back at the dorm, Stace."

Marla watched her leave. *Back at the dorm.* The three of them had had so much time for each other then, and now it seemed as if Brenda were in a hurry to get away from her. She turned to Staci. "It seems like a long time ago, Staci," she said. "I keep wanting to ask you if things are the same as they were, but I know they are. Just like Brenda said, it's only been a month. Less. A month used to seem like nothing."

Staci nodded, shifting her books from one arm to the other.

"I know. But things *have* changed, I guess. You're gone, and—"

"I'm not *gone*, Stace. I'm right here."

"You know what I mean."

Marla knew. It was a weight dropping inside her. "But I don't want—I don't know, Staci. I still want us to be friends like before, but I know things have to be different now." She paused. "Hey, maybe we can get together at the Keg 'n' Pizza some afternoon, just the three of us."

"That'd be great. Would he let you do it?"

"Sure. No problem." Marla glanced toward the entrance-way, hearing a buzz of voices. There was Keith.

Staci followed her gaze. "Even as we speak," she said, waving at Keith. "Got to go, Marla. I'll call you."

"Okay." As Staci left, Marla turned toward Keith. He wasn't alone, of course. He was never alone, always trailing an entourage of groupies, as Marla had taken to calling them. She didn't like to think of the short time ago when she had been one of them, rehearsing a question to get his attention.

But he seemed to be getting them trained. Breaking off an apparent debate on the worst movie ever made, he waved them away and came to Marla with a shrug and a sheepish grin meant to be comical. "Heavy academics," he said. "How's your friend?"

Marla accepted a "faculty-wife" kiss on the cheek. "She's fine and I'm glad to see you," she said, "but I've got just enough time to leave for class."

"Without lunch? Oh, no, you don't." He took the books from her. "Listen, I called your dad today, just like you've been wanting me to do, and one thing I promised him is that I've been taking good care of you. And that means lunch."

"You talked to Dad?"

"Uh-huh. He actually spoke to me. Things are looking up."

Marla knew how hard it would have been for Keith to call her father, or even to track him down by phone. Burton Latham owned three motels in Oklahoma City and one in Ardmore, ninety miles to the south, and lived in constant motion between all three in the conviction that none of his managers knew what they were doing. And he liked his managers. He didn't like Keith.

"Thank you for doing that. Really, Keith, it means a lot to me." She paused. "But I'm late for class."

"Aw . . ." He dismissed the objection with a wave of his hand. "That's Charlie Maxwell's class, right? I'll buy him a beer. Don't worry about Charlie."

"He may be Charlie to you, but he's still Professor Maxwell to me. I don't want special treatment, Keith."

"Then don't be so special."

Marla looked at him, really seeing him for the first time that day. *He's doing it to me again*, she thought. Somehow he made the midday shadow of a beard look roguish instead of scruffy, and he was using that way of talking to her that made it seem like the rest of the world had been shut out completely. The anger she felt toward him began to slip away, replaced by a feeling of foolishness, of having made a mistake.

Keith shifted her sketchbook to the top of the stack and began flipping through it. He came to the wrong page before she could stop him: a profile drawing of him, the harsh black strokes across it still leaving the likeness recognizable.

"It . . . it's not finished," she said, wanting to grab the book and hide it, tear it, burn it. "I wasn't happy with it."

Keith smiled, looking a little awkward. "It looks good to me," he said. "Except the eyes, maybe. Kind of spooky-looking."

"Are you going to feed me or not?"

He closed the book. "Anything for a starving artist."

They joined the remnants of the cafeteria line, Keith behind her with one hand lightly touching her waist. She was very aware of that hand.

"And what for you, Mrs. Ransom?" asked the hair-netted, grandmotherly woman behind the counter. Marla felt a rush of satisfaction. Hearing the name was like wearing a new dress.

"Take plenty," Keith whispered. "You'll need it to get through tonight."

Ransom grimaced, looking at himself in the full-length Woolco bargain-special mirror affixed to the bathroom door. The costume was finished, or at least there was nothing more to be done for it—orange-colored leotards; a pair of bedroom

slippers wrapped with stripes of ribbon; formal dress shirt
with ruffles at the neck, the tail left hanging out and the waist
tied with rope; and an old sport jacket with the sleeve cut off
to make a jerkin.

"A bloody deed!" he said stiffly to the door. "Almost as
bad, good mother, as kill a king and marry with his brother."

"I'll be out in a minute," Marla answered from inside the
bathroom.

Ransom tried bending to see if the leotards would split,
almost hoping they would, so he could stay home. But no
such luck—and no escape from the party.

Hopes had raged through the English Department that Dr.
Thurman would drop the affair after he had been "struck
down" by the flu and forced to cancel at Halloween, but the
famous Thurman Shakespeare Gala merely had been resched-
uled. Or reassigned.

"Give me six trips to the dentist to one night of this,"
Ransom said. "I *hate* this crap."

The door opened. "Oh, what a noble mind is here o'er-
thrown," Marla said, a tone of aching sympathy in her voice.
She wore a retailored red velvet bathrobe with a square-cut
neckline, the skirt angling in a stiff cone shape from her waist
to the floor; a double string of heavy white beads; and a small
white bonnet. She had parted her hair in the middle.

"Well, I hope you're having fun . . . Ophelia."

"I think it *is* kind of fun, Keith. How do I look?"

"Let's just go and get it over with."

"You could cheer up a little."

"Hamlet's supposed to be melancholy," he said.

"Hamlet didn't have a wife to straighten him out."

Ransom smiled, realizing with some surprise that he was
enjoying the banter. As bad as his mood was, as much as he
dreaded what lay ahead, he was having fun with the repartee
between him and Marla. His smile edged into a grin.

"That's better," she said.

"I perchance hereafter shall think meet to put an antic
disposition on." He flipped at his coattails. "That, and a
long coat. I'm going to freeze my ass in this getup."

The car started sluggishly in the mid-November cold. The
night had the blue-black sheen of metal, glinting with stars

and the sleepy, dull glow of the three-quarter moon. Ransom switched on the cold engine breath of the heater, cursing at it as he backed out of the driveway. Marla huddled against him.

The back tire jolted as he pulled into the street. A sharp, squalling sound pierced the air.

Marla stiffened, looking backward, as he hit the brakes. "Oh Lord . . . no," she said weakly.

Ransom started to say something, but she was already out of the car. Through the open door he heard her calling, "Here, kitty. Kitty?"

He caught up to her in the red glow of the taillights, the smoky fog of the exhaust. She pointed toward a section of shrubbery beside the house.

"It was that gray cat with the white face, the one I've been feeding," she said. "We hit it. It's hurt." Her voice tightened, and her mittened hands waved helplessly.

"Couldn't be hurt too much if it could run that far, that fast."

"We've got to find it, Keith."

"What we've *got* to do is get to the party. We're already going to be late," he said. And so what? he thought. He didn't care about the time, didn't care about the cat, didn't care . . .

About Marla? About making *her* feel bad?

"The best thing to do is to let it come out by itself," he said. "Cats take care of themselves." He reached out, clasping her and leading her back to the car.

"Are you sure, Keith?"

"I'm sure. It'll come out in the morning, and we'll take it to the vet."

She got in, clenching the collar of her coat. "I feel just awful," she said.

"Yeah. So do I," Ransom returned, shutting the car door. He walked around the back of the car. At the base of the left rear wheel a small pool of blood stained the pavement, reflecting a dimly white, three-quarter-round shape. Slowly and deliberately he scuffed the toe of his ribboned slipper through the pool.

For a moment, just a moment, he thought about reaching down and pressing his hands into it.

They drove with the radio throbbing. Ransom turned the sound up, the music battering away the worst of his guilt feelings. But a queasiness stayed with him. Perversely his mind interplayed the sight of the cat's blood with a vision of shiny black caviar spread on party crackers and bubbling cheese dip—a choice of dreading the thing left behind or the night still to come. And a question . . .

He thought of the angle, the shadows, the shine of the car's taillights as he had stood there, looking down. There was no way that the moon could have reflected so sharply from the dull surface of the pool. But he had seen it!

His hands tightened against the steering wheel. His heart raced at the fear of seeing frost again on the windshield, and eyes in the frost, and Marla through eyes that weren't his.

She sat reading a copy of *Hamlet* with a flashlight, now and then closing her eyes and repeating one of Ophelia's lines. The music blared, and Marla said, "To speak of horrors, he comes before me."

Ransom reached over and turned the radio down, forcing his mind away from the visions. "I'll be anxious to see how you work that line into the conversation," he said.

She closed the book, smiling. It was the kind of smile people give to each other in a hospital elevator, but at least she was trying. "Well, you picked an easy one," she said. "Hamlet. All you have to remember is 'To be or not to be.' Not very enterprising."

"*Dull* is the word. I strove for it and got it. Anything else might be misconstrued as a show of interest."

"It wouldn't hurt you to play the game just a little, Keith. Dr. Thurman—"

"Ah, yes. *Dr.* Thurman. I'll tell you *his* game so we can both play. You get ten points for knowing on sight that he is supposed to be—and get this, dear Ophelia—is *supposed* to be King Lear. Wire-rimmed glasses and all. That's *supposed* to be a secret, but it leaked."

"Okay." She paused a moment. "Now what I *started* to say . . . He *is* the department head, and you ought to try getting along with him. After all, this is only a party."

"Wait and see."

"To speak of horrors, he comes before me."

Ransom took the Lewis Avenue exit off the Interstate and turned south, on past 51st Street, where the city changed character as surely as if a sign had been posted there: "Now Entering South Tulsa. Neckties Required." Goldie's hamburger restaurant was the last sign of life as he knew it; ahead lay the favored land surrounding the gleam and glitter of Oral Roberts University, with its City of Faith hospital rising like a spotlit, gold-plated, high-rise prayer into the night sky.

"On your left, that popular tourist attraction, Six Flags over Jesus," Ransom said as they passed the evangelist's campus.

"Keith," she admonished, "don't talk like that."

"You expecting a lightning bolt?"

"I just don't think it's a good idea to make fun of religious things."

Ransom nodded. "Okay. But is it all right to make fun of Oral?"

He turned at 81st Street, following the directions on the party invitation, turned again onto a rolling, curved drive that flowed into a cul-de-sac faced by a ring of stone-fronted homes. Each had a two-car garage, a glass storm door, a yard light. They weren't oil-money houses, not that big, but places where the idea of a membership in Southern Hills Country Club might be taken seriously. Ransom had no idea how Morris Thurman could manage to make the payments on such a place; he only hoped that it hurt.

Already the circular curb line was crowded with the parked cars of other party goers. "Which house?" Marla asked.

Ransom pointed. "We'll take what's behind door number one," he said, and she reached for his hand as they walked past the yard light toward the door. As they approached the house he found himself thinking again about the moon's reflection, searching for an explanation. He found none. But the drive and the night air had been good for him; all he felt now was vaguely foolish to have been afraid of seeing ghost-like images in the glass again. *Again.* That was what bothered him: that the first time had happened at all. He couldn't dismiss the reality of it, just as he couldn't forget the eyes on the film screen or explain away so many other signs of something gone wrong with him. The sleeplessness. The nightmares. And now the moon. Now that he thought about it, he realized what had bothered him about that. The moon hadn't seemed to be reflected by the pool of blood; instead it had appeared to be . . . trapped inside it.

Ransom rang the lighted doorbell, suddenly wanting a drink very badly. Muffled voices filtered through the door, and laughter that would have suited a television sitcom. Ransom mimicked a cigar in his hand, gave a Groucho Marx roll of the eyes. "To flee or not to flee," he said.

Marla punched him on the shoulder and the door was opened—first the polished inner door, then the polished glass storm door—by Morris Thurman, wearing a gilt-edged robe and crown. A rented costume, Ransom thought, or more likely one borrowed from the Reinholdt Drama Department by a little rank pulling.

"When we are born, we cry that we are come to this great stage of fools," Thurman said, his head tilted back, his hair silvered and waved. "The fools are still here, but you've missed the reading."

"We had some car trouble," Keith said. "Dr. Thurman, I don't think you've met my wife, Marla."

"No. I think not," said Thurman, smiling at her as if he might give her a pat on the head. "My great regret is that I have such limited time these days to acquaint myself with the undergraduates. Please do come in, *Mrs.* Ransom."

Ransom was taken aback to see her curtsy with a flourish of her robe. "As the good King Lear commands," she said.

"Ah!" Thurman's smile this time seemed genuinely benevolent. "And let me guess. Of course. Juliet!"

"Of course," she said, smiling.

"And you, Ransom . . ." He closed the door behind them. "Who else but Hamlet, the same as last year, as I recall."

"Do not look upon me, lest with this piteous action you convert my stern effects."

"Yes. Hamlet." Thurman gestured toward the beige-carpeted living room. A white knit fabric pit group dominated the center of the room, but most of the people were standing; the furniture looked so little used that Ransom suspected even the Thurmans avoided sitting on it, afraid of getting it soiled. A stone-fronted fireplace flickered silently from a gas log at the far side of the room, flanked by shelves that alternated rows of books and conspicuously placed travel souvenirs, mostly Oriental.

"Do make yourselves comfortable," Thurman said. "The bar is in the kitchen, or . . ." He smiled again at Marla. "Ginger ale, if you prefer."

"Thank you, nothing for now," she said. But when Thurman had excused himself, she nudged Keith and whispered, "Get me a boilermaker."

"Don't say I didn't warn you about how this was going to be."

"What was that 'reading' we missed?"

"His wife recites poetry. We lucked out."

Marla scanned the room, the costumes. Here was an Othello, there a Macbeth, a Falstaff, a Portia, a Shylock, a Cleopatra. "Which one is she?"

"I don't see her," Keith replied. "Last year, when she finished with her reciting, she had to go rest for a while. The creative act is so terribly draining, you know."

"So what do we do now?"

"Throw our coats on the floor, I guess, and join the fun," Keith said.

Marla stood, rolling the glass between her hands, feeling the cold moisture, listening more to the soft clinking of the ice than to the conversation around her. The party had formed into "battle lines"—Keith's description—with the longest entrenched professors and associate professors in a cluster near the fireplace. Thurman was with them. The wives were mostly gathered in the kitchen, and the children had been relegated to somewhere out of the way, most likely a bedroom.

She turned again to Keith, who seemed to have taken some real interest in an argument about the plan to build a new state university in Tulsa; but then, she reflected, Keith could lose himself in a scratchy old jazz record, or a late showing of *The Day the Earth Stood Still* in murky black-and-white on TV. She envied him the ability.

Marla could tell by the set of Keith's jaw that he was poised to jump into the conversation again, as soon as Edgar Jackson, who taught freshman composition, might give up the floor, if ever.

". . . and mark my words," Jackson was saying. "There

is going to be a bloodletting. Tulsa does not have the popu-
lation to support another university. What with the junior
college expanding and . . .''

She wondered if it worried Edgar Jackson that he was going
prematurely bald. Surely he didn't have to make it worse by
combing what was left of his hair straight back. She was glad
to have avoided him as an instructor, glad she had heard and
heeded the things her friends had told her about his grading
policies.

He stopped talking abruptly, with a sharp nod of his head
that seemed to mean he had scored some particularly telling
point, but Keith missed his chance, and Gwendolyn Archer
took over.

Gwendolyn Archer was famous on campus as the daughter
of Tommy Archer, ''the high-volume dealer with a heart,''
whose used-car commercials blared over the AM radio channels. She countered her father's image with a soft but precise
voice that banished all traces of an Okie twang.

''That's absolutely correct. And we at Reinholdt *must* make
the legislature understand the consequences to this institu-
tion, as well as to the University of Tulsa and Oral Roberts
University. The very existence of private education cannot be
allowed to be jeopardized by . . .''

Marla tuned her out and studied the room. The costumes
provided the place with a carnival look, and it did have the
cheese-dip and snack-cracker trappings of a party. But the
party was missing. It was more like a test, with everyone
aware of being graded. At least *she* felt graded.

The sound of Keith's voice brought her back to the conversation. ''So education is too lofty a thing for comparison
shopping? Is that what you're saying? Maybe we should all
be wondering what we *do* here for anybody that's worth a
hundred and twenty dollars a credit.''

Jackson stiffened, and a series of creases, like ladder rungs,
measured the expanse of his forehead. ''What *we* do, I should
say, is a question for those who have tenure.''

Gwendolyn Archer was talking at the same time, something about cutting ''junk'' courses out of the curriculum,
and Marla burned with resentment at what she knew to be a
direct and personal attack against Keith and his film class.
Her glass felt cold in her tightened hands, in counterpoint to

the fire spreading across her face. She wanted to fight for Keith, but she was afraid to open her mouth and let the words come out, because she knew what those words would be. They pounded inside her.

Shut up! Just two words, but they so desperately needed saying. *Shut up!*

The voices outside her were no more than an insect buzz as she fought to control herself. What could she *really* do that would be of any help to Keith and not an embarrassment? The cost of going to college had never been a concern of hers; the only difficulty had been in deciding where to enroll, and in her father's refusal to consider any of the art schools on the East Coast simply because he had wanted her to stay close to home. And *tenure*—that was a puzzle to her. It was clearly more complicated than who could or couldn't be fired. It was all wrapped up in faculty politics and game playing, and the one fact about it that Marla grasped completely was that Keith could be in trouble.

But now Keith was grinning. He was grinning the way she had once seen her father look just before he had shot a deer.

"Canned tests and canned lectures," he was saying, "and how many people do you think are going to pay extra for a fancy label on the can?"

And Marla, her anger drained, was just . . . standing there. She was nothing but a weight that made her feet ache. She wished that Keith would at least give her a glance. What ever had made her think that he might need *her* to back him up, to be with him, when he hadn't so much as bothered to explain what would be expected of her?

A new resentment coiled around the old. She wanted to . . . what? . . . yank on his sleeve just to get his attention. To shout, "Remember me?"

Keith and Jackson were talking at the same time now, Jackson jabbing the air with his forefinger and Gwendolyn Archer pitching into the jumble of voices with an unnaturally shrill tone that caused heads to turn and conversation to die down across the room. Marla saw Thurman approaching, his gilt-edged robe swishing ludicrously against the carpet but with a cold and dangerous look of pleasure on his face, as if for him the pot had finally boiled. And she didn't want to be there. She didn't want to stand there feeling tongue-tied and re-

jected; and more than that, she didn't want to be used against
Keith, tricked by Thurman and the others into saying something stupid.

The quoting of character lines was a trifle that had long
since played out. The costumes seemed now to be just a way
of making people feel awkward in an already tense situation.
Next time she would *know*, would be ready, and things would
be altogether different. But for now . . .

She backed away, unnoticed, from the group, starting for
the kitchen, but the sound of whispered voices and whispery
laughter stopped her. No, she wasn't ready to deal with the
faculty, and she damn sure wasn't ready for a swim in *that*
tank of piranha.

And that left the hallway. The first door she passed was
shut, and Marla guessed it was the bedroom of the so terribly
drained Mrs. Thurman. The sound of a woman's cough from
beyond the door confirmed her suspicions, and she suddenly
dreaded to think of the door opening. She hurried down the
hallway toward a half-opened door at the end, toward the
sound of children's laughter.

Edging the door open, she saw two grade-school-aged boys
and a girl who looked a little older clustered around a *Star
Wars* game, and a baby wrapped in pink, asleep on the bed.
In a bentwood rocker a plump-and-then-some, round-faced
woman sat reading a paperback book titled *Love's Tender
Fury*; her flat white gown could have suggested any of Shakespeare's women, or none of them at all.

She looked up at Marla. "Friend or foe?" she asked.

Marla felt suddenly relieved. "I'm . . ." she started to say
but checked herself. She didn't want to make introductions.
If this was Edgar Jackson's wife, she didn't want to know. "I
thought maybe you could use some help."

"Is that an offer to take over here so I can go back to the
party?"

"Sure."

The woman closed her book. Reaching over and tucking
the blanket around the baby's shoulders, she sighed. "I was
afraid of that," she said.

It was Thursday, a day that had been so long in coming.
For Ransom the days since Thurman's party seemed hardly

to have existed; they had collapsed into the events of Marla searching and calling until she had located the injured cat under a bush in the back of the house, and running up a seventy-five-dollar veterinarian's bill, and naming the cat Strawberry. For Ransom they had been days of sleepwalking through classes, and nights when the buzzing confusion in his brain led to drink and more confusion, unfocused but filled with a kind of dread that led to three A.M. drunkenness in front of the television set, an ashtray overflowing with cigarettes and a Scotch bottle beside him.

Now he thought he knew the cause. He had a focal point for his dread, and he told himself this was what had caused it, the lifeless drifting of time spent in wait without being conscious of the thing for which he had been waiting. He reached over and took the folded pages of *The Reinholdt Ranger* from on top of his desk.

Wendy Layton, as editor of the campus paper, had come bubbling into Thurman's party, along with a scraggly-haired kid with the camera, the result being the photo that dominated the top half of the *Ranger*'s front page. The cutline read, "Dr. Morris Thurman, chairman of Reinholdt's Department of English, entertains party guests in the guise of King Lear. 'If you have poison for me, I will drink it.' "

Ransom turned the page over to find, beneath the fold, exactly what he had expected to find there—had dreaded, he now knew, from the moment he had noticed that Marla wasn't beside him at the party and that Wendy and the kid with the camera were nowhere in the living room—and the way Wendy emerged from the hallway smiling at him with such dark-eyed glee.

The photo was of Marla, surrounded by children. The cutline said, "Mrs. Keith Ransom as Juliet. 'Well, think of marriage now.' "

The paper slid lightly from his hands, and he pressed his hands against the ache in his temples. The ache meant a nightmare was on the way, and it was always the same one.

Always . . . the one with claws.

CHAPTER FIVE

Keith Ransom was beginning to feel a little high, and it wasn't a minute too soon. He had managed to throw back a couple of double Scotches before venturing out of his home, and now a half-empty pitcher of beer sat between him and Marla on one of the Formica-topped tables at the Keg 'n' Pizza.

How is it? he thought. Beer on whiskey, mighty risky?

He didn't care. Riskier by far, he thought, to stay straight, to have to think, to have to deal with the residue of one nightmare and the approach of another as the inevitable darkness fell. Sometimes, if he drank enough and stayed up late enough, he didn't seem to dream. Awakening with a Scotch-and-cigarette hangover had seemed small payment for a night without torment.

Then it had stopped working.

A couple of nights ago—Wednesday—he had awakened with the dull taste of nicotine in his throat and alcohol lurching in his stomach, awakened to find himself bolt upright in bed, sweat blocking his pores and stinging his eyes. He couldn't remember the particulars of the dream—even the images seemed suffocated by the darkness around him—but he knew what it had been. He knew. As his breathing had returned to normal he had looked over to see Marla still asleep, wrapped in bed covers.

The second night, after he had seen *The Reinholdt Ranger*, he hadn't been so lucky.

It was always the same dream, sometimes as vivid as the glinting of a piece of sharp metal, other times dark and murky, but always the same. It had become the play, the movie, and sometimes he viewed it from afar, and sometimes from the first row, and sometimes, at the most awful, terrifying times, he was in it.

That night he had awakened only when the pain snapped through his face, had opened his eyes to see Marla huddled like a terrified child against the brass headboard of the bed, holding one hand in the other and sobbing, and then he had realized the source of his pain.

"I had to," she had said then. "I had to . . . hit you. To make you stop."

"It's funny," she said now, not quite looking at Ransom, her thumb and forefinger rubbing at the moisture on the mug.

"What?" He could scarcely hear her for the jukebox's pounding and the laughter and talk of the Friday evening revelers.

"I said, it's funny. It's only been a month or so since the last time I was here, and the whole place seems different."

"I think they've turned up the jukebox."

"No, it's . . ." She tried a smile, succeeding only partially. "It's more than that."

He knew what she meant. The restaurant seemed different because she was seeing it from a different place, a table in the center, with the salad bar commotion right behind her—a place they had not so much chosen as felt resigned to take.

Years of tradition dictated that the west side of the Keg 'n' Pizza was the student side. The jukebox was on that side, flanked by the blinking screen of a video baseball game. The wall was a bulletin board papered with notes and Polaroid photos; the rough wooden supports defied anyone to find the room to carve one more name. Reinholdt Rosie, a department store mannequin dating back to the fifties, was propped in the corner as always, wearing a big-nose-and-mustache pair of glasses.

The east side was the faculty section. The red-and-white-checkered vinyl tablecloths were topped with candlelit lanterns on that side. Flames popped and flickered in the rough stone fireplace, and the air curled with the fragrant smoke of pipe tobacco.

There was, of course, no wall between the two, no line drawn across the floor, but the separation was generally respected by both sides. Students here, faculty there—and a half dozen tables in the middle for nobody in particular.

"You want to go somewhere else?" Ransom asked. And then, to soften the meaning: "It's going to take forever to get a burned anchovy in here."

She shook her head quickly. "I've been looking forward to this."

Ransom swallowed a long drink of beer. He felt a new guilt weaving through him, and he let it play, a fresh guilt at having robbed Marla of the careless pleasure of being a student. She should have gone out by herself, he thought. Next time she probably would.

They were coming apart, and he knew it. Not far apart, not yet, but the schism was there—and this time it was different. She was afraid of him. He could see it in her eyes. Ever since that night.

No!

He blocked the thought. It was bad enough to be haunted in sleep, when his defenses were lulled and the demons—the *demon*—crept in. There was nothing he could do about that anymore. But now he was awake and could fight it. He could make things right with her.

Sitting there now, the alcohol buzzing in his head, he resolved to show her, to make her happy again. She wanted him to go to a doctor? Fine. He'd go to the doctor, and the doctor would prescribe something for the nightmares, and if that didn't work . . . well, hell, he'd even see a shrink if that was what she wanted.

He closed his eyes and thought for a moment about how happy she would be once it was all over. He envisioned a scene in which he came through the door carrying a note from the doctor, giving him a clean bill of health, and he would be waving it, grinning, and they would embrace, and the night in the mountains would become a movie again, and the nightmares would be gone.

Ransom wondered why he hadn't thought of this sooner. He began to smile at the simplicity, the inevitability of it all, and a warm flush spread through him. Meeting Marla's eyes, he said, "You're right." It was almost a shout, a shout of joy and release.

She looked startled. "Right about what?"

"About lots of things." He held out the pitcher and refilled his mug. "Lots of things, my wonderful wife."

"Are you already a little pie-eyed, Keith?"

"Working on it."

She didn't smile. "So, then, what am I right about?"

"About me. About how I should see a doctor." He leaned in toward her. "Absolutely on-the-nose right."

"Keith, are—"

"No. I'm not humoring you again, not this time. I was just thinking about it, and it makes perfect sense, what you've been telling me off and on for the past month."

Marla looked relieved but still a little wary. "You'll do it this time, Keith? You promise?"

His smile felt good, the noise of the place felt good, the buzzing of the alcohol felt good, and Ransom felt good, good and giddy and redeemed. "I'll swear it on a stack of Bibles, of Uncle Scrooge comics, original lobby cards from *Casablanca*—anything you want, Marla. Now drink up. This is a celebration, by damn."

"Keith, if only I could believe it."

He reached toward the pitcher. "Believe it. More?"

"You know me," she said, putting a hand over the top of her mug. "Two beers and here comes the sandman."

"Then we'll make it an early evening." He nudged her hand away with the tip of the pitcher and poured the mug full. Lifting his own mug, he said, "To mental health—drink up or I'll kill you," and a shock ran through him as he realized what he had just said. An old, stupid gag, even under the best of circumstances, and with what was going on lately—

He started to stammer out an apology to Marla, but when he looked at her, he saw that her eyes were trained past him, behind him, and he realized with a beat of relief that she had not been listening. As he turned to look over his shoulder his attention was caught by the full moon, showing through the plate-glass window at the front of the restaurant like an unblinking, cold eye in the darkness.

Ransom caught himself rubbing at the cut on his wrist. It should have healed long ago but hadn't. Now a spot of watery blood came off onto his fingers.

The moonlight reflected against the glass doors at the front of the restaurant as they were swung open by a group of incoming students, Wendy Layton in the lead. She was wearing a soft, capelike beige coat that looked expensive, and faded jeans laced at the front: a queen with the common touch. The loose, dark ends of the bow knot invited untying.

"Well, look who just blew in," he said to Marla, trying to keep his voice casual, wishing like hell they had left before.

Marla's face was unreadable, and Ransom fell silent, awaiting the inevitable and feeling himself starting to lose the alcoholic buzz he had worked so hard to attain. His hands found the beer mug, and he was in the middle of a long draft when he heard Wendy say "Hi" behind him.

Ransom turned, and then he knew. It hadn't been Wendy that Marla had been watching so intently; instead it had been the student with her. The boy stood behind Wendy now, huge and towering, an awkward-looking grin on his face. Ransom had never had him in class—the jocks had their own group of professors at Reinholdt, tried and true—but he knew who the boy was. And he knew that Marla knew, too, that she had him secreted back in a part of her mind labeled "ex-boyfriend."

Ransom looked at them both for a long count, hoping to make them feel uncomfortable. It didn't work. The boy continued to grin, as if he were a not-too-bright child who nevertheless possessed some secret power. Wendy smiled, too, and the silence thickened until Ransom could no longer stand it.

"So where were you Monday?" he asked. "We had a test in film class."

Wendy turned a palm up. "Couldn't make it. Something came up."

"That's twice you've missed a test. It's going to be pretty hard for you to pass if you don't start showing up."

She gave him a look of—no, not innocence. The eyes were all innocence, but the smile made her expression condescending. "I'm holding out for the werewolf movie. You left us all hanging a month ago, and I never *did* find out what happened to that poor baby—you know, the one that was getting baptized."

Damn her! he thought. She seemed almost to know exactly

what had happened to him that night. But she didn't . . . she couldn't . . .

"I told you that the print had sprocket damage," he said. "I requested a new copy, but these rental agencies move slowly."

"Yeah? Well, maybe you ought to hurry them up a little." She spoke with a subtle arching of her eyebrows, as if to let him know that she had trapped him in a lie.

That was her talent, Ransom thought: to sense something wrong and make the most of it. A very finely honed skill.

"Look, can we sit down?" she said, taking the chair next to Ransom as if he had answered. The boy took the empty chair next to Marla. "So how are things?" she asked cheerfully. "Oh, by the way, this is Ben Taylor." She nodded toward the boy. "Ben, this is Keith Ransom."

The boy nodded. His smile had disappeared. Turning to Marla, he asked, "How are you?"

"I'm fine." Her eyes betrayed nothing. "How about you?"

"Good."

Ransom felt a sudden burning anger. His hands began to imperceptibly twitch, to loosen and tighten, under the table, as if the very cells of his skin had all begun to crawl in different directions, and he knew he had to do something *now*, something to get these people *out of here*. His mind raced. He and Marla could leave—that would be the easiest thing—but he didn't feel like running, not tonight, not now, not when he was on the verge of having everything together.

"Sprocket damage, huh?" Wendy said to him. "Is that what you said?"

"Yeah."

"It's funny they'd send a film out like that, all torn up. You'd think they'd have people to check."

He looked at her with a flash of anger that made his head reel. For just that instant his vision blanked to frost white, and against that white, in place of Wendy's face, there were spatters of red. His voice came from nowhere. "I want to talk to you," he said.

"Talk away. Just get us some beer first."

"I mean *now*." To Marla and Taylor he said, "We'll be back in just a minute."

"Back from—?" Wendy began, but he had her by the el-

bow, easing her out of the booth with a grip that let her know
he meant business. He struggled to keep his anger from
showing, but his blood was racing.

"Wait a minute, Keith," Marla said.

He turned, spoke through clenched teeth. "We'll be back
before you know it," he said, and turned before she could
protest any more, his hand still firm around Wendy's elbow.
They began moving through the tables.

"Mind telling me where we're going?" she asked, turning
to him.

"Outside."

She squirmed a little, and he tightened his grip. Her eyes
flashed anger but she kept moving, past the tables full of
students and out the door, into the night, with the moon round
and leaden on the horizon.

"This way," Ransom said. They went down the street,
stopping in front of his car. He let her loose then, and she
shook her arm irritably.

"What the—?" she began.

"Get in."

She got in, and he went around to the other side and
climbed in behind the steering wheel.

"So what the hell is this macho trip all about?" she asked.
"What's gotten *into* you?"

He felt his eyes narrow to slits. "Plenty. For starters, let's
talk about that little number with the paper."

"What?"

"Nice piece of imagery, that picture of Marla with the
kids, but about as subtle as a knife fight."

She took out a cigarette, tapped it impatiently on the dashboard, and lit it. Inhaling, she said, "Look, she was there. I
didn't set her up."

"Right."

"She was there and I took her picture."

"And the caption? Was that serendipity, too, or did you
have to work a little on that?" Anger began choking his
words; he started to feel an odd floating sensation, as if the
rage were buoying him up, making him weightless.

"Loosen up," she said irritably. "You know, ever since
little Marla came along, you've been a real dead-ass, you
know that?"

He felt the anger billow through him like smoke. "I want you to leave her *alone*."

"Poor li'l thing can't take care of herself, is that it?"

Again the frost in his eyes. She dimmed to a tissue-white in front of him, a flimsy thing, so easy to tear. He fought to control himself.

"What do you think, that it's some kind of *contest* with you? It isn't, Wendy, and it never was."

"Oh, right, I understand. You explained it before. It just doesn't do for a faculty type to get caught with his hand up the wrong skirt. He can slip once or twice, but then everybody's got to pretend it never happened. Unless—and, gee, Mr. Ransom, here's the part I don't understand—unless he marries the girl he's doing it with, and then it's okay."

The words jolted him. He feared that she might put the rest of it into words that he would have to answer. *Why not me, Keith?*

Instead she reached for the door handle. "*Mrs.* Ransom is waiting for you," she said.

Ransom's hands were on her before he knew it, had her by the shoulders, pulling her close to him. Her eyes, her mouth, inches from his, and for an instant there was a gleam of satisfaction in her face as she let herself be drawn into his arms. She tingled under his grip, and for a moment he wavered, but the words came of their own volition.

"This kid," he said, "this Taylor." The voice seemed amplified in his head, ringing and hissing and echoing.

"C'mon, Keith."

His hands tightened; they promised the strength to crush muscle and bone. "How long did it take you to think *that* one up?"

"Keith . . . let go of me."

"How *long*, Wendy?" He leaned over her, his fingers bands of steel around her throat. How easy it would be—

He saw the flash of her hand coming toward him, felt the sting of the slap against his jaw, but the pain seemed distant and softly focused. There was ice in the car.

Wendy wrenched away from him, breathing harsh obscenities, and he let her go.

Blood. There was blood spilling in a rivulet from the corner of her mouth, scarlet against the frost white of her face. He didn't know what he had done to her.

Cold white explosions went off in his head, and he couldn't think anymore, could only watch her run, hear the muted slapping sounds of her shoes against the pavement. Ransom reached for the steering wheel, grabbed it hard with both hands. It seemed to be melting within his grip. For a moment he didn't realize that the sobbing he heard was his own.

His wrist throbbed. But where the cut had been now seemed to glint like splintered glass. He could see through his arm.

It was—*true*!

He felt the concrete beneath his feet, unaware of having gotten out of the car. He was reaching toward the full moon, watching the light of it play through his hands, tasting and breathing in the light of the moon. He couldn't slow down, couldn't speed up, and it was the dream again, the dream that he moved through.

He saw his hand on the restaurant door. The lettering on the door melted and whirled before his eyes.

The door was open, and he was enveloped in warmth, the cottony drumming of the jukebox, the smell of food—but it was different now. One color washed over it all.

White. The bone-white color of death, of frost, of the full moon. Bleached and frozen, faces looked back at him.

Marla.

But he hadn't come for Marla, not this time.

Wendy.

He saw her standing there, Ben Taylor beside her, towering over her. And then he saw Taylor move toward him and Marla, who was grabbing at the football player's arm, trying to hold him back. Ransom felt the contractions of laughter in his throat, but there was no sound.

Then: amazement.

He moved with such grace, with such speed, with such power. He felt himself in motion, as if he were watching from the window of a machine, in awe of what it could do.

Talons flashing, the machine swung at Taylor.

The boy stood his ground, solid and confident. Ransom wanted to scream for him. Couldn't he see? Didn't he *know*?

Bone exploded against flesh, and Taylor's face jerked out of Ransom's line of sight. Taylor staggered backward, eyes jammed shut, one hand covering his face and blood running between his fingers. And Ransom lunged into him. Blood and frost, blood and moonlight. The machine of his body raged out of control. He felt terror, he felt joy, and they were the same.

Taylor, his mouth wide in a cry of rage, aimed a wide-sweeping hammer blow at him.

Ransom's response was effortless. An upraised arm, deflecting Taylor's fist, and a blurring strike toward the throat. The moment froze with the boy's look of dismay, his mouth opened as if to split the jaw hinges, his tongue curled backward. Frost glazed his eyes.

Taylor slammed back-first into the salad bar, arms flailing. His head snapped to one side, spattering red over the countertop, across the lettuce and crushed ice, and the bar toppled with him.

Ransom heard screaming; he didn't care. His eyes locked on Wendy, but even as he turned toward her he was falling. He fell as if he had charged a door only to find it open, with no floor inside. Mists and vapors thundered through him, and he was cold, so very cold.

The floor met him, hard, and he welcomed the pain. So good to feel pain. Pain was real.

There were hands on him, rough hands, holding him down. He opened his eyes, trying to focus.

The frost light was fading. Colors edged into his vision again, clots of color, taking shape as the people around him, looking down at him. Marla knelt toward him in aching slow motion, her eyes glittering with tears.

He reached for her. His hand felt stiff. The knuckles were bleeding, and the nail of his forefinger was torn back.

But the cut on his wrist . . . just a cut, no more than that.

He turned his head, saw Taylor sprawled motionlessly to the side of him. Funny, almost. Crackers and puddles of dressings, and Taylor there, like it was all a joke.

Get up, Ransom thought. Get up then, Taylor, damn you. Laugh about it. He twisted his head to escape the sight of the boy.

The full moon, framed in the restaurant window, burned into his eyes. And then he knew . . . the machine was not through with him.

It wanted the voice that had returned to him.

It turned his head, sought the crowd. It lifted his hand, pointing.

The voice raked his throat. ". . . the next time . . ." it said.

Sirens rippled in the distance, coming closer, and blackness took hold of Ransom. It dimmed away the people, dulled his mind, and he let it take over, welcomed it.

In the night sky he drifted. A black sky . . . with no moon.

CHAPTER SIX

Hurt looks. Puzzled looks. Looks of anger, betrayal, fear. Curiosity. Envy.

Ransom cataloged them all, checking them off in singles and groups as he crossed the campus of Reinholdt College. He listened to the quick beat of his shoe heels against the sidewalk, looked at the faces, and tried not to let himself think of anything else.

Last night a cold front had blown in, dropping unseasonable snow all over the area, and Ransom had sat up and watched the snow, watched the flakes swirling and dropping and covering the ground outside his home. He wished he was back there now, among the dark, white flakes blanketing everything.

In less than two weeks the story of Keith Ransom's fight with Ben Taylor had taken on the bigger-than-life qualities of a genuine legend. Ransom had heard and overheard so many different versions of it, each more elaborate than the one before, that he felt almost left out of the excitement. It was as if the people all around him were playing some sort of game, seeing who could make up the most frightening account of what had been done to Ben Taylor. They were talking, always talking, about a lunatic roaming the campus, and the lunatic had a name. That was the oddest part. Ransom couldn't comprehend it, so he tried always not to let it enter his mind. But he knew. They spoke of the campus monster in those same theatrical tones of reverence and fear as the villagers making

fools of themselves in the old Universal horror movies, and
they had named it Keith Ransom.

He turned toward McKendrick Hall, looking over the heads
of the crowd passing in front of it, watching the mid-morning
sunlight taunt him in glittering blue and silver, reflecting off
the remnants of the previous night's snowfall gathered on the
windowsills of the old redbrick building.

Second floor, third window across. That one was Thurman's, the one with a hand swipe across the glass, clearing
the condensation from inside. Ransom knew that the department head had been watching for him, wondered if he
watched now from behind the window, out of sight.

Ransom's heart quickened as he neared the front steps. He
saw some of the students coming toward him. Toby Harris,
Diana Kendall, John Walkingdeer . . . they were some of the
ones who had made a point of talking to him, of being seen
with him. Ransom knew they meant it as a show of support,
but sometimes, in situations like this, he could sense them
almost daring one another to be the first. *Run and pet the
biting dog.*

"Morning, Mr. Ransom," Toby said.

"How's it going, Toby? Diana?" Ransom pressed through
the crowd. He could feel the smiles they gave him being taken
away behind his back.

You can do without the paranoia, Ransom told himself, but
he kept on moving. The door flashed sunlight ahead of him,
and then, all of a sudden, there stood Wendy, blocking his
way.

"Keith . . ." She stepped toward him. "Keith, I've got to
talk to you."

"Later, okay, Wendy? I'm late."

The frost of her breath hung between them, and her red-
mittened hands were tightly clenched. "I've got to explain
something to you."

Ransom nodded upward, toward the second floor and Thurman's office. "Command performance up there," he said.

"*Please*, Keith . . ."

He moved to one side of her. "I don't think I'll be there
very long," he said. "I think I'll have all sorts of time pretty
shortly."

"Okay," she said, and touched his shoulder gently, as if she were breaking some rule. "I'll wait for you."

He nodded and pushed on through the door, thinking for a moment about the change in Wendy. It all could have been put on, he thought, and maybe it was. But it would have had to have been a particularly calculating and cold-blooded put-on, and he couldn't envision what she had to gain from it, from her suddenly being so damn *nice* to him.

Ransom had expected, after the fight with Taylor, to find the next issue of *The Reinholdt Ranger* splashed with prose detailing every blow of the atrocity, under banner headlines of the kind reserved for world wars and presidential assassinations. Instead there had been only a short, flatly worded account of it on the second page.

He started up the time-honored stairs, and they creaked under his weight.

The way she had come to his office. The things she had said to him: "My fault. My fault, Keith. I was hurt, and I wanted you to hurt too. I set it up with Ben to be there. I put the pressure on you. I feel sick at what happened. I caused it. My fault, all my fault. . . ."

He had never seen her cry before, somehow had never thought her to be capable of tears.

The stair rail shook as he held on to it, climbing.

She had taken the blame to herself, and she would have kept it, all of it. But he couldn't do that, hadn't been able to let her do that.

It wasn't you, Wendy. It was me. It was something . . . inside of me. I can't explain it. Something wrong with me.

He reached the top of the stairs. Thurman's office awaited him at the end of the hallway, the door closed as always.

Life was a circus, all right, Ransom thought. Not a stage in the grandiose Shakespearean sense but a circus full of freaks and clowns and colored lights, with shadowy people in the background always ready to take down the tent. Nothing real but always a new act.

He had found, in amazement, that he could *talk* to Wendy Layton. She wasn't like Marla; she wasn't afraid of him. And he needed so much just to talk.

All my life, Wendy . . . obsessions. Obsessions, one after another. Collections of things. There were baseball cards that

I wanted so much, I couldn't sleep. Dumb baseball cards. Comic books. Christmas tree ornaments. Can you believe that my hands would literally shake at the thought of some damn thing like that? Kid stuff, fun stuff. But . . . I never seemed to have any fun, really, with it. I just had to have it.

She would listen to him, just listen. There were never any questions.

I feel caught. Pushed, driven—whatever the hell you want to call it. Compelled . . . but toward nothing. I don't know what's taken hold of me.

She would come to his office or they would meet for coffee. Sometimes they would just talk in the hallway between classes, but then the conversation was never as intense. There was nothing clandestine about it, nothing sexual, nothing wrong.

Then why not tell Marla? Ransom had asked himself that question time and again over the past few days, but he knew the answer. It was because there *was* something wrong, something that felt like a pain he was trying to pretend didn't exist, an ache he was trying to wish away.

Or was he only afraid to let go and believe, in some small way, in a change for the better? Ransom considered that possibility. *A change for the better.* It slipped from his mind like the cold touch of the old brass doorknob as he took the first step into Thurman's quarters.

Thurman's secretary, Virginia Beale, regarded him with the look that had earned her the campus nickname of Iron Eyes. The deep creases at the corners of her mouth gave her the appearance of constant disapproval, which made the soft, almost melodious tone of her voice seem to be coming from somewhere else in the outer office.

"Good morning, Mr. Ransom," she said. "Please have a seat. Dr. Thurman will be with you in a moment."

Part of the game, Ransom thought. He could picture Thurman sitting there, a few feet away behind the closed door of the inner office, calculating just how long a wait would be enough to humble the visitor appropriately.

Mrs. Beale returned to her typing. The keys struck in cycles of rhythm, clatter-and-stop, clatter-and-stop, never slowing, a clockwork sound. Ransom sat in a chair of creaking vinyl next to a short, polished mahogany table. A brass planter of ivy at the center of the table was surrounded by a carefully fanned arrangement of magazines—*The Chronicle of Higher Education, Time,* and *World Literature Today,* interspersed with past numbers of *The Lyric Echo,* Reinholdt's quarterly of poetry and "serious" fiction. Thurman was credited as editor in prominent script on each *Echo* cover.

Ransom, alone among the English Department faculty, had never submitted to *The Lyric Echo.* Also alone, his poetry, an occasional by-product of his songwriting attempts, had been accepted by *Bitterroot* and *Rolling Stone*—a point of aggravation to Thurman either way you looked at it, Ransom liked to think.

But now he could feel himself building to exactly the level of tension that Thurman must have wanted. His hands drummed the armrests of the chair, and he discovered that his mouth had gone dry. The game was Thurman's now, and Thurman was winning.

Ransom had not allowed himself to wonder too deeply why the department head had suddenly wanted him. He was sure that Thurman was aware he was supposed to be teaching a class at this hour. But earlier, on the phone, Mrs. Beale had simply said, "Dr. Thurman would like to see you at ten o'clock," and that had been that. Ransom assumed Thurman would send a substitute.

Whatever the reason for the urgency, nothing good would come out of their meeting. Ransom was sure of that. But the worst would be—what?—that Dr. Thurman had finally seized upon the means to get rid of him? Ransom tried the words in his mind. *You're fired, you're fired. Fired.*

He wanted, for Marla's sake, to care. But he didn't. He just wanted to be done with it—and done with it, he decided, on his own terms.

Getting up, he treated himself to a glance at Mrs. Beale as he pushed open the door to Thurman's office. Her eyes widened in astonishment as the typewriter stuttered to a halt. "Don't bother," he said. "I'll announce myself."

The door swung open, swishing against the carpet inside, thudding against the wall. Thurman didn't turn. He stood, hands clasped behind his back, looking out the window. "You really don't have to try so hard to make me dislike you, Ransom," he said, and turned slowly and precisely. His silvered hair matched the gray, pin-striped suit. He looked as if he were made entirely of metal.

"Close the door," he said.

Ransom ignored him and narrowed the distance between them.

"Very well. We can make this just as public as you want, Ransom. I am pleased to say it loudly." Thurman leaned across the neatly stacked papers on top of his desk. "You are *through* here, Ransom," he said. "Finished. Out."

Fired. You're fired.

Ransom fought it but his face flushed, denied it but his breath caught, refused to let the words hurt him but they did.

I don't care. I don't . . .

He jammed his hands into his pockets, where the trembling wouldn't show. "You don't have the authority," he said.

"No?" Thurman's mouth bent to a smile. "Let me show you what I *do* have." He slid open the top drawer of the desk. Withdrawing a tabloid newspaper, he slapped it onto the desktop.

Ransom scanned the cover. *The Midnight Enquirer.* There was a photo in the center of Joan Collins beaming toward Michael J. Fox, and a row of teasing headlines to the side. Thurman's finger jabbed at one of those headlines. It read: COLLEGE PROF ON THE RAMPAGE. MOON TO BLAME?

Ransom grabbed up the paper. He ripped it open to the page touted by the headline. The words floated like sparks in front of him.

At the top, in bold letters: MOON MADNESS STRIKES COLLEGE PROF. Underneath: "It was the night of the full moon—a night of sudden violence—the night of a bizarre attack by Reinholdt College professor Keith Ransom upon the Midwestern college's star football running back, Ben Taylor."

The printed words blurred into Thurman's voice, taunting him. ". . . *surprised*, Ransom? You seem to have fallen behind in your supermarket reading."

Ransom's head reeled. "How did . . . *this* get in *here*?" he heard himself asking.

"That's a fine question, isn't it? The point is, it did." Thurman's voice was rising. It seemed to come at him from every direction. "I tried, Ransom," he said. "I tried, not for you, but for the reputation of the college, to put a lid on your little incident. *That's* why no charges were filed. And *that's* why you weren't kicked the hell out of here. We didn't want the publicity. We didn't want the college to come off looking like a lunatic bin. But now we don't have to worry about that, do we?''

Thurman crossed toward the door, giving Ransom a sweeping wave toward the opening. ''You're right,'' he said. ''I don't have the authority. The vice president for academic affairs has the authority, and you can take it up with him if you'd like. But I must tell you that Ron Hatton has a copy of this same newspaper, and he's very aware of what's going on.'' Thurman paused. ''So see him. You have the right to appeal, to waste time, to drag it out. Or you can do it intelligently, Ransom. You can resign.''

Ransom's mind was a confused jumble, thoughts racing through like shooting stars and flaming out in the fog. Dumbly he handed the paper to Thurman.

''Keep it,'' Thurman said. ''Keep it and think about it, Ransom.''

Ransom nodded and turned to go. As he passed Thurman he heard the man's voice: ''I would very much like to see your letter of resignation on my desk this afternoon,'' it said.

He stood in the hallway, too sick to run. He stood reading about the monster that shared his name.

He read the words of the monster and remembered when he had said those words, and each one of them sliced through him.

I feel caught. Pushed, driven—whatever the hell you want to call it. Compelled . . . but toward nothing. I don't know what's taken hold of me.

''Keith?''

He looked up from the paper.

She was crying again. Real tears. Poor Wendy.

''Keith. Oh, God, Keith. I'm sorry,'' she said.

And the red mittens lay softly on the **hardwood** floor, scattered like the dozens of other articles of **clothing** around the apartment, and the smell of food and perfume and marijuana, Ransom sucking on a hand-rolled cigarette and coughing, trying to cough out the day, his life, and Wendy, the tears still in her eyes, slipping off her blouse, and Ransom finally seeing what he had thought about seeing for a long time, the sight leaving him curiously empty. She was tanned all over, even in autumn, and she came to him with joy and penitence and a kind of inevitability, and even as she reached for him he thought of Marla, and the next thing he knew, he was running in the sunshine, the cold air stinging his nostrils, sad because he hadn't done it but proud from having left the woman with the dark hair trailing over her naked shoulders, and what could have been.

CHAPTER SEVEN

I hope you feel proud of yourself, you son of a bitch! We who care about college football and the winning tradition—

Ransom put the letter down and reached across the littered desktop for the bottle of Scotch. He poured himself another drink, the amber liquid splashing loudly in the midnight silence.

They were all the same, he thought, folding the letter carefully and putting it back in the envelope, wondering at the same time why he didn't just throw them all away and go to bed. There weren't going to be any surprises, not with this group.

Dimly he heard the sound of the television set from the bedroom adjacent to his study, and he thought about Marla, whether she was still awake at this hour, waiting to be needed by him, or whether the television was playing to no one now. She had probably given up and fallen asleep long ago, he decided.

Three days. It had been three days since the nightmare at Thurman's office, and still, he was no closer to a decision. He hadn't written a letter of resignation, and he hadn't talked to the vice president for academic affairs. He had simply taken the line of least resistance and stopped showing up for classes. And for Wendy.

Ransom cleared his throat and brought the drink to his lips, gazing at the pile of still unopened mail in front of him, and then at the stack already read, or at least scanned. After the first dozen or so, after the initial shock had worn off, he hadn't needed to go past the first line to know what was coming. Curlicue lines on floral stationery, IBM type on letterhead, penciled scrawls on notebook paper; some obscene, some arrogant, others raging or subdued or threatening—all carried the same message. Reinholdt's best running back is out for the rest of the season, they said. A sure early-round draft pick, they said, but now, thanks to you, you son of a bitch, Ransom, a young man's career is ruined, and worse, Reinholdt has no chance now, no chance at all, to win the conference.

Why was it so *important* to them? Ransom tasted a sudden acid bitterness. Were their lives so damn meaningless that the loss of a football player on a second-rate college team threw them into written violence? He clenched his teeth, feeling for the first time something like anger at his unseen but very real antagonists. Worthless lives, he thought, worthless lives in worthless shells that filled the stadium on Saturday afternoons and bought pennants and seat cushions and hurled oaths at the opposing teams and then went back to their homogenized, bland lives, awaiting the next feverish outbreak, quietly smoldering all the while. And now they all had a focal point for their collective hatred, something to make their insubstantial lives worthwhile. Him.

He got up and walked into the kitchen, breaking some ice from a tray into his glass. All right, maybe that wasn't fair. But he didn't care. He didn't *want* to be fair; he wanted to be angry, to have something to focus that anger on, something real and tangible.

Then he realized that he wanted to be just like them.

Back at his desk, he picked up the next letter and opened it.

Dear Sir,
    I have always thought that our college teachers are supposed to set examples for our students. So it was with great puzzlement that I read of your "fight" with that fine Reinholdt College student and excellent football player, Ben Taylor. What could you have been hoping to prove, Mr. Ransom? It is clear to me, as it should be clear to you, that you need psychiatric help, especially

after I read the recent national newspaper story about you. A young man's career is ruined—

Ransom nodded slowly, glancing at the rest of the letter long enough to see that it was unsigned, putting it back inside the perfume-scented envelope. The stab at anger hadn't worked; it had settled into his bones with a heavy, sad weight. He blinked a couple of times, focusing his eyes on a spot just below the desk lamp. The light from it seemed haloed and fuzzy.

Marla had wanted him to come to bed a long time ago, had been by turns reasonable, seductive, and petulant, and had finally gone off without him, hoping, Ransom was sure, that he would soon realize he didn't want to do this thing and would be following her. But he had sat at the desk facing the stack of mail, and the routine had settled down as he reached for a drink, a cigarette, another letter, his movements becoming more and more leaden. And as the opened envelopes piled up, he kept going—hoping, perhaps, for one that might somehow erase the effect of those that had gone before and in a moment of burning truth bring sense to everything.

Now he knew it wouldn't happen. He was going on scholar's determination only, opening one after the other as the November night wore on outside his window, the feeble desk light the only illumination in the room.

He opened one, shook the sheet of paper, and scrawled obscenities crawled in front of him like angry spiders, suddenly and shockingly. Reflex made him crumple the paper into a tight ball, and he sat there for a moment, staring out his window into the blackness. Then he carefully laid the paper on top of his desk and smoothed it out with the side of his hand.

Why am I saving these things? he asked himself, putting the letter aside. *What am I doing to myself?* He searched his mind for a reaction, an answer to his questions, but found nothing. All he knew was that he would have to read them all, and then maybe he could sleep.

The next envelope on the stack bore an out-of-state postmark.

"Well, now," Ransom muttered, "change my luck, maybe." His words were sucked into the darkness outside the lamp's glow and died to the sound of ripping paper. He took a final drag on his cigarette and snuffed it into the over-flowing ashtray.

He shook the envelope, and a pamphlet fell out, a note paper-clipped to it. The note read:

Dear Mr. Ransom,
   The Devil is alive and real on Earth, and it is Satan that caused your troubles. If you accept Jesus Christ as Your Personal Savior, you can drive the Devil away. Please read this book. I am praying for you.
                                   In the Holy Name of Jesus,
                                   Mrs. F. O. McQuarry

At least that was a kind one, Ransom thought. The first. He turned the pamphlet over in his hand, opened it. It was full of rows of neat type with Bible verses in boldface, and "Four Steps to Salvation" on the back, with a picture of a man at the bottom of the steps, and Jesus at the top, his arms extended in welcome.

Ransom looked at the woman's note again. Out of the whole stack, the first decent words, the first writer who had assumed he was something more than a wild-eyed, unregenerate lunatic; something more than a monster named Keith Ransom.

I am praying for you.

Something old and nearly forgotten stirred in Ransom then, and he suddenly remembered the old women in the church of his youth, their kind, weathered faces and their bright dresses; and the men, standing outside the building between Sunday school and church time, smoking cigarettes and visiting. He remembered being baptized—nine years old he'd been, and all the kids in his class already saved—and the feeling of his minister's strong hands on his back as he went down, the water filling in over his face.

Now he wanted to believe again. He wanted to believe all the things the church had taught him that had fallen away as he had grown up, in stages, like dead skin off an insect. He wanted to believe in Hell, in Moses, in Lazarus coming back from the dead, in the two thieves on the crosses beside Jesus, and the one who had repented and joined Jesus in heaven.

And he remembered, back to what seemed an eternity ago,

joking with Marla as they passed Oral Roberts University. He suddenly felt bad and remorseful, realizing now that he wanted to believe in the evangelism of Oral Roberts, too, to accept it all and clasp it to his chest and feel the cynicism flutter away from him.

Then he could believe in the Devil and he could be saved.

The Devil . . . ? Ransom took another drink, the ice clinking against his teeth as he sucked at the liquid. It would be so good and so right if it *were* the Devil. Then he could pray, and the good people of the world could pray for him; he could follow the "Four Steps to Salvation" and send money to Oral Roberts and make the dreams go away, leaving him whole and unashamed again, facing the world smiling and scrubbed and confident.

He rubbed his head with the back of his hand, closing his eyes. He squeezed the lids together and was surprised to feel moisture underneath them, and a thickness in his throat. His eyes still closed, he leaned his forehead against the palms of his hands.

"Help me," he whispered, swallowing. "Please . . . help me . . ."

"Keith?"

The voice echoed through him like a cannon shot. He whirled around to see Marla, her eyelids heavy, standing in the doorway.

"Marla," he said, shock still coursing through his body. "You just about scared the living hell out of me."

"I'm sorry." Her voice was husky.

He shook himself. "Lord, give a guy a little warning."

"When are you coming to bed?"

He stared at her for a long moment. "Soon," he said.

"But when?"

"You go on. I'm thinking right now. I couldn't relax, anyway, you know that."

"Stop thinking," she said in a sleepy child's voice. Her steps toward him were heavy like a sleepwalker's. Reaching around his shoulders, she squeezed him. "I'm worried about you."

His voice was muffled against the fabric of her nightgown and the flesh underneath. "Not to worry. I'm fine."

"You sure?"

"Yeah."

She smelled of perfume and powder and sleep. He gently eased her away. "Now go on, okay? And if I'm not there in five minutes, start without me."

"I'll try to wait."

"Okay."

She brushed a lock of hair out of her face and bent over to kiss his forehead. "Come to bed soon," she whispered.

"Count on it."

He watched her walk unsteadily away, through the study doorway and into the darkness.

Is that my salvation? he thought. *Marla—my wife?*

But no, she couldn't be, because she had been terrified and impotent, too, just like the rest of them, the frozen tableau of faces that night, watching him or the thing that was him. Marla . . . Wendy—

He turned away quickly, going back to the letters.

And what of *the* letter? The one he was supposed to have already written, the one Thurman had wanted on his desk *that* afternoon? Ransom hadn't written it that afternoon, nor the afternoon after that, and now, three days later, he still had not written it. A part of him wanted to get it out and be done with it; another part urged him to wait, told him that somehow everything would work out and that he would remain at the college, and besides, since when had he knuckled under to the likes of Dr. Thurman?

Ransom knew time was running out. Thurman was leaving him alone for now, but that wouldn't last much longer. His silence seemed more malevolent to Ransom than any other action he could imagine. The day after he had walked out of Thurman's office, he had half expected the man to come storming into one of his classes with a squad of campus police, bent on ejecting him forcibly from the podium. It hadn't happened, and Ransom's initial relief had turned into wariness that grew until today, when he had simply not shown up for any of his classes.

The line of least resistance, Ransom thought, and cursed himself for a coward. He took another drink and began shuffling through the letters again, determined to divert his attention to them. He found another one with an out-of-state postmark, hoped it was another soul who might be unaware of the all-pervasive influence of the Reinholdt Rangers and their conference standing.

This one didn't look too promising. The address was scrawled in big, scratchy letters—the work of a child or a barely literate adult. Inside, the paper was folded irregularly, corners hanging out. Ransom unfolded it and read the top line.

"Its the moon, Mr. Ransom."

The next line read: "I know because it happened to me and I dont know what to do but its the moon you can bet."

Ransom's eyes focused on the lines, but his mind was somewhere else. He was suddenly seeing the headline at the top of the tabloid story: MOON MADNESS STRIKES COLLEGE PROF.

He forced his attention back to the letter, to the irregular, half-printed, half-written lines.

"We got to help each other before it does it again—I thought I was the only one." A name and phone number below, and beside that, "Call collect."

Ransom stared at the letter for a long time, then got up and plugged in his phone. Two days ago he had disconnected it, when the ringing at all hours and the angry voices on the other end got to be too much. They had started weeks ago, immediately after Taylor was hospitalized, had built to a maddening crescendo and then died away to only a few a day, only to be revived when the supermarket tabloid had hit the stands. The power of the press, Ransom thought.

Before Ransom could dial the number on the letter, the phone rang.

"Hello," he said, knowing what was coming at this hour.

"Is this the bastard that beat the kid up?" The voice was full of drunken, but uncertain, rage.

The air was quiet around Ransom. "This is the bastard, yeah."

"Well . . . well, listen, you werewolf motherfugger, you want a piece of *my* ass, you just come ahead on."

"You're pretty tough, aren't you?" said Ransom.

"Damn right," came the voice from the other end. Ransom could hear, behind it, music, the clinking of glasses, and people muttering. The guy was calling from a bar, all pumped up with alcohol and false bravado.

"Well," Ransom said, dropping his voice and speaking slowly and calmly, "I know who you are, and I know where you live. And you know, you can lock that front door and all your windows, but none of that can stop me. You're right. I *am* a werewolf. And one night I'm going to come right through the wall of your bedroom while you're asleep, and I'm going to come right to the head of your bed and sink my teeth in your neck, and I'll stand there and laugh while you die."

The man started to sputter, but Ransom hung up before he could say anything. He knew that if the guy wanted to, he could find out where he lived and come over with his drunken buddies and make a lot of trouble. He was also pretty sure he wouldn't do it. That's why they wrote letters and made phone calls—they were scared of coming face-to-face with the monster.

The phone rang again, and Ransom unplugged it. Going back to his desk, he looked at the letter again.

I thought I was the only one.

He stared at it for a long time, put it down, and looked out the window. On this night the moon was half full, glowing in the star-dotted velvet of the sky. He looked up at it, and then he reached over and snapped off the desk light. Now it was just him and the moon, and a dawning within him that began deep inside and grew and pressed until it thrust itself out, arcing a path to the heavens; and the barren half-moon caught it and sailed it back to him in a straight even line that pierced his heart and his mind and his soul with the dead certainty of a cold and quiet blade going in.

CHAPTER EIGHT

"It's Thanksgiving," Marla said. Her tone of voice was like a coin balanced on edge, about to fall. She was either hurt or angry; he couldn't tell which.

He didn't really care.

Ransom sat cross-legged on the circular braided rug in the center of the living room, the letters arranged in front of him in a series of stacks that followed the curve of the rug pattern.

"You *told* me that you were going to throw that junk away," she said.

Ransom ripped the end off another envelope. He glanced at the letter, his mouth twisting and tightening, and then he slapped the page onto one of the letter stacks. Papers fluttered. "Football," he said. "And *this* bunch . . ." He jabbed at a second stack. "Nut mail. Religious tracts. Do-it-yourself exorcism—$10.95 for a book that tells how. Just what I need, wouldn't you say?"

"I would have fixed a turkey," Marla said. She turned from him, picking up a music box from his collection that rested on top of the bookshelf beside her. "If I'd known that we weren't going to go anywhere . . ."

"And these!" Ransom's finger traced an *X* across the top letter of a third stack as if he were holding a scalpel. His hand clinched and came down against the center of the mark, hard.

Across the room Marla's cat, Strawberry, jumped almost sideways at the sound and sudden movement. It hissed at Ransom, its ears flattened, green eyes as sharp as needles.

"Crazies," Ransom said. "Lunatics. And *me*? I'm just one of the boys. Welcome to the club, Prof."

He read from the top letter, " 'Its the moon you can bet.' " The next down, his voice rising: " 'Something in the moon can twist a man.' " Then the next, stapled to a clipping from the *Midnight Enquirer*: " '... madness? Oh, no, Mr. Ransom. You are not mad. You are merely alert to the racial memory of the moon. The primitive in you responds to the song of the full moon. You *remember*.' "

Marla knelt beside him, not touching. "Shitty, damn newspaper," she said, the words thrown like rocks. A sweep of her hand blurred the stacks into a jumble, littering the floor.

"Oh, I'm even more famous than just the *Enquirer*," he said. "Or didn't you notice? I made the wire service." He sorted out two other clippings from the clutter on the floor. "Denver, this one, and Philadelphia." Studying one of them, he said, "Here's a catchy headline: WEREWOLF TEACHER ARRESTED ON NIGHT OF FULL MOON."

Marla snatched the clipping from him, looked at it a moment, and wadded it up.

"Hey," Ransom said, "give me that."

"Why, Keith? *Why?*"

He took it from her and smoothed it out. "I might want to press it in my Bible."

There was silence for a moment, and Ransom knew that Marla was near the breaking point. He looked at her, her mouth working. Finally she said, "Don't they have to let you *know*?"

"Who?"

Her voice threatened to shatter like china. "The papers. If they're going to do this to you, they should have to tell you, give you the chance . . ." Her voice caught. "The chance to say . . . something . . ."

"Say *what*? That it never happened? That I woke up and it was all a dream?"

"It's just not fair, Keith. This . . . *thing* in that supermarket newspaper; they made it sound like you came right out and called yourself crazy, when you never said that to anybody. I still don't know why you won't get a lawyer. They can't just make up the words and get away with it." Her fists clenched. "They *can't*."

Ransom doubled forward, hands clasped at the back of his neck, suddenly remembering Wendy Layton and her part in all this and how she had looked that day on campus. To dispel the memory he said quickly, "I just want it forgotten."

"Okay. Fine. Forget it, Keith, and *here*—" She thrust a handful of the letters toward him. "You can start with a trip to the garbage can."

He took the letters and methodically began to sort them again: football, religion, the crazies.

Marla stood. He could feel the frustration—the contempt?—exude from her, settling over him like a cloud of ether. "It's Thanksgiving," she said. "I'm going to go buy a turkey. We're going to have a turkey."

He tried to make a joke of it. "Turkey today, and turkey again Sunday. We'll be a couple of stuffed birds ourselves."

He watched as she grabbed her coat from the bentwood hall tree. "I guess *I'm* the oddball around here. I *like* the holidays. You can sit here and brood yourself into another drunk, but you're not going to ruin the day for me, Keith. And I'm *not* going to say that Thanksgiving is Sunday, just to make it fit into my dad's goddamn *business* schedule."

The door slam knocked a framed and signed photo of Dick Miller off the wall, the glass shattering, and Ransom felt something deep inside him crack and splinter the same way.

Marla stopped outside the door. She drew in a breath of the cold air, tasting the promise of more snow. Turning as if to go in again, she was startled by the winter-chilled touch of the old brass doorknob as her hand closed around it. She stopped and wiped at the streaming tears that stung her face.

No. There was no going back, Marla told herself. There were no apologies due from her, no making up to be done unless Keith cared enough to come after her—but of course he didn't.

Guilt floated around her like the frost of her breath as she walked with forced steps toward the car. But she knew—oh, *how* she knew—there was nothing she could do to bring him out of the brooding gloom that he almost seemed to enjoy, that he had built up like a wall to keep her away.

Maybe feeling bad was what he needed, she thought. Not sympathy. Just as well, because she didn't have much sympathy left; it was all pouring out of her, and none was coming back.

She didn't like getting into the car. It was Keith's car, and it felt like Keith. It was cold all over.

The engine rattled to a start but died when she put it in reverse. Coaxing it into running again, she sat there, the motor idling, the heat vents spilling a pool of cold air across her legs.

She didn't want to go shopping. The only store she knew that was open on Thanksgiving lay clear across town, and she felt wrong about spending money in a place that would make its employees work on a holiday. But it *was* Thanksgiving. Her first *married* Thanksgiving, and it was supposed to be special. Damn it, Keith!

She jammed the gearshift into reverse again. The car lurched down the driveway, spattering gravel.

He *knew* what the day meant. How many times had she told him? She had grown up with her birthday always being moved up a week, or back a week, so as not to interfere with her father's business trips and meetings or some convention going on at one of his motels. Thanksgiving, too, and sometimes even Christmas, postponed to a "better" day.

But not this time, Marla thought.

The street seemed to shimmer, the old frame houses blurring to smears of white and yellow, and Marla wiped at her tears again.

All morning she had waited for him to announce his plans for Thanksgiving dinner. She had half expected something outrageous from him, some surprise, like driving across the state line just to eat, or going into Tulsa to some little ethnic restaurant, maybe eating Greek or Vietnamese food while everyone else was going traditional. Maybe even, she had hoped, a little gift for her.

Well, she had been surprised, all right. What a surprise to watch him as he sat there, mesmerized over a goddamn stack of goddamn letters.

Forgive me, God, she prayed. *Forgive me*. There was no excuse, no need, for profanity. *Thou shalt not* . . .

Forgive me.

She felt weak, drained, and confused. But the back tires squealed when she hit the gas pedal, and the anger of the machinery meshed with her feelings, making her almost glad.

Ransom yanked open the door as the tires sounded, but the Datsun had already swerved around the corner before he opened his mouth to call to her. He didn't call; he didn't have the words for it. Standing there, staring at nothing, he realized he had never seen her so angry before, and his throat began to burn, urging him to give in, to begin bawling like a baby over a smashed toy.

But it wasn't a toy to be broken and fixed, broken and fixed again. It was Marla. And one time—maybe this time, he thought—he would break *her*, and the damage would last forever.

He shut the door and, through the square of stained glass in the center at eye level, saw the empty street in rippled shades of blue and orange, a dream street, a neverland.

He remembered what he had said to her moments before: "I woke up, and it was all a dream. . . ." A cliché, a laugh, an excuse lousy writers used in lousy stories when they were stuck for an ending. Just wake up, that's all, and your troubles would be gone. Ransom wondered what it would take. Would pinching help? A slap in the face? A knife across the wrists, maybe?

In the kitchen he grabbed a glass out of the cupboard, a tumbler with a decal of Bugs Bunny on it, and splashed it full of Scotch up to the rabbit's cheerfully waving, three-fingered hand.

. . . *brood yourself into a drunk.*

The liquor scalded his mouth, and with it came the burning image of Marla's face, the sound of her voice.

. . . *into a drunk.*

He set the glass on the counter and tapped it with his fingers. He could brood, yes; he could drink; he could make his wife cry. Three proven accomplishments. Now, what else could he do?

The fingers stopped tapping and moved around the glass,

tipping amber liquid into the drain. The rest of the bottle followed it, and Ransom, watching, felt a curious mixture of relief and fear wash through him. The smell of the whiskey was acrid, and it seared his nostrils. He walked away from it and rummaged in the pantry until he found the popcorn popper.

"You can't be unhappy and eat popcorn at the same time." It was one of his grandmother's old maxims, and it usually worked.

Soon he had a bowl of popcorn, and he took it into the living room, setting it on the footlocker that served as a table in front of the saggy sofa, where Marla would see it first thing when she stepped in the door. From behind a stack of books he brought out the necklace he had bought for her in the Ozarks, a gold chain with a tiny, golden-apple medallion. He had conceived it then as a Thanksgiving present, something to mark their first married holiday together . . . so carefully chosen, so cleverly hidden, so damn near forgotten.

He draped the necklace next to the popcorn bowl and stood back to evaluate the offering.

A stack of letters crinkled under his heel.

Ransom twisted his foot, grinding the papers underneath. The football letters, the mail-order salvation—

Marla was right. They were shit, and you don't bring in shit and spread it on the living-room floor.

So why had he done it? And not just once, but compulsively.

Compulsively.

Ransom took in the room with a pivoting gaze. The room, and the house—his life, for that matter: a patchwork of compulsions.

The books that he *had* to have. There! First editions of all the Oz books. All the Mars books by Edgar Rice Burroughs, in dust jackets. He could total them up in meals skipped, rent payments missed, furniture sold, appliances hocked, just to fill a blank space on the bookshelf.

And up on the ledge that ran around the living room, across the tops of the windows and doors—the model steam engine he had built, machined piece by piece the summer before his junior year in college, when he should have been working toward the next year's tuition.

The oddly shaped little engine still ran perfectly, although he seldom thought to start it. It was a model of the 1829 Rocket that set the multitube boiler standard for steam locomotives of the next century, and it was precise to the twelve spokes on the oversize drive wheels. And, Ransom recalled, the engine was to have run on an exactly detailed, O-gauge layout of the Rainhill level near Lancashire, England, where the Rocket proved its worth to the Liverpool and Manchester Railroad.

He couldn't remember, though, where he had picked up an interest in the Rocket to begin with, or what had become of the partially completed layout. Or why the compulsion to build it had drained from him so suddenly that some of the sketches and plans stopped making any sense at all.

But *they* could have told him, Ransom thought, stirring the papers beneath his feet. "Moon madness," they would have said. What a marvel, how simple an answer can be. "You're insane. Just like us. Nothing to it."

Ransom scooped up the letters in wadded-up handfuls and began cramming them into the wastebasket next to the rolltop desk that had come with the house. There were letters still on the floor, though, and the wastebasket was stuffed full.

The moon-crazy letters were the ones left—perversely the ones most deserving of being dumped. But a trip to the cans in the alley would take care of them too.

You see, Marla? I cleaned house.

And then he would clean out his mind just the same way. He would take all the fever-dream images of the frost-eyed thing on the roadside, the eyes on the movie screen, the horror on the face of Ben Taylor, the ride in the back of a police cruiser, the gray floor of the jail cell, the *Midnight Enquirer* thrust into his hands by Thurman—all of these he would take to the alley and be rid of them. He would be *clean* again. Ready to start over.

In fact, he already felt different. In control again. The letters were nothing to worry him—they were pathetic scrawlings, that was all. From now on they would go straight into the trash unopened. And before long they would quit coming.

Ransom thought of asking the mailman to quit bringing anything to him that wasn't properly addressed—one envelope had ready simply "Keith Ransom, the S.O.B."—but then he wasn't sure if the carrier was trying to be helpful, or if he might have written the letter himself. One of the football letters.

Nothing wrong with a little paranoia, Ransom thought. Under the circumstances.

As for his mailbox at the college, he probably wouldn't be bothered with *that* much longer.

But the thought of the college was a saw blade against the framework of supports he had so confidently erected. Good intentions wouldn't change a thing there. He could resign, or he could appeal to Ron Hatton, the vice president of academic affairs; he could ask for a hearing. He could "drag it out," as Thurman had said.

Resignation would look better for him the next time he applied for a job, if he could make it *look* like a resignation and not like running away. A hearing? The outcome of that would depend on Hatton, and Ransom just didn't know the man that well. He did know that Hatton had been more or less in favor of the film class, but also that Hatton and Thurman played a regular Thursday night game of backgammon.

Come off it, Ransom. What could you possibly say that would make any difference?

He imagined himself facing Hatton, and Thurman there, off to the side, teeth and eyes gleaming in the shadows.

Every class full. Every class filled early. And check the enrollment. These aren't the slide-throughs, the skates, looking for an easy grade. They come in with a four-point-oh, a lot of them, and they work like hell to keep it.

Ransom caught himself pacing the floor, gesturing and muttering and changing the emphasis on his words, like some minor-league Perry Mason in front of a jury.

Translation, he thought. *Hey, don't you see that I'm loved? There's nothing wrong with me. I'm a good teacher and a valuable member of your staff. Except every now and then I try to kill someone for no reason at all. And I get some screwy mail.*

Why fight for a job that he didn't want, anyway? And then he thought: For Marla. He owed it to Marla.

Really? Then why hadn't he told her that he was about to be sacked, dumped out on his butt? Didn't she have the right to know?

He bent to grab the last stack of letters.

Of course he would tell her. Just as soon as he could formulate some good ideas of where to go and what to do next, so he didn't come off sounding like nothing but one more freak with a head full of green cheese.

The letters snapped out of his hand, fluttering across the room. *Great move, Ransom*, he thought, surprised at the sudden anger that had propelled them. *That helps a lot.*

He began to pick them up again. It was like clearing the floor of dead rats.

Get a grip on yourself. You're not one of them. You're not like them at all. Look. See for yourself.

He studied the page in his hand. It was nearly illegible, written in wandering, thick pencil strokes on a piece of brown paper that might have been torn from a grocery sack.

See?

The letter had something to do with the moon being a hole in the sky, and the next one—written in such a tiny script that he couldn't imagine what clenched, bony hand might have produced it—rambled on about UFOs beaming psychic waves onto earth from the moon's "volcanoed" surface. Ransom almost wished that he could meet the "volcanoed" writer in person, to prove the difference between himself and a genuine lunatic.

Because there *was* a difference.

See?

The letter in his hand now was a two-page gem, neatly fastened at the left corner with a paper clip. There was an oddness about it that escaped him for a moment, then seemed obvious. The writing looked like a sample page out of an old *Palmer Penmanship* textbook: clear, precise, flowing in straight lines across the paper, and never a word crossed out. Nobody wrote like that anymore.

He imagined that Mrs. Whoosis—Ida Milburn, the signature read—must have written and rewritten the letter she sent him until it was perfect.

But why go to such trouble?

Just like you, came the answer. *To keep from looking nuts.*

The letter rattled softly in his hand. As he read, his head began to throb, as if each of the words hurt in a new way.

Dear Mr. Ransom,

I am writing to tell you something I think you need to know. It's not much but I think it might help you. Don't blame yourself. What you did is not your fault. It was the full moon that made you act that way. I know. I am going to tell you how I know, even though I don't expect you to believe me.

The first night it happened—

Ransom read to the end of the letter. Then he read it again, and the second time he couldn't keep from laughing. It was the kind of laugh that burned in his throat. Mrs. Ida Milburn, Mrs. Milburn of the painstaking pen, was, of course, totally insane.

He envisioned her living up in the high terret of a mist-shrouded, haunted castle, silhouetted against the razor-edged disk of the full moon, her robe flapping in the shadows. He imagined all that, and then the return address on the envelope stopped him cold. It was a rural route outside of Arcadia, about a half hour's drive from Oklahoma City.

He and Marla would be driving to Oklahoma City on Sunday.

Ransom's breath quickened. His face took the blood rush, and he wiped at the sweat that had popped out in tiny beads on his forehead.

He-ee-eere's Ida.

There was no other way. He would go to her. Talk to her. *Be* with her. And it wouldn't take long. She would show him how it was to be insane. She would scare the hell out of him. And then he would *know*; he would know that the sickness had nothing to do with him.

Shock treatment.

He folded the letter in half as the front door rattled. Quickly he tramped the letters that were already in the wastebasket and stuffed the moon-crazy letters out of sight behind the desk.

Marla came in, elbowing the door open. Her cheeks and the tip of her nose were brushed pink by the cold outdoors.

She had an armload of white sacks with the tops rolled shut, reading, "Yum! Take me home!"

She looked at him, and then away. "I sort of . . . backed down on the turkey," she said. "Do you want the cheese-burger deluxe or the hickory sauce special?"

It was his idea later to break a French fry and make a wish. And she gave him what he wished for.

CHAPTER NINE

The rural mailbox, affixed to a silver-painted post, jutted up out of an old rusted milk can beside the dirt road. Painted on its side was the name Milburn and the route and box number, the letters and numbers faded to dark gray with age.

Ransom checked the numbers against the return address on the envelope just once more, then nodded to himself. An hour's drive out of the city this morning, then another two hours running up and down country roads, tracing box numbers, had finally brought him here. He still might have been looking if not for the old man at the dusty grocery store on the highway a mile away, who had just happened to know Mrs. Milburn.

Known her practically all my life, son. Lives just down the road a ways.

Ransom checked his appearance in the car's mirror. His eyes looked a little bloodshot, but otherwise everything was fine. He'd even worn a tie along with his corduroy jacket, hoping to put across a professorial look.

And what would Mrs. Milburn look like? Pulling away from the mailbox, he cut the wheels onto a dirt driveway, thinking again about what he might find at the end of it.

One illusion was dispelled when he looked ahead toward the house. Ransom remembered thinking about a haunted castle, a mental image of Mrs. Ida Milburn scurrying among the turrets, hopelessly insane. That was what had come to mind when he had first read her letter. Driving down, he had imagined a big Gothic two-story, the dull gray of weathered wood showing through patches of white paint.

But the reality was different. Ahead of him now, partially obscured by the pendulously bare mimosa trees lining the drive, was a little pink clapboard home. The naked branches of the trees scraped the top of his car like claws as he slowly drove toward it.

There were "cat ladies" everywhere; every town had one. Eccentric, lonely old women. But now, as he drove, a recent newspaper story popped into his head about a woman who had allegedly run a "pet adoption agency," taking people's unwanted pets and promising to find them good homes. According to the article, she had been revealed as a sadist who took the animals to her house and systematically tortured them to death.

He was sorry he had thought of that story, and he told himself that Mrs. Ida Milburn would not be like that woman. Her house probably would smell of cat excrement and animal odors, but he tried to convince himself that she would be simply a garden-variety cat lady—just an old woman who fed her cats out of cans, smiled at them with motherly smiles, and talked to them at night.

There was one difference, though, he reminded himself. According to Mrs. Milburn's letter, *her* cats talked back.

Ransom stopped the car beside another one, an old yellow Rambler wagon with rust spots on the sides at the end of the drive. From where he sat, he could see the corner of a wooden front porch. He looked at the lace curtains in the front window, and past them, for any sign of life inside. There was none.

Now what? he thought, suddenly remembering Marla back in Oklahoma City, her blank look when he had told her that morning that he had to leave for a while. She had propped herself up in the bed in her old room, her hair fanned out against the pillow, and her blank look had turned to one of hurt and bewilderment when he had refused to say where he was going. He had tried to reassure her that everything was all right, but he knew she hadn't bought it. God only knew what had been going through her mind when he left, and what was going through it now.

And her father—she would have to make excuses to him

because he would have questions, too, and how could she make decent excuses when she didn't even know what was going on? Thank God the old man had still been in bed when Ransom had slipped out.

Maybe he should have told her. Maybe she already knew, or had a good idea, even though he had tried to keep the letters, the lunatic ones, from her, pretending not to be interested. And they had been getting along so much better, ever since Thanksgiving.

But it had to be done, Ransom thought. *And so let's do it.*

He got out of the car. The morning was crisp, the tiny November sun almost translucent in the sky. From somewhere came the pleasant smell of burning leaves. He walked around to the porch, and the first thing he noticed was the row of large cardboard boxes, ten or twelve of them, in a line against the house, broken only by the newly painted screen door. His foot touched the first step of the porch, and the boxes stirred and exploded in front of him, cats streaming out—dozens of them, all sizes and colors, running away from him and past him, leaping and bounding and sailing off the porch and across the yard, disappearing in seconds through a barbed-wire fence into an overgrown pasture. Ransom recoiled, grabbing at a post for support. In a moment there was no sound but his throbbing heart.

"You sellin' somethin', young man?"

Ransom whirled at the sound of the voice. The woman stood in the doorway, holding the screen open a crack. She was in her fifties or sixties, with the heaviness that comes with being buxom in youth. Her hair was pulled back and tied with a ribbon, and she wore a housedress, faded to light purple. She wiped her hands on a dish towel.

"I'm sorry," she continued, "but I ain't in the market for anything today, if you're a-sellin'." The sunlight reflected back at him from her octagonal-lensed, wire-framed glasses, as if she were shooting tiny bolts of light from her eyes.

"N-no, ma'am," Ransom said, stammering. "I'm not a salesman."

"Lost?"

"No, I—"

"One of them Jehovah's Witnesses?"

This time Ransom smiled. "No. My name's Keith Ransom, Mrs. Milburn. You wrote to me."

She was silent for a moment, regarding him. Finally she said, "I should've known." Glancing toward the pasture where the cats had disappeared, she nodded. "Come in," she said.

Ransom walked across the porch to the doorway, glancing down at the boxes. Inside each one, old towels and rags were piled up, coated with dirt and cat hairs. He mentally prepared himself for the overwhelming animal smell he expected upon going inside and was surprised to find only a faint antiseptic odor.

The house had bare wooden floors, polished to a high gloss, and in the living room a large oval rug lay in front of an overstuffed deep crimson sofa with a woven blanket thrown over its back and doilies on its thick arms. The furniture and lamps and tables were of an old style but well kept, with two antimacassared chairs facing the sofa.

"I got to turn down my beans," Mrs. Milburn said. "Make yourself at home."

Ransom looked around as she left. Another mental image shot down. From the precise handwriting and near perfect grammar contained in the letter, he had envisioned—what?— a cultured woman expensively dressed? In Arcadia, Oklahoma, on a rural route?

He smiled at himself and sat down on the sofa. The house was dark, and it took him a moment to notice that the sides of the chairs near the floor were shredded and torn. The smile fell from his face as he bent over to examine the legs of the coffee table in front of him, running his fingers over the wood and finding deep grooves. They had been stained over in an attempt to make them less noticeable, but they were still there. Ransom leaned back, his elbow resting on one of the sofa's arms. Reaching across, he lifted the big doily. Underneath it were jagged tears, white stuffing oozing through.

"They don't know I got the doilies," Mrs. Milburn said from the kitchen doorway. Behind her, Ransom could see an enameled stove with pots on the burners. "They've doggone near wrecked th' furniture, and all I can do is try to hide it best I can." She walked across the room and took a seat in one of the chairs. "There's little tricks I've learned," she continued. "That blanket behind you? Lift it up and you'll see th' same thing. Cat scratches. I can turn the cushions over, but there ain't much I can do about th' backs and sides." She spoke with weary resignation.

"The . . . the cats did this?"

"Yes, sir. That's a fact, and that ain't th' half of it."

Ransom stared at her, trying to form a question. He could see her eyes now behind the thick lenses, unfocused and watery, like pebbles at the bottom of a clear stream.

"I oughta get rid of 'em all," she said, and for just a moment the eyes flashed hard before settling back down. "But I can't. I can't haul 'em off, and I can't kill 'em. I ain't never liked to kill any livin' thing." And then, almost to herself: "But sometimes they make me."

"In your letter," Ransom said, "you told me that the cats talked to you."

"That they do. For a fact, they do." She nodded to herself. "And you're the first person I ever told that." Unexpectedly she chuckled a little. "Ain't even told my boy. He come down for Thanksgivin' a couple of days ago, and I'm tellin' you it was touch and go, wonderin' if he'd leave before the moon got full and them cats started in."

Ransom was aware of the bubbling of the pot of beans on the stove in the kitchen. Warm cooking smells drifted in.

"Sooner or later I'm gonna get caught," she continued, "and he'll probably be th' one to catch me. But if I get caught, I get caught. Meanwhile I can't tell him or anyone else that them cats *talk* to me. I'd get put in th' 'sylum, for sure."

"You told *me*, Mrs. Milburn."

She nodded slowly, biting her lip. "I saw that story in th' paper about you, 'bout how th' moon made you crazy, made you do things you wouldn't ordinarily do. And I thought, 'That's like me. That young feller's just like me.' It was almost like we was kin." She waved her hands a little. "I know it's crazy, but it was sorta like bein' hit by lightnin', like all of a sudden I knew I had to get in touch. And th' cats said it was all right too."

A tingling started at the base of Ransom's neck. *Almost like we was kin.*

"This is somethin' I've always figured I got to handle on

my own, Mr. Ransom. I do what I can, scrubbin' th' floors and stainin' th' table legs an' tryin' to hide th' rest of it.''

"You do a good job," said Ransom.

She shrugged. "Best I can. My boy keeps sayin', 'Mama, how come you don't get rid of them stinkin' cats? Look what they're doin' to your furniture, Mama.' You wouldn't figure they could do that much damage in such a short time, just the few days around the full moon.''

It felt suddenly cold in the room. "Only under a full moon," Ransom said. "That's the only time you have . . . problems?''

"Yes, sir. Right before it and right after it, but th' worst is th' night of th' full moon. I 'spect they'll be startin' up tonight.''

"Please, Mrs. Milburn. Tell me about it.''

She exhaled. "Well, it all started a while after Floyd died. That'd be . . . let's see . . . eight years come January.'' She stopped suddenly. "Mr. Ransom," she said, "this is gonna be a little harder than I thought. I got a little homemade wine back in th' kitchen, and I believe I'll have me a glass. Can I offer you one?''

Ransom nodded, aware of the tightness in his body. "Yes, ma'am. And may I smoke?''

"I'll get you an ashtray." She got up and went slowly into the kitchen, wrapped in the fabric of memory. Ransom heard her fumbling among bottles and jars.

So now what? he thought. She didn't seem crazy, not really—but no one, he reminded himself, *seemed* crazy, especially the truly insane ones. The real crazies always carried that patina of respectability, of hyperrespectability almost. They moved among other people, mad secrets burning in their heads, nodding and smiling and making small talk, and it was only when the secrets exploded that anyone knew anything was wrong. Ransom recalled newspaper interviews with neighbors and friends of mass murderers, and the phrase *a respectable, quiet person* was almost a cliché in them. Madmen didn't go mad.

Mrs. Milburn appeared at his side, handing him a jelly glass filled halfway with a dark purple liquid, and took her seat on the other side of the room. Ransom sipped at the wine. It was sugary, but lighter than he expected.

"Thanks," he said. "This is good." He shook a cigarette out of his pack and lit it.

"I put up a few bottles every year. Not so much since Floyd passed away." She took a drink. "Got my own grapes growin' along th' fencerow."

Ransom nodded, and she fell silent. Taking off her glasses, she rubbed at the lenses with the hem of her dress, put them back on, and blinked a couple of times, taking another drink. And then, without preamble, she began.

"We always had a cat or two 'round th' house. Out in th' country, you jus' kinda naturally keep a lot of animals." She brushed a few gray strands of hair away from her forehead. "Floyd died eight years ago come this January, like I said, and the boy had growed up and moved out by that time. I was here by myself, tryin' to adjust to not havin' someone around th' house, when this big tom showed up on th' porch one evenin'."

"This was soon after your husband died?"

" 'Bout three months. I figured th' cat had come here 'cause of th' other cats I had 'round, couple of cats that lived in th' barn. But he seemed to want to stay close to th' house. He was different."

Ransom flicked an ash from his cigarette. "In what way?"

"Smart. Real smart. Y'know how cats'll kinda howl and whine? Well, sir, when this one howled, it was almost like he was talkin'." She took another drink of wine. Behind the glasses her eyes seemed to sparkle. "It got to where I'd talked myself into thinkin' he *was* talkin', sayin' *food* when he was hungry or *in* when he wanted in th' house. I was alone for th' first time in my life, and anything livin' was good company."

She leaned forward in her chair, looking away from Ransom at a spot on the faded rose wallpaper-covered wall. "And then one night, he *did* talk. He said, 'Lemme in this house *right now*!' " The last two words exploded from her with unexpected force, as if someone else were using her vocal cords.

"And on that night," Ransom said, "there was a full moon?"

"I don't recollect. But I imagine so."

"What did you do, Mrs. Milburn?"

"I jus' stood there in th' doorway and looked at him, and

then he said it again, plain as day. And I let 'im in.'' She sighed. ''That was th' start of it.''

With a sudden motion she picked up her wine and drained the rest of the glass. In the hallway behind Ransom, a floor furnace kicked on.

''It's amazing what them cats *do*,'' she said, swallowing. ''They start comin' 'round about the time th' moon starts looking round and yellow. Maybe three nights before it goes full, for sure. Then, night of th' full moon, I have to let 'em in, and they have the run of the house for a few nights after that, me waitin' on 'em hand and foot, then they go out and don't bother me again till next time. But, Lordy, the mess they make while they're here! Takes me all month practically to get th' house back into shape.''

''You say you *have* to let them in, Mrs. Milburn?''

''I *got* to.''

''Why?''

''All of 'em—they all talk. And they threaten me, show me things, just like I was watchin' a movie or something. They show me what they'd do to me if I didn't do what they said.''

Ransom's mind reeled, the pungent smell of wine in his nostrils. Hurriedly he lit another cigarette. ''But . . .'' he began, ''I mean . . . they're *cats*. Just cats. After the full moon couldn't you . . . get rid of them?''

Mrs. Milburn smiled a little. ''You sound just like my boy now. But you saw how many there was out there, didn't you? Weren't they on th' porch when you came?''

''Yeah. They ran away.''

''Always do when a stranger comes,'' she said. And then, ''There ain't no way I could get rid of that many, even if I wanted to. Oh, I used to think about puttin' poison in their food, or havin' someone come out and shoot 'em, but it wouldn't do no good.''

''I don't understand,'' Ransom said.

The woman suddenly shook her head, smiling. ''This is th' part I hated to get to, but I guess you need to know it all. C'mon out back.'' She pushed herself up out of her chair and led him through the kitchen and out the back door. Behind the house, beyond the backyard, a barbed-wire fence bounded an overgrown pasture where a pole barn sat squatting in the morning sun. Mrs. Milburn pushed open a gate made out of an iron bedstead and walked out into the pasture, onto a path where the dead grass and weeds had been beaten down by footsteps.

Ransom wrapped his corduroy jacket tighter around him. A northerly wind whipped across his face, rippling his jacket and flapping the dress against Mrs. Milburn's body.

In front of him, she motioned toward the pole barn. "Barn's jus' goin' to waste," she said above the noise of the wind. "Didn't raise no more stock after Floyd passed away, and th' cats kill all th' chickens. Can't have a chicken on th' place."

As they walked around the side of the barn Ransom scoured the pasture for signs of cats. There were none, but the pasture was so overgrown that anything could have been hiding in it.

"Right here," she said. Ransom looked down at a place beside the barn. It was a neat plot of bare earth, dug out like a garden plot. He walked to it and bent down, the tangle of thick, dead vegetation scraping at his pant legs. Rows of crudely made crosses pierced the soil at intervals. Some stood relatively straight, but most of them were twisted and tilted at different angles, as if they had been batted around and pushed up from underneath.

The woman stood beside him, her voice coming from above. "Each time they come in," she said, "I have to kill one of 'em with a knife. Kill it, take it out here, and give it a Christian burial."

Ransom's mind flashed on the story he had been thinking of before meeting Mrs. Milburn, the one about the woman who had killed the cats on the pretext of helping them, and he now wondered if he was in the presence of simply a garden-variety sadist. It would make things so much easier if that was the case. He could deal with that.

"All th' others gather 'round, and I bury th' cat and make it a little cross. Every full moon."

He glanced up at her. She was almost smiling, and the sun was reflecting off her glasses again. "But," she said, "it don't do no good. They always come back."

"You mean—out of the grave?"

"Well, I ain't never seen that. All I know is, th' same number's always waitin' for me on th' porch when that moon comes out, and whichever one I buried last full moon is always back, with nary a scratch on it.''

The chill wind shivered through Ransom. He turned back to the jagged rows of crosses, pushing at the ground with one hand. It felt soft and loose under his palm. Clenching a handful of soil between his fingers, he fought a sudden urge to choke.

Out of the dead grass, behind the crosses, a cat's head popped up out of the brush. The head was yellow, and the eyes, regarding him, gleamed agate-brown. The eyes and the head were as still as death, and the sharp wind barely rippled its fur.

The voice, behind and above Ransom: ''That's him, Mr. Ransom. Th' ol' tom. He told me it was okay to write you and to tell you *everything*.''

For only a second, frozen in time, the cat's head seemed to nod, and Ransom saw himself reflected in the agate eyes.

CHAPTER TEN

Where had he been? Why wouldn't he answer?

Marla watched him through the half-opened door of the bathroom adjoining the room that had always been hers as a child. He was shaving before dinner, staring into the eyes of his reflection in the bathroom mirror as if there were demons in the glass. He looked suddenly old to her, forcing Marla's realization: *Ten years' difference between us.* It was, in truth, almost twelve, but ten was the most that she could accept. There were lines in his face that she hadn't noticed before, hard-edged lines that buried themselves in the shaving foam.

Still, he could change. She had seen him do it. He could change in one smooth motion from bleak and silent to attentive and charming, and she hoped to heaven that he could make the switch in time, *this* time. One maddening, beguiling transformation, please, to go.

Best to just leave him alone, she thought, straightening the fold of her blouse at the waistline. For now, at least.

She felt some small part of her wanting to hide under the pink-ruffled quilt of her bed, a child again surrounded by stuffed toys, here in the room that her father had kept and maintained as a kind of museum, a shrine to her childhood. It was a room with no place in it for a man's clothes draped across the bed, the sharp scent of Grey Flannel cologne, the bulky gray suitcase in the corner.

Each time she came home she could see that the room had been changed in subtle ways, but always to the same effect. Each time it belonged more and more to the past. The pen-

nants and posters from high school left the walls as if they
had simply faded away; forgotten dolls and playthings and
picture books settled onto the shelves again, until she felt like
an intruder into her own yesterdays. In this room she could
almost hear the voice of her father reading to her about the
Pokey Little Puppy and Scuffy the Tugboat, and she ached
with a formless guilt. It was the feeling of having done something very wrong and very disappointing to him, simply by
growing up.

And now it was the worst of all—grown-up and married.

Keith emerged from the bathroom, dabbing with a wad of
tissue at a cut on his chin.

"Haven't nicked myself in I don't know how long," he
said, and stretched his hand toward her with a comically ex-
aggerated tremble. "Nerves. You'd think I was planning to
ask him if we could tie the knot."

"He would have said no."

"*Really?* Before or after he punched my lights out?"

"I think he'll come around to you, Keith," she said. "He
just takes some knowing."

Keith nodded and finished dressing. His necktie, as always,
was lopsided (probably on purpose, she thought). As she
straightened it for him, his arms folded lightly and hesitantly
around her, as if he expected that she might push him away.

"I want . . . a long talk with you," he said. "I've been
putting it off, trying to get everything settled, all figured out
and explained to myself first. But I want you to know what's
going on, Marla. Everything. On the way back home, okay?"

She must have smiled a little. Her face felt tingly. "Okay,"
she said.

"Now let's go bait the bear."

"It's called 'having a talk with the father-in-law.' And it
goes with the lady, sooner or later. Can't be avoided forever."

"Not because I didn't try," Keith said.

And then she watched him change, and the change took no
longer than the walk down a hallway from Marla's bedroom,
through the living room with its massive, leather-upholstered
sofa anchored in front of the fireplace, and toward the dining
room. Keith had taken her arm with an assurance that would
have been called elegant in one of those Victorian love stories

she sometimes liked to read, except for what he whispered to her as they neared the table: "Any of youse guys make one move, an' th' dame gets it, see?"

They stood in the archway, the burgundy silk of her blouse interlocked with the tweed of his sport coat, as Marla's father directed the efforts of a catering staff that outnumbered them two to one.

It was the kind of spread that only her father would have arranged, in which only her father would have felt comfortable. To him the object of a holiday observance was not just to enjoy the day but to seize it as the chance to make up for past slights, for time not taken, letters not sent, presents not given, phone calls never made. The table all but sagged. A huge, bronze-roasted turkey dominated the center in a throwaway aluminum pan, surrounded by plastic bowls of mashed potatoes and giblet gravy, cornbread-and-oyster stuffing, sweet potatoes, pearl onions in butter, cranberry sauce, and hot rolls with individual pats of butter beside them.

The rising steam dissipated as Latham negotiated with the caterers over something or other that hadn't been satisfactory, giving Marla time to notice that he had framed one of her oil paintings. It was a still life of a violin and a fruit bowl that she had completed during her first year at Reinholdt, and it hung beside a crayon drawing of a flower—a circle in the middle surrounded by loops for petals—that she must have done some time in grade school. The combination stirred a confusion of feelings within her, from which she tried to isolate the good.

She wasn't aware that the catering people had left until her father said, "Well, come and get it, kids." He motioned toward the table, adding a shrug at the end of the gesture, as if to apologize for not having enough.

They sat, and her father offered grace, but Marla kept her eyes open, enduring a pang of conscience for the chance just to look at him. His hair seemed a wispier white than it had been the last time she had seen him, more of a contrast against the stark black of his eyebrows. Those eyebrows imparted a look of such sternness that she imagined him ending the prayer with *or else* in place of *amen*.

She studied him, looking for some small reflection of herself but finding none.

She knew, more from photos than from memories, that she resembled her mother. But how could she? Her mother had left him—left the two of them—and long before it had become fashionable for a woman to abandon her family in favor of "making it" up the ranks of a marginally important career (something to do with a chain of department stores on the East Coast—that was all Marla knew, or ever wanted to know).

She remembered her father as a different man entirely during the hazy-dim time of her childhood, while her mother was still around. She recalled him as playful, childlike himself. And now she wondered if the change in him was only an altering of her own perceptions. Or was it the result of a man's emotional crippling, of being left for dead and trying to salvage some meaning from the experience, some lesson?

She was startled to realize that he was looking back at her. The grace had ended.

"Well, now," her father said, "I'd take you to be a drumstick man, Keith."

"Drumstick sounds just fine with me," Keith said, although Marla knew better. She caught him giving a forlorn glance toward the shimmering-moist slices of white meat at the side of the platter, and they traded winks across the table.

They ate, the dinner conversation mostly controlled by Latham and aimed toward Marla. He talked about her relatives: the cousin in California, the aunt in Hawaii. Safe talk, anecdotes Marla had heard countless times before about his own childhood and his own Thanksgivings as a child, the year they hadn't been able to afford a turkey and his father had gone out the night before and shot a jackrabbit, his mother baking it, fixing it up like a turkey, with stuffing and all. Although Marla thought Keith must be bored to death by the talk of people he didn't know, she noted with pride that he interjected things from time to time, encouraging her father to keep talking.

Afterward Keith helped her carry some of the dishes into the kitchen. On one trip he rolled his eyes upward and heaved a sigh, and she whispered, "Doing fine." The next, he kissed her on the back of the neck.

She waited in the kitchen, making a slow job of cutting and serving three wedges of pumpkin pie. But he didn't reappear, and as she stood by the kitchen door she could hear them talking, Keith and her father.

". . . this commotion at the college," her father was saying. "I won't ask you what happened. That's not my business, not at this point. I just want to know one thing." There was the tapping sound of some piece of silverware against the table edge, one of his nervous habits. "Have you still got a job there?"

"Yes." Keith's voice.

"Because if you don't, I won't stand for Marla to suffer from it. You tell me. I'll see to it that everything is . . . handled, and she won't need to know where the money came from."

"I still have a job." The voice had gone flat. "And some savings. We're okay."

Marla knew that the savings weren't much and weren't really savings at all—just what was left of some money Keith's grandmother had left to him. Keith seemed to have grown up with her more than with his parents. He never talked about them; they were dead, for all Marla knew.

That had been one of the first things to deeply attract her to him, Marla thought: the fact that he shared with her a kind of disjointed upbringing and that it hadn't seemed to bother him very much. He was a day-to-day assurance to her in that way, living proof that people did manage somehow to grow up and get on with it, regardless of how or by whom they were raised.

"I'm going to be blunt, Ransom, simply for lack of time," her father said. "I would have appreciated a talk with you this morning, instead of trying to shoehorn it in now. But, of course, you weren't here this morning. . . ." His statement, not quite a question, hung in silence for a moment. A coffee cup clicked against its saucer.

"I don't trust you," he continued. "Maybe I'm wrong. I don't really know you, and that's my fault as much as it is yours. But I want the best for Marla. Do we agree on that?"

"I'm sure we do."

Didn't they know she could hear them? Marla wondered, feeling the small, awkward honor of being discussed as a concern. As if she couldn't take care of herself just fine, thank you.

"Then I'm going to ask how much in savings. Because from what Marla tells me, you've got a lot tied up in . . . a number of little interests. *Hobbies*, shall we say."

Marla heard herself gasp and backed quickly away from the door, afraid they might have heard it too.

"And how much would you trust me," Keith asked, "if I let myself be pushed into answering questions like that?"

Good, Marla thought. Way to play it.

"Funny books," her father said. "Bubble gum cards. You can see where I might be concerned."

"Collectibles, Mr. Latham. A good investment, if you know the market."

The clink of a coffee cup again. "I suppose there's always somebody to pay a few dollars for just about anything."

Keith laughed. It wasn't natural-sounding for him, but it was convincing, Marla thought. Like Maverick on the old TV show, bluffing at poker.

"Let me give you an example of a funny book, Mr. Latham. *Detective Comics* from May of 1939. I paid five hundred dollars for a copy a few years ago, wrapped it in plastic; it's in a bank drawer now. I could sell it today—*today*—for close to four thousand. And that could be Marla's tuition, if you want me to take over the payments."

Marla recognized the ploy. She knew that Keith had no intention of selling his beloved *Detective Comics No. 27*, which he had displayed to her with all the ceremony of an unveiling at the Louvre; she recalled being ashamed afterward for having made fun of the crudely drawn, garishly colored little panels inside the magazine. And she knew—and had told Keith—that her father took much pride in being able to send her to Reinholdt, which was far more expensive than any of the state universities would have been.

No, Keith's objective simply had been to change the subject. And it worked. She all but laughed out loud at how well it worked.

"Four *thousand*!" The astonishment in his voice carried, and she tried to picture his face. "What would make it worth—"

"The first appearance of Batman."

"The guy with the pointy ears, and the kid trailing after him."

"Robin."

"The boy . . . the *Boy Wonder*! Sure, sure. I remember. And 1939 . . . I might have had that very same book."

"You should have kept it, Mr. Latham."

"Batman and Robin," Burton Latham said, and for just a moment Marla heard a tone in her father's voice that matched the way she remembered him from the best times of her childhood, when he would read to her, and they would plan in secretive whispers just to jump in the car sometime and go see Disneyland, although they never did.

But Keith seemed to sense, as well as she, that her father's change in mood was a painful slip, a loss of control that demanded recovery.

"The point is, I haven't put any money into collecting that I can't get back, and with a profit," she heard Keith say. "And I'm ready to pull out. It used to be fun, but it's gotten to be a business, with a lot of people and a lot of money involved, and you can't seem to trust anybody not to steal from you the first chance that comes along."

"Amen to that," her father said, and Marla listened as he launched into one of his favorite subjects, that of the necessity of counting and inspecting sheets delivered to his motels from the laundry, because they would short the count and try to charge for unacceptable work. And all the things that people stole out of the rooms: not just the linen and light bulbs and toilet paper, but even the little screw caps that held the lamp shades in place.

She returned to the counter and picked up the plates of pie, thinking of excuses she could give for being gone so long, if they asked. They probably wouldn't ask, though.

She felt an odd respect for Keith's ability to smooth past her father's hostility, although, of course, nothing was settled. They merely had been sparring; the main event was saved for some future date. But not today—thankfully, for this Thanksgiving, not today.

She emerged from the kitchen balancing three plates at once. Keith smiled at her, lightly applauding the act.

And the smile chilled her.

He could turn on the charm like a light switch, she thought, and she knew that, but she'd never had such a good chance before to see him make it work on someone else.

And, moments before, she had been *cheering* for him. Never stopping to think, until this precise moment, of how often he might have played that same game of dance-away with her, smoothed past her, even lied to her, all of it accomplished so very easily.

A long talk, he had promised. On the way home. But would it be a real talk or just another misdirected charade, a distracting sleight of hand?

She wanted to scream at him, suddenly, a hundred questions.

CHAPTER ELEVEN

"Did you mean what you said to my father, Keith?"

It was dusk, and they were almost out of the city now, cruising down the ribbon of interstate highway. Huge fenced plots of range- and farmland with ranch houses set back in the distance replaced the concrete, steel, and prefab of shopping centers and franchise restaurants and multileveled office buildings. Ransom felt relieved, as if some of his tension were dropping away as the city receded.

He had told Marla: No questions, no serious subjects, no nothing until they were out of the city. She had remained mostly silent, even when he had stopped at a suburban convenience store for a six-pack of beer. He knew she didn't like him drinking while he drove, and he remembered guiltily how, just a couple of days ago, he had poured the Scotch down the sink.

But beer wasn't really drinking, he told himself as he opened the door, putting the six-pack between them in the front seat. He knew better, and he knew Marla knew better.

Now he opened one of the cans. The pop was pleasant to his ears and he thought, *By damn, I deserve it*. A day with Marla's father hadn't exactly been like a week in the country, and the worst part of the day, he thought, just might lie ahead of him.

Well," Marla said, "did you mean it?"

"He drank, putting the can between his legs on the seat. "I guess it *is* time," he said. Drinking again, he held up the can. "Care for one before we launch into this?"

"Not right now."

He nodded. "Okay. Now, was I serious about what?"

"About what you said to my father."

"Which time?"

"The part about selling your collection."

"Oh," Ransom said, drinking and pursing his lips. "You heard that, did you?"

She smiled a little. "I heard. Were you serious?"

"Sure. If things get that bad."

"Uh-huh." She reached over unexpectedly and took the beer from him, sipped, and handed it back. "If you'll pardon my saying so, I think that's a crock."

Ransom looked at her, at the knowing gleam in her eyes. It made him angry. She thought she knew every damn thing there was to know about him, about what he did and what he was and how he'd act in any situation. He felt like telling her she didn't know shit.

"You do, huh?"

"Keith," she said, "you love that stuff. I don't think you'd part with any of it for anything."

"If we needed the money, I would," he said coldly.

There was a short silence as they drove, the autumnal light dying to darkness around them like the slow dropping of a curtain. Ransom searched the sky for the moon. It would be nearly full now, he thought, almost time now for—

For what? Time for another scene? Time to be jerked like a marionette toward God knew what? Time for him to lose his sanity—or for his sanity to leap from him, screaming into the night? He thanked God that the dreams hadn't started again.

Yet.

He was aware of Marla's voice.

"What?" he asked.

"I said, are we going to need the money?"

He looked over at her. The gathering night silhouetted her hair, her face. "You mean, have I quit my job?"

"Something like that."

"Well, you seem to have heard everything else I told your father. Didn't you hear what I said about that?"

"I want you to tell *me*."

"No." He finished the beer quickly and reached for another one. "I mean, no, I haven't." Not yet, he added mentally, beginning to feel the old, familiar edginess, the feeling of waiting. His lips were suddenly dry, his throat constricted.

He glanced at Marla again. She stared straight ahead, and he knew she was worried and trying to form words that would either dispel that worry or bring it out in the open. She was waiting too.

C'mon, Marla, he thought. *This is our discussion. The one you've been waiting for.*

Didn't she understand? The college was insignificant, was nothing, a tiny mound of concern next to the mountain he faced. *Ask me, Marla*, he thought. *Please ask me where I was this morning so I won't have to tell you first.*

He was running out of time. He lit a cigarette, and she asked him to crack his window. Another irritation. She didn't like the smell of cigarette smoke, and he felt like asking her: "Why, Marla? What's wrong with a little smoke? Where there's smoke, there's fire."

Her problem was that she had no vices. His problem was that he had too many for both of them. *Vices, habits, obsessions, and compulsions*, he thought. *You name 'em and I've got· 'em.* He blew out a stream of cigarette smoke and took another drink.

"Keith?"

"Yeah."

"How do you . . . feel?"

Ransom felt his jaw clench. "You mean, am I going nuts again? Am I going nuts right now, this very second, sliding right off the edge?"

"Please, Keith. I didn't mean that." Frustration colored her voice. "You've been under a lot of strain, and I'm sure being with my dad didn't help things. And you seem so distant now."

Ransom turned the can up, thinking, *Now's the time to tell her. Guess what, sweet thing. We're taking a little side trip.*

He checked himself from saying it out loud. He felt the weight of so many times of hurting her—not openly, not in ways that she knew, but in words of cutting cruelty, sneered in the darkness of his mind.

"Marla . . ." he began.

She squeezed his arm, and the unexpected gesture made

him shiver. "I love you, Keith," she said, touching her head to his shoulder. "I want you to be happy. That's all. I'm on your side."

Ransom pitched the empty Coors can into the backseat, wondering if he really had wanted the beer, or if he had bought it with the intention of starting a fight with her.

Because he would rather get into a loud, stupid fight with her than to sit and answer questions, and because—

"Keith?"

"Yeah?"

"This isn't the road back."

"Aha! And the doors are locked and—what's that? We're leaving the ground! Yes, foolish mortal, I am not your Keith Ransom, but an emissary from another—"

"Quit it, Keith."

The exit ramp joined with a frontage road, coming to a stop sign at the intersection of the state highway that ran toward Arcadia. Marla stiffened and pulled away from him as he made the stop too abruptly.

He knew what she must be thinking: Here it comes again. The props were all in place—the empty road, him acting screwy as hell, driving in jolts and lurches, and the moon—

The moon was waxing full now. They were five nights away from another full moon; Ransom knew the date exactly, having checked it with a call to the college's Astronomy Department. But it already *looked* full, white and haloed above them, partly hidden by the drifting bruise of a cloud bank.

Why didn't she just *ask* where they were going?

He reached for her hand. She really did love him, Ransom thought. She made it look easy.

But it wasn't easy. Not for him. Oh, no. For *him* there was a maze to blunder through every time he thought of her, a grand maze of dead ends and wrong exits. Now and then he would luck onto the right course, and he would come to the point of purely and simply *loving* her; and he would think, whatever made it so difficult? But even as he thought it the maze would change, and he would be back at the start of it, threading his way toward another wrong turn.

She made it seem easy. And he almost resented that.

He said, "I want . . . I need you to see something. Something out here. . . ." Faltering, he let go of her, rubbing at his forehead with the back of his hand. "Someone," he finished.

"Something or someone. Keith, it's late, too late to be playing Twenty Questions. I'd really just like to go home."

"It's the woman I . . . went to see this morning," he said, and thought, *There. It's out. And it sounds just as bad, just as awkward, as I knew it would.* "I'd like for you to see her, Marla. Just to see . . . what you think of her."

"See *her*? A *woman*?"

Marla's voice was laced with hurt and suspicion, and it caught him so much by surprise that he couldn't help laughing. For once, if only for *this* time, he could reassure her.

"Saw her this morning," he said. "Yep, I sure did. But I don't think it's going to work out. She's not quite my type—around sixty, I'd say, and with the mind of a squash soufflé."

Don't you wish, he thought. *Don't you pray.*

Marla said nothing, but the silence was a question in itself. What was left of Ransom's confidence dissipated into the night outside, gone in an instant. He let out a long, slow breath. "One of my pen pals," he said. "One of the people who wrote to me . . . about the moon."

"Oh." Her voice was a soft eruption in the gloom.

Ransom pulled onto the old state highway, taking the turn toward Arcadia.

Very quietly she said, "I wondered where you were."

So now you know, he thought, but the quiet of the night sounded better than speaking.

"I wondered. My father wondered. We sat around all morning wondering," she said.

"I'm sorry, Marla. That doesn't sound like much, but I really am. I just had to find out."

"Find out *what*, Keith? *What?*" She turned toward him, not just her head but her whole body, shifting back against the car door, cornered.

Ransom knew that he had to sound calm. Like in front of a class, that was it; just calmly explaining, one more time, the influence of Beatrice on Dante.

"Find out if she was . . . crazy or not," he said.

There now, class. That makes sense, doesn't it?

Marla leaned back; he heard the crinkling of the car seat. "Well," she said, as if she were looking under a bandage. "And what did you find out?"

"I'm not sure."

"That's too bad."

Ransom's throat tightened. He thought she might scream at him at any moment, and he wouldn't have blamed her.

"I think I was . . . maybe . . . too open to letting my own mind play tricks on me. I don't know." And he told her the whole story, all about the cats and what Mrs. Milburn had said about them, and the scratch marks in the house, and the little graveyard out back with the tomcat and his piercing eyes.

"So what do you think?" he asked when he was finished.

"I think it's too late for Halloween stories, but that's a good one."

Ransom turned off the highway, onto the farm-to-market road that led to the Milburn place. He could almost feel the glow of the moon on his face.

"You really mean it," she said. "We're going out to this place. We're just going to *drop in*—that's your idea, right? And I'm supposed to pick out who's the craziest. God in heaven, Keith."

The headlights cut a swath of white across the road, sweeping over the dried clots of grass and weeds along the roadside.

"Okay. Okay, then, we won't stop. We'll just drive past. I want to see the place at night, when all this—"

"Keith!" Marla pointed through the windshield.

He saw it barely in time to swerve. The cat's hindquarters had been crushed, and it was scrabbling wildly with its front feet, trying to pull itself off the road.

The Datsun wobbled as he brought it back into the right lane. Ransom thought he saw the twin glint of animal eyes, caught for a second in the headlights, trained toward him from the roadside.

"Keith, *stop*! We need to help it."

He saw a low, dark shape rush across the road, just beyond the range of the lights.

"Help . . . ?"

"The cat. That poor cat back there."

"Marla, that cat was as good as dead."

"You don't know that."

"We're not going to stop out here on a dark road in the country and look for a mashed cat in the bushes."

"Oh, no. I guess that wouldn't make sense." Her words were drenched with the cold anger that had finally taken hold. "And we *do* try so hard to make sense—by going out on a dark road in the country and looking for crazy old women."

It should have been funny, Ransom thought, but he couldn't laugh. "You can't stop and save every cat on the road, Marla," he said.

"You mean Strawberry. You never liked Strawberry, anyway, did you, Keith? It would have been just fine with you if she would have died under the—"

"Marla, listen to me!" Ransom's temples pounded. There was a ringing in his head, and he knew that he must have been yelling at her. "It's . . . important. I *need* this."

There was a brown-striped cat running alongside the road; another darted almost under the car's wheels.

"I need to know the truth about her," he said.

"And suppose that she is. Insane, I mean." Marla's voice had softened to a tone of patient urgency. "I don't even like that word. What does it *prove*, Keith?"

"Maybe that I'm not."

Ransom slowed the car. Ahead, at the top of the rise, was the Milburn place, orange light showing from every window of the house.

Marla sighed. "So what are we doing?" she asked.

"We go up there and we see Mrs. Ida Milburn. Probably we make a couple of fools of ourselves."

"Just drive past, you said."

"Drive past and . . . maybe stop. Just for a minute. Knock on the door. I want the whole effect, Marla. I want the dead of night, and the moon, and I want you with me. I got it all wrong this morning; I can see that now. I need the moon up there, if it's supposed to be such a big part of the story. And I need you to make sure . . . to *con-firm* . . ."

"Confirm that we've rattled some half-witted old woman out of her bed and scared the cats."

"Right," he said.

But there was an alternative to that scene, and Ransom saw it in his mind now. He saw the cats surrounding him, regarding him with wise and ancient eyes, and one of them—the agate-eyed old tom—baring its animal teeth at him. Telling him, "Bury me. *Bury me*—and I'll show you a *secret.*"

And Marla. *Marla*, trapped in that nightmare.

He caught himself whistling, almost but not quite tune-lessly. It was "If I Could Talk to the Animals." Good old Doctor Doolittle.

The twin beams of the headlights speared Mrs. Milburn's mailbox. He slowed to a stop. "Here," he said to himself as much as to Marla.

"Keith . . . ?"

He turned into the graveled driveway, the lights sweeping along the dark skeletons of trees. A mimosa limb scraped across the top of the car.

"Keith, I don't like this. I mean, you've got me good and spooked, and I know it's all just stupid, but then I think: *What if . . . ?*"

And in some parallel universe, Ransom thought, another Keith Ransom had thought better of taking the Arcadia turn-off, had gone straight home instead, and was feeling pretty good right now.

"What if, huh? Like, what if we find a bunch of talking cats trying to break down the door?" He gave her what passed for a grin. "We tell her it's too bad Ed Sullivan died, and get the hell out of Dodge."

The car rumbled beneath them.

Ransom wanted it over with. He wanted once and for all to witness the demons of Mrs. Ida Milburn for what they were—pathetic delusions and twists of the psyche having nothing to do with him.

He glanced toward Marla. She sat with her hands between her legs, arms still and head bowed as if she were freezing, and he suddenly, desperately, regretted making her a part of this, his self-prescribed little healing ritual.

"It might be better for you to wait in the car right—" he began, cut off by the thud of something hitting the car's hood.

The cat seemed no more than a bristled wad of black fur as it bounded off the hood again, running toward the house.

There was a movement in the grass to the side of the car, a skittering of white and orange.

Ransom saw a shifting row of eyes trained toward him, tiny glints of fire, from under the chassis of Mrs. Milburn's old Rambler wagon, parked alongside the front porch.

"Keith, I think I wet my pants. Honestly. When that cat hit the car . . ."

The Datsun's engine knocked. Ransom's eyes shot to the lighted dashboard, where the fuel gauge needle rested almost against empty. He pictured with taunting precision the store where he had bought the beer, the bright yellow Root-'n'-Scoot sign and the gas pumps to the side of that, where he had meant to fill up. But his mind had been keyed into the prospect of coming back to the Milburn place, and on whether Marla would make a fuss or not. And the beer—so damn important then.

He shut off the engine.

Marla yelled his name in protest as, out of habit, he punched off the headlights.

And in that second, he saw—

The image drifted in front of him, a frost-lit thing in the darkness, a thing of light and shadow, captured in his eyes and in his mind.

He saw—a jumble of moving shapes to the side of the house. Crawling, tumbling, multicolored, shining eyes and white teeth, hiding there.

Hiding in the darkness now.

Ransom groped for the headlight switch.

"Keith, we're getting out of here. Right now. Do you *hear* me?"

And in the doorway now, the woman, standing behind the screen and looking down, the porch light reflecting from her glasses.

"Keith!"

The woman looked up in the direction of the car. Ransom jabbed at his eyes, but his vision was clouded, frost-edged.

It wasn't the old woman anymore.

It was—*Marla*, he saw.

Marla, standing above the cats, the hem of her dress hanging in tatters, her legs streaming blood.

"Bury me." She called to him. *"Bury—"*

He was out of the car then, everything soft around him. He tripped, running. Saw the hissing gray cat at his feet. Kicked and caught it in the head, sent it cartwheeling sideways, squalling. But where there was one, now the ground filled with cats, howling and mewing, sliding past him, toward—

—the opened door of the car.

Ransom jerked around. The car horn blared, and he saw here, there—Marla—still in the car, and he saw what she didn't, as one of the cats, now two, now three, converged on the car door.

Marla, still in the car.

Still in the car. His mind fought for an anchor, clung to that reality. The frost cleared from his eyes.

From behind him he heard the screen door slam shut.

The porch light went out.

At the side of the house—he saw the ground move. The darkened, black mass of it shifted, rose up, and came toward him, sparkling with eyes, coming closer.

Ransom made a clumsy leap for the car door. His foot twisted, spilling him onto the ground, into the warm, hissing breath of the old yellow tom. The cat's eyes pierced him, twin moons in the centers of those eyes.

It opened its mouth and yowled, and the ragged sound melted, congealed, became a word.

Soon.

Ransom scrabbled to his feet.

Soon, it screamed. *Sooooon.*

He ran. Something caught at his pant leg. Something needlelike tore at his skin.

He plunged into the car, slammed the door shut. It made contact with a dull, crunching sound, and there was a thud, and second impact, against the metal.

And Marla. She was crying, squeezing his face between her hands, covering it with kisses. Warm lips on him.

"I . . ." he heard himself whisper. "Get us out of here." And somehow, then, he was on the passenger's side, the door locked, looking through the windshield as Marla backed the Datsun out, sobbing and bumping against things in the night.

He saw the cats massed, clawing against the screen door of the house, and then the car cleared the driveway and took a backing turn onto the farm road.

The Milburn place was behind him, and he could run from it and never see it again.

But the moon was unchanging.

CHAPTER TWELVE

Ransom unlocked the door, stepped in, and snapped on the light. The bulb in the front hallway's ceiling was a 150-watter, and it lit up the far side of a headache within him. He could see through the hallway, past the framed poster of *Viking Women and the Sea Serpent*, and into the living room with its bookshelves and toy train and the permanent little decorated Christmas tree in the corner. His collection of antique ornaments dangled from its branches.

All during the drive home his mind had been fixed on this moment, imagining how wonderful it would be to come through the door—*his* door—and be home again; he had clung to the promise of security and well-being that surely would be his once he stepped through the doorway.

But it didn't work that way.

The house and its surroundings only served to put a new and harder edge of reality on the night, on the fever-dream of the Milburn place, on the angers and fears, the words and the silences that had followed that grand little stop in the country.

He stepped inside and the house let him know, with the hiss of the furnace kicking on, that the night had come in alongside of him.

He said nothing to Marla. She passed him as he stood there, and she snapped on more lights as she moved through the living room and into the kitchen. As he watched, she started a pot of coffee.

She must feel it, too, Ransom thought. Sleep was out of the question that night.

Marla reached for a cup from the wall rack of coffee cups that he had begun saving some time during his first year at the University of Missouri. The cup—fashioned in the shape of a striped cat with the tail curling to form a handle—slipped from her hand, and when it cracked on the floor, something small cracked in the back of Ransom's mind too. She didn't pick it up. She just reached for another.

Pick it up! he thought, but he didn't speak. The coffee began to perk, and he stood in the archway, and she sat at the kitchen table, and they listened to the bubbling as if it were telling them something.

"Is there anything more we should . . . talk about?" he asked.

"A lot. I think, a lot more. I just . . ." Marla shook her head. She poured the coffee.

"I know." Ransom joined her at the table. "I think we're both pretty well talked out, and we still haven't said anything."

She sat, tapping a spoon against the tabletop.

"Marla, you saw the cats. I know you did. Shit! You can't tell me now that you didn't see what was going on there."

He had said it before, almost the same words before, over and over; but he tried it again, hoping that maybe *this* time . . .

"I saw . . . *you*. I saw *you*, Keith."

They had stopped for gas at a Conoco station off the Interstate; got a couple of cans of Coke so cold that there were little ice crystals floating in them, and she had lost it, right there in the Travel Shop, screaming at him. *"It wasn't the goddamn cats! It was you!"*

Now Ransom reached to stop the clacking of the spoon. "You've got to *know* what's happening," he said.

"Oh, I do. I do, Keith. It's all very clear to me. You need help."

"*Say* it, then. I need—what?—I need to pay some pretentious jerk-off in a paneled office full of wonderfully well-tended plants, need to pay for somebody to listen to me and nod and tell me that I'm going to need a *regular* appointment for a long, long time? *That's* what I need?"

"Keith"—her voice was soft but tense—"I don't see that an analyst is any different from any other kind of doctor."

"That's because you've never been to one."

"And you have . . . ?"

It was a rock he hadn't meant to tip over, the underside crawling with beetles and worms and things that should stay in the dark. "A long while ago," he said.

Marla was quiet, waiting for him to continue.

"Grade school. Because I wasn't . . . fitting in. My mother's idea was always that an afternoon of babbling out her life's details to kindly Dr. Bergman was better than a ball game, so I got the treatment too."

At least it was getting them onto a different track, he thought. It was breaking the pattern, and if it took a little pain to break the pattern, that was all right too.

"I suffered . . . compulsive behavior. So said the doctor. I had to be shown that a compulsion could be cut off and nothing bad would happen to me—that was Dr. Bergman's advice."

Ransom swallowed. Amazing that such an old memory could still pull the strings, he thought. He shrugged, smiling a little.

"I had a ten-gallon tank full of tropical fish. The whole thing was balanced and self-sustaining, and I was spending a lot of time just watching the fish, studying them. And dear old Mom, boy's best friend that she was, dropped them all, one by one, into the john, and flushed them away. I cried, I think, for every one. And she said, 'There, now. Dr. Bergman will applaud you.' "

Marla clasped his hand softly. "Surely you can see, Keith. That wasn't the normal . . ." Her lips moved with no sound, in search of the word. "Normal way."

"It was for her."

"I feel . . . so *helpless* sometimes, Keith, so much in the dark. There's so much about you I don't know."

Ransom lit a cigarette that he didn't want. "Well, that's about all of the fish story, the ones that got away," he said. "That was the year that the old girl remarried, and she wanted some time to get settled with her shyster lawyer—sans me. I guess she never got settled. My dad's grandmother—Grandmother Rose—took me in. And the brilliant Dr. Bergman, shame that it was, never got the chance then to diagnose what really was wrong with me."

"Which was?"

"Penis envy," he said.

Marla's expression went blank for a second. "A joke, right?"

"Right."

She poured seconds, or maybe it was thirds, of the coffee and started a second pot, which Ransom took to be the signal of some very heavy talk about to begin.

"You know," she said, "I think that's the first thing you've ever told me about your folks."

Ransom shrugged. "Never any reason to. I liked my dad just fine, what I remember of him. He died a very long time ago. Up until a few years ago I got a Christmas card from my mother with whatever surname she had that year. Those stopped, and I don't much care."

"No other contact?" Marla asked.

Ransom blew on the coffee, shaking his head. "I have this fantasy or daydream—whatever—that she's in some supermarket a couple of weeks back, and she picks up a tabloid while she's waiting at the checkout counter. And there I am, her son, the full-moon prof. Know what I see her saying?"

"No."

" 'Dammit. If only he'd gone to Dr. Bergman just a few more weeks.' " His chuckle was dry, low in his throat.

She squeezed his hand again, and the conversation took a turn toward silly things, safer things, of her father's phobia concerning miscounted motel sheets, of final exams and great moments in successful cheating, and why he'd never be able to persuade her to eat a raw oyster. He told her about getting into the fight with another kid over a Wayne Terwilliger baseball card, and they traded turns guessing the ingredients of McDonald's Secret Sauce, getting more and more outrageous.

He wouldn't have ruined the moment, and he didn't. She did. The sleeplessness-and-caffeine roller coaster took them up, laughing, and dropped them down again, and after a period of silence she spoke.

"Keith, I'd like to know what's going on with your job," she said. "I think I have the right to know."

He told her straight out, "I just about don't have one," and it wasn't so bad, after all. He knew, even as the words flowed out of him, that he *wanted* to come straight with her on something of consequence.

And so—the college. What was wrong with the college, with its inflated tuition and aggrandized self-image as the pristine oasis of culture on the plains, the faculty politics, the senseless mire of policies and requirements, was all wrapped into the person of Morris Thurman.

When he was finished, she said, "I think you should quit, Keith. I really do. I'm behind you."

"I can't quit, Marla. No more than I could throw away those books over there, or the coffee cups, the damn stupid coffee cups, or the baseball cards that I never look at."

"Just call up and quit and be done with it."

"It's not that easy."

"Why not? There's the phone."

"That phone?"

"That's the phone."

"You know what? I think you're right. What a great idea."

"You could . . . Keith? No, wait. Wait! What are you doing? I didn't mean call him *right now*. What time is it? *Keith!*"

Ransom hung up the phone. Taking a swallow of black coffee, he tried to smile.

Marla tried too. But more than the smile, he saw the redness and worry in her eyes.

"So, now that I've done it, I wonder if I did the right thing."

"I think so, only . . . maybe not the right way."

Somebody laughed; Ransom guessed it was him. But it set her off, too, and they put their heads down on the kitchen table and laughed, not knowing why.

"Should've heard him, Marla," Ransom said, coughing, trying to catch his breath. "Sounded like he had a mouthful of mattress."

She gave in to a deep yawn. "You too. And me," she said. "This isn't going to hit me, really, until after I get some sleep. But you know what?" She leaned toward him, smelling of yesterday's perfume and a night's worth of coffee and cigarette smoke. "I feel"—she yawned again—"better. So much better."

"Well, then. Let's do this again real soon."

"Thanks all the same. What time is it?"

His wristwatch had stopped in the night, the winding neglected. He glanced toward the old glass-fronted railroad clock that hung over one of the bookshelves. The clock hummed, as if in reproach of having its insides turned electric, and he still meant, sometime, to rebuild the original workings.

"About six," Ransom said.

"Hmm. Guess I could sleep for an hour, but I think I'd feel better if I just took a shower."

"A wise choice."

She turned toward the stairway, a little shaky on her feet. "You know, I haven't stayed up all night since . . . I guess not since the senior prom."

"It's what you call a cheap high," Ransom said. And it was, or even better. There was no drug in the world that could do as much for you as a good, long denial of sleep, he thought. It dulled the sharpest edges.

He had just quit his job, and he couldn't care less. The whole night seemed to have happened to someone else, its agony blunted, drained away.

"What about you?" Marla asked. "Are you still going to be teaching today or what?"

"Nope. Dr. Thurman said it would be entirely fine for me just to evaporate. Or words to that effect."

She leaned against the banister for support. "I think I'd be scared if I wasn't so tired."

"I know."

"You want to talk about what happens now?"

He got up and went to her, putting his arm around her shoulder and guiding her up the stairs, one slow step at a time. "I'll write a letter. To make it official. Then we go from there."

She leaned against him. "It's the 'go from there' that worries me."

"Yeah."

They reached the bedroom at the top of the stairs and sat down on the edge of the bed, still holding on to each other.

"Keith," Marla said, "I want you to know that it meant a lot to me just to talk to you." Her voice was slow and languid.

Ransom reached across the bed and fluffed up the pillows beside the headboard. He urged Marla up on the bed.

"What are you doing?" Marla asked with all the resistance she could muster.

"Let's just lie here together a minute. It feels awfully good."

"Okay. But don't let me go to sleep."

He hardly heard her. A thought had hit him back there on the stairs, an idea that made such perfect sense, he wondered why he hadn't thought of it before.

A book. He'd write a book. Ideas and details tumbled through his sleep-deprived mind.

All that crap in the papers—he could use that to his advantage. And the letters, there was a reason for having them now, as studies, case histories—or at least starting points for research.

Ransom was more awake than ever now, as his mind burned with possibilities. None of the old werewolf stuff but true stories of true people maddened by the moon. What *possibilities*! And giving it all credence, the fact that it was written by the moon-mad professor himself! He saw himself on radio and television, plugging the book, holding it up before audiences, and the title . . .

Full Moon. What else?

And why couldn't it happen? he asked himself. He could write, he knew he could, and the public—the great unwashed masses out there who swelled the coffers of the supermarket tabloids—they'd eat it up.

"Marla," he said, "I've got an idea." After the emotional ups and downs of their long night he hated to introduce anything new to her, but he had to. She had to know that all of this, all the letters that he had saved, had a purpose now, a sensible, rational purpose. "I'm going to do a book, Marla," he said.

He turned to her. Sleep, denied for too long, had taken her quickly, quietly, and gently, and she lay beside him now, her regular breathing barely audible. Ransom watched her for a few moments, thinking about waking her up so he could tell her what burned in his mind. But no, he decided, she'd had enough for a while. Let her sleep.

Ransom closed his eyes. Mrs. Milburn was just the start.

He would *find* those people, the letter writers, find them and study them and publish the results. . . .

The warmth of Marla beside him soothed him, and he drifted, just for a second, into that region of half sleep in which a second is long enough for the darkest of dreams to come out of hiding. He thought he was standing again outside the Milburn farmhouse, but the moon was full now, and the roof of the house seemed outlined in cold white against the night sky. He could see Mrs. Milburn standing in the lighted doorway, and the woman looked like Marla, but Marla didn't wear glasses; and then he could see that Mrs. Milburn wasn't wearing glasses, either—that her eyes were round and yellow with slitted pupils. And her teeth, long and thin, impaling the furred body that was clenched in her mouth. And the jaws squeezed together—

The vision ended. His eyes snapped open.

As Ransom disassociated himself from the vision he realized that it had been no more than a sample of the dreams that he would have had, if he had slept that night—the dreams still to come.

He shook the thought away and pushed himself up and off the bed, careful not to jostle Marla. Shedding his clothes, he padded across the threadbare old carpet, into the bathroom, and turned on the shower. The water stung, and the steam and the haze of his mind became one and the same.

He was glad Marla had fallen asleep, but he also knew, when she awakened, that there would be no holding back anymore, not if he was going to do the book. He would have to be careful to balance things. The good thing, the book, would have to be very good, better than what would come with it. The traveling, the people he would see—true lunatics, and him the biggest one of all. He would have to tell her that too. All of it. All about the vision that had seized him that night in the Ozarks. About the change that had come over him, hurling him into Ben Taylor with the mindless force of a thrown knife. And then she would see why he had to do that book; she would *have* to see.

But, he thought, what if she didn't?

He cranked off the shower. The air felt cold, the tile floor colder. Toweling himself dry, he found his robe hanging from a hook inside the door and shrugged it on.

How would she take it? he asked himself, looking at her sleeping form. He didn't want, couldn't have, any more arguments, any more scenes.

And as he sat down beside her, the springs creaking slightly under his weight, his mind flickered darkly again, just for a moment, giving him another look at the cat-eyed Mrs. Milburn, taking him back again to the pit of the night.

Driving. They were driving so fast that the car rattled.

"Marla, you saw. You saw. At the door, they were up at the door. Clawing—"

Onto the Interstate. The bellowing horn of the semi as she pulled out in front of it. And Marla, her voice broken. Racking, dry sobs in the night.

"Jesus, God, damn the cats. It was you!"

No control left in her, and Ransom, afraid to look, to move, to open his eyes, and at the same time *wanting* to, to reach out and—

Ransom found himself staring at Porky Pig, who grinned from an old Looney Tunes poster on the bedroom wall. It took him a moment to realize that he had descended into the darkness of his mind again, and he was still dealing with the residue of that journey when he heard a knock at the front door.

At this time? he thought. Who . . . ?

The knocking came again, and he crossed to the bedroom window, looking down toward the front steps of the house, darkened except for the spill of the porchlight.

A girl was standing there. The hair registered first: long and blond, swinging across her shoulders as she shifted from side to side, her arms folded against the cold. She had on jeans and a denim jacket. He didn't know her.

Beyond, parked against the curb, sat a battered van of almost the same deep blue as the morning's darkness. Ransom saw it first as no more than a silhouette, then—splotches that must have been rust on the back fender, and a devil's face painted on the side.

The girl uncrossed her arms and knocked again.

Ransom took the stairs down, past the movie posters lining the staircase, and opened the door to her. The face smiled at him awkwardly.

"Keith Ransom?" she asked.

He nodded, still trying to place her. Nothing fit.

"I'm Freedom," she said. "Elizabeth Garland, really, but they call me Freedom." The smile flickered. "Can I talk to you?"

Something about her compelled him—something in her face, which would have been pretty but for the sharply fixed shadows under the cheekbones. The blue eyes seemed almost innocent, but they were sunken, as if held captive, into the shadow-darkened sockets. She looked like she needed a fix, Ransom thought. Maybe not drugs, but something . . .

"It's not even seven yet," he said, startled to find that he had backed away from the doorway to let her in.

"It's not me, really," she said. "It's Rooster that needs to talk to you, but he's out in the van." And then, looking around the room, she said, "Hey, this is some kind of circus."

"Talk about what?" Ransom asked.

"Look, I know it's early, and you're not even dressed yet and all that, and it's cold and dark out, but Rooster . . . he can't come in, and it won't take but a minute for you to see him. Okay?"

Ransom hesitated, feeling a formless apprehension where there should have been only annoyance.

"Please," she said. "Okay?"

"If it's all so important, then why can't . . . ."

"Rooster."

"Why can't Rooster come up to the door, then?"

"You'll know when you see him. You've *got* to." Her voice took on the shrillness of desperation, and Ransom's first thought was that she would wake Marla up. He didn't want that, not now.

Grabbing an overcoat, he slid his bare feet into a pair of shoes that he'd kicked off just inside the doorway. "All right," he said, "let's go."

Holding the door for her, Ransom saw as she passed him the tiny heart-shaped tattoo on her right cheek, like a teardrop, and the way that her jeans laced in the back like something from Frederick's of Hollywood. No, he thought finally, he didn't know her at all; not a chance.

She walked in brisk, long-legged strides toward the van, and he followed in bathrobe and overcoat, feeling like some kind of custard-pie clown. A clown, he thought, and then he remembered the maxim attributed to Lon Chaney: "A clown isn't funny in the moonlight." At the same time he came close enough to the van to see that the rust splotch above the back fender was surrounded by a peppering of holes. Buckshot.

The girl slid open the side door of the van, and the screeching of heavy-metal rock music sliced against the cold air. "Rooster, here he is," she said, and the music went dead.

Her hands fluttering, she turned toward Ransom and gestured toward the open door. He stepped to the side to read the license plate, what was left of his adrenaline beginning to seep through his body. A local plate would have been the tip-off to another Reinholdt football nut still looking for blood over the Taylor thing. It would have told him: "Last one back to the house is a rotten egg." The word *California* on the plate gave him no assurance. Now it could be anything.

Hesitantly Ransom bent into the van.

The dome light was on inside, more as if to throw shadows than to illuminate anything. The air was thick with the scent, the feeling, of sickness, confinement, engine heat; of dust, smoke, alcohol.

The tip of a cigarette flared from the far end of the van. Ransom saw him then: the pale face stark white against the red spikes of the beard. The wheelchair, anchored by cinder blocks against the wheels. The half-lidded eyes. The halo brace circling the man's head, the bolts from the brace connecting to the skull.

"Boogie on in, man."

To Ransom it was as if the other man hadn't even spoken; nothing about him seemed to move. His voice was a labored whisper.

"What's this about?" Ransom asked, ready to turn and run if the situation called for it.

"Talk, man. Just talk. You can see . . . I'm not much to be scared of, right?" The man's left hand moved slowly, falteringly, to his mouth, taking the cigarette and dropping it to the floor of the van. "A little rap here . . . do us both some good."

Ransom found a seat against the side of the van, scarcely aware of the girl sliding into the driver's seat behind him.

Rooster said, "You're the one in the newspapers, right? Kicked shit out of some dude, night of the full moon."

"I don't talk about it a whole lot before breakfast."

The other man wheezed in what might have been laughter, but his face and his voice went slack again just as quickly. "How'd it feel, man?" he asked.

Outside, there came the rumbling of engines. Ransom heard two, maybe more; he caught a glimpse of one of the cycles through the side window of the van.

He needed to get out of there. "It felt . . . real crazy, *man*," Ransom said, edging toward the door. He felt a coldness in his throat. "And now I believe I'll boogie on out the way I boogied on in."

"Not yet."

"Look, I don't know what you want, but I haven't slept all night, and I've had enough trouble to last me for a while. I don't need any—"

"*Trouble?*" Rooster's eye's flickered wide open, moonwhite. "Hear 'im, babe? The man's got trouble. Like we don't."

The girl spoke with a painful softness. "He might think we're not making much sense, Rooster. He wasn't there—"

Rooster looked for a moment as if he might surge to his feet, knocking the wheelchair behind him. But he didn't. Only his left hand clenched and loosened, again and again, on the arm of the chair. After a moment he said, "Show 'im the picture."

Freedom reached to the sun visor above the driver's seat and unfolded a piece of notebook paper, grease-smeared and torn at the edges. "The best I could do," she said, handing the paper to Ransom. "Good enough that I don't like to look at it."

It was a pencil drawing of a man's face, almost childish in the heavy scribbling of the beard. Ransom saw it and felt his body stiffen, a spreading coldness beginning in the pit of his stomach. The hiss of his breath seemed like thunder.

The eyes!

"You *know* 'im," Rooster said.

"No. No, of course not."

The eyes—cold and blank, just the same as the drawing

Ransom had seen of himself in Marla's sketchbook, the one she had tried to hide from him.

"Don't lie to me, man. This ain't no *game*."

"Who is he?" Ransom asked.

Rooster held him with a look as sharp and hard as a knife blade. Ransom stared back.

"You don't know?" Rooster said. "You don't want to know. Leave it at that."

Ransom's eyes flashed back to the drawing. His mind was a fog, but somehow, he thought, that picture held the answer to what was happening to him—and yet it told him nothing. Nothing at all.

"This . . . man," Ransom said. "You're trying to find him." It wasn't a question; it was the one clear part of the whole scene.

Rooster's hand flapped toward the brace around his head. "Just the way he *found* me."

"And the moon. What's the moon got to do with it?"

Rooster's face registered a flash of surprise. "Let it go, man," he said. "Take it to the house."

Ransom sensed fear from the other man, and it surprised him. *Why?* Ransom thought. *There's no way I could hurt him any more than he's hurting already. There's nothing I could do, except . . .*

I could laugh at him.

"I want to know," Ransom said evenly. "Like you said, it's no game."

Rooster's voice dropped to a whisper. But not for effect, Ransom thought. In weakness and pain.

"Only see 'im . . . nights of the full moon. Maybe a couple of nights before the moon goes ripe, if the sky's right, no clouds, and the moon's like on fire. Maybe a couple nights after. But the night of the full moon—*then* for sure, man."

"Where?"

"Phoenix. Out on the desert roads, used to be. Not anymore, though. Tore hell out of a little shithouse town outside Amarillo; hit the Interstate comin' this way. I figure next time he shows up, it'll be close to here. Real close."

Ransom chilled. "Because of *me*? Is that it?" Sure, he thought, sure. Birds of a feather and all that.

"Maybe. Maybe so, man. It's nothing but a feeling I got,

but it's the kinda feeling that bangs you upside the head. What I'm saying—a little friendly advice, maybe—I think you oughta keep your ass covered.''

"I'll do that," Ransom said. "But you didn't come just to tell me that, did you? I'd like the rest of it. Why did you and your entourage''—Ransom jerked his head toward the two men on cycles who were now in front of the van, their bike engines rumbling at idle—''come all this way to look me up?''

Rooster gave him the snap of a grin that, just for a second, made them equals. "Tell you, it's going to blow your wheels," he said.

Ransom reached for the pack of Camels balanced on the arm of the wheelchair. "Well, this hasn't been much of a treat so far, anyway," he said.

The cold air, the sharp, clean taste of it, burned his lungs as he stepped from the van into the now sunlit day. Ransom wanted nothing more than to run up the walk, taking the front steps three at a time; to be inside, the door bolted behind him. But he couldn't let it show, not under the sullen watch of the two shadow-masked figures that flanked him from the sides of the van, their faces blank and unreadable.

Freedom, following Ransom out of the van, introduced them as Randy and Joseph. They didn't talk, though, and neither did Ransom.

The girl twisted and tugged at the collar of her jacket, her eyes flickering toward and away from Ransom. "What he said . . . about the doctors that let him out of the hospital, that wasn't exactly the way of it, Mr. Ransom. We, like, we sneaked him out one night, because he told us to. He would've tried it by himself, and it would have been worse for him.''

"He's dying, isn't he?"

Her face tightened for a moment as if she might cry, and her eyes shimmered, but there were no tears. "I think . . . sometimes I think that we're helping him to kill himself by doing this," she said. "And sometimes I think he'd be dead right now, anyway, except for being out on the road where he wants to be, and except for . . . having a reason.''

Ransom caught himself doing a little hop-dance against the

cold. He quit it, glancing toward the motionless forms of the two men on the cycles to see if they were watching.

"Rooster, he's Scorpio, you know what I mean?" the girl continued. "When he's friend, he's all friend; but you cross him and he's going to come after you, and nothing else matters."

"The rest of the story—it's all true, the way he told it?"

"Straight true. The first time—out there in Arizona—made Rooster like he is. And then . . ." She shivered and turned away. "Yeah, it's true."

Ransom's mind flashed white. White, then dark; and in the darkness—something moving.

He heard her voice, trailing like a vapor. "Hey? You okay?"

It was like another black-out, another blink of a dream, another slide into twilight sleep. But he was fully awake now. He could feel it happening.

"Hey!"

Awake, but he couldn't stop it.

Rooster's story replayed in his mind, the second meeting with the Moon Rider, the whole grotesque business about the rest stop, and he couldn't control it.

Ransom saw it through the crippled man's eyes. He could feel the rattle of the van beneath him, see the blood-red taillights of the bikes cruising in a wedge of three in front of the van, cutting through the night, and the silver-dollar moon up there, white as the centerline of the Interstate.

The image crystallized and was solid. Ransom was *there*.

He was a dying man named Douglas Arnold Jarrett, whose mother still called him Dougie, maybe because she was blind and had been for most of his thirty-six years, and still clung to the memory of him as a grade-school child, bringing her his papers and reading them to her.

The other kids had tagged him Rooster, not Dougie, making a joke of his red hair. But Tony, his big brother Tony, had made a badge of the name, and that was part of the memory too.

You're a tough li'l rooster, aren't you, kid? You and me. We're a couple of scrappers.

And Tony had built up the cycle shop in Martinez, and had started the Satyrs.

And Rooster had done, and was doing, his damnedest to
be what Tony expected of him.

You and me.

What was left of him, what was left of the Satyrs—they
were barrel-assing toward Amarillo now. They were tearing
the road—"throwing sparks," Tony would have called it—but
there was no joy in the ride, only the miles and the butcheries
left behind.

Left behind in a place called Mitchell, Texas. Just a fly-
speck on the road, a two-pump Texaco with an old sign lit by
a tin-shaded bulb at the top; a grocery store with a splintered
wood porch and a sagging screen door ripped loose at the
top hinge; the sparkle of glass scattered all to hell in front
and clear across the highway.

Mitchell, Texas: Place of a big yellow dog sprawled dead
on the store's porch, the eyes big and bright like a teddy
bear's, the mouth wide open. Seen through the porthole set
into the side of the van, everything looked bent and distorted
and smoky; unreal. Especially the old man, lying twisted at
the base of the Texaco sign, overalls undone, arm extended,
fingers splaying into the dark-stained grit, straining toward a
lump of something just out of reach.

And Randy then, checking it out. Picking the foot up, getting hold of it by the big toe, like he was playing This Little
Piggy. Randy saying, "Here, man—pull yourself together,"
giving the bloodied thing a toss toward the old-timer, who
didn't move, wouldn't ever move again.

Mitchell, Texas—rid of it now. Making time toward Amarillo, over the smooth, gray blur of Interstate 40—

Ransom tried to stop the ride, to come back to his own
time, his own place. It waited for him out there, but he
couldn't stop the vision. He was swept along, even as he tried
to move his body, his feet, *something* to bring himself back.
His head jerked back, and he saw the early-morning moon
now, transparent and almost full, over him.

And then it wasn't the same moon at all. It was full and
silver-bright, and he saw it through the windshield of the van,
and the sound of the motor throbbed under floorboards.

He was Rooster again—desperately wanting the codeine
now but refusing it. It could dull the pain, but it would kill

his mind, too, and he couldn't lose that, not now. Not so
close!

Rooster—with the grip of the .357 hard and cold against
the fingers of his left hand; Rooster—sweating for the strength
to lift and fire it.

Straight ahead, past Freedom's shoulders (damn, but the
woman could drive!), he could see the lead bike—Shovelhead's—veer to the right, taking the turnoff into a rest stop.
Shovelhead's arm locked and pointed. *Here! Here!*

Then, the bikes flattening to the right, taking the sudden
turn.

The van couldn't make it. Freedom hit the brakes, and the
back end looped around in a broadside skid, and the chassis
lurched sideways, jolting the wheelchair painfully against the
side of the van, Rooster the clapper of the bell.

Something *changed* at the base of his skull then. It didn't
hurt much; it just changed. It was a whisper inside him.

Die, it said. *Die now.*

Freedom horsed the wheel around, crying out once, a brittle and angry oath, lost to the scream of the tires. She took
the van straight on, across the spattering dirt of the median,
toward the open, paved sweep of the Interstate rest area.

The headlights of the van bleached the scene ahead, and
Rooster saw it all.

A cream-over-brown Chevy sat there, an Airstream trailer
hooked behind. The windows of the car had been broken out,
even the vent windows, as if someone had gone around the
car with a hammer saying, "And now you." Smash. "And
you." Smash. "And you." And the hammer shattering glass.

There was a high sometimes just in tearing a thing up.
Rooster could dig that. But the light through the open door
of the trailer . . . it wasn't right, wasn't natural. It was an
orange, flickering light that spilled out the door, across the
handlebars and the beetle-black tank of the Harley that sat
propped alongside the trailer.

The van nosed to a stop even as Joseph, already off his
bike, lumbered up to the trailer door with Randy and Shovelhead right behind him. Sharks after the whale.

Rooster screamed in rage then, as if to scream life into his
dead legs, but it was no good. It only made Freedom swivel
toward him, blond hair whipping across her face, dealing him

the look of a sweet little mama whose kid had just run crying into the house. He was the kid. If he'd had a strong arm, he would have used it then, to knock her face off.

The light flared.

Rooster saw—thought he saw—a fireball explode out of the trailer's door, bursting against the ground. But then he saw it rise and a part of it move toward Joseph; and Joseph, for all his size, scrambling backward. The flaming thing twisted and flailed on the ground, and smoke coiled around it, but not enough, not—

Sweet Lord!

—not enough to hide the truth of it. Man or woman, Rooster couldn't tell. But there were hands, pleading hands, in the writhing mass of fire.

Then the trailer door went black, a looming man-shape in the doorway blocking the light.

He knew that shape. He knew it the moment it shifted, coming forward, spider-legs of fire crawling along the sides of it.

Rooster's hand clenched until it quivered around the handle of the Dirty Harry revolver.

Somehow Freedom had gotten in back of him—he could feel the chair shake from the way she had hold of it—and he liked that; it made him feel strong and alive. He was still the John Wayne of the Satyrs; she was still his old lady; and given half the chance he ached for, he could still blow the balls off any son of a whore on the road.

The Moon Rider sprung from the doorway, arms outstretched. There was a glistening movement of black leather edged by the yellow and white of the fire; the trailer rocked behind him.

And Rooster saw: the heavy black boot that swung with a sound like a gunshot, that would have had Randy's guts opened up and spilling out if he hadn't seen it coming. The toe caught Randy in the side as he tried to spin away, slammed him face-first into the side of the trailer.

The burning thing on the ground, not moving now, provided a merry crackle for the dance.

And Rooster saw: the cut-off .12-gauge extended from the locked arm of Shovelhead; saw that arm bent like soft clay within the black-gloved grip of a shadow that merged with it.

There was a white burst like a flashbulb going off between them, a muted *whump*! sound, a sudden black spattering. And Shovelhead stood there for just a moment, looking down at what had become of him, and it was almost funny, Rooster thought; it was a friggin' cartoon, and it couldn't be real, he couldn't have seen it—the flicker of firelight showing right through the middle of one of the best friends he'd ever had.

It was a laugh, all right. It was har-de-har time. But the sound coming out of him was a ragged and escalating bellow, churning up from the pit of his stomach and sending zig-zagged lines of red across his vision.

Through those lines he saw the Moon Rider coming toward him in long, loping strides. Breaking into a run, leaving Joseph behind as if in contempt of him.

Rooster tried to raise the revolver. A thousand uncalled-for demons pulled his arm downward.

The Rider lunged forward, throwing the force of his body's momentum into the black fist aimed at the windshield of the van.

And Rooster thought his mind had stopped like a broken clock then. He thought insanely that he might have died at that moment, and that what he saw as a series of spasmodic images must have been the last faltering connections made by the brain of a dead man.

He saw the fist strike the glass. He saw the crack lines of glass radiating outward from it; curious, questing little things, skittering here and there.

He saw the glass explode so slowly that he might have counted the glistening shards as they spun toward him.

He saw the face of the Moon Rider, rising above the rim of the dashboard, and the eyes—

I'm dead. I'm dead and gone to hell.

The eyes a flat white. Crystalline. Lifeless.

The face an ice carving, almost.

Rooster's mind pulsed. Back to fights he'd been in, when his body had seemed to move with no conscious effort, smooth and fluid and so fast that it almost freaked him out. Or at last summer's bike meet outside of Goleta, that time when the two bros ahead of him had spun out at sixty on the curve and he'd cut right between those dudes, right into the dust and the bikes doing cartwheels on both sides of him;

didn't think for a second, just did it. And the next thing he knew, there was crazy-man Stoney shoving a Bud longneck into his hand, and some ol' lady he'd never seen before—the front of her painted with a skull-face, flames spilling out between the teeth, and tits bouncing in the eye sockets—she was telling him, "*Man*, you move like a *rocket*!"

But not now.

Every inch that his arm moved, he knew it. The muscles responded like bags of wet sand. The weight in his hand— the revolver—was almost beyond endurance. His jaw shook. His pulse thundered.

But the gun came up.

The Rider's head tipped back in silent laughter.

Rooster's hand quaked like a bum with the D.T.'s. The nerves were a half-deadened tangle. He couldn't sort out the fingers, couldn't find the line to work the one that pulled the trigger.

And the Moon Rider reached toward him, going to take the popgun away from the little rug rat.

Like hell! Rooster thought, and never felt the tension of the trigger, only the bone-jarring shock of the recoil.

He didn't see what happened after that. Not really. But he knew what should have happened.

"For Tony," he said, so softly that it might have been only a thought.

"And tell me again . . . what happened," Ransom heard himself say. "After the shot."

He opened his eyes just in time to see Freedom's hand flinch from his shoulder, came out of it with a jolt of realization.

"*Jeez*, man!" she said. "You were *out* of it."

How long had he stood there in the cold morning air, replaying, *feeling*, Rooster's story in his head? "I was . . . I had kind of a dizzy spell," Ransom said, stammering. "I'm okay."

"I thought you'd tripped out."

The images still in his mind had turned murky and shapeless, clearing the way for a dull, throbbing ache. "How long?" he asked.

"I don't know. Maybe not even a minute, but there was—"

She backed away from him, laughing a little, the way people laugh at an injury that just couldn't have happened. "—your eyes went crazy. Like—"

Ransom interrupted. "What happened after the gun went off?"

Joseph's voice rumbled like the start of a cold engine. "Th' Moon Goon played ghost on us, is what. Disappeared. I figured that .357 of Rooster's would take the fugger's head off—and mine with it, 'cause I was right behind him. I took a dive for the ground. And he was just *gone*, man, out of sight, before I could spit."

"You mean, somehow, he got past you," Ransom said.

"Yeah. Somehow. He jumped, he flew, he turned himself into smoke. All I know is, I didn't see shit of him until I heard that bike of his kick fire. Way back by th' trailer. I turned around, and there he was—just starin' me down, and the fugger's eyes—eyes were like—" Joseph's melon-sized fist thudded against the handlebar in front of him; it made the whole bike jolt. "—eyes you wouldn't *believe*."

Ransom believed it. He'd seen the moonfire eyes of the thing on the road in Arkansas.

"And he took off again then," Ransom said.

"Yeah . . . like he was the cat and we were the mice. And the cat, he'd taken his fill of blood and meat and wasn't hungry anymore. He'd save us for . . . some other time."

"You don't think he was hurt? Not even a little?"

"Might've been. Hope to hell he *was* hurtin'. But there wasn't any blood around; not any of his, anyway. I mean, you don't *wing* a dude with a .357 hollow-point. You blow the wing clean away. And that was point-blank, right into his face. But there wasn't any blood, just . . ."

"The glove, Rooster said."

"Yeah. One black glove. Th' fugger's gonna need a new pair of gloves. Makes you wonder where he *shops*, don't it?" Joseph's laugh rumbled bitterly. "Th' glove, and that scrap outa some newspaper."

Ransom froze. "Scrap?" His glance shot from Joseph to Freedom. "Rooster didn't say . . ."

The girl gave him a look, frozen somewhere between innocence and bad news. "It's . . . how we found you," she said.

Freedom held out a wadded lump of black that Ransom knew she had been holding all along, ever since they had gotten out of the van. He had been too keyed up to notice before.

"Rooster said to give this to you," she told him.

Ransom took it, and the glove unfolded in his hand as if it were a living thing. And there, as if gripped in the palm of it, was a crinkled and rough-edged piece of newsprint.

The headline read: WEREWOLF TEACHER ARRESTED ON NIGHT OF FULL MOON.

He'd seen it before. Somebody—one of the moon crazies—had mailed him a clipping of the same newspaper wire story, but which one? *Which?* So damn many letters, and he hadn't kept track of the junk that had come enclosed with some of them. And the piece was nothing but a hole stuffer, a filler; it probably ran at the bottom of some inside page, so the newspaper's name wasn't on it.

Joseph said, "Take care of yourself, man," and the biker next to him nodded before they both wheeled back out into the street. The motors gunned, shattering the cold silence of an early Monday morning on Rockford Street.

Ransom felt numbed. "Where?" he asked. "Where are you going to be?"

The girl was still there, beside him. She shrugged. "Around. You might not see us, but we'll be around." She backed toward the van. "Until Rooster says otherwise."

"Get him some help, will you?"

"We'll try. *I'll* try. I'll do what I can for him, because that's what I'm here for. But he won't rest. No way. Not until . . ." Her voice trailed off to nothing.

She was scared, Ransom thought. Scared to the bone, but she was going to be there, at one with her man, no matter what. She must have been Scorpio, he thought.

"You're some woman," he said.

Not like some, he almost said. Not like some who don't try to understand, who expect all roses and cream out of life, who aren't there when you need a friend, a woman—not a girl but a woman to stand by you, right or wrong.

She gave him a little smile and disappeared into the van. Ransom stood watching as it pulled away, trailing a wisp of white exhaust.

When it was gone, he walked to the front door. Marla, in the doorway, startled him.

He looked into her sleep-reddened eyes, at the bathrobe she had hurriedly thrown around her. "How long have you been here?" he asked.

"Just a couple of minutes. I woke up and you weren't there, and then I remembered classes. And I went to the window and—Keith, who *were* those people?"

"It's a long story. I don't think you'd enjoy hearing it."

"I was scared, Keith. They looked rough, and the way those two had you hemmed in with their motorcycles, I was about ready to call the police."

"Don't *ever* call the police for me," he said quickly, roughly.

"Keith, what—?"

Ransom felt his guts knotting in anger, and the face of the girl named Freedom played across his vision. Going back to help her man, no questions asked. He fought back the anger. *Think it through.*

"It's okay," he muttered.

He forced himself to be rational, sensible. *You've built up a fine case against your wife, with just one little flaw: There's not a shred of truth in it. Marla listened. She listened all night, and it's not her fault that you weren't saying anything. Think it through; let it go. You want to trade her for some motorcycle mama?*

Still, he could not bring himself to touch her, to be gentle and soothing. He stood awkwardly, looking away from her toward the corner, where the van had disappeared moments before.

He said, "We'll talk again," and wished for a cigarette.

Silence passed between them like a fog.

"I've got to get ready for school now, Keith," she said. "Are you all right?"

"I'm all right," he said, and turned to go in, only then realizing he still held the glove.

"What's that?" Marla asked.

Ransom palmed the newspaper clipping with one hand and held the glove up with the other. For the first time he realized the size of it. It dwarfed his own hand. If he were to put it on, he would have looked like a kid playing dress-up with one of Daddy's big gloves.

"A glove? Who dropped it?" Marla asked as Ransom pushed past her into the warmth of the house.

He thought of trying to tell her then, thought of leveling with her right there, shooting straight with her, starting all over again with a new horror.

He turned to her. "Cinderella," he said.

CHAPTER THIRTEEN

Ransom stood silently, numbly, watching out the window as Marla got into the car with Brenda and Staci and left for school. There was snow in the air now—thick, heavy flakes of it that clung to the window glass, melting slowly into droplets that ran down, only to freeze again along the window ledge.

He watched as Brenda's candy-apple-red Firebird jerked into the street. The engine gunned, blue smoke spun from the rear wheels, and they were gone: Mrs. K. E. Ransom and associates embarked upon another day in higher education.

Ransom told himself that he ought to feel glad that she was taking up with some of her college friends again, although he didn't particularly care for those two. Brenda-Staci; they were practically inseparable. And Brenda, especially, had the intelligence to be a top student, but she would rather just—

So what? he thought. *What do you care? You don't teach. Not anymore.*

He stood, watching the snow, wondering what they were talking about, what they were saying about him.

What *she*—Marla—might be saying.

His fist broke the glass. He saw more than felt it go through, his fingers still locked into the stiff black leather of the Moon Rider's glove. Blood dripped from his wrist, spattering onto the ice of the window ledge, but it wasn't a new cut.

Ransom squeezed the inside of the glove against the welling red line—the cut that seemed never to heal, that closed and reopened just like his thoughts of that night on the road.

He could just as well have killed her that night.

Or a moment ago, he thought, in the doorway. Ransom knew—and chilled at the thought of it—that *something else* had just forced his hand through the glass. Not anger—not *just* anger. He could have thrust his hand and torn through flesh and bone just as easily, and it would have felt . . .

Just fine, he thought. Fine and dandy.

Fine and dandy, just like candy.

He lifted the edge of the glove, recalling how, once before, he had seen that cut as a splintered crack in his arm that seemed sculpted of ice. But now it only bled, and the bleeding had slowed to almost nothing, as had his mind. He couldn't surprise himself anymore.

He found himself thinking analytically as he lifted the edge of the glove that he would have to fasten some cardboard over the window, or better still—

The glove, wadded, neatly plugged the hole.

Big damn thing, that glove. It was a cartoon glove, Ransom thought; it was made for Black Pete.

Had to be a joke.

Yes, sir, a man fires a .357 into your face, what you do then is drop a glove. Most natural thing in the world, right? Drop a glove and a piece out of the newspaper.

Ransom fumbled the newspaper clipping out of the pocket of his bathrobe. WEREWOLF TEACHER ARRESTED . . . it read, and below the headline:

Tulsa, OK—Reinholdt College instructor Keith Ransom, after giving a lecture in film class on *Curse of the Werewolf*, seemed to have fallen under the evil spell of the full moon himself Friday night, police said.

Never mind that the lecture had been weeks before the night of the arrest. It made a better story to imply that he had stepped right out of the classroom, begun to slaver in the moonlight moments later, and scarcely had tarried to set aside his roll book before knocking the hell out of "star running back Ben Taylor."

Not that he hadn't been given the chance to tell his side of it in print and on the local television stations, Ransom thought. Until they started calling him, he hadn't realized the number of news reporters in town. But he hadn't felt like talking to them, gabbing it up to some reporter or manicured newscaster. He hadn't felt like talking about it at all for publication.

Except, of course, to Wendy Layton.

Wendy, who wanted to screw him, and finally did.

Ransom crossed to the kitchen. He found some coffee still in the pot, left over from the night before, and drank it cold.

The glove and the clipping. He could choose to believe them as nothing but the fragments of a dying man's insanity, or as something even more insane.

He could choose to believe that the Rider *existed*—murder and madness, inhuman, taunting the Satyrs to follow him, prolonging the hopeless agony that would end in death.

Phoenix!

The whispery rasp of Rooster's voice, telling him, "Phoenix, out on the desert roads . . ."

Ransom was in the living room almost as fast as the thought came. He shoved the rolltop desk away from the wall, grabbed for the bundle of moon-crazy letters that he had hidden behind it. His hands shook as he sorted through the papers and envelopes, until he found it: the one postmarked "Phoenix."

The first line of the letter inside read, in block-printed letters, "You got the moon inside you." The corner of the letter was bent and torn, as if something might have been attached to it—a newspaper clipping, Ransom thought; he could almost remember pulling loose that scrap of a wire story.

At the top of the letter, between the Harley-Davidson shield to one side and the circular BMW emblem to the other, was a line of heavy lettering that read "McNutt's Cycle Repair." The address was underneath, but the telephone number had been marked out with the same black felt-tip pen that must have been used to write the letter.

Ransom read it.

"You got the moon inside you. Its alive. Did you know that? Its alive and inside you and people say it makes you crazy, but it dont. It makes you top of the line."

Ransom couldn't help laughing at the ending sentence:

". . . top of the line." Just like a machine, he was *top of the* . . .

Like a machine, a machine that had gone for the throat of Ben Taylor.

Ransom went to the phone. He dialed Phoenix information, asked for the number of McNutt's Cycle Repair. Disconnected, he was told. The number for Charles McNutt? No such listing.

"Try McNutt the nut, then," he said. There was a pause, and the phone clicked dead.

He poured himself another cup of coffee, laced with an inch of apricot-flavored brandy, the only liquor left in the house. Flipping through the letters, he checked for other Phoenix postmarks. The only one close was from Globe, Arizona, and the letter itself was illegible.

Ransom's head buzzed from the brandy-and-cold-coffee mix; his stomach fought the combination.

He was on to another collection. Got the cat lady, check. Got the motorcycle loony, check. Who's next?

What would Marla think?

But Marla didn't *know*, damn her, didn't understand. Marla hadn't seen the ground moving, glittering with eyes. She didn't know . . .

Didn't know that her loving husband had put his hand through the window glass that morning. Or what he might have done to her if she had been there at the time.

Ransom made it to the sink before he gagged. He turned on a wash of cold water, and when the sink was clean again, he let the water run over his head.

He lay on the sofa then, trying to sleep, but it was no good. The closing of his eyes transported him back to the highway outside of Eureka Springs. He felt again the rattling of the car, smelled the apples in the backseat, heard the song playing through his mind—

"Used up and gone, but the silence lives on, in the heart of the vampire night."

That—and the single, wet, snapping sound of Marla's neck.

Ransom awoke on his feet. He forced his legs to move. His hands felt wet and sticky, and he was afraid to look at them, even though his head had cleared enough to tell him the wetness was nothing but sweat.

He was shuffling in circles like a wino, and that wouldn't
do, so he put a stop to it.

Go someplace.

The desk was close, and he went in a straight line toward
it. The back of the desk chair was cold under his hand, cold
and hard, good and real.

Ransom sat. He could look at the beige-painted wall behind
the desk and watch blurred little swimming things, cellular
things, floating across it. He could—

Do something.

He reached for the letters. The letters needed arranging.
They needed some order.

So.

To the west—Phoenix and Globe. To the south . . . to the
south . . .

He thumbed at the stack. *To the south.* There had to be
one from the South. A collection of crazies; there had to
be one from the South. There had to be—

Beaumont, Texas. No, that was the Southwest. That wasn't
the real South.

Baton Rouge, Louisiana. All *right*. And Chattanooga, Tennessee. *Bless you, suh!* And to the east—

Ransom tensed for the fever to take him. He wanted it,
wanted it all, and he could feel it coming, the nebulous heat,
building all through him. He felt it now, gathering into his
mind, where, if he let it, the fire would compact to the white-
burning ache of another obsession, another *gotta*, against all
other thought, against reason.

And to the east—

Columbus, Ohio. Meadville, Pennsylvania. Providence,
Rhode Island. And to the north—

Hastings, Nebraska. Des Moines, Iowa. Salina, Kansas.
Great Falls, Montana.

The letters were separated into four neat stacks on the
desktop now, only a few left in his hand. He arranged those:
two from Los Angeles; one from Fairbanks, Alaska; one from
Hannibal, Missouri.

Ransom smoothed the last of the letters into place. The
adrenaline had done for him what coffee couldn't; the blanking of thought had been something like sleep.

The burning was still there, but now it made sense.

He reached for a notepad. The sheets were printed with a cartoon of Ziggy at the top; the caption read, "Things I should have done yesterday." Ransom wrote, *"Full Moon."*

He circled the words, wrote them again.

Full Moon.

Marla thought he was crazy, but Marla was wrong. The book would set things straight again.

It would be the terminus of what had come clear to him now as just one more compulsion. All the same, grab all the cards, fit all the pieces, finish the set, fill up the shelf. Write the book.

If he could *find* those people . . .

Sixteen letters. And the one from Ida Milburn (I-da-cat Milburn); that made seventeen, all seventeen telling him that something went wrong with them on nights of the full moon.

And suppose that it did.

Ransom didn't have to ask himself how willing he would be to set foot on the Milburn place again, on the night of the full moon, at lunchtime on a Tuesday, anytime at all. He'd see it in dreams for the rest of his life but never again for a second of waking time, not if he could help it.

But the others . . . oddballs, maybe. Or worse. But they couldn't affect him, not the same as the Milburn place had. The book would supply him a *function*; he would be the reporter, the writer, detached from the scene. Aesthetic distance. It made exquisite sense, just like it had when he had first thought of it, turning to Marla with it.

She had been asleep and unhearing then. What would she have said if she hadn't been; what would she have thought? What did she think now, for that matter? She had seen her husband come in from a tête-à-tête with a motorcycle gang, had seen him surly and uncommunicative—just another fine lunatic morning. And she had lost herself in the motions of getting ready for class, and thus saved herself . . . what?

"But it's okay, Marla. It makes sense now."

That's what he'd tell her. The book made everything all right.

Then he remembered her voice, bursting out in the dead, surreal night just past.

"It wasn't the goddamn cats! It was you!"

So maybe she wouldn't listen, wouldn't understand. But

what did she expect him to do? Sit around the house, just
rattle around the house, mailing off résumés, trying to sneak
into some piss-ant of a college where nobody ever read the
newspaper filler stories, let alone the bellowing black headlines of the *Midnight Enquirer*?

Instead he could make some good of being the ''werewolf
teacher.''

*Sure, Marla. Me and P. T. Barnum, right? We know what
to charge for a look at the freak.*

Full Moon.

Ransom crossed to the window. The snow had turned to
dry, dusty-looking swirls of white, powdering the yard, giving his car the look of a white-on-red Christmas ornament.

He touched the cold glove where he had jammed it into the
broken glass.

Then he thought of Marla and knew the one reason, the
one real compulsion, forcing the book.

He didn't want to be home with her.

(Image of Lon Chaney, Jr., as Lawrence Talbot, the Wolf
Man, begging to be locked away.)

The moon was coming full again. He didn't want to be
home with her.

Ransom backed the car out of the driveway, still looking at
the note pinned to the front door. The wind caught a corner
of the paper, and he stopped the car, intending to go back
and fasten the note in some better place, or to take it inside
the house and put it somewhere she'd see it.

He didn't want to go back inside the house. He didn't even
want to see the note again, because if he did, he would read
it again, and the words would sound flimsy and mindless.

Better to go. Just go.

The last thing he saw of his home was Marla's cat, Strawberry, watching out of the upstairs window, come out of hiding to see him off.

He tried the brakes, testing the slickness of the street. The
Datsun fishtailed. But the weather service had told him that
he ought to run out of the storm about ninety miles to the
east, if he was damn fool enough to be out on the highway,
and that fit the course that he'd marked in the atlas.

Chattanooga, Hannibal, Des Moines, Salina, back to Tulsa

again. He figured about seventeen hundred miles round trip, shorter than one way through Phoenix to Los Angeles. He could finish the loop in a week.

He would come back and *know* then if there was any real case to be made for the idea of *Full Moon*.

Or he would come back with nothing to show for himself but a glove compartment full of MasterCard receipts, and Marla would be totally pissed off at him, and he would have to plead himself the victim of a midlife crisis and hope for the best.

Either way he could deal with it. Either way put him on top for a change.

Top of the line.

He was almost to Fort Smith on Interstate 40 when the car hit a rough patch of ice, spun sideways, broadside down the highway, finally nosing into the median.

Ransom felt like a kid at the wheel of a toy car on a carnival ride. He could spin the wheel, he could ring the bell. Nothing mattered. *Gee, but it's fun to pretend that you're driving.*

But the ride didn't stop there. He was sliding over the median. Ransom jammed his foot against the brake pedal, tensing until he was off the car seat.

From the westbound lane, coming toward him—the gleaming of headlights.

Ransom saw the lights wobble as the driver of the pickup tried to pull to the right, out of the way, the truck's rear end trailing a plume of blown snow.

The car slid ahead, caught the pavement, and snow sprayed the windshield.

There was a rush of wind, the blast of a horn.

And silence.

Ransom sat, one hand still gripping the wheel, one clenched between his legs, watching the pickup truck's taillights blur into a wake of snow.

He was back on the road again, and very nicely, thank you, except that he now was pointed in the other direction, back toward Tulsa, as if the fates were trying to tell him something. He gave the Datsun just enough gas to edge forward, and it lurched from the shaking in his knee.

The car steadied. He felt in control of it.

He felt something else, too, something out of place, something to laugh at—the bulge in his pants. As he maneuvered the car he found himself thinking of red mittens and warm hands; soft lips and questing, smooth tongue; perfume and the woman-smell of her. Jasmine, he thought, although he wasn't really sure what jasmine smelled like.

He could almost have touched her then, as he negotiated a sliding turn toward the exit ramp and crossed the overpass.

She was on her knees, long hair spilling forward, nothing but white all around her, and she was begging him.

From behind, from behind. I want it . . . !

Ransom snapped on the radio, and it covered the sound of her, the quick and high cries and the catching of breath that he heard as he thought of her.

There, Wendy. *There!*

Rain laced the snow, spattering the front plate-glass window of Irlene's Home Style Cookin' of Fort Smith, Arkansas.

Ransom watched the precipitation through the window. The name of the restaurant was lettered on the glass in a half circle around the scarlet image of the Arkansas Razorback, emblem of the University of Arkansas football team. Menu items reflected the owner's apparent preoccupation with the team, but Ransom had passed on a Razorburger. A half glass of milk had been challenge enough for his stomach.

He paid the check, took a toothpick for no good reason, and went to the pay phone at the back of the restaurant.

He dialed, and the call was accepted, collect.

"Ransom?" The voice crackled. A bad connection. "You off in the Himalayas, chum, or what?"

Ransom gave in to a sigh that brought a coolness to his chest. The news of his quitting the college seemed not to have spread yet from Thurman's office—at least not across campus to the Department of Physical Sciences, which only meant that Thurman was not trusting to the grapevine. There would be an announcement in order, skyrockets and marching bands. But not yet . . .

"Fort Smith, David," he said. "A little bit east of Tibet, I think it is."

"Ah, the places you've been, and the things not worth seeing. And . . . ?"

"I need some advice on what's going to be dumped on me, going east from here."

"*Expert* advice."

"The weather service flubbed it."

"Poor souls, they do try."

Ransom could picture David Holstrom in his paper-littered office on the third floor of the Physical Sciences Building, looking out of the corner window toward the frozen fountain in the oval court of Reinholdt's campus.

Holstrom taught freshman geology, which bored him, and a class in meteorology, which he talked about endlessly, given a beer and the smallest encouragement.

Ransom could hear the droning of a weather service monitor playing in the background.

"Freaky weather, chum," Holstrom was saying. "Hard to call, even for me. But I'd say you're about out of the worst of it."

"That's what *they* said."

"Trust me."

Ransom turned at the sound of a foot scraping the floor behind him. There was a bearded guy, broad-brimmed hat pulled over his eyes Charlie Daniels–style, clicking a dime and a nickel.

Ransom nodded to him. "Be just a minute," he said, but Holstrom was off and running.

"First snow of the year was October twelfth, and that's *freaky*, my man. That's bizarre."

"Blame it on the moon," Ransom said.

"Maybe so, maybe so. I have a theory—"

Holstrom *always* had a theory.

"—that the pull of the moon fools around with the level of meteoric dust in the atmosphere. Now, add to that the tendency of higher precipitation just before the moon comes full and you've got yourself a subject that I would be pleased to expound upon, if you want to reverse the charges."

"You mean it. You're serious," Ransom said. He felt his hand tighten on the phone receiver. Behind him, the cowboy was scratching a dime against the wall.

"Not really," Holstrom said. "I've got to run off to class here, and you know how that goes."

"Yeah."

"Just chalk up the moon and the snow to the Devil's eye."

"The *what*?"

The jukebox was thumping out "Elvira," and the cowboy sang along softly, taking the bass part.

"For shame, Ransom, for shame," Holstrom said. "Aren't you supposed to know literature, myths and legends, and stuff like that? Devil's eye. The moon is the Devil's eye, and that explains everything."

The cowboy was singing louder, "Giddy-yap, a-*oom*!-pappa-*oom*!-pappa . . ." punctuating the beat, striking his fist into a cupped hand.

Ransom jerked toward the cowboy. "Give it a *rest*, okay? Hi-ho, Silver, away."

The cowboy tipped back the brim of his hat, showing red-rimmed eyes. "You tryin' to be funny, mister?" he asked.

Ransom pressed toward the phone. "David! If you say that there's some connection, that the pull of the moon is getting stronger, affecting the weather—"

"Well, then, chum." Holstrom laughed, a crackle of phone static. "You'd about have to say that the Devil's winning."

The phone clacked to silence.

Ransom looked. The cowboy's hand held down the receiver hook.

"Time's up, funny man," he said, and Ransom didn't argue.

CHAPTER FOURTEEN

Holstrom had been right about the storm. It broke to the east of Fort Smith, as sharply as if a blade had been drawn across the sky. Ransom followed the edge of that blade and then broke away, under a suddenly blue sky dotted here and there with cumulus clouds. Minutes shuffled and became hours; the level of cigarette butts in the Datsun's ashtray multiplied to a foul-smelling grayish heap. And still Ransom drove down the mostly two-lane road, thinking road thoughts, telling himself that soon now he would have to stop and sleep.

Around nightfall the thoughts began to get ugly.

He thought of the cowboy back in Fort Smith, the dull red eyes challenging him to make a move. And he thought of how he simply had turned and left, walking swiftly until he was out the door and in the car and on the road again, checking a couple of times in his rearview mirror to make sure that the man hadn't followed him.

I could have taken him, he thought now, as the sky dimmed around him. *He didn't know . . . who I was.*

I can take anybody. Top of the line.

He shook the thoughts away. Between cities now, no lights anywhere, just the light of the moon growing brighter above him as he drove.

He remembered talking once to a student of his, a long-distance trucker who was taking night school and who had, surprisingly, written one of the best five-paragraph essays on Eliot's "Love Song of J. Alfred Prufrock" that Ransom had ever seen. In talking with the man, Ransom had brought up the subject of long hauls, and the man had been more than happy to talk about it.

Drive a man crazy, Mr. Ransom, and that's no bullshit. Gets lonely out there. No one to talk to, and you get to seein' things. Loneliness is what does it.

Loneliness. Ransom knew he should pull over. His stomach skittered on the edge of nausea, and the inside of his mouth tasted sickly-sweet and felt gritty. It wouldn't be long before lack of sleep and miles of road would be making him see things, too.

That—and the moon.

It looked full now, even though Ransom knew true fullness was still a few nights away. But it was full enough, heavy and pregnant in the sky—full enough to *hurt* him.

Keep driving. Don't think about it.

Loneliness, like the trucker said. Loneliness was causing the feeling that threaded through him, the raw ends of anger, of rage, winding around, punctuated by the hum of the car.

There was nothing he could do about it. No one would have wanted to go with him; no one was around to count on when he really needed it.

Marla? No way. He tried to make himself feel guilt about leaving her—any emotion to replace the madness boiling in his gut. He pictured her in the house, pacing, crying, wondering—

Your own damn fault, he thought. *If you'd tried to understand—*

But she *had* tried. He had been the one to blow that one, by going with no forewarning, leaving her alone with no explanation except a note pinned to the door. What a B-movie gesture *that* had been. The doomed romantic hero taking it all on his own shoulders, striking out alone and selflessly for everyone else's own good, even though everyone else would never understand. Bogart in *Casablanca*; John Garfield in *They Made Me a Criminal*; Keith Ransom in—

Full Moon.

Really existential, he thought. What a man.

Ransom wiped at his eyes. Funny. It looked as if the storm were starting again. It was getting hard to see, and ice was forming around the edges of the windshield. Not ice but . . . frost.

It was everywhere. Outside the car and inside. Ice crystals
swam around the periphery of his vision, and the anger, the
madness, glowed like a hot coal within him. He was cold,
though, the coldness of rage—at Marla, at the cowboy in the
restaurant, even at David Holstrom, with his damn little smug
university theories.

Ransom knew it then. He wanted to *hurt* somebody. Anybody.

The ice, the frost, clouded his vision. Something told him:
Keep the car on the road. It's your only chance.

His thoughts jumbled. He was the car, the machine, and
he had to stay on the road. The car hummed, and he vibrated
with it, eyes locked on the broken white line down the pavement that ran into forever, miles of forever, around dark
curves and up hidden hills. Time became meaningless, dropping away as he drove. The only important thing: *Stay on the
road.*

Ransom drove, enveloped by ice, bulleting through the
darkness.

Sometime in the night, she said, "It ends where you want
it to end," and he looked—or thought he looked—across the
seat, to see Wendy Layton smiling at him out of the darkness
and the frost, her eyes glowing.

She said other things. She said, "You wanted company and
here I am." She touched his cheek. "Frankly I'm a little sad
that you didn't ask me on this trip. You know *I* understand,
Keith."

The frost all around him. Part of him.

"Did you know you can do it in the car? Have you ever
done it in a car?"

It was as if he were seeing her through a snowstorm, or on
a television with bad reception. He saw her hand at her throat,
unbuttoning her blouse, button by button.

"It's fun to do it in a car, especially while you're moving.
Look at me, Keith."

Stay on the road.

Her blouse was gone, and she moved to him, was on him.
Lust surged within Ransom, and the lust was rage. He
grabbed at her and she was gone, leaving behind laughter
like a vaporous trail in the darkness.

Ransom heard the car before he felt it, tires squealing as it headed for an embankment. He wrenched the wheel with ice-cold hands, shot back onto the road, skidding. The ice crystals were jagged now, solid, suspended raindrops, tiny knife blades, teeth. Ransom rolled down the window felt the rush of cold air on the side of his face. He stuck his whole arm out the window, the palm of his hand up.

There was no storm. Nothing touched his hand but air. The frost, the ice—same as before, same as all the befores.

It's not real!

He drove like that, one arm out the window, until the moon faded above him and the sun glowed redly on the horizon, showing him Chattanooga in the distance. That was when his strength left him, and he pulled into a roadside parking area, pushed the seat back as far as it would go, and let sleep take him like death, sudden and swift, black and dreamless.

Sometime in the lunatic night Ransom had crossed into a different land entirely. The tangle of kudzu vines above and around the car told him that.

The broad leaves were everywhere. They snaked up and over the telephone poles beside the road, spreading out onto the wires. To his right, runners of them attached themselves to the natural rock that held up the rest stop's picnic-table shelters.

Ransom remembered Kafka writing about the terror of opening your eyes after a night's sleep, the fear that something would be changed. But he wasn't Kafka; he was supposed to be where he was.

Or, more specifically, he was supposed to be in Chattanooga, which lay just ahead.

Ransom glanced at his watch through sleep-clouded eyes, did a double take. Four-thirty? The unreal glow of the afternoon sun, low in the sky, confirmed it.

Everything had caught up with him. The two nights without sleep, the road, the emotional strain—his body had simply said ''Enough'' and demanded ten peaceful, dreamless hours.

Ransom slowly adjusted the seat back to its original position, stretching his body as the seat came up to meet it. All things considered, he felt pretty damn good. Opening the door, he got out and walked around the car, smelling the foreign smells of another town, flexing his legs. In the distance he saw the city of Chattanooga.

After a moment he got back in the car and drove toward it.

Ransom stopped twice on the way to his destination. The first time was at a convenience store on the outskirts of the city, where he bought a microwave sandwich, went to the rest room, and found out that the address he was looking for was on Lookout Mountain. At the base of the mountain he stopped again for gas and more specific directions, and the young attendant was more than happy to oblige.

"The McGivern place?" the kid asked. He squinted and had dark, oily hair that hung across his forehead like spider's legs. "That where you're goin'?"

Ransom nodded from inside the car. "That's right."

The kid spit through his teeth and grinned at Ransom. "Sure, mister. Just head on up, straight to the top, and you'll come to this ol' high brick fence. Me 'n' my buddies use ta try an' climb it. I got almos' all th' way up, once—cut my hands somethin' awful." He spit again. "Don't try an' climb th' fence."

"Thanks," said Ransom. "I won't."

"You a reporter, or what?"

That was a curious question, but Ransom let it slide. "Just a what," he said.

"Okay. Way back behind th' fence you'll see what looks like a big ol' department store up there but with some o' them high columns in front an' a bunch of chimneys, an' that's it." He pulled the hose nozzle out of Ransom's tank, recapped it. "That'll be eight-fifty."

Ransom gave him a card, signed the slip that the boy brought back, and started his engine. "Thanks again," he said.

The kid slapped Ransom's hood as he pulled out. "Just tell 'em Ernie sent ya," he shouted, laughing. That was the last thing Ransom heard as he pulled away.

Now the Datsun coughed and rattled its way toward the top of the mountain, straining up a slope intended for better-tuned automobiles. Ransom tried for second gear, and the car threatened to die and roll backward. Behind him, the driver of a sleek white Lincoln contributed a discreet, single honk of the horn, the apparent extension of an irritated sigh. Ran-

som rolled to the curb line, braked, and gunned the motor.
The Lincoln cruised past him with a superior air.

He glanced to his right. Through the trees, still swathed in
fall colors, he could see the city below him, rimmed with
highways and forested countryside, as if it were a toy train
layout. Farther, the misted gray of the horizon. Marla would
have loved it, Ransom thought, but Marla wasn't there. In
her place on the car seat were some tourist brochures he'd
picked up for her at the convenience store, a few more sug-
gestions for places to see sometime. They told about the Rock
City Gardens and Mother Goose Village up on the mountain,
and about the Revolutionary and Civil War battles fought
around Chattanooga. Places she'd like to see—if she ever
wanted to see anything with him again.

He didn't want to think about that, not now. There were
more important things.

Glancing into the rearview mirror, he saw more than just
the now clear road. He saw the redness in his eyes that ten
hours of sleep hadn't been able to expunge, and the black
stubble of a two-day beard. He saw his face juxtaposed against
the crisply trimmed shrubbery and sharp, white-painted window shutters of a two-story redbrick home in the background
of the reflection. Brushing ineffectively at the matted disarray
of his hair, he thought, *Great, Ransom. Just great. One look
at you and they'll pull in the front walk.*

He thought for a moment about going back down the
mountain, checking into a motel, getting a long, hot shower,
and making another try, all clean and presentable. He considered all that at the same time he was coaxing the car into
first gear and starting up the slope again.

So close now, so close . . .

The higher he went, the bigger and wider the houses got,
as if they had all taken a deep breath and stretched out after
the climb. There were wide lawns separated by neatly edged
spacious driveways, and the side streets all had fairy-tale
names, such as Peter Pan and Cinderella.

The fence that the gas station attendant had told him about
now came into view, unmistakable, and a chimney-studded
roof in the distance behind it. Ransom gave a low whistle.
He had expected something big, but the McGivern estate was
massive, looming, the mansion rising like a frowning head

on the shoulders of the mountain. Again he checked himself in the mirror, feeling suddenly dwarfed and inadequate. It wasn't too late to turn around, he told himself. A good shower, a change of clothes . . .

But, almost as if he were being tugged, he followed the fence to a turn-in, which was blocked by an ornately scrolled iron gate. The gate was flanked by a pair of brick pillars topped with a matched set of gleaming bronze eagles, and a speaker was set into one of the pillars. Ransom pushed the button under the speaker, catching himself and wishing that it was a call button at a McDonald's drive-through.

Nothing happened. He waited a moment and pushed the button again. This time, finally, the speaker responded with a crackling snap, followed by a woman's voice. "Yes?" it asked doubtfully.

"I'd like to see Mr. McGivern."

"Is he . . . expecting you?"

"My name is Keith Ransom. He sent me a letter. It's very important for me to talk with him." Ransom pulled the folded letter from his shirt pocket, as if to show it to the speaker. *I'm in worse shape than I thought*, he told himself, and then he saw the TV camera lens trained on him from higher on the pillar.

"Unfortunately Mr. McGivern is not here. And not expected," said the voice.

Ransom snapped the letter open, reading from beneath the blue-engraved C. M. McGivern letterhead. "He makes a point in this letter of saying that he never leaves the house."

"He also never sees anyone, Mr. Ransom. I'm sorry. Good day."

Ransom slammed his fist against the button. "Look," he said. "*Look*. I've come a hell of a long way just to get here, and maybe I should've arranged an appointment, all right? And I'm sorry for just showing up like this, but I want to see him!" His voice had become a shout. "I'm not leaving until I see him, or until *he* tells me to leave!"

"Don't force me to call the police, Mr. Ransom."

"Don't force me to come over the gate."

The speaker went silent. Ransom felt a chill building in his body. *Police again*. They would haul him to the station and run a routine check, and then they would discover they had collared *the* Keith Ransom, nationally celebrated wacko. He might make the *Midnight Enquirer* again, this time the cover, right there with whatever celebrity was having an affair or a tumor removed.

He forced his voice down. "Please, ma'am. Just tell him I'm here. Keith Ransom. Please do that for me."

After what seemed an eternity, the speaker crackled. "Wait where you are," said the voice.

Ransom lit a cigarette and sank back into the car seat, the letter mashed in his hand. He loosened his grip on it, smoothing the paper, scanning the words again.

"Dear Mr. Ransom," it read. "Be aware. You are not the only one. Something in the moon can twist a man. I have the proof."

There was something odd about the letter itself, something Ransom hadn't quite been able to put his finger on, no matter how many times he reread it. Now, rubbing the paper between his thumb and forefinger, he knew what it was. The paper was heavy and crisp with the expensive feel of a cockle finish, but the typing was awful, some of the words exed out and some run together.

"You know, of course, that the very word *lunatic* translates to 'made crazy by the moon.' "

Ransom looked at the bottom of the letter. There were no secretary's initials, which meant McGivern must have typed it himself. The man obviously could afford an entire office staff, but he had struggled over a typewriter instead. Why?

And then the thought came to Ransom: *Because he didn't want anyone else to know.*

The clanking of the gate startled him. The noise changed to a humming, and then the gate swung open, untouched. Ransom looked to the speaker for directions, but it was silent, so he drove ahead, hesitantly at first, as if something else might clank and hum and yank him back. The smooth, paved entranceway took him on a curving sweep through a section of shrubs trimmed to arrowhead points and delivered him to the front of the mansion. In front of its double doors a woman with starkly pulled-back gray hair in a stiff white uniform waited for him.

Ransom snuffed his cigarette and got out of the car. He walked to the door, the woman regarding him with eyes that were both somehow dull and piercing at the same time, eyes that weren't going to give anything away. "Mr. McGivern will see you," she said flatly, and he recognized the voice.

"I'm sorry," Ransom said, gesturing at his face, at the wrinkled condition of his clothes. "About my appearance, I mean. I didn't have any time to—"

"It doesn't matter." She turned, and Ransom heard her mutter, "Nothing matters here." She stopped before the closed door, taking a cloth from beneath her belt, and began rubbing at the center of the diamond-shaped glass set into the center of the door. In the same low tones she continued, "I can't do it all. I can't keep up with it. I tried to tell him not to let the rest of them go, but he just wouldn't listen."

Talking to herself, Ransom thought. The whispery tone she used—almost a second voice—intensified the edginess he already felt.

She finished wiping the glass, tucked the cloth back into her belt, and pushed the door open, standing aside to let him enter. Her eyes were fathomless, almost marblelike.

Ransom followed her as she led him through the marble-tiled foyer and across a high-ceilinged room lined with white colonnades. The furniture, mostly Louis XV as nearly as Ransom could tell, was placed as if to emphasize the opulent distance from one piece to the next. It was a room made for the furnishings, not for people, he thought, but then he changed his mind, because standing flush with the wall was a carved walnut cabinet and mechanism almost seven feet high with a small crank to the side. Ransom stopped as if tethered. It was the first one that he had ever seen outside of a museum, although as a onetime collector of music boxes he could not have failed to recognize it: a Symphonion upright disk music box, German-made, probably late nineteenth century, easily worth four to five thousand dollars. Ransom suddenly longed to hear it play. It was exactly the way he would spend that kind of money if he had it, and it instantly gave him a liking for the mystery man, McGivern.

He walked to it, touched it. "Does this work?" he asked.

But the woman was silent, waiting for him at the far end of the room. "You may sit here, Mr. Ransom," she said, indicating a stiff, high-backed chair to the side of a closed door. "Go in when the door opens."

Ransom said ''Thank you'' to her retreating back and watched her depart past the landing of a curved staircase, noting that a rope, trailing the barest wisp of a cobweb, had been strung between the banisters. The stairway seemed to go silently up into darkness, apparently unused for a long time, although it must have been a central passage to the rest of the house.

He sat, watched the door, paced awhile, then sat again, thinking about lighting another cigarette but spotting no ashtray. The room dimmed to a hazy yellow as the last of daylight strained through the partially curtained high windows. Ransom forced himself not to look at his watch. He was aware, however, of silent minutes passing, of the feeling of being the only living thing in the house.

The light from outside weakened to grays and pooling shadows. Inside, no lights were on, and Ransom glanced toward the cut-glass chandelier that hung like a darkened carnival ride from the center of the ceiling. He stared at it as if he could will it to come on, to throw a little illumination into the room.

Then it hit him. *A snipe hunt.* He sparked with anger, almost grateful for the emotion. It was obvious. *Stick him in the dark long enough and he'll go away.*

He rose from the chair, slapping his hands against his legs, defying the silence of the room. He faced the door. Slowly he reached for the faceted glass knob, tried turning it. Locked. As he raised his hand to knock, a voice behind him said, ''No!''

He whirled around, making out the figure of the woman.

''I had hoped he would see you before nightfall,'' she said. ''As it is . . . please, go, Mr. Ransom.''

Her face was indistinct in the darkness, but Ransom thought he saw the glimmer of tears in her eyes. ''I don't want to go without some answers, Mrs.—'' He stopped. ''Who are you, anyway?''

''Mrs. Bennett. I was . . . I *am* the head housekeeper. I have been in charge of the McGivern household for well over twenty years, Mr. Ransom. I . . . live here.''

She reached past him, pressing the chair back to a firm position against the wall. ''That's the trouble with me,'' she said, her voice dropping again to that odd, flat whisper. "I live here."

"We could use a little light in here, Mrs. Bennett," Ransom said, and then startled himself by putting the unease he felt into a word. "Please."

"Mr. McGivern does not prefer the light."

"When will he be willing to talk with me?"

"I'm afraid I don't know, Mr. Ransom," she said. "I have tried to tell you. Mr. McGivern has not met with anyone, myself included, not since—"

The door in front of Ransom clicked and swung open. At the same time a man's voice crackled through a speaker somewhere near the ceiling. "To answer your question," it said, "the easy one at any rate: Yes, it does work. It plays ten different disks and two bells. Come in, Mr. Ransom."

Ransom peered into the open doorway. Beyond it, the darkness was solid and unmoving.

"Come straight ahead," the voice ordered, this time from the bowels of the room.

Ransom took a step in. *You're not thinking right*, he warned himself. *You shouldn't be doing this.*

And then: *The book. Remember the book.*

He stopped, blocking the doorway, holding his ground. The light from behind him was scarcely enough to coax his shadow into the darkness beyond.

"Did you know, Mr. Ransom, that the light of the full moon is ten times as bright as the light of the first quarter?" the voice asked. "Just say that I've had all the light that I . . . want!" The voice was broken by a small gasp of pain.

"Mr. McGivern?"

"Straight ahead."

Ransom took another step into the darkness of the room, his mind racing, all the horrible scenarios he had ever imagined flying through his head. He held one arm out in front of him, touching nothing.

The door swung shut behind him.

His first impulse was to spin around and slam against the door, to *get the hell out*, whatever it took; but even as he started to turn, a greater fear hit him.

Don't turn your back.

He straightened in the darkness, and the air seemed to close in around him, heavy and stale. The breathing he heard was his own.

The voice was a bolt. "I never should have written you, Mr. Ransom." A pause. "Perhaps I wanted . . . *needed* . . . help. However, I don't think there is any."

"I need help too," Ransom said, his voice a detached echo. "What you said in the letter, about having proof . . ."

From somewhere in front of him there came the creaking sound of a weight being shifted in a chair, or so he guessed. He thought of a large chair, upholstered in leather, and added a big wooden desk to the image, calculating from the faintness of the sound and the hollow tone of the voice that the room was large and that McGivern was a good distance from him. He tried to envision McGivern, but nothing would come except half-formed, malevolent images.

"I've got proof," said the voice. "Of lunacy, moon madness. Yes." Again Ransom heard that low, hissing gasp. "I set up a grant, got the university going on it. A couple of universities, in fact."

"And the proof?"

"Just about what any good bartender could have told you. People go nuts when the moon is full."

The chair, or whatever it was, creaked again. Ransom thought of McGivern leaning forward, then had a far colder thought: *He's getting up. Coming toward me.*

Ransom strained his eyes against the darkness, seeing nothing. He scuffed his foot against the floor, discovering that it was thickly carpeted. A man could walk across it, making no sound, and Ransom thought about moving to the side a few steps, just to change his position; then his mind locked on the easy way that McGivern had been able to hear him—to see him as well, he felt suddenly sure—admiring the music box. The place was wired for sight and sound, the door behind him had closed electronically, and McGivern clearly had the money for whatever gadgetry he wanted. Did he also have something to see with in the dark?

"Homicide," the voice said. It struck Ransom with a chill and relief at the same time, coming from across a distance that still seemed vast. "Homicide rates go up double when the moon is full. Arson doubles. Assault and suicide, traffic fatalities . . . anything bad, the full moon makes it worse."

Ransom still could make out nothing in the room, no trace of light, no trace of movement. *Keep the man talking*, he told himself.

"Bleeding ulcers bleed more," the voice continued. "People die more from those things than can kill you in bed, asleep. Crib deaths . . ."

Suddenly Ransom realized that to stay in this room, with this disembodied voice rambling on about death and murder, was against all reason. He tried to will himself back toward the door—maybe it wasn't locked—but he could not move. In that moment he told himself that it was equally against all reason to come here, to *this*, from halfway across the country. The word *compulsion* imprinted on his mind, and in it was the sound of Marla's voice.

But if McGivern had anything but talk in mind, Ransom thought, wouldn't he have tried something before now? Was he waiting for something? For the *right time*?

"They take all that data, Ransom, and they run it through their computers, and analyze and cross-check it, and it comes out in pages of figures. You know what those figures say? They say that people go nuts. *Say something, Ransom!*"

There was fear in the command, and Ransom thought, *Maybe he's as scared as I am.* Quickly he said, "I still don't know your interest in all this, Mr. McGivern."

"*Interest?* That's very diplomatic—" The voice broke off into a dry wheeze of a laugh, trailing into what sounded like a moan. "My . . . *interest* is the same as *your* interest. You wouldn't be here if the moon didn't *do* something to you."

Ransom's mouth was dry. "That's right." The fear was leaving him now, being replaced by an emotion he couldn't define, one just as strong.

"It does something to me too. It puts a voice inside my head that's not mine."

The words fell into silence. Ransom felt a tiny ringing in his ears, and pinpricks of white light danced in front of him. They were still there when he closed his eyes.

"A voice . . . all the time," the man said. "Right now. And it *hurts*, Ransom. It's words and it's hot knives. The sound of it cuts. I can feel things . . . coming loose inside."

Ransom's words were a rasp. "What does it say to you?" he asked.

The response was slow. "Ransom, let me tell you something about myself. I wasn't born into this kind of place. My old man worked his whole life to hold on to a dirt farm that would've fit into a corner of this room. 'I don't know the answers,' he used to say, 'just don't know the answers,' and sometimes he'd laugh, and sometimes he'd cry. But that's what he taught me, Ransom. Get the answers." The voice tightened. "The way to do it, I found out for myself. I studied, read books. Put what money I could scrape together into the right places. Made money. Made enough money to go to the people smart enough to do the research. Made enough, *they* came to *me*. And I got the answers."

"About the voice, you mean?"

"I mean stocks, Ransom. Pipelines. Coal mines. And the moon—that too. There has to be *something* that makes it all make sense, some real *answer*. That's the best I can tell you. Has to be, but . . . I've run out of time." The voice unexpectedly frayed to an angry sob.

Pinpoints of light still swam in front of Ransom. He fought back the urge to venture deeper into the darkness, find the man, *touch* him—

Then, with shock and revulsion, he realized his emotion, the one he had been unable to define.

It was a kind of joy.

He was . . . *happy*. Happy that the man suffered, happy that he was there to witness it, happy to find someone who was giving in to it. McGivern, for all his money and power, was weak. Not like Ransom. He was strong, top of the line. *Top of the line*.

Ransom bent the joint of his left thumb down until it hurt. He wanted the pain. He had to feel human again. The white dots jumped before his eyes, and he bit his lip.

After a moment he felt in control again and forced himself to speak. "All this research," he said. "No answers? No connections?"

"Too many connections," returned the voice, "and nothing but guesses. It's the bright light of the full-moon cycle that causes lunacy; it's the pull of the moon's gravity, electromagnetic tides and metabolism imbalances; it's some kind of high-frequency noise coming out of the moon; or it's all because somebody looked at the full moon over his left shoulder one night. Any of that clear things up for you?"

In the floating darkness Ransom's mind flashed to the thing as he had first seen it, etched in moving frost on the car's windshield; and later, in the restaurant, pointing out Ben Taylor, and the vision, the blood rush, the webbing of *her* blood between his fingers. The fear was back inside him.

"No," he said.

"I've read them all—*memorized* them, Ransom, and you're right. None of them makes a damn bit of difference."

Ransom braced himself for the question that had to be asked, blinking at the dots before his eyes. "What did the moon do to *you*, Mr. McGivern?" he asked slowly.

In the quiet that followed, Ransom could hear the sound of his own temples throbbing, could almost feel the emotions warring inside him.

"It started . . . just a whisper," McGivern said. His voice was quieter, turned inward. "So soft. I just took it to be my own thoughts, it was so soft. I started thinking about little things, but they were things I never thought about before. About dying. The voice told me . . . whispered to me . . . said that the brain lives on, longer than anyone knows, and that I . . . that I would feel the worms in me."

Ransom felt a surge of emotion, and he made ready to bend back his thumb again.

"Dying. I got obsessed with dying." Ransom heard a soft, repetitive scraping noise even as Marla's word, *obsession*, rose up again in his mind. There came the soft clatter of some small metal thing being dropped, followed by a wet intake of breath.

The voice continued. "At first I tried to tell myself I was just depressed. I'd just sold out most of my business interests . . . that was Kate's idea, to sell out and travel." The voice stopped as if considering something new. "It wasn't so much that she wanted to go anywhere; she just wanted to come back and talk about it. But I loved her. You can't look for answers to everything, Ransom. Oh, Lord, but I loved her."

Ransom felt a new emotion: panic, rising like a sickness. He yearned to see light, to feel and taste light, to run in the light. He felt he could splinter the door behind him with a scream.

And run to what? To the moon?

"Mr. McGivern . . . what does the voice tell you now?"

"Choices." The word came like a curse. "Ways. Things I can do to keep from dying. Oh, it's very imaginative. It's almost a laugh, some of the things I've done to try to get it to leave me alone. Sometimes I thought it would leave me alone if I was wearing the right clothes, or not wearing the wrong clothes. Or . . . other things. I can tell you this, Ransom—it wanted you here. It wanted you here all along."

Ransom felt a chill that seemed to rush from the darkness of his heart.

"It's using you, Ransom—against me. It knows that I'm . . . desperate . . . for answers. Answers I think you might have, or might get for me. So it's letting me talk to you. But it gave me a choice. Don't talk to you . . . or talk . . . and pay the price. That was the choice. Isn't that right? *Isn't it? Say it, you bastard!*"

There was a crackling, splintering sound from that end of the room, and then a sudden, fierce scream exploded in waves, the noise of it slamming Ransom back against the door. It built and crested and echoed into silence.

"Sometimes . . ." The voice was louder now, a deranged quality to it, shrill and then restrained, as if the man uttering the sounds were fighting something deep inside him. "Sometimes it has . . . ideas. About other people. And I just have to fight it. Hell! I fight it, Ransom, and now I've got just about everyone cleared out around here except the housekeeper, and she flat won't go because her mind's broken. Her mind's broken, Ransom, and that's why she stays. But you, Ransom. It knows about the book you want to write and— *you'd better get out of here!*"

The doorknob was slick with sweat under Ransom's hand. He gripped it even more tightly. One more question. "The moon," he said quickly. "I've got to know. How *exactly* does the moon affect you?"

The voice seemed—no, *was* closer. "The first time it . . . screamed at me . . . was the night of the full moon. That voice. Not man, not woman. Not human. *Ransom! It's screaming now!*"

Ransom whirled around, jerking at the knob. It slipped in his hand. Behind him came the swishing sound of feet moving against carpet. He turned the knob again, pulled, and the door cracked open, a shaft of dim gray light bolting into the room. He looked over his shoulder, saw the pale shape moving toward him; saw, frozen as if in a camera flash, the slack, tortured face, blood dried and clotted in a smear around the right eye, the bare chest glittering with pinheads.

The shape was on him. A hand swung down hard against the side of his face, and Ransom was suddenly weightless again, aware of the door slamming beside him, the room plunging into darkness again in the split second before his head and back struck something hard and angular with a sound like a gunshot. He slid to the carpet, scrabbling to hold on to consciousness. Beside him, above him, an animal scream rent the darkness. He opened his eyes in time to see the door crack open again, saw that the scrabbling noise he heard was hands on the door, and then the ache in his head closed his eyes, drove him down in the frigid darkness.

He lay there a moment, his face in the carpet. Silence jelled around him. Haltingly he struggled to his knees and then to his feet. For a moment he stood, wavering, trying to get his bearings, and then he took a tentative step forward, a swimmer in dark, silent water. He suddenly envisioned McGivern, crazed in the grip of the voice in his head, waiting out there in the darkness, perhaps one step away. He tried to force the thought out of his head, but it clung. Was that breathing he heard in the room?

The feeling of power had deserted him as quickly as it had come. He was no longer anything but afraid. The doorway was somewhere close—if only he could find it.

He took another step, and his leg struck something solid in the room. Running his hands out in front of him, he grazed the desktop and felt around it. There . . . a telephone, a penholder, a lamp. *Lamp!* He fumbled for the switch, found it, and snapped on the light. A dull yellow beam flashed in front of him, spreading over the desktop with sudden, almost blinding, ferocity.

There, in the center of the desktop, was a thick, legal-sized brown envelope with his name scrawled on it.

Ransom gazed around the room, straining as his eyes adjusted to the dim light. Outlined against one wall, so faint that he could hardly make out the shape, was the chair

McGivern had been sitting in, and a sofa along another wall, as far as he could tell. Everything was cloaked in shadow. Nothing moved.

Ransom's head ached. He reached back, gingerly touched the still swelling knot, then turned his attention to the envelope, keeping one eye on the door. His body fairly screamed at him: *Get out!*

Instead he emptied the envelope.

On top was a bound, half-inch-thick sheaf of photocopied paper labeled "McGivern Project" on the front. Ransom let it fall open to a chart headed "Homicide Frequency Relative to Lunar Cycle." Lines of different colors zigzagged across the chart, all merging to a high peak at the lane arrowed "Full Moon." A code box at the bottom of the chart identified the lines by color: New York City, Dallas, Memphis, San Francisco, Boston . . .

Ransom glanced back toward the door. There was no movement, no sound anywhere. His hands shaking, he flipped through the pages, scanning them. A passage jumped out at him, and his eyes locked onto it. ". . . increased maniacal behavior, which in turn accelerates the metabolic process, including beard growth. Thus the full moon brings on fits of wild behavior, altering both the *personality* and *physical appearance* of the patient."

Ransom turned the page. Next came a section of letters from directors of mental hospitals, statements from ambulance drivers and police dispatch officers ("You know you're in for a night of it. Oh, yeah, watch out for the full-moon loonies").

Under the bound study Ransom found a loose array of other papers. They were copies of newspaper articles mostly, the first a wire-story account of his own arrest. Seeing *that* brought a sick thrill of recognition back to Ransom, and he turned it over quickly, revealing another clipping that told of a researcher's theory about Jack the Ripper driven to madness by the full moon; and another, a letter to Dear Abby, asking if "moon madness" could be for real.

The clipping on the bottom of the stack was the obituary of Mrs. Chester (Kathryn) McGivern, with the accompanying story explaining that she had died in a fall down a stairway at home.

The rope across the banisters, Ransom thought.

Attached to the obituary, an almanac page with the date of the full moon circled. It was the date of her death.

Ransom leaned against the desk, bone-weary and sick and hurting, wanting to run, wanting to collapse on the spot. It was all there—all the research, the statistics, the examples. It was something he could build his book around, the book that had seemed so important, the book that he had driven down miles of road for, pushing himself through all the fear and insanity.

This was it. And it told him only one thing.

So much worse than I ever imagined.

Ransom slid the papers back inside the envelope, his hands still shaking. He would take the envelope and get the hell out, just as quickly as he—what was *that*?

The far edge of the envelope, out of the light, seemed to glisten. He shifted the lamp toward the back of the desk. The light from it glinted weakly off the blade of a golden letter opener, the tip of it submerged in a thick splotch of . . .

Blood.

Around it, smaller drops and spatters. And beside it—

Ransom reeled. Gagged.

Beside the blade lay a man's severed thumb. He thought he saw it twitch.

And then he saw it through ice, the ice in his heart, the ice that clouded his vision like frost edging a windowpane.

At the door he thought he heard blood dripping somewhere, rhythmically, the heavy drops falling, and the music box played as he tore past it, heading blindly for the outside.

The iron gate hummed shut behind him. Ransom dumped the papers onto the empty seat, squeezing his eyes together to regain his vision, and threw the stained envelope out the car window, where the moonlight caught it.

CHAPTER FIFTEEN

"Did you sleep any?" Staci asked.

Marla, sitting on the edge of the bed, shook her head. "I don't think so," she said, "but I . . . I don't know what I would have done"—her throat tightened—"if you hadn't . . ."

The tears came again, and once again she couldn't stop them. Staci's arms were around her, and Marla cried until the sobs gave way to coughing that hurt, and then quiet.

There were voices in the hallway, the beat of a stereo playing in the next room, footsteps above. The radiator hissed.

Dormitory sounds. Gerber Hall in the morning, and, Lord, but she had missed it—missed being one of the "Gerber babies," missed the trading of clothes, the date talk, the room parties.

"I know what *you* need," Brenda said from across the room. She had slept on an air mattress on the floor, giving Marla her bed. Now she held a skirt on a hanger but dropped it onto the top of a cinder-block-and-wood bookshelf and pulled a chair under the ceiling light. Standing on tiptoe on the chair, she reached over the circular rim of the light fixture. She wore yellow panties imprinted with a daisy pattern, the seam ripped at one side, cloth drooping.

Marla, give me a break. Please! Don't say any more.

She could hear him, just as if he were there in the room holding her, only the two of them.

And she could hear, as if from an impossibly long-ago memory, the sound of her own voice, peppered with laughter.

But it's true—

Stop! Let me have my fantasies.

—that girls in the dorm don't lounge around in silky underwear. They don't run around topless. You've been to too many drive-in movies, Keith. Do you know what they really wear?

I don't think I want—

Baggy bathrobes. Knee socks. Things that sag and drape and droop.

And you thought I was funny, Keith. You thought I was everything. You said that you wanted me and wouldn't leave me, not for a second.

Keith? Keith, maybe you couldn't help it, maybe you couldn't help lying to me. But why did it have to be now? I need you . . . so much. Keith, help me! Be with me. Lie if you have to, but stay with me now.

The chair clattered sideways, bringing Marla back, as Brenda hopped to the floor, a plastic bag of grass waving from the hand above her head.

"Maybe Marla doesn't want any," Staci said. "You think a little pot'll cure everything, but—"

"Puts a shine on *my* morning," Brenda said, interrupting, sitting on a bed corner and rolling a cigarette with practiced motions. "And, you know, you *need* something, Marla. Something to mellow you out a little."

"I need . . . someone."

"Yeah, well. He's cute. I mean, *really* cute, Marla. He's right up there in the double digits when it comes to looks." She lit the joint and inhaled, holding the smoke. "But I think you've got to ask yourself what kind of asshole—if you'll excuse my saying so—would go off and leave you . . . and, I mean, last night, of all the god-awful nights in the world."

"You're a lot of help, Brenda," Staci said.

Brenda continued. "What with the police being there and . . . and all." She offered the joint, and Marla shook her head.

"But I lit it for you," Brenda said.

Marla felt the burning in her throat again, the stinging of tears. She clung to the image of Keith in her mind, not daring to lose his face. It was all that kept her from seeing, again and again and forever, the blood on the front steps.

The blood—spattered across the porch, on the door, where she had found the note pinned that evening, after a day of classes and a trip out for a beer with Brenda and Staci.

Do you know what they did with the pin, Keith? They sealed it up in an envelope. They called it evidence. Isn't that something? They asked me for the note, and they took that too. More evidence. And they cleaned up the blood, but I don't think they got it all. I think you could still find some spots of it, so we're going to have to paint, you know, paint over . . .

Blue would be nice, I think. Don't you?

Don't you, Keith?

Ransom awoke lost. He awoke to the scratchy sound of a voice demanding, "Lu-*cee*, what haf you done *now*?" and pieced the room together from that: the TV set on the low desk across from him (Lucy and Desi there, Fred and Ethel, ageless); framed imitation painting of a flock of ducks flying over the bed, screwed to the wall at all four corners; a nearly empty fifth of Jack Daniel's on the bedstand.

He sat up slowly, trying to remember. His head throbbed and his mouth felt chalky as he reached for a cigarette to make it worse. The pack was almost gone; a crumpled one lay beside it, next to an overflowing ashtray.

He could almost remember having checked into the place, could almost remember . . . Pa-hoo, Pa-doo, Paducah—that was it. Paducah, Kentucky.

Checked in, went to sleep with the television going. He glanced at the bottle and the ashtray again as smoke filled his lungs. Wild times in Paducah.

But before . . . ?

His mind was a fathomless blank. He remembered leaving Chattanooga, driving hell-bent, and then—

Darkness, as if someone had turned off every light in the world.

He was almost used to the nightmares now. They frightened him with their power, but they didn't frighten him as much as not knowing, as not being able to give himself an account of his whereabouts.

Ransom got to his feet. His legs steadied. He didn't know how long he had slept, but there was daylight now. Switching off the television, he walked to the bathroom and took a shower, letting the hot water spray into his mouth, washing out the sodden residue of liquor and tobacco.

When he was finished, he unfolded a clean shirt out of his suitcase, trying not to look at the papers scattered on the floor, spilled from the binder that he must have thrown, must have pitched against the wall. Some of the papers were smeared with a rust color. He finished dressing and picked them up. They seemed to smell of decay.

Got to get it together, Ransom. Get professional about all of this.

What had *happened* the night before?

The voice shouted from a corner of his mind: *Ransom! It's screaming now!*

He needed to write that down, before he forgot, not that forgetting was likely. He needed proof, and he only had himself.

Himself and the scattered papers.

Ransom looked at his watch. Nine A.M. Early enough for a department store to be open somewhere, one that would take his credit card in return for a cassette recorder and some notepads, things he should have had all along.

As he thought, he began to realize that there was an oddness to the room, and it took him a moment more to isolate the reason. The lights. Every light in the place was switched on, from the bedside lamp to the fluorescent tube over the bathroom sink.

He drew the drapes fully open. The window overlooked an emptied swimming pool and a Coke machine across the way, but there was sunlight, almost enough . . .

His head reeled from the sharp blue of the sky.

. . . almost enough to make him believe that Chester McGivern had been nothing but a bad—a very bad—joke.

Almost.

If he had had a recorder then, he could have played it back now. But the only evidence of his visit were the papers and his memory.

He picked up the papers, telling himself that he ought to stop and read them, and that he would—soon. But not right away. Later, when the touch of them didn't make the skin crawl up his arms, his neck; when the sight of them didn't make him want to scream.

Ransom stopped at a shopping mall a half hour later and bought a tiny, pocket-sized recorder that played even tinier tapes, and stocked up on yellow pads and pens. He set everything in the backseat, on top of the sheaf of papers, and began almost immediately to feel better. Organized. A man with a purpose once again.

The Datsun snapped a water hose on the Interstate west of St. Louis, but he lucked out and found a replacement at a gas station not a mile's walk away. The walk did him good. He felt the healthy stirrings of an appetite even as the car kicked to life again—the reward, he thought, for having actually *fixed* something. The black smears of engine grime, the slightly bloodied scrape across the knuckles of his right hand, only made it all the better, because now he could *wash up* before lunch. He could look at his hands as if to apologize to the waitress, and when he got back from the washroom, there would be a cup of coffee waiting for him on the countertop. He could deal with that, with being normal, or at least looking normal.

Ransom turned north onto Missouri Route 61 at Wentzville, drove through Flinthill and Moscow Mills, and finally stopped at a diner outside of Auburn, where the scene played out almost as he had imagined it. Except, alongside the coffee when he came out of the rest room, there sat a bowl of grits. He found he could deal with that too.

"How far to Hannibal?" Ransom asked the man at the cash register on the way out.

The old man chewed thoughtfully on a toothpick, his bearded face framed by a card of Alka-Seltzer packages tacked to the back wall. " 'Bout . . . fifty miles," he said finally.

"Still the way Mark Twain described it?"

"Wouldn't know," the man said. "Never been there."

Ransom thanked him and left, heading back down the road and refusing to let himself question the sense of it. He told himself he had the tools now, the research tools, and that the book was taking shape, trying not to think about how the moon would look on this night and what it would do to him— or what it had done to him the night before, the night he could not, would not, remember. He drove, glancing now

and then toward the east, as if there might be a break in the
trees that would show him the Mississippi, although he knew
that the river was miles in the distance.

Passing a billboard advertising TOM SAWYER'S CAVE—JESSE
JAMES'S HIDEOUT, he thought about Marla and how she would
have had a brochure for the place tucked into her purse. He
thought of how, if she had been there, the car would have
smelled of perfume instead of stale smoke, and the backseat
would have been crammed full of suitcases and paper sacks
creaking and rattling, and probably some oil paints, too, because she would have loved to stop and paint something like—
over there, that ramshackle barn of leaning gray wood, stripes
of sunlight showing through the cracks in the boards.

Sunlight.

The sun was edging toward the western horizon. Another
couple of hours and it would be evening. And then . . .

The cats would be gathered at the door of the Milburn
place. Rooster and his bunch would be prowling the highways
like Ahab and his doomed crew in search of a quarry beyond
belief. And Chester McGivern . . . God knows, Ransom
thought. God only knows what would be going on with him
in that darkened tomb of a mansion at the top of Lookout
Mountain.

And for himself: another stop, another call to pay, as if
there were so little pain in his life that he had to go and seek
out some more of it.

What would happen to *him*?

Ransom prayed for some better way to go, some plan he
had never considered, something that would give him cause
to turn back. Tonight, as the night before, there would not
be one lunatic and one dispassionate observer taking it all
down for posterity and the titillation of the masses. There
would be two lunatics.

Put *that* in the book.

Always two lunatics, for as long as the moon was full and
there was a new letter to check out, a new crazy. They didn't
know, but Ransom did. He was the *X* factor.

Pulling into the parking lot of a shopping center, he sat
and looked across the rows of cars toward the smiling, freck-
led face of a Huck Finn, painted on the window of a bakery,
and welcomed himself to the city of Hannibal. After a mo-

ment he fumbled in the glove compartment, withdrawing the folded letter that had brought him to this place. It was written in pencil on a sheet of lined paper, and Ransom read it carefully, as if the words might have changed.

> To K. Ransom—
> You can't help it what the moon does to you. Makes a man owlish as hell, and that's a fact. Me, it takes me a week in the tub afterward to get the moonstink off me . . .

Another one, Ransom thought, resisting the urge to fling the paper away from him. *How many more can I take?*

And then he thought: *What the hell else did you want? What did you expect? The book. Remember the book.*

He read the address, folded up the letter, and went into the bakery to ask directions. In the window of the store was a white-frosted cake in the shape of a steamboat, with "Happy Birthday" written on the paddlewheel, and even as he got back in the car and drove off, the image of the cake stayed fixed in his mind. It would be Marla's birthday soon.

A wrong turn took him past the Mark Twain home and museum, up toward Riverview Park, and he couldn't help stopping. From the turnout he could look across the Mississippi, flowing with flecks of gold from the low sun. Ransom had crossed the river in darkness going east toward Chattanooga; crossed it in daylight going into St. Louis—but there he had seen more of the bridge and the traffic than of the Mississippi, and the river had seemed just a flat gray beneath him, a vague part of the concrete ahead. But now . . .

So *wide.* All the times he had talked in class of *Huckleberry Finn,* of Jim and Huck on a river raft, he had pictured them drifting down the likes of the shallow-bottomed Arkansas River that ran through Tulsa. That was nothing like this.

Ransom could half close his eyes and imagine a steamboat plying the river, stern wheel churning with the sound of a waterfall, towering black smokestacks, billowing dark clouds, and fiery cinders. He could imagine the biggest ship that would fit his mind, and then the river turning mad, the currents racing, and the ship being swept aside and crushed. Like a boat made of white cake and icing.

The moon could rise at its fullest and brightest and play its reflection across the top of the river, and the river wouldn't feel it, wouldn't care. And maybe that counted for something, Ransom thought. Maybe so.

He turned the car, heading back through town, out onto Fulton Avenue. The sky was turning to bronze along the tops of the trees. It seemed to have done that in a blink, but now Ransom saw that some of the oncoming cars already had their headlights on, as if to taunt him, to warn him with their round lights of the moon, the night.

The houses thinned as he headed south out of Hannibal. Soon he came to the place that seemed to match the letter's address.

But there had to be some mistake.

He pulled to the side of the road, staring ahead at the spotlighted sign made of a half dozen uneven boards joined together and painted yellow. The lettering was done in a splotchy red, ending at the bottom with an arrow that pointed up the driveway. The sign read:

HERE IT IS! ! !
INJUN JOE'S HOUSE! ! !
WORLD FAMOUS! ! !

Ransom checked the address again, and the signature. Charles Pautz. He pulled into the driveway, parking on the flattened brown grass of the front yard alongside a green Chevy with an Iowa license plate.

Ransom grabbed his coat from the backseat. The air was cold and evening was settling as he walked toward the front door of the redbrick-fronted home. The door stood open.

A slack-jowled face thrust suddenly into the doorway and gave Ransom a grin that made the eyes crinkle shut. The man gestured to him with a pudgy arm. "Come on, come right in, mister," he said. "You're just in time. Tour's about to start."

Ransom stepped back for a moment, flashing back to the image of Chester McGivern's pitch-black room. But he could see through the doorway that the house was brightly lit inside, and there were other people: a man in a topcoat, a hefty-looking woman, a couple of kids.

The man in the doorway hustled Ransom inside, putting a friendly arm around his shoulder. "Three bucks for the tour, and they all say it's worth it," the man said, holding a thick hand palm up toward Ransom.

Ransom dug a five out of his wallet and the man took it, stuffing the bill into his shirt pocket, where it rested as a small lump atop the swell of his stomach.

"Mr. . . . Pautz?" Ransom asked.

"Right this way. Right this way, folks," the man said, bulling through the front hallway. From the back, nothing showed of his low-set head but a fringe of yellowed white hair.

One of the kids, a piggy-eyed boy of five or six, whined, "I *said* I gotta *go*," and the woman answered, "Shush!"

"Injun Joe's House. Right here!" the man in charge intoned loudly but respectfully, indicating the living room with a slow sweep of his arms. He took a deep breath and nodded. Purple veins webbed his nose.

He pointed toward an overstuffed chair, its pattern a faded floral. "Injun Joe's chair," he said. "Ol' Injun Joe, he'd sit right there, scheming on how to get the best of Huck Finn, he would."

"I'll be darned," said the man in the topcoat.

"And here"—the tour guide scooped up a carving knife that rested on the end table beside the chair, holding it by the blade point—"Injun Joe's knife. The very knife he used to skin cats in the cemetery. Oh, he was a mean 'un."

Ransom saw that Injun Joe must have been peeling an apple a few moments before, but he didn't say anything.

"Now right this way, folks." The man led the way past a dusty-screened console television, onto the buckled linoleum of the kitchen floor. The kitchen was painted a dim yellow and smelled cloyingly of cabbage and something like old flowers.

"Mark Twain would stop by sometimes to shoot the breeze, and him and Injun Joe'd sit right there—right at that table. Sometimes they'd drink coffee, and sometimes they'd get into a poker game. But when they played cards, ol' Mark, he was always the one to know which way th' wind blew. He'd never play for nothing but matchsticks. Like these right here."

"Don't touch those, Jeremy," the woman scolded.

The tour progressed to the back porch through a rusted screen door, and from there to the bedroom, where the guide kicked a copy of *Knave* under the sagging bed.

"Any questions now, folks?"

The boy tugged away from his mother's grasp, latching on to the knob of a closed door that sealed off what Ransom guessed to be a second bedroom. "What's in there?"

"Injun Joe's *secret* room," the man said, shooing the kid aside. "Injun Joe locked it up himself before the posse hung 'im, and nobody ever goes in there, except maybe . . ." He leaned into the boy's face, whispering at him through clenched, blackened teeth. ". . . the *ghost* of Injun Joe. And some nights, yes, sir, some real quiet nights, you can listen at that door, and you can hear the crunchin' of Injun Joe a-gnawin' away at the bones of some poor young lad that he stole off the street. *Hear* 'im?"

The kid blanched. His little sister (the family resemblance was like a rubber stamp, Ransom thought) whimpered and clung to the woman's skirt.

"Well, then," the man said, straightening. "You folks come again, and tell your friends." He ushered the visitors back to the gray-carpeted living room and the front door of the house.

"Do you have any postcards?" the woman asked dully.

"Better 'n that." The man reached into a cigar box on the arm of Injun Joe's chair, withdrawing a white feather. "From Injun Joe's own headdress," he said. "Show this to the folks back home and they'll know that they've seen somethin'."

"I'll be darned," the man in the topcoat said again, but this time his tone was brittle. Ransom figured the change in tone came with the transparent flimflam of being presented a chicken feather dangling a five-dollar price tag.

"Can I have a feather?" asked the boy, looking up at his parents. "Can I have one of Injun Joe's feathers?"

"Certainly *not*," the man said, eyeing the feather with disgust. "Let's go."

"Please, Daddy?"

The man began hustling his family out the door. "The Chamber of Commerce will be receiving a *stern* letter about *this*," he threatened, glancing backward, trying to lock eyes with the host of Injun Joe's house. But the old-timer was rocking with laughter, a squeaky and rasping hee-hee-hee that made his head settle even lower into the slump of his shoulders.

The other man paused a moment and then slammed the door, and the last thing Ransom heard of the family was the boy's voice whining *"Please,"* then fading away.

The old man's face was sparkling with tears when he finally look up toward Ransom; his voice was choked, his nose running. "That—" he said, breaking off into laughter again. "That's almost m'favorite part."

"Mr. Pautz?" Ransom said.

"M' *favorite* part." The man wiped at his eyes. "Sometimes they buy the feather."

"I'm Keith Ransom."

The grin slackered. "Keith Ran—the hell you say."

"You wrote me about—"

"I know what I wrote." The man straightened, crystal-blue eyes trained on Ransom. He backed toward the center of the room. "Wasn't looking for you to show up on th' doorstep, though."

"I just want to talk to you."

"Tried to do you a mite of a favor, that's all. I don't want no trouble over it."

"No trouble. Just a few questions."

Pautz gave him the half-lidded, sly look of a practiced horse trader. "Guess I ought to feel honored, you being so famous and all, right on the same page with Dolly Parton, best I recollect it." He warmed to the subject. "Yes, sir, I read that, and I thought . . . here's a man got some of th' same wild hairs that I got."

"You said in your letter . . . about the *moonstink.* I don't know what that means."

"Don't you, now? Don't you?" Pautz rubbed at the side of his face with a blunt-tipped finger, the fingertip trailing a wake of white across the slack ruddiness of his cheek. "Well, sir, can't say as I've ever just out an' talked about that before, and I don't see no reason to start now."

"I've come a long way, Mr. Pautz."

Pautz shook his head. "Not on *my* say-so, you didn't."

"And I didn't ask for that letter, but you wrote it, or else I wouldn't be here. I think you *owe* me—" Ransom caught

himself. He had no right in making demands, coming on like
Morris Thurman, shouting out rules. "Two dollars. Two dollars in change from when I came in here."

The old man gave a pat to his shirt pocket. "Didn't say I
wouldn't talk about it. Just said I didn't see no reason."

"Because . . . I need to know." Just great, man, Ransom
thought. Smooth talking at its finest.

"Sure. Sure you do. 'Cause, mister, you've got a thing
goin' here that I don't, and that's an angle. You're up to something."

Ransom drew a breath. He could *feel* the old man's secret
as if it were a thing he could grasp in his hands, a card that
had been dealt to him facedown, and nothing mattered but to
bend up the corner of it, to read the suit and number. There
was a burning throb in his temples.

He glanced toward the window, past the curtains once beige
but now mottled with brown-edged water stains, not at all
surprised to see the eye of the nearly full moon glaring back
at him.

Ransom told the man about the book.

Pautz nodded when Ransom was finished, with a grin that
seemed to creep out of his shirt collar. "Pretty sharp," he
said. "Pretty sharp, at that." He turned toward the kitchen,
motioning for Ransom to follow. " 'Course, if I was to be
in this book of yours, and you sold it for money . . . Have a
seat."

Ransom pulled up a chair at the table where Mark Twain
used to shoot the breeze, according to Pautz, except the table
was plastic-topped with an imitation wood-grain finish.

"I ought to be in for a cut of the profits, seems like,"
Pautz said, striking a series of stick matches to start the gas
burner under the coffeepot. The air smelled of smoke and
sulfur and—

And perfume, Ransom thought. *Perfume!* It wasn't from
the woman who had been in there, either. The odor was thick,
and the sweet, sticky smell was so out of place, he almost
hadn't recognized it.

"Agreed?" Pautz asked.

"We could work that out."

The old man poured a couple of mugs full of coffee so
black that it had to be weeks old, Ransom thought.

"Good, sharp idea, that book." Pautz clattered the cups onto the table and sat across from Ransom, right where Injun Joe used to squat across from Mr. Twain. The old man tapped at his temple. "And I know a good, sharp idea. This place right here bein' one."

Sloshing coffee and slapping the tabletop for emphasis now and then, Pautz spun out the story of Injun Joe's house—how he'd been sixty-seven and still out on the road selling one thing and another when the first of a couple of heart attacks knocked him flat; how the second one left him at home with the TV and a garden for company, and just about enough of a check from the government to pay half the bills.

"It was the statue that done it for me," he said. "Right downtown—maybe you seen it—that statue of Huck Finn and Tom Sawyer. Never thought much about it before, many times as I'd seen it. But this time, I'd swear to you, it was like ol' Tom gave me a wink and a wave, and he said to me, 'Charlie, some folks will buy anything.' "

Ransom suddenly wished he had brought his tape player in with him. He didn't want to go outside again, but he did have his pad and a pen inside his coat, and that would do. He took them out, trying to appear casual. "You saw this," he said, "on a night of the full moon?"

Pautz gave him an odd look. "I saw this at noon on a Friday. What do you take me for, mister? I don't mean I *saw* the statue move; I'd've had myself locked in the squirrel cage for *that*. I mean, it was an *inspiration* come over me."

"Sorry," Ransom said.

"I did some more lookin' around then, and I saw the river-boat rides and the Mark Twain Museum. Tom Sawyer this and Aunt Polly that. And I asked m'self, what kind of business could I start, given th' resources at hand, which was some ol' boards out back and a can of paint."

"The sign for 'Injun Joe's House,' " Ransom said.

"Worked right away." Pautz leaned back with a creak of the chair. "Prob'bly do even better once I get around to readin' th' book. Like I said . . . a good, sharp idea. I like a good, sharp idea. And this book of yours, it couldn't hardly help but sell, wouldn't you say?"

"That's what I'd say." Ransom stopped himself from drumming his fingertips against the table edge. A sickness had jelled in his stomach. The perfume smell, now that he was aware of it, seemed to hang in the air like a thick-globuled, slow-falling rain.

"Well, then," Pautz said. The chair banged forward. "If it's such a sure thing, and I've got a cut of it coming to me, I'd favor to take my share now." The old man's lips compressed into a straight line, as if never to open again.

Ransom eyed him. "That would be, maybe, another ten dollars."

They sat looking at each other, saying nothing. The silence of the house seemed to whisper to them.

Then, under Ransom's gaze, the old man's expression suddenly went dead.

"No . . ." he said.

"*Damn* you!" Ransom was on his feet. A warm stickiness trickled into the palm of his left hand. His arm was bleeding again.

"Better you just go on now," Pautz said.

There were crystals of frost on the tabletop, threads of frost, reaching out, linking over his notepad, over the table.

"You want money? *Money?* Here!" Ransom yanked out his wallet, slamming it onto the tabletop. The ice sparked.

Pautz didn't move. "No, I . . . don't want . . ." His head strained upward, eyes on Ransom. "You feel it. You feel it, don't you?"

Ransom heard the tiny, hollow plipping sound of the blood running from his hand, falling onto the linoleum.

"The moon," Pautz said. "Ain't so funny when it happens. Ain't so funny anymore." He slid the chair back, picking up Ransom's wallet and handing it back to him. He touched the end of his thumb to the small pool of blood on the tabletop.

"You got it . . . maybe worse than me," Pautz said. "I think . . . maybe *a lot* worse. Don't want you anywhere close to me, mister, night of the full moon."

Ransom saw frost spreading up the greasy yellow walls. He jammed his eyes shut. The frost was gone a moment later, but there were snow-sparkles of white and silver in the air.

Pautz stood facing him, oddly straightened, as if gathering strength. "I don't want you here now," he said.

"I don't want to be here," Ransom said. "I want an answer, though. What the moon . . . does to you."

The slightest of smiles, a funereal smile, crossed the face of Charles Pautz. "Guess that's why I wrote to you in the first place," he said. "Guess I wanted to tell, wanted to . . . say it in so many words, only I couldn't. Didn't have those words in me; don't have those words now."

Pautz shuffled toward the bedroom hallway. "Moon comes up, big full moon . . . I can smell it. Always could. But it seems t'be worse now, and worse every time, so it's more than a smell now. It's the *air*. It's the taste of the air."

Ransom forced himself to follow the man. They stopped in front of the locked door.

"Smells . . . cold," said Pautz, without looking around. "But what does that tell you? Smells like a dead thing all frozen. Smells *white*, you know? Thick and white. And dead, but not dead."

Pautz withdrew from his pants a jangling wreath of keys. He fitted a key to the door lock, shrugging. "Used to be . . . I thought it was *me*. Come time of th' full moon, let me tell you, I was th' cleanest kid in Marion County. Used to scrub myself with a boar's-hair brush till I looked to the point of bein' skinned, but it didn't help."

He clicked the lock open, and the door swung inward with a snap of weather stripping. The inside was dark, and Ransom made a sound of revulsion, startled by the impact of the far side of the hallway against his back as he recoiled. The old man seemed not to notice him.

Pautz reached into the darkness, fumbled a moment, found the wall switch. The ceiling light flicked on with a dull yellow glow, spilling light into the hallway.

And along with the light came a rich, ripe aroma, the smell of flowers and spice, pine, vanilla and roses, incense and musk oil, a heavy, coiling mixture of scents drifting leadenly onto the gray hallway carpet, lifting itself like some thick-coated creature arisen from sleep.

Ransom's stomach lurched, even as he leaned toward the opened doorway.

"I just gotta do what I can," Pautz said.

Inside, the walls were lined floor-to-ceiling with shelves, and the shelves sagged with bottles: bottles of amber and rose-colored liquids, bottles gold-capped, bottles topped with atomizers, bottles shaped like swans and motorcars. There were spray cans and incense burners, candles, garlic, balls of colored soap.

Pautz reached to the nearest shelf. His hand struck a bottle of English Leather after-shave, and it toppled and smashed onto the floor. He grabbed a petite spray mist, aimed it into his face, and pumped the nozzle, clouding himself with a spray that Ransom briefly recognized as Chantilly—Marla's favorite—before the delicate scent was driven into the stench of the room.

"I do what I can," Pautz said. "Keep the moonstink offa me. To keep th' moonstink off. Got to . . ." He dropped the empty spray mist, reached to the shelf again. "*There's* somethin' for your book, mister. Write what a fool he is, Charlie Pautz. Write what he does to himself."

Pautz poured a palmful of cologne. He slapped himself, hard, across the face with it, and his cheek reddened. A trickle of blood ran from his mottled nose, crossed his lips, stained the edge of his shirt collar.

He held the opened bottle toward Ransom. "And how about you, mister?" he said. "Maybe *you* could use some."

Ransom looked past the trembling bottle, through the ice crystals between them into the old man's eyes. Slowly he took the bottle, spilling some of the stinging liquid across his own hands.

"Maybe so," he said.

The night air seemed oddly thick, and Ransom was afraid of the smell of it. He lit a cigarette inside the car, sitting until the crystalline flecks were hazy with smoke, and then he drove.

He pulled into the nearest motel. It was called the Tom 'n' Huck Inn, and even though the grandmotherly desk clerk with the too red fingernails recoiled at his approach—the smell, Ransom knew, and he hoped it was only the mixture of colognes—she still tried to sell him on taking one of the "special" rooms. It was off-season, she said, so he could have his choice: the Tom Sawyer Suite, the Huck Finn Suite, the Becky Thatcher Suite, the Injun Joe Suite.

Ransom took just a room, found his way to it through the

icy haze around him, stopped beside it to get a Butterfingers bar from a machine.

He sat on the hard bed eating the candy bar, squeezing his eyelids together to try to rid himself of the icy dots that swam everywhere he looked. He tried thinking of other things.

The Injun Joe Suite the woman had tried to sell him. Probably even had a feather in it, he thought, and then he felt torn between crying for Charlie Pautz and laughing at the old man's showmanship. In the end he did what he thought Charlie Pautz would have wanted. He picked up the ashtray on the bed table, read, "Stolen from the Tom 'n' Huck Inn" on the bottom of it, and dropped it into his suitcase—a souvenir for Marla.

Marla.

She seemed so far away from him, both in miles and time, and it seemed as if someone else had made the decision for him to have it that way, someone selfish and out of control, someone that wasn't . . . him.

His hand went to the phone.

What could he say for himself? That he was right—at least that much. Right about what he was doing. And more, right to be away from her on this night, and the next, and the ones that had gone before. But she wouldn't believe, wouldn't want to hear that.

Ice crystals shattered from the telephone dial as his fingers found the appropriate holes.

The phone rang on the other end. Rang again.

Clicked.

"Hello?" she said.

Pretty Marla. Suddenly, desperately, he wanted her; and just as much, he knew that he dare not touch her, that he might somehow hurt her by only the touch of his voice.

"It's Keith," he said, and the words seemed to come from somewhere else, behind him, above him.

A cold, faint sound whispered through the receiver, then a cry from the other end, a shrill rush of words.

"Keith! Oh, Lord, Keith, where are you? He's *dead*, Keith. Dead, he was killed—"

"Who? What are you talking about?"

Ransom was looking across the length of the motel room,

toward the mirror mounted over the low desk. The glass was frosted now, the reflection dim and white, like a phantom.

"Him!" she shouted.

The reflection moved. It stood, shifting forward, as Ransom watched.

"Don't you *know*?"

The sound of her voice dimmed as the receiver slipped from his hand, clattering off the edge of the bed stand.

It was a doll's voice now.

"Ben Taylor," it said.

CHAPTER SIXTEEN

Ransom sat transfixed, watching the thing in the mirror as it came toward him out of the white glow of the frosted glass.

He knew what it was. He knew what it wanted. He knew of the murder that shone from its eyes.

His hands felt for the base of the phone and yanked it free, ripping the cord from the wall. He pitched the phone into the swirling silence of the mirror.

But too late.

Even as his throat burned with terror and rage, his voice was cut to silence as if by the smooth stroke of an icy blade, and the eyes of the thing drew him in.

"Keith! Marla shrieked into the phone—his name, again and again, until it had no meaning.

She felt the receiver being pried from her hand, turned to see Staci listening to it, jabbing at the phone cradle.

"Nothing," she said after a moment. "Dial tone."

Marla wanted to cry, but she was sick of crying. She wanted to wrap her arms around her head. She wanted to throw something, break something, but the salt shaker was a bad choice; it only snapped open when it thudded against the wall, spilling a blizzard of granules, and left her feeling weak and foolish.

"Shit," Marla said, and she was giggling a little, ashamed.

"Shit is right," Brenda returned, setting a box of books and art supplies on the kitchen table. "Listen, is there anything to drink around here?"

Marla felt grateful to her for a simple question, easily answered. "No," she said. Keith had poured out all the bottles, had made a point of leaving the empties in the trash where she couldn't help seeing them.

"I think we could use something," Brenda said. She buttoned on the white fur coat that made her look like a snowball. "I'll make a quick run to the happy store. Be right back."

"We'll be through here in a minute," Staci said. She stood beside the sofa, folding clothes into the open suitcase on top of it. "We can stop on the way to the dorm."

"Be right back," Brenda repeated.

"Sure. Go on," Marla said, because it was easier than saying the truth. *You're afraid of me. You don't want to deal with me anymore. You think I'm going to pieces again, and you don't want to be here for the breakdown.*

The front door opened and closed with the whine of the wind from outside, where the storm still raged. Marla felt the anxious touch of Staci's hand on her shoulder.

"It's . . . all right," Marla said. "I just want to finish up and . . . get the hell out of here."

Staci nodded and went back to her work. Marla made a final trip upstairs, up past the movie posters and Keith's collection of antique mechanical banks in a showcase on the landing. She brought down an armload of clothing on hangers and draped that over the sofa, next to the suitcase.

She tried not to look around at the house. It was Keith's house, not hers. It would never be hers.

"I think that's all I need. For now," she said.

Staci looked at her helplessly. "Shouldn't you maybe . . . call your dad?"

"And tell him *what*? Hi, Dad. Guess what? Keith took off and left me. And remember Ben Taylor? You sort of liked him, Dad. He's dead now. What's new with you?"

"Keith . . . didn't even tell you where he was?" Staci asked softly.

"No." Marla answered in kind, as if to prove that she *could*, that she didn't have to say everything on the verge of tears.

She was ready to leave and remembered that she couldn't, because Brenda had the car.

Brenda, I could have done without you leaving, she thought.
I could have done just real *well without being left here.*

Keith's old railroad clock hummed in the stillness of the
house, and the wind spattered sleet against the windows.

The house—the very *presence* of it—kept pulling her back
in time. There was nothing about it that she could see or
touch or sense that didn't lift her out of the present and force
her back again to the evening before last.

Sometimes that evening seemed to have happened years
ago and to someone else; sometimes only a moment before;
sometimes *now,* and very much to her. And still going on.

She could still feel the cold slash of the wind against her
face as she had stood on the porch, books clasped in front of
her, reading the note pinned to the door, Brenda and Staci
already out of the driveway and down the road.

She hadn't believed the note. It was later, looking at Keith's
place at the kitchen table, the plate and silverware set for
him, the chair empty—the fact of his leaving had struck her
only then, with a pain like that of a cut so deep that it hadn't
hurt at first.

Guilt had twinged at her then. If she hadn't gone out with
Brenda and Staci after classes, she might have been able to
stop him; instead she stood in an empty house, the beer on
her breath condemning her.

Still, she told herself he would be back at any moment,
that he wasn't crazy enough to take off on some idiot hunt
for lunatics in the middle of the worst storm of the winter.

She listened for the sound of the Datsun pulling up in the
driveway.

Listened . . .

Sat with a book, reading the same few sentences over and
over, feeling the come-and-go of emotions: now anger, now
loneliness, now guilt, now the fear that something must have
happened to him.

And then the sound of a motor from just outside the house
but not the soft rattle of Keith's old car. It was a sudden,
rising scream of machinery that brought her to her feet, sent
her rushing to the window.

Something hit the front porch when she was no more than
halfway across the living room. Something heavy.

And when she opened the door . . .

Marla broke herself away from the awful memory before it could rush back and trap her again. She focused on her hands, clenched together on the tabletop.

"Want some hot chocolate?" she asked Staci.

"Sure. I guess."

"I'll make it."

"I will. I mean . . . no problem."

Staci filled a saucepan with water, set it on the stove. Marla envied her those motions and the absence of thought that went with them, the simple doing of simple things, a moment's escape.

But now, in her mind, the door opened.

It opened to the whipping of the wind, the stinging cold of rain and sleet. And red—so much of it. Vivid. Electric. So bright, it seemed to burn. There was steam rising from it, delicate, smoky vapors that lifted between the gusts of wind, coiling from the scarlet opening of his mouth.

His head was twisted backward so that he lay stomach-down on the porch boards but was looking directly at her, eyes incredibly wide, as if he were showing off a new trick.

Just like you, Ben. Always fooling.

And voices now. Odd, Marla thought; she could still hear those voices, every one of them, but there was not one clear, single face to match any one voice. Instead there were disjointed images—the flashing red and blue lights of the police cars and the ambulance, lights glancing off the snow-covered ground, people *(neighbors!)* gathered like specters to watch from behind the rope the police strung around the front yard, the swarming of uniformed strangers; and the television trucks then, the cameras, the news reporters, police, neighbors, voices, voices, *voices* . . .

Where is your husband, Mrs. Ransom?

Gone? Gone where?

You're not helping, Mrs. Ransom—not him, not you, not us. Or don't you care?

"Chocolate's ready," Staci said. "Marla?"

"I've got to stop this, you know. I didn't used to cry like this. I've got to *stop this* ."

"You can't help it."

"Yes, I can, Stace." Marla wrapped her hands around the

hot cup, welcoming the pain against her palms, because it hurt but she could take it.

"Crazy Brenda. There's no telling what's become of her," Staci said.

They sat, and the clock hummed. Marla's cat, Strawberry, brushed against her leg, purring.

"We could sneak her into the dorm," Staci said, kneeling to pet the cat.

"You think so."

"Sure. They had a goat upstairs once. Remember?"

"I remember." Marla rolled the cup between her hands, the gold of her wedding ring clacking faintly against the porcelain. "Ben . . . the time he got the high score on a whole row of machines at the games place. Berzerk, Defender, all of those, and he put in my initials. And it seemed . . . it meant something. I don't know. Pretty dumb, huh?"

"You were close to being solid with him. I know that much, Marla."

"Until Keith . . ."

"It's okay," Staci said. "You can trust me, and you need to let it out, just to say what you're feeling."

"I don't know what I feel."

"Ben . . . he must have been coming to see you."

Marla shook her head, and the motion stirred an ache across her temples. "I think . . . he was coming after Keith. To get even. I think . . . another fight."

" *Jeez*, Marla. You didn't tell that to the *police*, did you?"

"They knew it. They said he'd been talking it up in the hospital even, how Keith was going to be sorry . . ."

"And now they're after Keith."

Helping him run is just making it worse, Mrs. Ransom. Worse for him when we find him. Worse for you.

I'm not . . .

Material witness. You wouldn't like it in jail, Mrs. Ransom. Look—here, drink this. Back off it, Larry. Look, we don't mean to scare you, Mrs. Ransom. But you've got to help us. If you really don't know where he is, make us believe that.

She wondered if the phone was tapped. If they tapped the phone, wouldn't they have to tell her? But if they'd been listening . . .

Keith, Keith, she thought. What if they heard? They must

think you're insane, Keith, and maybe you are. I think that's what I hope, that's the best I could hope for you. Be a long ways away, and be out of your mind.

"Marla, you don't think . . ." Staci's voice went soft; she sucked at her lip. "That Keith . . . could have done . . ."

"I thought you said talking would help," Marla said. She lifted the cup, nearly dropping it then at the sudden, shattering ring of the phone bell.

Marla grasped the receiver so tightly that her fingers hurt. *"Keith!"* she shouted into it.

The receiver crackled.

"Keith, I—"

"Mrs. Ransom?"

The voice was not his. It was a rough but steady voice, controlled, emotionless. Marla's heart fluttered, leaving a chill in her throat.

"Yes . . ." she said.

"My name is McGivern. Your husband was here with me. Yesterday. Is he there now?"

She didn't know what she had meant to say; she only heard herself gasp.

There was a knock on the front door, light but insistent. Staci yelled, "Brenda, just come in, dammit!"

"I didn't think that he would be," the voice said. It was followed by a muffled, hissing sound. "How I know doesn't matter, Mrs. Ransom, but I know quite a lot about your husband and his . . . research, let's call it. Now listen to me."

Movement registered in the corner of Marla's eye. Staci, leaving the kitchen, the quick sound of her footsteps diminishing toward the front of the house, and a hard rapping against the front door. All this as Marla was saying, "Where *is*—"

The voice interrupted. *"Listen.* I can't talk for long, Mrs. Ransom. Two things. Your husband is not a suspect in the killing of Benjamin Taylor; my attorneys have taken care of it. And tomorrow, look for a check in the mail. Fill it in for a comfortable sum."

From the voice Marla envisioned a strong, big man, shirt cuffs rolled back, a man accustomed to giving unquestioned orders. She felt numb and heard herself say, "What are you telling me? Is this some kind of *game*?"

"No games, Mrs. Ransom. No big mystery. My reasons
are selfish, and money . . ." A thudding sound carried to her
through the receiver, again and again, soft against hard.
"Money is all I've got left that still works. Tell your husband—"

Noises intruded; the clack and creak of the front door
opening, the moan of the wind, floating voices.

"—stay with it. I'll do what I can for him, and he can do
as much for me. Tell him that."

The receiver clicked to silence. Again, Marla thought. As
if it were supposed to work that way, as if the phone itself
took pleasure in hurting her, contrived to do this to her.

At least, she thought, Keith never had gotten around to
replacing the standard desktop phone with the smiling Mickey
Mouse model he had talked of wanting. She couldn't have
taken it, coming from Mickey Mouse.

Marla slammed the receiver down hard enough to break
something inside it, at the same time hearing Staci softly call
her name. She turned to see her standing in the kitchen doorway, hands plaited awkwardly.

"It wasn't Keith," Marla said. "It was some . . . I don't
know, nut case, I think." She reached for her coat, which
lay draped over the back of one of the mismatched dinette
chairs. "Take some of these books, would you, Stace? I just
want to take what the three of us can pick up on the way
out."

Staci was motionless. "It wasn't Brenda, either, Marla. I
think you'd better see . . ."

A second figure stepped into the doorway behind Staci,
so huge and so strange that Marla couldn't take all of it in
at once. The boots registered first, the shuffle and thud of
the scuffed black engineer's boots; then the massive legs in
faded denim, keys on a loop of chain at the belted waist,
stomach a mountain of zippered black leather. Finally the
face, looking as if it had been set on top by mistake,
framed by curly dark hair twining down over the hulking
shoulders.

The man spoke. "Got no place else to go," he said. "Got
to get him inside."

Marla felt a clinging rush of cold air across her feet. As
the huge man stepped aside she saw a wheelchair being wres-

tled through the front door into the living room, trailing
streaks of snow across the hardwood floor. She saw a blond-
haired girl of delicately slender frame maneuvering the front
of the chair as another man pushed it into the room. That
man looked toward Marla momentarily, ice glistening from
his eyebrows, gloved hands loosening stiffly from the handles
of the chair.

Marla's first reaction was simply a dull astonishment,
tempered with the feeling that she *knew* these people, had
seen them somewhere before. She looked at the man in the
chair. He seemed dead; his eyes were closed, his mouth
slack, his face almost the color of the snowflakes that were
melting now into the red of his beard. Beads of water se-
quined the tangle of red, glistened from the metal brace that
circled his head.

Even as she watched, he moved. The eyes opened slowly.
The lips parted, and Marla felt herself a part of the silence
that hung over him.

"How about gettin' the fuggin' door closed," he muttered.

The man behind him turned quickly toward the door as the
blond girl fussed with a frayed blanket that lay over the lap
of the crippled man. He fixed her with a glare that stopped
her dead.

That same look swept to Marla. "Where's Ransom?" the
man asked.

Marla had thought she would scream if anyone else asked
her that question. She didn't scream. Bewilderment gave way
to anger, cold anger that froze her voice to a whisper.

"Get out," she said.

None of them moved.

"Staci . . . call the police." Marla went to the doorway,
as if to block them if they tried to keep Staci away from the
phone.

The crippled man tried to push himself forward, shoving
against one of the wheels with his left hand. The chair spun
sideways, and even as he cursed it the blanket on his lap
caught and slid to the floor, revealing the hard blue gleam of
the biggest revolver Marla had ever seen.

It was pointed toward her.

Marla felt fingers grip the flesh of her arm. Staci, beside her now, said, "Maybe they'd like some hot chocolate."

The crippled man grinned. "Yeah," he said. "We'd like that. We could use that."

Marla tightened her arms across her breasts.

The blond girl said, "I don't think she knows anything about us, Rooster. At least, we need to . . ." She awkwardly crossed toward Marla. "They call me Freedom," she said, pulling back a sleeve of her too large Army jacket and extending a hand.

I've seen her somewhere, Marla thought, slowly accepting the greeting. *All of them, maybe. But where?* She felt the girl's cold hand in hers, trembling slightly.

The girl continued. "This is Joseph. Randy. Rooster. We're not—" She gave a small shrug. "We don't mean to scare you. We need help."

"And Keith . . . knows you?"

Of course! Marla remembered in a rush, watching through sleep-filmed eyes as the motorcycles pulled away, the girl retreating to the old van. *That* girl. Freedom.

"World's full of surprises, right?" Rooster said. His low, rasping voice seemed to drift in from a great distance away. "Can't move, and it's too friggin' *cold* to sit still."

"We've never been this far east before," Freedom said. "Joseph, he's never so much as seen it snow before."

"I'm freaked," Joseph said politely, glancing around the room as if in search of approval.

"I'll just, uh, start the water," Staci said, but Marla was scarcely aware of her.

"Going east? Going where?" Marla asked.

Rooster's hand fell to the butt of the revolver—a reflex action, Marla thought. "Right here, pretty lady," he said. "Right here we'll wait for 'im."

Marla flinched, feeling suddenly out of balance.

"He means the Rider," Freedom said.

"Moon goon," Joseph added.

"What?"

Rooster fixed her with another stare. "Who do you think took that dude apart out here and played fifty-two pickup with the pieces of 'im?" Randy held out a lit cigarette to him, and

Rooster took a drag, expelling the smoke in a long sigh, his mouth compressing slowly into a tight line.

In her confusion Marla felt herself again thrust back to *that* night. But now, as she saw again across the yard, the barrier of the police rope and the crowd there beyond it, she saw the glint of spoked wheels. The oddness of it: a wheelchair out there in the snow.

"You know . . . who did it?" Marla asked.

" *Saw* 'im. Lost 'im." Rooster spat a fleck of tobacco. "I wouldn't have said any man could move the likes of that devil's bastard. But I know 'im now. Wants th' hellwind on 'im."

Marla struggled to make connections. The man seemed to be talking a different language; she wanted to cry at him, "Make sense!"

"Moon's about full tonight," Rooster continued. "I'd say someplace on the storm edge, someplace where the road's dry and sky's clear, they're about to get th' life tore out of 'em. But then he'll be here again. Right here."

Marla thought she caught a look of fear in the big man's—Randy's—eyes. That look made him seem strangely vulnerable, as if the heavy black eyebrows and the chisled, angular cheekbones were just a disguise. He straightened then, leveling toward her the half smile of a secret promise, and she saw that his jacket was zippered open now, the T-shirt beneath reading, "If You Ain't a Biker—You Ain't SHIT!"

"So, pretty house mouse," Rooster said. "Like it or not, you've got company."

The door clicked open and Brenda stepped in, cradling a six-pack of Coors Light and a bottle of tequila.

The bottle dropped, smashing against the floor. Brenda made a little squeaking sound as Rooster spun the chair toward her with astonishing speed, his hand lifting the gun then.

"I . . ." Brenda started. "I saw the bikes and . . . I figured you had company. Maybe I should go get . . ."

Randy took the six-pack from her, tossing a can across the room to Joseph. Rooster's arm fell to his side, hand locked on the revolver, his face glistening with sweat. Before Marla knew what she was doing, she had rushed to his side.

Freedom was beside her. Their eyes locked.

Marla thought then she would always remember that moment. The sudden and totally open look of gratitude the woman gave her, deep and painful. And Brenda just standing there, trying to finish her sentence, looking at each of the visitors in turn, as if they were shadows that would melt away if she could only get them in the proper angle; watching Joseph take care of the first can of beer in one fast, loud swallow.

". . . another couple of six-packs," Brenda finally managed. "So we'll have enough, you know."

CHAPTER SEVENTEEN

Ransom awoke on his feet. The room came into focus with startling clarity. He took a dazed step forward, and something crunched under his shoe.

It was a shard of mirrored glass.

Now he saw that the glass was everywhere. Jagged planes of it cast back his reflection from the desktop, the faded green of the floor's carpet. The frame of the wall mirror hung at a broken angle in front of him, nearly wrenched away from the wall.

He tapped at the frame. It swung momentarily from the single top corner screw still left in place and then fell, cracking the glass of the desk's surface beneath it.

Only then did he see the blood spatters on the glass top, and on the wall where the mirror had been.

His stomach lurched at the sight of his hands.

Some of the cuts reopened as he forced his hands under the full, cold pressure of the water in the bathroom sink; it swirled into the drain, turning pink as it passed his hands.

His right hand, the worst one, stung and throbbed as he wrapped it with a washcloth, looking away from it.

Ransom turned, taking stock of the place: the scattered, broken glass; the overturned desk lamp; the phone on the floor in the middle of the room, trailing a snapped cord.

And the smell.

The stench suddenly smothered him, a cloying, confusing mixture of garlic and roses, pine and Chantilly. His lungs were stuffed full of it. He was drowning in the smell.

229

But this time he knew the feeling. It was the same slipping of time and place that had made him a living part of the biker's nightmare account, and now it was trying to take him again. It wanted him back in *that* room, shut in there until he could smell the frozen white of the full moon the way poor Charlie Pautz did.

Ransom knew the feeling, and he fought it.

The smell burst around him. The air thickened to black, and he was trapped again in the library of the McGivern mansion, screaming against the door.

His hands scrabbled along the polished wood of the door, found the handle, yanked.

Outside, they were waiting for him, a silvered, writhing mass in the moonlight. The screen door was shredded, and the first of the cats leapt into the torn opening. Ransom grabbed for the cat, the old agate-eyed tom. His hands locked to break the cat's neck; but now it was Ben Taylor there, Ben Taylor dying within his grasp. Ransom watched the eyes film over, going dead, and they became Marla's eyes. A bright, bloodied froth ran from her mouth. "I love you, Keith," she whispered. "I love you, love you . . ."

Ransom heaved into the sink. Running the water again, he picked up the half squeezed tube of Colgate toothpaste, marveling just at the touch of it, then the minted taste, the touch and taste of something real.

He jerked in fright at the three quick knocks against the motel-room door.

Cracking it open only slightly, he peered out.

She was all sunshine out there, with sun-colored, curled hair and a smile matching the white of her apron. "Good morning," she said. "Checkout time is in thirty minutes. Will you be staying over?"

Ransom glanced quickly toward the shambles of the room and made the crack in the doorway even slimmer.

"No. I'll be leaving," he said.

He picked up the glass shards, wiped at the spatters with a cold, dampened cloth, and replaced the phone and the lamp. For good measure he made the bed.

Ransom checked the contents of his wallet. He couldn't begin to pay cash for the damage, couldn't imagine the management being happy to settle up with a check or a charge card, didn't want the confrontation, anyway.

He took off his wristwatch. It was an expensive, gold-plated one that his grandmother had given him as a high-school graduation present, carefully kept in repair. Smoothing it out, he laid it on the desktop.

Time didn't seem to matter much, anyway, he thought; at least not time measured in hours and minutes. The only time he cared about anymore could be measured only in the phases of the moon.

He missed the watch immediately as he pulled out of the Tom 'n' Huck Inn parking lot.

Highway 63 took him rolling north into Kirksville, Missouri, alongside Thousand Hills Park, every dip of the highway registering in the small of his back, the pain slid like a weight into his right leg, and he found himself driving either too fast or too slow; the miles, at last, were catching up with him.

Ransom felt not even vaguely hungry now, but he forced himself to pull into a drive-in at the town's edge.

He sat waiting for his order—the Show Me Deluxe with cheese—watching, here and there, a stray fleck of snow dissolve against the windshield from a sky that had darkened steadily ever since he had been on the road. He sat in silence, and the silence brought to him the damning question of the broken mirror. He couldn't doubt that he had smashed it; the muted red stains that crept through the cloth on his right hand and the naked cuts on his left were proof enough of the obvious.

But . . . *why?*

And in place of the answer, another question: *Do you really want to know?*

Eyes closed, Ransom could feel himself at the brink of a darkened corridor. The answers were there, all in his mind, the memories daring him to come in search of them.

He sensed something worse in the darkness, something harder to bear than the sick desperation of two nights gone blank for him, something eager to be found. The glimmering of frost eyes . . .

And Ben Taylor was dead. But he hadn't, couldn't have,

any involvement in *that*. He remembered Marla's voice on the phone, as if from far away, very far away: "He's *dead*, Keith. Dead. He was killed—" A thin edge of hysteria in the voice, somehow tied in, Ransom knew, with the unblinking white eyes, glowering now from a dark corner of his mind. . . .

"That'll be three seventy-nine."

Ransom stared dumbly out the side window for a moment.

"Three-seventy-nine," the woman repeated, clacking at the window with the corner of the tray she carried, sloshing some coffee from a Styrofoam cup in the process. She was wearing the most obviously fake black wig that Ransom had ever seen, more like a hat than a hairpiece; she delivered to him a thick, steaming burger dripping heavy melted cheese over crisp lettuce, one of those miracles to be found only in the unlikeliest of places.

Afterward Ransom wanted nothing so much as to let back the seat and to sleep like . . .

Normal, he thought. Just to sleep like normal people, and to wake up feeling better.

He didn't dare. He couldn't be trusted to sleep like normal, and his muscles tensed with the knowledge. He was glad for the anger, then—the anger that came with knowing he might rampage around and *break* things; might sleep himself right into the news. Again.

Read all about it, folks. Ransom goes on another rampage. *The Nap of Terror.*

He was a joke, a clown, a fool. At the best.

Consider, class, the ridiculous plight of the tragic figure cursed by the awareness of himself as a tragic figure. And name three. Oedipus, Elmer Fudd, and . . .   .

Might as well make a joke of it, Ransom thought. Laugh or scream. Or why not both?

A surge of anger brought his fist down. It rebounded against the steering wheel.

That's good. That's right. *Break* something.

Ransom sat, looking at the mess in the car, the mess he had made of things: ash tray spilling over with cigarette butts, the litter of candy wrappers and fast-food bags, crinkled, lonely-looking envelopes of ketchup. It looked like an assassin's living room.

He then drove in search of a car wash and vacuum. He could do that much; he could straighten up the car. Driving, he remembered what his grandmother used to tell him about making sure he had on clean underwear before he went out anywhere. That way if he had a wreck, the people at the hospital wouldn't think he practiced bad hygiene.

He could do the same with the car. That way, if anybody looked in, they wouldn't think he was crazy. They'd say, "What a clean car. The person who owns it must be a real straight guy."

He could at least do that, for sure. He could keep up appearances.

Ransom thought for a moment that his grandmother would be proud as he pulled into a self-service car wash and plugged a quarter in the slot next to the wand.

And he could do something else, he thought, as the spray mist clouded the windshield. He could damn well do a better job on the book he was supposed to be trying to write. Because *that* was for real; at least it could be, despite his having made such a half-assed job of it so far.

He didn't need any more proof of the moon's effect—at least not for himself. But he hadn't begun to prove it in a way that would make sense to anyone else, had not assembled even the proof he'd require for a passable term paper. So much to account for, so little to show.

The McGivern papers. He still had those, and Holstrom seemed good for an elaboration on the full moon's effect on the weather. But his own thoughts were blurred now, images running together. He couldn't trust himself to hold on to the madness, to remember the feelings and fears, and then to be able to stand outside it all, finding the precise and correct words necessary to describe the experience of sheer lunacy.

He hadn't turned out to be much of a note taker.

Ransom stopped in town. He found a drugstore that would sell him not only the medicine and bandages he needed for his hands but also carried the tiny cassettes he needed for his tape recorder. He bought a half dozen of those, just in case he ran out of the first batch. The clerk took his MasterCard without question, leaving Ransom feeling good about the trust of small towns.

He was passing the front of a small, brick-fronted antique shop—toying with the odd numbness that had dropped like cold sand into the soles of his feet—when the gleaming thing caught him from its place in the store's window. It was a dusty glass ornament, at over a foot the longest of its kind he'd ever seen. It was made of a series of globes that became smaller and smaller toward the top, finally smoothing to an elegant point.

The door swung open against a jangling bell as Ransom entered, looking around at the clutter inside—an old water-fall-style headboard, a mounted deer's head, a cathedral radio. The girl behind the counter was reading a Harlequin romance; she glanced up reluctantly.

"What's the price on the treetop ornament?" Ransom asked, motioning toward the shop's window.

Her glasses slid the length of her nose. "Whatever the tag says."

Reaching down, Ransom flipped the tag over. Five dollars. He blinked and read the price again, feeling a tingle up the sides of his neck.

"That can't be right," he said. "Do you know what you've got here?"

"Merry Christmas," she said.

"From Lauscha, Germany . . ." He picked up the ornament gently, held it. "I'd guess 1840 or 1850. Hand-blown, all from a single piece of glass."

"I wouldn't know."

"I thought I was lucky to have just a few of the glass balls from that long ago, but this . . . ." He turned the spire slowly. Each of the segments was pressed with a different reflective pattern. "It's worth a lot more."

"It sells for what the tag says. That's what they tell me. I just work here." She folded the covers of the book, keeping her thumb in place between the pages. "You want it or what?"

Ransom pulled the five ones out of his wallet, trying not to look at how little was left. But now he had something for Marla, something to show for the trip and himself. He could think of going home.

The tape recorder helped shorten the miles as he drove
north across the Iowa state line, through Ottumwa to catch
Interstate 80 into Des Moines. It excused him for talking out
loud to himself.

"Two places to check out yet. Des Moines . . . the letter
is from a Peter Troyer. Something about voices, and something about the 'magic dome.' "

Ransom reached into the glove compartment, finding the
letter. He looked toward the highway—straight and clear—
and fumbled the letter open.

I read a lot, Mr. Ransom. I like to read. Sometimes,
when I was a kid, I'd read something by Edgar Rice
Burroughs or E. E. Smith, and I could cover my eyes
and rub them real hard and I'd be there in the place I
was reading about. Did you ever do that?

Yes, Ransom thought. But a long time ago, when the *gotta*
of the time was the run of Burrough's *John Carter of Mars*
novels. Ransom had traveled and charted the surface of Mars
just as clearly as any other fourteen-year-old in his neighborhood might have known the streets of Tulsa.

I'd invent things too. I wouldn't tell anybody, but that
was how I got the farm chores done when I was a kid.
I'd go out to get the eggs and pretend they were golden,
or that the chickens were from another planet and that
they could talk to me.

Ransom couldn't help laughing. In his case the talking animal had been a cocker spaniel named Fluff, who had turned
into quite a philosopher.

Then a different thought, hard-edged, forcing its way in:
Ida Milburn and her cats.

Ransom, realizing the tape player was still on, reached over
and flipped it off. The action cleared his mind, and it settled
back.

Fluff. Ransom had been five, perhaps six, years old; he'd
almost forgotten. It was all make-believe. Of course, make-
believe. But now he could hear very clearly the gruff, rasping

sound of Fluff's voice, there at his bedside, telling him, "I could sure use a little snack-o, Keith, buddy. What say?"

And hadn't the dog's jaws moved? And wasn't it the night of the full moon?

The car rattled. Ransom was on the shoulder, veering straight toward the bar ditch on this side. He whipped back onto the highway again. Trying to keep his concentration on his driving, he found himself drawn to the letter again, almost against his will.

> Our old brood mare—she was a unicorn, really, and the barn was a magical cave where she lived, with fine silver-braided halters hanging up for her. And a dragon, way in the back. Sometimes I would ride her, trying to find the dragon.

Trying to find the dragon.

Chattanooga. Hannibal. Next, Des Moines. Trying to find the dragon.

Ransom slowed to pass a black, horse-drawn buggy that rolled along the shoulder of the highway. The sight of it startled him, as if he had fallen back in time to a hundred years ago. Then he realized that this was Amish country.

He glanced at the wagon and driver as he passed, got an image of the buggy against the gray sky, farmland drawing a straight line across the horizon. Black horse with a white-starred forehead. The driver, bearded, wearing a black, flat-brimmed hat.

Ransom waved; the driver nodded in return.

What would *he* think of Peter Troyer? Ransom thought as he passed the man. Or of me? He might say that we're too wrapped up in ourselves, too wrapped up in the things of this world. We've got too much time, maybe, to worry about what's wrong with us.

He watched the Amish driver recede to a dot in his rear-view mirror, fighting a longing to stop the car. He thought of what it would be like to stop and get out. He could wait, then, right there on the highway until the buggy wheeled alongside him.

And the driver would ask him, "Are you lost?"

"I've been lost a long time, sir."

"You don't have to be."

Ransom could hear the creaking of the buggy as he lifted himself into the seat beside the black-garbed driver. Then the snap of reins and the smooth, rhythmic clopping of the horse's hooves against the pavement.

No, sir. You don't have to be.

It would all be so simple, then. The maddening swirl of contradictions, delusions, and senseless things in the world would all give way to an ascetic life, with simple pleasures and warm rewards. No collections, no obsessions—except perhaps the purest obsession of all, that of resisting the temptations of the world. Ransom figured he could do that just fine.

He came out of his reverie just in time to see himself coming up hard on the tail end of a pickup. Whipping around it, he looked again in his mirror, to see the quiet image of the Amish farmer replaced by the florid face and shaking fist of the pickup's driver.

He floored the accelerator. The air vents whistled cold air at him, and the pickup diminished to a dim green blot in the mirror.

As he drove, the thoughts of the Amish life reluctantly receding from his mind, he began wishing for some of the hills and curves that he had come to curse only a few hours ago. The flatness, the sameness of the land, seemed numbing. There was no sense of movement, despite the whining protest of the car's engine. He was pushing it too hard in an effort to feel motion.

Slowing he snapped on the recorder again.

"So . . . Des Moines tonight. Salina tomorrow. Salina . . ." Reaching over, he picked up another letter off the seat and rattled it open, reading through it again in glances traded between the highway and the crumpled piece of paper.

"Salina . . . for a visit to the inviting home of one G. Naisbitt. The letter seems to have been wadded up before he—or she—mailed it. Maybe G. Naisbitt threw it away and then had second thoughts. It says, in part, '. . . spiders in the wall. I can hear them moving all up and down, inside the walls, across the ceiling. There is a crack in the ceiling. I can't help what I do. Night of the full moon, they drop through the crack, and I watch. They are white, white like pearls. I don't dare to move. Not until morning. Then I break the webs. But they are bigger each time, and the webs are hard to break. One time, I know, I will not be able to break away, and they will have me. I think it will last for a long, long time.' ''

The tape recorder hummed. Ransom silently dropped the letter aside.

Night of the full moon. Tonight.

He thought of the first time he had read those letters, the ones from Peter Troyer and G. Naisbitt—and the others. Ida Milburn, Charles Pautz, Chester McGivern—like a trip through a carnival freak show, safe in the knowledge that all the exhibits were probably fake. And reading them again, a little less sure. And now . . .

One time, I know, I will not be able to break away.

Still, there was such a thing as delusion. Paranoia. Sickness of the mind.

Take your choice, Ransom, he thought. *Which applies to you?*

Tonight he would have proof, one way or the other. Tonight, a last chance to show that there was nothing the matter with him, nothing he couldn't control. And that was the real point in going on. To show there was nothing wrong with him that he couldn't handle; to go home clean. Wasn't it?

He could turn around right now. Of course he could. He could be well again right now. He could be *top of the line.* He could leave the collection unfinished.

Dr. Bergman will applaud you.

Hands clenching the steering wheel, Ransom tried to envision the windshield frosting to white, tried to force himself to see the glittering crystals. Nothing.

The turnoff onto the Interstate was directly ahead of him; no frost, no eyes, no monsters, just a green-and-white sign pointing the way to Des Moines.

The car tried to stall as he made the turn. Lights fluttered red on the dashboard, but then the engine caught again and he gunned onto the westbound highway.

A dead car in the middle of nowhere. *That* was something to worry about.

Not the damn moon.

Des Moines reached out a welcome of neon. The motels and restaurants along the Interstate were just beginning to turn their lights on as Ransom neared the city.

The motels promised him cable television and "continental breakfast," and the traffic was rush-hour heavy. Civilization at last.

He pulled into a gas station that looked like the real thing, with a sign out front that read, MECHANIC ON DUTY. Ransom stopped the car and went in to find a leathery-faced old-timer behind the counter.

"I'm having a little trouble with my car stalling out," he said.

The man looked up from his sandwich just long enough to assess Ransom's Datsun through the station window. "We only do American," he said.

"Oh." Ransom turned away from the man, fighting anger. There was a city map tacked to the wall above a drinking fountain, and he looked at that. It was peopled with a scattering of happy-looking little cartoon figures seeing the sights in Des Moines: running through Heritage Village at the fairgrounds, admiring the Victorian stateliness of Terrace Hill mansion (HOME OF THE GOVERNOR!), pointing excitedly toward the Iowa State Capitol. The map seemed to have everything except the street he was looking for.

"Need gas?" the man asked him.

Ransom opened the door to the station. "Naw," he said. "Your gas probably wouldn't work in a foreign car, anyway."

He got back in the Datsun and drove along the frontage road, stopping finally at a place that promised nothing but cheap gas, self-service. He filled his car and went to the bathroom, and when he came out, the girl in the pay booth told him how to find Peter Troyer's address by following I-235 into the city, close to the Capitol complex.

"You know," she said after she had finished giving him directions, "You look like . . . what's-his-name. In the movies. You're not in the movies, are you?"

She wore more makeup than was necessary for night work at a gas station, Ransom thought, but it wasn't badly applied. Her blond hair was mercilessly curled.

He passed his credit card to her. "Now and then. I always try to get an aisle seat."

"By yourself?" She looked at him the way he used to catch some of his students looking at him in class. Like Marla . . . a long time ago.

"Yeah," he said, signing the slip and pocketing his card. "Thanks." He turned to go.

"Christopher Reeve, I think. That's who."

Ransom didn't look back. But some of the road dizziness cleared from his head, and his legs seemed steadier.

His hand touched the cold of the car-door handle, but that feeling was lost suddenly to the white flash that blanked his mind. He was lost in the white, or was part of it.

The white narrowed, took shape, became the full moon that he saw rising above the silently screaming neon and platform lights of the station.

The moon filled the side window as he drove toward the center of the city. It dwarfed the light-spattered horizon. Ransom knew that the size of it must have been an illusion; it had seemed to grow, and still seemed to be growing, as it lifted higher into the night sky. But the illusion held, as always. The Devil's eye was on him.

Crossing the dark wound of the Des Moines River, he exited into an area of old two- and three-story wood frame houses. Once they must have been the pride of some grand families of Des Moines, Ransom thought. Now they were mostly converted to apartments, mailboxes clustered like clinging beetles alongside the big front doors. And looming over them all, the five floors of the chunky brick Capitol View. Peter Troyer's address.

Ransom parked on the street, wheels grinding against the curb line. He found himself thinking about the girl at the gas station. How simple it would have been, how easy; he could have taken her . . .

He slid from the car, locking the door. His head seemed to be floating, held to his shoulders only by the weight of a drumming pain.

But he would do it right this time. Introduce and explain himself, ask for an interview, bring out the tape recorder from his coat pocket, pose the kind of questions that would call for a quotable response.

That done, he would go have a decent supper and a good

night's sleep, priding himself as he slipped between the sheets on having done a good day's work, having done what he was there to do.

Taking the concrete steps in front of the old apartment house, he let himself into the yellow-lit foyer. There was a lumpy green trash bag outside one of the facing doors, a bicycle chained to the stairway banister.

He started up, bandaged right hand tingling against the worn-smooth stair railing.

. . . could have had her. Could have dropped the gas nozzle and let it run, set it off with a cigarette; could have watched the pretty curls blacken and snap, and her face, the dying amazement on her face.

Ransom steadied himself against the grime-smudged wall of the second-floor landing. The image of the burning girl dimmed from his mind, as if he never could have imagined such a thing. He wouldn't have known, could not have described, the way her face had come off in peeling layers of black, like burning tissue paper, showing bright pink underneath—he had never *seen* that happen. So why, now, did he know exactly the look of it?

He forced himself to climb the stairs. Apartment 5-C; that was Troyer's. Just take one stair at a time. Nothing hard about it, nothing wrong . . .

Third-floor landing. The air here was thick with cooking smells. Tomato sauce and garlic. From behind one of the doors came the muted sound of a television playing.

Ransom's breath was coming heavily. He stopped himself from charging the stairs, taking them two or three at a time.

Fourth floor. The landing was glazed. The stairway for the next floor started next to a frost-glimmering window that faced the Capitol.

Magic dome.

Ransom reached toward the window, forcing it open, shoving against the screen. It broke from its hinges, cracking and clattering somewhere below.

I just pushed too hard, Ransom told himself. *Nothing wrong with that. Nothing crazy. It was old. That's all.*

He looked at the Capitol dome. It caught the moonlight and shimmered there, across the river, a haloed blur of gold.

Smaller spires flanked it like helmeted guards. And there—there, at the peak of the dome, something moved.

Ransom saw it for only a moment: a dark, unfolding thing stretching outward from the golden surface. Then it vanished.

The dome seemed to flicker like the dying of a candle flame, the color turning dull. Ransom was aware, suddenly, of traffic noises.

His feet scuffed glitters of ice from the landing as he turned toward the last flight of stairs. The frozen railing burned and numbed his hand.

Fifth floor. *Top of the line.*

Ransom glanced toward the window of the top-floor landing. Lines of white crisscrossed the window glass, more and more lines by the moment, even as he watched. White, bead-like things skittered along the outside edge.

He knocked at the door of 5-C and was answered. But not at the door. The voice came from above him.

Hey-y-yy. We've been waiting.

It made itself heard over the rhythmic thud of stereo music overhead.

Waiting for you, teacher, C'mon. We can have fun, teacher.

The voice was cold satin, cold touch, cold promise. He could feel it drifting over him.

Ransom tried the door. The old brass knob hesitated, locked. He twisted his hand and the lock broke; pressed the door and the chain inside snapped in front of his face.

It was a metal chain, but it could have been anything, could have been muscle and bone. It was all the same. Nothing would have stopped him.

Ransom heard himself laughing. All *wrong*, he thought. He didn't feel like laughing. He didn't feel anything—just an emptiness and a gathering strength.

The door swung open.

A step took him into the room. No one was there.

He saw an unmade bed with a checkered quilt rumpled on top of it; a closet door, opened, showing a row of neatly hung shirts; a tiny kitchen set apart from the larger room, the sink cluttered with dishes, faucet dripping. And books, jammed and spilling over from an unpainted, pressed-wood book-shelf, scattered over the hardwood floor, piled under the bed. They were paperbacks, mostly, with covers of red and orange and silver, lined across the top of the scratchy-surfaced old bureau, dropping off the side to the sagging, overstuffed chair.

Ransom read just a few of the titles—*Dragonflight, Windhaven, The Silmarillion*—before the words faded and all the colors around him froze to white.

The full moon appeared, centered in the window across the room, a looming face that suddenly split open with the zigzag of white teeth.

And the voice again: *Hey-yy-y, teacher. Party time, teacher.* It came from the other side of the ceiling.

Ransom crossed to the window. The glass had been raised; a rush of cold wind made the blinds shudder. Outside, the Capitol dome gleamed blindingly, and he leaned toward it, into the night.

Something caught his hair then, raked the sides of his face. There were hands clutching at him, grasping at him from above. Choking sobs impaled the darkness.

He wrested sideways, looking up.

The top of the building was ten feet above him, up the moonlit surface of weathered brick. And there, at the top, something twisted and fought as it was dragged by its heels up the side of the building. Pale hands clutched the edge of the rooftop, grabbing for a hold, losing finally to whatever force lay beyond sight, beyond the wall and the night shadows.

A last pleading cry from an unseen face, and the scrabbling hands and arms were wrenched over the top.

Waiting, teacher . . .

Ransom tried to make his voice work, to call for help. But even as he tried to pull back he felt the ice-smooth motion of muscles that weren't his. He was standing on the ledge outside the window before he even knew he had moved. He watched as crystal talons found holds between the bricks, and the wall slid beneath him.

He rose and dropped like a mist onto the rooftop.

Talons, *hell*! He stretched out his hands, already a mess, now bleeding from the fingertips. The nail of his right forefinger, just above the bandage, was torn off completely.

He jerked toward the edge, looked down. The ground seemed to waver in a dizzying blur.

"Mister . . . ?" This time a different voice, one with no

magic to it. Just a voice in the darkness. "Help me," it said. "*Please*, mister."

Ransom moved toward the sound, his feet crunching against the graveled rooftop. The surface was studded with pipes and wind vents, TV antennas.

A shape rose in front of him. Ransom gasped, arms raised in a shielding motion, even as the form took shape and Ransom saw he had nothing to fear.

It was just a kid. Or more than a kid, but not by much. Maybe a year out of high school, with a heaviness that gave him a vaguely unhealthy look, as if he had waited too long to shed his baby fat and now it was going to be with him for good. White, thick hands protruded from the sleeves of a knife-edge-pressed shirt, the paisley pattern clashing wildly with the check of his slacks. Ransom's first thought was: This boy should be home, where someone could take care of him.

"Peter?" Ransom asked.

The kid's mouth hung open, his face slack. "My name," he said. "How did you know . . . ?"

"From the letter you sent me. About the moon."

"Keith . . . Ransom."

"That's right."

The kid took a step forward, hands working constantly, now interlocked, now tightened to fists. "I don't believe you," he said. The wind whipped around them. "You're another one, just another one."

"I want to help you, Peter."

"*Petey.*" The kid straightened. "Just laugh at me, why don't you? Call me Petey, little Petey. What's-wrong-with-Petey. See if I care. 'Cause I'm scared, mister, scared, but I'm through with being hurt."

Is that what you think, farm boy?

The voice came as part of the cold, slicing air. Ransom looked from side to side, then behind him. Nothing.

"You . . . *heard*," Petey said. "I thought—" A tortured smile twisted his face. "I thought . . . I was the only one."

Ransom surveyed the rooftop again. He saw the silhouette of a lawn chair, the amber glint of scattered beer bottles. There had to be some way down from the roof.

"Let's get the hell out of here," he said.

No, farm boy. Her voice cut deeper than the cold. *You don't want to leave. The party's just starting.*

Petey was turning now, awkward steps that took him in circles, as if he were "it" in blindman's buff. "You stay away from me," he shouted, his voice growing louder as he turned. "*Hear* me? *Stay away!*"

Then go, farm boy. But I might bring you back. Think about that. If you go, then I might bring you back—and you know what? I might drop you the next time. I might let you fall all the way to the pavement.

Music wavered all around them, the bass striking the rooftop like the beat of some huge, awful heart, pounding from the center of the building. The kid still whirled in circles—then, suddenly, his head snapped backward and his feet rose from the surface, and he was whirling, faster and faster, in time to the beat.

Ransom saw frost glaze the roof in a shimmering wave, until it was white, all white, catching the moonlight and blanking the stars and the lights of the city. Petey's figure danced in the midst of it, caught in the arms of a ghost-white figure. She was spinning him, moon-white hair streaming in glittering strands behind her. She was laughing in chimes that repeated and doubled, becoming a chorus, blending with the music, surrounding everything.

Ransom heard her. *Fly, Petey, fly,* she said, through smiling white teeth that never opened. The kid's eyes were rolled up so far that only the whites showed, and she whirled with him down into the party.

The party. For the first time Ransom saw that there was a party going on. Young men in business suits, ties loosened above their vests, sat on chromium stools at a long bar, lanterns bobbing around them. They mingled with young women in clinging dresses. A smattering of other types stood around the room and at the bar: intellectuals in blue jeans and gray sweaters or corduroy jackets over T-shirts; older women wearing strings of pearls, sitting correctly in modernistic chairs.

Ransom saw the party through a white-misted haze but in perfect detail, right down to the trays of finger sandwiches and the record spinning on the turntable under a clear plastic cover.

The people were laughing now, laughing at Petey as he danced, whispering secrets, pointing.

The room had no ceiling. Above it hung the moon, seeming to shine through the party goers—except for Petey—making them transparent. As Ransom watched, the voices and party sounds faded along with the figures themselves, and the music died as if borne away, like the sounds from a long-ago ice-cream wagon disappearing around the block.

Fly-y-y-y-y-y-y, farm boy. She floated up, still twirling the kid. Without warning she let him go.

Petey hit, slid, and rolled, tearing at the gravel of the roof, ending up with his legs thrust over the edge, kicking out into space. Clawing for a hold against the tar seams, he looked up at Ransom, his eyes begging.

Ransom wanted to go to him, help him. He tried. But even as he tried, he heard laughter bubbling deep in his throat, just as he had when he had wrenched the kid's door off below. The laughter was a living thing, issuing from his mouth, wrapping around him, rumbling into the air.

The girl smiled at Ransom then.

He let her come to him.

She was smoke and light, ice and the chill of the moon. Her face swirled and shifted. She was Marla; now Wendy. She was other, half-forgotten girls—Marilyn, Ginger, Gail, and faces with no names; she was Julie, the first one, trying on faces, slipping into bodies that weren't hers.

She offered him Wendy's breasts, lifting, cupped in her hands, laughing in a hundred different voices.

He reached toward her. His left hand, outstretched, beckoned to her, bending from the splintered wrist.

She lifted his hand to the chill of her lips. Kissed it. Guided it then down the inward curve beneath her breasts, letting it slide between her legs.

Want me, teacher?

Ransom felt his fingers thrusting. His lips moved. No sound came. But she smiled then, as if having heard him say, *I want you.*

Then have me.

His hand tightened. Lifted. Her eyes shot open wide, and she screamed from all sides of him. The air split and echoed her shrieking. He was killing her over and over.

The talons sunk deeper, clicking inside of her.

She gave him the face he remembered as Wendy's, blood spilling from her mouth as he lifted her past him, above him, until his clawed hand broke through her back.

He dropped his arm then.

She fell in a burst of white light at his feet, still screaming. Nothing left but the screams.

Ransom turned toward the kid. He had managed to pull himself back up onto the rooftop, where he stood now, at the very edge. Around him and behind him, the gold-gleam of the magic dome turned the sky to fire.

And, again, something moved on the dome.

Ransom clinched a handful of Petey's hair, forcing him back, watching his feet slap and scrape against the metaled edge of the roof. He looked past the kid's contorted face, toward the dome's peak. Black, jagged shapes rose from the gold-gleam, one shape a Phoenix from the fire.

It had burning red eyes that lifted above the dome. A huge, triangular head atop a coiling neck.

Then the wings snapped down with a sound like a whip crack, and it flew. Blacker than the sky, it rose until it was out of sight—except for the eyes. Ransom still saw the eyes, glinting the color of fury.

It glided above the roof, close enough that Ransom could see the jaws open and the teeth gleam, like a shark in the sky. Then the head of it drew back with a doubling of the long, glistening neck, and flames spurted white and red and yellow out of its mouth, spattering the rooftop with liquid fire.

"Oh, Lord," Petey said, gasping. "Oh, Lord, what have I done?"

The dragon's wings slammed the air; a concussion hit with a blast of gravel and glass.

It wheeled in the sky, balanced for a moment as if riding on top of the moon. Then the eyes flashed, the wings locked out. It dived straight at them, streamers of fire splitting around the flat snake head.

Somewhere on the ground a woman was screaming.

Fire crackled and licked at the rooftop.

Petey crouched at Ransom's side, crying. "I can't make it stop. I can't make—"

The dragon fell upon them, a roaring mass of wind and fire. The tail whipped, and the jewels embedded in the thick white underbelly were like bursts of colored flame.

It swept down, and its claws enfolded Petey.

The wings beat, sweeping a sheet of fire across the rooftop, a storm of ash and cinder. Long after the night sky had cleared, the building still seemed to shake.

It took some time for Ransom to realize that he could not breathe. The choking smoke engulfed him, even as he heard sirens in the distance. Fire crawled at his feet. His mind showed him again how it would look to burn alive.

He was not aware of when or how he had fallen, just the dull whistling of the air past him, the whipping of his clothes, the blur of brick and lighted windows, the top of his own little car on the street.

He tried to see frost. He tried to see the moon, tried to feel the awful strength of what the moon did to him, tried to feel invincible.

Nothing . . .

He thought, though, that he saw white, glittering fragments on the pavement, just as the impact shattered his legs.

CHAPTER EIGHTEEN

Ransom keyed the ignition. The engine caught and died. Ahead, he saw the flashing red lights of a fire truck rounding the corner, and a second truck behind it, sirens ripping the air.

He pumped the gas pedal, kicked the engine over again. It whined to life.

A hard, tire-burning turn took him careening away from the trucks and the Capitol View. His rearview mirror showed him the street, washed in oranges and reds, fire beating against the upper windows of the apartment building, people running, jamming, falling out the front door.

A police car wailed past him toward the fire. He saw people on the curb line, kids on bikes, old women in housecoats taking in the excitement.

He felt that they were watching *him*. And not just them, but people behind every window of the big, decaying houses that lined the street—and the buildings themselves, as if they might close in to stop him, the killer of one of their own.

Then he turned, and the sound and fury dimmed behind him. Soon he found his way back onto the Interstate, the traffic lights blurring to a kaleidoscopic spattering.

Something tightened deep inside him. Something pulled, contracted, with a grinding white pain that made him want to fold up and cry. With a superhuman effort he managed to stay on the road.

He knew what it was. He had been feeling the pain ever

since the moment when the pavement rose up to meet him. Grinding, tearing, straightening.

He was mending inside.

His legs still felt as if they were made of splintered ice, but they worked. Oh, yes. Like it or not, they worked just fine.

Ransom knew they'd been broken. *That* was no delusion, no craziness. He'd seen all too clearly the shard of white, glistening bone, jabbed through his pant leg just below the knee. And the other leg, twisted, and twisted again, beneath him, as if there were no bone at all in it.

But the moon-thing inside of him had taken care of all of that.

It left him the pain, but it mended his legs. It needed a body that worked.

Because now it *was* inside him.

Maybe it always had been—a little deeper, a little more firmly entrenched with every compulsion, every obsession, forcing him on to the next one. Until, finally, Marla. It had used her like a scalpel, cutting him wide open.

The dashboard was frozen white, and crystals of ice framed the windshield. But his hands were taking color again. The slash on his wrist was a red, bleeding line that looked good to him—like something normal, so long as he didn't think of how he had gotten it. Placing his left hand in front of his face, he tore the bandage off with his teeth. Under it, the cut places were receding, filling it with new flesh.

Soon he would be whole again.

Normal—that was the word.

The highway was a *normal* thing, taking him out of Des Moines, a very *normal* place, so long as he didn't think of how close he'd come to dropping Peter Troyer off the top of the building, so long as he didn't think of the thing from the dome swooping out of the night sky, talons grabbing—

Ransom snapped on the radio, spun the dial through crackling static.

"—on the scene. Bob, can you make any sense of what's going on down there?"

"They've called in a second alarm. They're hosing water over the neighboring building, trying to contain the fire to the Capitol View."

"Any more on those, uh, sightings?"

"At least a dozen, a dozen people here saying—*swearing*—they saw some kind of UFO just before the fire broke out. I'm still talking with . . . Just a moment, Frank."

"We've had calls to the station—"

" *Dragon?!* Wait, wait, get him back here. Frank, we've got a man here claiming what *he* saw—"

Ransom killed the radio.

The night had turned out to be wonderful, just wonderful, for the Des Moines news media, Ransom thought. They owed him one.

The pain up his spine caught him by surprise, and he screamed, veering onto the shoulder, knowing it didn't matter—that even if the car was torn apart, he would mend. From the inside.

Time and distance melted together, meaningless now, things of no shape and no substance.

He had to make a decision when he saw the sign indicating the Salina turnoff, and he did.

Screw it, he decided. Leave the spiders to the spiders.

Anyway, he didn't need to drive halfway across Kansas to look at spiders. He could look at spiders in the car.

Pretty things, really. The webs shone white as frosted crystal, forming a lacework that ran from his arms to the car seat, crisscrossing in front of him, draping over the dashboard knobs and swirling, like a small wind, to form a white nest in the seat next to him.

He didn't think they would bite, though.

Not if he was very, very still and didn't swat at them, not even at the light flicking of legs just above his right eye.

Something moved in the nest then.

It was a surprise.

He would save it for Marla. *Look, Marla. See what I brought you. Or no, no, better yet—*

Hold out your hands and shut your eyes, and I'll give you a big surprise.

Rooster always slept sitting up. Ever since the accident it had been impossible for him to sleep any other way.

He was sitting up now, but he had done no sleeping for the

past two nights. Instead he had been waiting. Watching.
Standing watch—except that he wasn't standing, knew he
could never stand again.

Not much longer, Rooster thought now, glancing toward
the window. The moonlight-laced blackness of the sky had
begun to gray at the edges. Soon the sun, and then the heavy,
unblinking yellow eye would grow lighter and lighter with
approach of day, until it was gone.

That was just fine with Rooster. Much as he hated to admit
it, that was just fine with him.

The Rider hadn't come, at least not this night. Rooster let
his hand relax around the butt of the revolver for the first
time in several hours. The grip was sticky with sweat. Rooster's head felt thick and cottony as he slowly reached for
another cigarette and lit it, never taking his eyes off the door
across the room. Ignoring the poisonous taste of the first puff,
he flicked ashes at the ashtray beside him. It already over-
flowed with the dusty remnants of two-plus packs.

He liked it this way, he thought, taking another ragged
drag. Just him. The old lady and the house mouse dreamin'
away like kids upstairs; Joseph and Randy gone, sleeping out
under some bridge in town now that better weather was here.
He'd told them to go—and to keep an eye out, find out what
they could. He'd take care of things here.

And he could. He could, by damn, take anything that came
up. He could outlast them all. If anything was going to get
into this sonuvabitchin' house, it'd have to come through him.

Rooster grinned. It'd come sooner or later, his chance. Just
a shot. All he wanted was a—

Something thudded against the front of the house, and the
revolver flipped up and pointed straight out in front of
Rooster, as if by its own volition, leveling just at the place a
man's heart would be. The air seemed suddenly full of tiny
electric noises.

Then nothing, and Rooster knew what had made the sound.

Placing the revolver back on his lap and snuffing out his
cigarette, Rooster slowly and painfully began wheeling toward the door. When he was just in front of it, he moved
around to the side and swung the door inward, using both
hands.

He was proud of that. A couple of days ago he had first

discovered that his right hand was able to move, and he se-
cretly exercised it every day. Hell, maybe he was coming
back, after all.

The predawn air, crisp and cold, filled Rooster's lungs as
he spied the rolled-up newspaper, resting at an angle against
the base of the house, just beside the front step.

It would be a little easier to get it this morning. Not like
yesterday, when the paperboy had thrown it too hard and it
had angled off the house and landed in the yard. And he—
Rooster—who had ridden through hell and most of Texas, had
made what felt like one of the longest trips in his life, ago-
nizing and sweating down and back up one tiny step, one
bump in the doorway—just to get a stinkin' *newspaper*.

Now he maneuvered his wheelchair over the doorsill,
reached stiffly down with his left arm, fingers groping for the
paper. The halo brace sent evenly measured waves of pain
through his skull and down his back as he grabbed the paper,
placed it on his lap. He closed his eyes until the pain sub-
sided, and then wheeled backward into the warmth of the
house.

There was nothing on the front page that looked like the
Rider's idea of fun, nothing on the page that followed—
nobody wasted on the road, no little out-of-the-way towns
torn apart. Zilch. Like the day before.

Rooster kept scanning. It *had* to be there—at least it did if
he had things figured right, if there *was* some connection
between the prof, Ransom, and the Moon Rider. The way
Rooster saw it, the Moon Rider had come looking for Ransom, and maybe killed the college kid by mistake. Or just to
leave a calling card, a little attention getter. But then the
storm had hit, and even the Devil had to dig in. Or get the
hell out.

The pages rattled, grocery ads and the television schedule.

Maybe it was wrong, all wrong, to think the Moon Goon
followed any kind of pattern. Maybe it was like trying to
make sense of what some wild animal did. But Rooster
couldn't go with that. He couldn't accept that he'd lost the
damn ghost again. No, what made sense was that the Rider
had cut out ahead of the storm and gone. South, probably.
And that he'd be coming back.

Gone . . .

He flipped the city-state page, and his eyes locked on a one-column story at the bottom of page three, section B. It may have been just a throwaway, words to fill a hole, but every word tightened his gut one more turn.

Rose Bluff, LA—State authorities are continuing to beat the countryside here in search of the "monster" claimed responsible for the killings of a rural family west of Rose Bluff.

Grady Landers, his wife, and two children were found killed and dismembered. Their bodies were discovered by a neighbor, who told police that he heard the family screaming from a quarter of a mile away, ran to investigate and arrived only in time to witness a "black thing" escape into the woods nearby.

The neighbor, not identified, told police the "monster" turned and "roared" at him, before it disappeared into the night.

Sergeant J. T. Hammer, in charge of the investigation, refused to speculate . . .

Rooster caught himself laughing. Gone . . . to Rose Bluff, Louisiana. And coming back.

He didn't know much about newspapers, but he knew the *Tulsa World* had blown it on this one. Somebody had glanced at the thing just enough to catch the nameless neighbor babbling about a monster, had ripped it off and slapped on a headline, never guessing that this particular bit of news had a local angle. Or would, before long.

He felt suddenly good. The friggin' house was safe for another day. He'd done *his* job while the rest of them had slept—even convincing mama Freedom to shack it out upstairs instead of curling up like a puppy at his feet, so he could watch in secret silence, watch for trouble. And he'd been right. There was trouble to watch for, but now it was close to daylight and he could let go a little.

Rooster folded the paper in his lap, open to the comics. His nerves had been stretched catgut-tight through the night. Now, they were loosening, making him suddenly sleepy, and he had to concentrate heavily just to focus on his favorite strip. It was *Calvin and Hobbes*. Rooster liked to imagine having a tiger for a playmate, although the tiger he imagined had longer teeth than Hobbes— *much* longer teeth.

And the tiger had flowing muscles that rippled beneath the sheen of its striped coat, and it moved the effortless way Rooster had been able to move . . . before . . .

The sound of a motor broke into his thoughts.

Quickly Rooster dropped the paper, fingers locking again around the revolver. He glanced out the window, saw the tentative first rays of the sun spreading whitely out into the sky.

The engine drummed directly outside now, but it was a puny sound. Couldn't be the Rider. But then, who— Ransom?

Well, now. Wouldn't it be a kick to come face-to-face with the prof again? Rooster thought. He kind of liked Ransom. Didn't trust him—hell, even the man's own wife didn't trust him. But Ransom thought he had some kind of answer going, and he was smart. And he *had* listened.

The doorknob rattled. Rooster held the gun between his legs, leaning tensely forward.

The door opened.

The first thing Rooster saw was glowing eyes, filmy and red. He'd seen eyes like that before, would see them forever in his nightmares, and the revolver swung upward. Rooster had almost squeezed off a round before he took notice of the rest of the body—stooped, haggard, clothes rumpled and bloodstained—and the face.

The prof.

He stood in the doorway facing Rooster, eyes flickering wildly, hands cupped around something that glistened. He seemed not to care about the gun leveled at him. After a moment he spoke, and the voice was dry, cracked.

"What—" it said. "What are you doing here?"

Rooster kept him covered. The dude didn't look like he had the last time they'd met, that was for sure. Crazy. Freaked.

Ransom took a step forward. "I said, *what are you doing here?*"

"Take it easy, my man." Rooster held eye contact, even though Ransom's eyes unsettled him. Rider's eyes. He spoke

softly. "I been watchin' the house while you were off doin'
. . . whatever."

The trembling began in Ransom's face, spread to his shoulders and down his arms. His hands, wrapped around the glittering object, shook as if palsied. "This is . . . *my house*,"
Ransom shouted in a quavering voice. A drop of saliva appeared at the corner of his mouth, trailing a line down the
side of his chin.

Suddenly Ransom crossed the room, moving faster than
should have been possible, a shifting of cold, silvery light.

And Rooster felt the same hard weight of fear and disbelief
that he had so long ago, back on the desert highway, watching
the Rider come for him, knife-smooth out of the shadows and
moonlight.

It wasn't going to happen again. The .357 would make sure
of that. The bullets were hollow-point this time, maybe not
the silver kind that would put down a werewolf but magic all
the same. There was a little trick they did called "hydrostatic
shock"—hit a man almost anywhere and the impact would
jolt a wave of blood into his heart so hard that the heart would
tell him *So long, sucker,* and just blow to pieces.

That was what he'd heard, anyway.

"Where's my wife?" Ransom stepped forward—too close
now—gritting his teeth like a wounded dog.

Rooster knew he had to stop him. The man was *gone*. Stark
raving. He was going to do some damage, and the hell of it
was that Rooster couldn't blame him. You don't come home
to find some braced-up freak in a wheelchair in charge of the
place, not without a few questions.

"Your wife's okay," Rooster said. "And you'd better just
back it off a minute, prof."

Ransom leaned forward, his whole body shaking now, his
face level with Rooster's. Rooster held the revolver steady.
Ransom hadn't seemed even to notice it.

"Pull the trigger," Ransom said, his voice an oily whisper.
"You won't *believe* what happens next."

"Don't try me, man."

He leaned even closer to Rooster, eyes glimmering wildly.
"Bury me . . ." he said.

Rooster burned for the strength to throw one good punch,
to put the bastard down with a broken jaw. But he didn't have

that. All he had was a choice: He could let one more crazy break up what was left of him, or he could let the gun change the color scheme of the walls and ceiling.

"Bury me . . ." Ransom's voice was singsong now, a dead chant. "Bury me . . . I'll show you a secret . . . bury me." And now his mouth was over the end of the gun, cold white teeth against the blue steel, grinning at Rooster, daring him.

He flushed with rage. It was coming fast. It was all coming down right now, and in another second he'd have to squeeze the trigger and blow away this lunatic, and the hell with whose house it was. He flashed on the idea of *getting out* of this place, wondered if he could be quick enough, if the old lady could get him to the van and out of town before—

"Keith!"

Rooster jumped at the sound, watched as Ransom jumped back awkwardly, trying to straighten, as his eyes flashed away from Rooster's and up toward the stairs behind. Ransom's body got stiff, and then it was like he couldn't move anymore. He just stood there and shook, right in front of Rooster, jerking like a hanged man.

"Keith!" The voice said again, and then quick steps behind Rooster, and the girl stood beside the wheelchair.

"Marla. I—I'm home."

Holy shit, thought Rooster.

As he watched, the girl reached out as if to touch Ransom, drew back her hand.

"Are you . . . all right?" she asked.

"I brought you something, Marla," Ransom said slowly, holding out his cupped hands.

"Keith—what is it?"

Rooster turned his head painfully, trying to see what was in Keith's hands.

"It's a Christmas ornament, a beautiful old Christmas ornament." Rooster saw Ransom try to smile, but it was like a wolf skinning back its lips.

"Oh . . . Keith."

"I'm—I'm sorry about the webs, Marla. The spiders made them. I tried to brush them all away, but some of them stuck, I think. I did the best I could, though."

Rooster didn't see any webs, and he bet that the girl didn't, either, as she took the bauble from Ransom and held it up.

"Do you like it, Marla?" The voice cracked into a sob. "I got it for you . . . for us."

As Rooster watched Ransom he saw something happen in the eyes. It was like they lost their gleam and went dull all in a second, the second before the pupils rolled up and Ransom crumpled to the floor, his hand stretched toward the artificial Christmas tree in the corner of the room. Then the girl was down on her knees beside him, stroking his hair, his now slack face, bawling to beat all. In her other hand she held the ornament up as if to keep it from breaking. Rooster studied it for a moment.

He had to say something. Crying women made him uncomfortable, uneasy, like it was he who was responsible. Relaxing his grip on the revolver, he leaned over toward her as much as the brace and the chair would let him, and touched her on the shoulder with his right hand, the first time he had used it in front of anybody since the accident. He doubted that she'd notice.

She looked up, her eyes luminous with tears, her breathing ragged sobs.

Rooster nodded toward the ornament. "That'll look real nice on your tree, won't it?" he said with as much tenderness as he could muster.

CHAPTER NINETEEN

The dreams—all part of one massive, thick dream—were an ocean, and Ransom was pinned to the bottom, faceup and gasping. The colors floated black and white and red above his frost-edged vision for a day, a night, and most of another day, and when he struggled to awaken, it was as if his head were clamped in a vise, allowing no movement. Once he had perceived light around the vague edges of drawn curtains, a reality he had struggled toward, but when he had tried to get up, he had seen and felt chains locked around him, pulling him back down to the bed, to the cold ocean's bottom. They were part of the dream too. He had started to cry out for release but could not remember finishing.

When he awoke for sure, sometime in an afternoon, Marla was there beside him, sitting and watching him, and there were no chains.

"I . . . I need a shower" was the first thing he could think of to say as he struggled with his grogginess.

She nodded. "All right." Then: "How are you?"

With an effort he raised himself up. It took another, greater effort to smile. "I'm fine. And, Marla, I've got everything I need for the book now. It about . . . did me in, but that's okay. *Everything's* okay."

She grabbed him then, as if he were drowning, and began to cry against his chest. He let her cry for a long time, held her, kissed her, made love with her, and lay beside her for an even longer time, neither one of them saying much, and then he got up, took a shower, and shaved.

259

He nicked himself with the blade of his razor, half on purpose, and felt a surge of joy and relief when he saw the tiny drop of blood spread slowly over a corner of his chin.

Everything *was* okay. He grinned as he daubed a shred of tissue paper on the cut, and then he left the bathroom, went to his study, and began working on the book.

It was Robert Penn Warren, Ransom remembered, who talked about the wonderful secret of work in one of his books. "Work kills time," he had written—more eloquently, of course, but that was the gist of it, and that was the secret.

Sitting at his rolltop desk, Ransom was reminded of the wisdom of that observation. Hell, he didn't even know what day it was, what week. He was cut off, isolated from the rest of humanity, with this study his only true reality. He looked around it now, at the piles of letters, newspaper clippings, the tape player with a few tiny cassettes strewn around, the ashtray in need of emptying, and three used coffee cups next to the typewriter, their insides stained a filmy brown.

Marla was good to him. Marla understood. She brought him his lunch, and sometimes his dinner, when he didn't go downstairs to eat. When he did join the others at dinnertime, he was polite but distracted; although he listened to the conversations and made the appropriate responses, not much of him was really there. He was back in his study even when he was away from it, organizing, studying, coming up with facts, theories, mentally shuffling note cards even as he talked with Marla and the other two. Somewhere in his mind the conversations and infrequent interruptions of his work were all stored, to be played back sometime, and sometimes they *would* play back, the time sequence all jumbled. Ransom would listen to the voices then, pausing at his desk, feeling like some kind of holy man, an isolated lama stuck back in a crevasse on top of a mountain, doing his holy work.

Now Ransom looked at the portable alarm clock behind the typewriter: 8:34. Funny. He didn't know whether it was morning or evening, but it really didn't matter. All that mattered was the book.

This was one obsession that was going to pay off.

(Mental playback: Ransom at the dinner table. Marla to his right, the girl—Freedom—to his left, dressed in some of Marla's clothes. She could've passed for a coed now, if she'd wanted to. And at the other end of the table, the crippled biker, Rooster, who had almost killed him. Or wanted to. But a little explanation had taken care of that, and now the guy didn't seem so sullen. Almost a nice fellow, all things considered. Talked to Ransom about collecting Daredevil comics as a kid. Ransom talking a little about the book but no specifics.

"It's been a good day. I keep up this pace and I'll be through the first draft in a couple of months."

Marla: "Are you finding out anything . . . new?"

God bless her; she had never asked for explanations, specifics, details of his trip, although she must have been burning to know.

"Lots of theories, Marla." Ransom, smiling, feeling himself smile. "I think it'll help us all, this book."

Glancing at Rooster, and the biker saying, "Dunno how a book'll help us with th' Rider. Not unless it's big enough to knock the sumbitch over th' head with." And laughing a little.

Marla joining in.)

Marla was good. She had gotten him his own little coffee maker for the study, after she had cashed the check.

("Sure, Marla. He's got the cash, and he wants me—us—to use it. I got a lot of my research here from him, and I'm carrying on where he left off."

"But for how much, Keith?"

"I figure a year. A living wage for a year."

"Are you sure? That's a lot—"

"Marla, listen. I told you—I'm carrying on for him. It's like he hired me or something. And he'll get a big acknowledgment in the book. He's a philanthropist, okay?"

"But a *year*?"

"I get a first draft done in two, three months. Another couple of weeks to polish, and then out it goes. Even if I find a publisher immediately, which isn't likely, it'll be several months before we see any advance. I don't know a whole hell of a lot about the publishing business, but I do know that the writer's always the last one to get paid. So, a year."

"What about Rooster and Elizabeth—Freedom? They haven't got much money, and what they do have's running out."

"Enough to feed them too." A chuckle. "We'll chalk it up to 'research expenses.' "

"You're sure?"

"Chester won't mind a bit. Now get your pretty self down to the bank and let me get back to work."

"All right, Keith."

"You're damn right, Marla." The voice warm, reassuring. "Everything is just all right.")

Marla. What more could a man ask for? In his isolation he thought about her in an idealized, abstract way, like a soldier remembering his girl back home.

She fielded all his telephone calls—he had unplugged the phone in his study—telling callers that he couldn't be disturbed, pushing notes under the study door with names and numbers so he could call back if he wanted.

So far only one call had had to be taken.

("Keith, I'm sorry. You're going to have to come to the phone."

Ransom, lost in a fog, stumbling downstairs.

"This is Lieutenant Larry Donaldson, Mr. Ransom. I heard you were back."

Ransom picturing the caller, the dry, dandruff-flecked shock of hair curled over the forehead, incongruous gold-framed glasses over piercing eyes.

"That's right, Lieutenant. I'm back and I'm very busy. I have a lot of research to compile and edit—"

"Right. I'll make it quick, Ransom. You've got your ass pulled out of the fire twice. The first time wasn't so bad—we play ball with the college as well as anyone. But you're not with the college now, I understand. And there's an unsolved murder on my books."

"I know all that. But Mr. McGivern told you where I was on the night of the . . . crime."

"Mr. McGivern said 'frog,' and a lot of people around here jumped. So you've got an alibi. But I'm still investigating the killing."

"Okay."

"Your wife told me she heard a noise outside your house

the night of the murder. Engine noise, like a big motorcycle. I understand you've got a couple of biker types staying with you.''

"We have two houseguests, yes.''

"That what you call 'em?''

"That's right, Lieutenant. One's a cripple and the other's a young lady, and neither of them had anything to do with the killing.''

"Maybe I ought to just take myself off the case and let you handle it, Ransom. Might save the state a couple of bucks.''

"Is there a point to this conversation, Lieutenant?''

"Yeah. Make sure your 'houseguests' stick around your house, and don't be taking any long outings yourself. We're watching you, and we're watching those other bikers that're out sleeping under the bridge. We may all get together for a little chat real soon.''

"Anytime, Lieutenant. Good-bye.''

"Stay put, Ransom.'')

Curious, now that he thought about it. As far as he knew, there hadn't been all that many phone calls, and Marla's notes indicated they had been from people he knew, nonthreatening types. He figured that Marla unplugged the downstairs phone when she went to class, but still . . .

There should have been more. It was strange that there hadn't been the wave of threatening, abusive, condemning calls he had received before, after the incident with Ben Taylor.

That was something good to think about, something for the book. Simple assault and battery had dozens of people on his butt; death, though, had rendered them silent, stilled.

There were two possible reasons. He had not been charged with any crime in Taylor's death, and maybe people bought that, figured that he was indeed not guilty.

Ransom, however, wasn't altruistic enough to believe that.

The second reason was more plausible. Maybe all the eight-ball shooters and stadium bums had figured they could match up with Ransom after the first incident, could step into Taylor's cleated shoes and give that crazy, damn pointy-headed prof a dose of the medicine he needed. But none of them wanted to be surrogates for Ben Taylor after he lay sprawled out in the snow, his last breath gone from him. None of them were ready to deal with the force that could have done *that*.

If this had been Universal Pictures' version of Eastern Europe, circa 1930s, the villagers would be under his window right now, torches raised, demanding justice and retribution. The movies, however, weren't real life, and anyway, it was fifty years later, the wedge of technology driven now between neighbors, stuck deep in the heart of all humanity. Instead of carrying torches, everyone around him was more likely to be inside watching television. And if they *were* keeping wary eyes on him, they were peering out of solitary windows afraid to get close, like animals on the outskirts of a campfire.

Then there was a third possibility. Marla could be keeping it all from him. He knew she had to be keeping the reporters away; even if they got by her, none but the most stouthearted would want to deal with the biker in the living room, crippled or not.

Marla. Marla was good to him.

(Ransom, coming downstairs for dinner, Marla on the phone.

"No, Dad—it's too late to get it annulled.")

She ran interference for him, kept him from having to deal with people while he was doing his work. He had only had to leave the house once since he'd been back, and he'd hated it, but it had to be done. That had been . . . what? A week ago, maybe.

At first he had thought about going to another library. Tulsa University's was fairly close, and there was little chance of his being recognized there. But whether because of defiance or simply a pull toward familiar surroundings, he had found himself on the third floor of the Reinholdt College library one crisp and cloudless morning, checking through their newspaper files.

Although he had mentally prepared himself in case someone recognized him, he did his best to be surreptitious, timing his trip to coincide with the middle of a morning class, when there would be fewer people walking around on campus. He went to the third floor via the stairway, which was shut off from the rest of the library proper, instead of going inside and using the elevator. Feeling that he had reached his floor undetected, and still preoccupied enough to feel a little otherworldly, he jumped a little when Wendy Layton touched him on the shoulder.

Now, lighting a cigarette, he remembered that conversation.

("I startled you, Keith. I'm sorry." A concerned look from her, as if she had awakened something better left asleep.

"It's okay. I didn't hear you come up."

An awkward silence.

"I saw you from the student union and . . . I just wondered how you were doing."

"I'm fine, Wendy. Thanks."

"I've been trying to call you almost every day. I get Marla, and she says you can't be disturbed."

"That's right. I'm working on a book."

Wendy biting her lip, looking for all the world like that woman on the roof in Des Moines, like a woman in a fantasy, a woman that couldn't hurt him now.

"You sure you're all right?"

"I'm all right. I'm just . . . sub-rosa for a while, okay?"

"Sure."

"You can do something for me."

"What?"

"Spread the word to my friends, if I've got any left around here. Tell them I'm fine, and I'm working, and I'll be back in touch after I'm finished."

"How long, Keith?"

"As long as it takes to get the job done."

"That's it?"

"That's it."

"Sure. I'll do that for you."

"Good. Thanks."

"See you, then."

"See you."

Watching her walk away, his mind already folding back, detaching. The movement of her hips less pronounced now but somehow more enticing because it seemed real. A stirring of lust; a quick, hot montage of images. Black hair fanning over tanned flesh. The face, hands, body of the girl on the roof in Des Moines. *Want me, teacher?*

Ransom turning back to the papers, smoldering pictures of Wendy crackling like cellophane in his head, fading away.)

Ransom had been lucky on that day. She had been the only one he'd seen that he knew, and he'd found what he needed and gone quickly back to his study, his cave, his womb.

As Ransom smoked his cigarette he shuffled through some scattered notes, found the photocopy of an article he had located that day, the day he had seen Wendy. It concerned a motorcycle gang that had attacked a fishing camp in Texas, on the Toledo Bend Reservoir. At least the theory was that it was a gang, although none of the men staying there had seen any more than one rider. A huge man, they said, on an equally huge bike. He had attacked at night, killing one man and landing five others in the hospital with everything from broken limbs to second-degree burns. The proprietor's description was of special interest.

> Cal Burleigh, owner of Burleigh Landing, claims he was awakened by loud roaring around midnight. When he got up to investigate, he found men running out of the blazing cabins and saw a figure on a motorcycle speeding away through the flames.
>
> "All the men were hollering," says Burleigh, "and this damn guy was laughing while he rode away. I ain't going to forget that face soon, that's for sure. All white and glowing. I mean, glowing like it was lit up inside."

Ransom lay the clipping aside. "You could even say it glowed,"—where did *that* line come from? Then he remembered: A kid's song. "Rudolph the Red-Nosed Reindeer." What a connection.

But not really so strange, after all, Ransom thought. It had to be getting near Christmas by now, and he would take a break, get out his collection of Christmas albums, and loosen up a little.

He remembered, then, the other clipping.

(Marla bringing him the letter one day, the first letter he had seen since he got back. Inside, a neatly folded clipping with a note attached. The note was written on a rich-looking sheet of paper, monogrammed in gold at the top, and read, "Thought this might be of interest to you."

The signature: McGivern.

The story:

MUSICIAN ATTACKED BY "GHOST"

Clarksville, TN—A musician, hitchhiking to Nashville last night, was attacked by a man he describes as "ghostly" and "a demon."

Ralph Jennison, a self-described gospel musician from Loogootee, Indiana, was on Interstate Highway 24 about four miles north of Clarksville when a "small, foreign car" stopped to pick him up. Jennison opened the front door of the vehicle, and then, according to the hitchhiker, a "white, icy hand" reached for him.

"I looked at the face, and the eyes were shining like the fires of hell," Jennison says. "A ghostly force came out of those eyes, pulling me toward them."

Jennison says that he began to pray then.

"I prayed loud and looked the thing straight in the eye. Then I slammed the door and took off."

Jennison, who spent the rest of the night in a pasture outside Clarksville, notified police earlier today of his encounter. A search failed to turn up either the vehicle or its driver. Authorities believe that what Jennison saw was an hallucination, possibly caused by light from the bright, full moon on that night.

But Ralph Jennison has other ideas.

"I think the Devil is trying to keep me from recording my music," he says. "It tells the good news of Jesus Christ, and Satan doesn't want that to get out. I believe he sent one of his demons to try to stop me from getting to Nashville."

Jennison denies that the alleged experience is a publicity move to call attention to his songs, none of which has been recorded as yet.)

Ransom closed his eyes, trying to remember what had happened that night between Chattanooga and Paducah, Kentucky, just as he had tried to remember scores of times before. If he tried very hard, he could conjure up a wavering clot of lights and buildings that must have been Nashville. After that, nothing.

And that was as far as he ever got when he tried to recall that night. There was also another night to account for—the night in Hannibal, Missouri, although he was fairly sure all he had done *that* night was stay in his motel room and tear things apart.

(The registered package arriving, and Ransom opening it to find his watch inside, wrapped in a bill for damages. Return address: The Tom 'n' Huck Inn in Hannibal.)

He turned his attention back to the book. The tapes were transcribed and collated with the rest of his notes, and *Full Moon* was definitely beginning to emerge. The scientific theories in appendices, case histories in the main body, all woven together with a first-person narrative line. It was a matter of putting it down on paper now, of placement, of getting the right stories in just the right places, of making *Full Moon* one of those rare books that would be of interest to scholars as well as thrill seekers.

If, indeed, it would end up being called *Full Moon*.

He looked at another sheaf of notes in the stack he had mentally labeled "Theories." That bunch outlined, among other ideas, David Holstrom's notion concerning the pull of the moon, how it was getting stronger and affecting the weather, along with his comment—as well as Ransom could remember—about the moon being "the Devil's eye."

He'd have to check further with Holstrom, but for now the man might have given him an even better title than *Full Moon*.

The Devil's Eye. The gospel singer had said as much about what *he* had seen, and Holstrom gave it credence. There were even literary allusions to explore. Ransom knew that would be a pretty sensationalistic title, especially if he wanted to appeal to the academic crowd, too, but he thought he'd be able to take care of that with a colon and a subtitle.

The Devil's Eye: Studies in Aberrant Behavior Under the Full Moon.

That would do it.

Ransom pushed himself away from the desk, lighting another cigarette. Whenever his mind wandered away from the book for too long, he sometimes found his attention turning inward, and he would begin to wonder what would happen to him under the next full moon. He told himself at these times that he would, could, overcome its influence, because the book was more important. The book had to be finished, and he wasn't going to let *anything* stop that.

But in case the worst happened . . .

He reached in a desk drawer, picked out an envelope marked "To Be Opened in the Event of My Death," and read it for the dozenth time.

The note said:

> Because of the effect the moon has exerted on my be-havior, I have found it necessary to take my own life, so that others will be spared pain and, perhaps, death.
>
> I hereby leave all my worldly possessions to my wife, Marla, with the stipulation that she sell them and use the money to complete her education. I also ask that she donate a part of the proceeds to help advance research into "moon madness," as she sees fit, so that future victims of this strange, and so far inexplicable, malady may not end up as I have.
>
> Keith Ransom

He felt good every time he read that note. It reminded him that even if the very worst happened, the book would go on, and he would be responsible. And he would be vindicated with Marla's father—in a way it pleased him to think of the man looking on with shock as Marla showed him what kind of money the comic books and toy trains and autographed pictures brought.

The worst was not so bad, after all, Ransom thought. And he was prepared, now, and had prepared things for Marla.

He put the note back in the envelope and placed the envelope on top of the vintage World War I Stevens pistol, that lay in his top desk drawer. It was a beautiful thing, a collector's item, and although it was only a single-shot .22 caliber, Ransom was certain it could do the job.

For now he had his own job to do, and after looking at the pistol for a moment he closed the drawer on it and went back to work.

"Keith?"

The voice at the door was soft, and it said his name a second time before Ransom was pulled from his thoughts. He had been thinking about Peter Troyer, and how his name had not shown up in the list of dead or injured in the recent Des Moines fire. And why not . . . ?

"Yeah," Ransom said. "What's up?"

Marla came through the door wearing an old work shirt and jeans and smelling freshly scrubbed and powdered. She kissed him on the cheek. "You were up before the chickens again this morning," she said. "Or did you ever even come to bed?"

Ransom had to think a moment. "Uh-huh," he said. "I went to bed awfully late, though, I think. I'll be able to start the first draft just as soon as I figure out where to put a couple of things. I'm going to have to go back to the library and do a little research, but I think I can go ahead and fire up the old Olivetti this afternoon."

"No," Marla said.

"Pardon?"

She made her voice light. "I said no, Keith. Don't you remember promising two nights ago?"

He didn't remember. "Promising what?"

"To take off for a couple of days on Christmas Eve."

"Oh, sure. Sure. I said that and I meant it. And I will. But right now—"

"My dear, foggy husband, it *is* Christmas Eve."

"Okay," Ransom said. "I get it."

"Two days," she continued. "That's all I'm asking for. One day for us, and one day to go see my dad." When he started to balk, she said, "You know the only way I've kept him out of our faces is by promising that we'd go see him on Christmas Day. You haven't forgotten *that* too?"

"No, of course not," he lied.

"I've taken care of all the gifts and stuff. All you have to do is be there. And listen, Keith . . ." She lowered her voice. "I've asked Rooster and Elizabeth to go get their two friends who are out there under the bridge and bring them in for Christmas Eve. I mean, it's not right for people to be out in the cold on Christmas, I don't care *who* they are. They need to be in where it's warm, where there's music and food and good cheer."

"I'm convinced, Marla."

"Great."

He got to his feet, and they embraced. Brought back to reality in this way, he felt a warm rush of emotion, as if he had just reentered the slipstream of human life and found it good. Still hugging Marla, he said, "We can have a real old-fashioned Hell's Angels Christmas. Just like at Grandma's. Stringing together beer cans, hanging chains around the—"

"Keith!"

"Sorry." He drew back, looking into her eyes. "I really love you, Marla," he said, holding eye contact so she'd know that he meant it.

"I think you're right," she said.

"You bet. Now scram. I'll be down in a couple of hours, and we'll play enough Christmas music to glaze the eyes of Frosty the Snowman."

"If you're not out of here by noon, I'm coming in after you."

"Come and get me, copper," he said, and she smiled and closed the door behind her.

The moment she left, the vacuum rushed in and sealed around Ransom again. As so often happened lately, he found himself replaying conversational lines in the silence.

". . . music and food and good cheer."

"I've taken care of all the gifts and stuff."

Gifts. It was Christmas Eve and he hadn't gotten Marla a gift.

Ransom began to pace, thinking. He couldn't bring himself to deal with the insane, last-minute Christmas rush, not after so many weeks of solitude. He just wasn't ready to do that yet.

But Marla deserved something. Hell, he thought, she deserved the *best* for all she had done, and was doing, for him.

What, then? Possibilities flashed through Ransom's mind, and soon the right idea came.

He got out a blank three-by-five file card and put it in the typewriter.

THIS CARD, he typed, GOOD FOR ONE FREE TRIP—WITH HUSBAND (IF YOU SO DESIRE)—TO ANYPLACE YOU'D LIKE TO GO, FOR AS LONG AS YOU WANT TO STAY. ALL EXPENSES PAID. VALID AFTER THE BOOK IS COMPLETE.

He looked at it, then added:

P.S. TRIPS TO SEE YOUR FATHER, LIKE THE ONE TOMORROW, ARE FREE AND NOT PART OF THIS OFFER, SINCE THEY'RE NOT VERY MUCH FUN, ANYWAY.

He pulled the card from the typewriter, found an appropriately sized envelope, and put Marla's name on the front. Then he stood up, looking over the sea of note cards and yellow lined tablets and scratch paper once more, and pulled the rolltop down over them with the finality of a curtain dropping after the last act of a play.

A few minutes later Ransom came downstairs, the envelope in one hand and a dusty guitar case in the other. Marla saw him first.

"Merry Christmas, hermit," she said. And then: "Keith, you've got your guitar."

He reached the end of the stairs, hefting the case. "I bet you thought I didn't remember where it was," he said. "But I found it in my closet. I hope the strings aren't too old." He sat down and opened the case on a years-old Ovation, plunking tentatively at the strings. "Who knows. We might get some live carols going."

"You play that, man?" Rooster asked. He sat in a corner, a cigarette smoking in an ashtray on an arm of his chair, an ice chest beside him. Someone—Freedom, Ransom was sure—had washed his hair and changed his clothes, and he didn't look bad.

"Used to," Ransom answered. "How's it going?"

Rooster hefted a beer can. "Hey, it's Christmas, and we got the cheer."

Ransom said, "I'll take one of those, if you've got plenty," and set the guitar aside, going to the tree, where he placed the envelope between two limbs. The house smelled of pine needles, and turkey and dressing cooking away in the kitchen.

Marla, beside him, smiled when she saw her name on the envelope. "Keith!" she exclaimed in a happy child's voice. "What's that?"

"What does it look like?"

"A gift?"

''That's right. It's a new Mercedes, and it was hell getting it in that envelope.''

She kissed him, and Rooster said, ''Hey, man,'' from across the room. Ransom looked toward him just in time to see a beer can arc toward him. He grabbed it with one hand.

''Thanks,'' he said to Rooster.

''Your tree—the artificial one—is in the closet,'' Marla said. ''I hope you don't mind, but that tree's up all year, and I thought it'd be nice to have a real one for Christmas.''

The beer can was cold against Ransom's palm and fingers. He looked at the tree and below it, where a sheet sprinkled with pine needles and glitter was spread, colorful packages anchoring it.

Marla touched the envelope's edge. ''You didn't need to get me anything,'' she said. ''You already got me something beautiful. This.'' Her hand went to the ornament Ransom had brought back.

That trip seemed to belong to another era now. Ransom touched the ornament, too, squeezing Marla's hand. He could not conceive of that twinkling bauble as an object of terror. It was for Christmas, for celebrating, for feeling good and wishing joy for all humanity.

And damn if he didn't have that feeling now. The clouds that had ringed his mind for so many days, cutting him off from the world outside his study, were thin wisps now, allowing new thoughts and images and feelings to come in. He had stepped down those stairs into another time and place. In front of him the tree glittered, all winking lights and strings of popcorn, silvered icicles hanging between colored bulbs of all sizes and shapes. Most of those had hung on the artificial tree all year, some of them for years before that—but he had never really *seen* them before.

''We put the whole thing up after dinner last night, when you went back upstairs,'' Marla said. ''We thought it would be a nice surprise.''

There was a noise from the other side of the room, next to the stereo. Ransom looked over to see Freedom, who had come in from the kitchen holding up an old record jacket that read, *The Beach Boys' Christmas Album*. She was wearing one of Marla's blouses and a pair of pressed jeans, and Ransom thought she looked much more like an Elizabeth than a Freedom on this day.

"We found your album stash," Freedom said, carefully taking the record out of the jacket and putting it on the turntable. "Marla said you wouldn't mind."

"Of course not."

"This one okay?" she asked as the opening strains of "Little Saint Nick" filled the room.

"Fine. Just great."

And it was. Keith Ransom, the moon-mad prof of Reinholdt College, popped the top of his beer, kissed his wife, and felt the Christmas spirit settle over him like a Bethlehem snowfall.

They had sandwiches and beer and pop for lunch, while the holiday feast cooked on in the kitchen, and then Freedom left to find the other two members of the Satyrs. Rooster and Ransom sat down to watch a football game on TV, and Ransom bet a dollar on the game with Rooster just for fun, even though he didn't have the slightest clue as to which team was better. Midway through the second quarter, he slipped away and found Marla, busy in the kitchen.

Tiptoeing up to her, he waited until he was just behind her before grunting loudly, "Food! Now!"

She whirled, saw him, and relaxed, but not before hitting him a fairly good clout on the shoulder with her open palm. "You—!" she began.

"Take it easy. I give."

"Don't do that," Marla said. "You surprised the hell out of me."

"I'm full of surprises." He kissed her lightly and went to the countertop, shaking some potato chips into a bowl. "It looks to me like you're working entirely too hard for a holiday."

Marla wiped her forehead with the back of her hand. With her hair back in a ponytail, she looked like a schoolgirl. "I want everything to be nice for you—and for them. I mean, I've really gotten to kind of like those two since they've been here."

"You're not going to be disappearing into the sunset on the back of a Harley anytime soon, are you?"

"You're pretty silly, you know that?"

"I've been told."

"You know, Keith," she said, "I suppose it's a little weird for us to have motorcycle people hanging around—"

"I'd say so."

"—but they're not that much different from anyone else, really. After I got over the initial shock of having them here, I began finding out a little about them. Elizabeth and I really have a lot in common. Do you know that she spent two semesters studying art in college?"

"Doesn't seem like the kind of curriculum for a future motorcycle mama."

"No. But she doesn't have any parents still around, no one to give her money, and so she found out that the easiest way to get money to go to school was by dancing."

"I gather you don't mean ballet."

"More like freestyle."

"I'll bet."

"Anyway, she was dancing in this bar when she met Rooster. She fell for him hard—sort of like I fell for you."

Ransom nodded. "She's sure stuck on him."

"She's a strong woman. I can't say I'd want to trade life-styles, but we sure have some interesting conversations." She adjusted the flame on a stove burner and lowered her voice. "And do you know what? Rooster—he won't tell his real name—helped us decorate the tree."

"I'm amazed." Ransom chuckled. "I don't imagine he'd want that to get out."

"He did seem a little uncomfortable. Looked over his shoulder a lot."

"Anything I can do to help you?"

"Later on, maybe. Right now you can go back out there and keep our guest company. He looks a lot better than he did when you came home, doesn't he?"

"Yeah. But then again, so do I."

"I'll go along with that."

Suddenly the door chimes rang. Ransom and Marla shared a quick look, and then he went out of the kitchen, through the living room, and opened the door, aware that Rooster had his eyes fixed balefully on the doorway.

A woman stood there, and Ransom almost didn't recognize her.

Mrs. Ida Milburn had a shoe box in her hand. Behind her, in the driveway, Ransom saw the old Rambler, puffing exhaust vapor against the sunlit backdrop of the day.

"Hello, Mr. Ransom," she said.

He looked at her. She didn't seem the least bit malevolent now, just a nice old granny lady in a blue wool dress, smiling uncertainly.

"Mrs. Milburn," he said.

"I brought you by a little something for Christmas." She fumbled with the top of the box, got it open. "Homemade preserves. Do you and your wife like homemade preserves?"

"Yes. Sure we do. Won't you come in?"

"Can't, thanks. I was on my way to see my boy. Lives up at Chelsea. I figured since I was sorta passin' through, I'd stop by an' bring you these."

Ransom looked inside the box to see four squat jars, wrapped with thin red ribbons that were curlicued on top. "Thank you," he said.

"I heard . . . about your trouble. Read it in th' papers." She looked away. "I 'spect I added a little to them troubles when you came by that night a while back, an' I been feelin' awful about that."

"It's okay, Mrs. Milburn."

"Well . . . anyhow, I figured I'd bring you by these here preserves, just so's you wouldn't think I was *too* terrible."

Ransom smiled. "Thanks again. I don't think you're terrible at all." He took the box from her just as Marla appeared beside him in the doorway. Ransom looked at her to see if there was any recognition in her eyes. He didn't find any. "Marla," he said, "this is Mrs. Ida Milburn of Arcadia."

If Marla was shocked, she did a good job of covering it up, Ransom thought. "Hello, Mrs. Milburn," she said. "Are these for us?"

"Yeah. A little somethin' for Christmas."

"Well, thank you."

"Gotta be goin'. You all have a merry Christmas, now."

"Same to you," Marla said.

As Ransom watched her turn and begin walking away, something inside him made him ask the question: "Who's taking care of your cats, Mrs. Milburn?"

She looked over her shoulder at him, and for a moment, just a moment, her glasses caught the sunlight and glinted as they had at her house on that night. "Them cat's'll be all right," she said, a pale smile creasing her lips. "Them cat's'll be *fine*."

"How about that," Ransom said when she had gone.

Marla took the box of preserves from him. "A nice old lady. I really don't see why you had to bring up the cats, though."

"So you knew who she was."

"Of course I did. I'm not blind."

Not wanting to darken the mood, Ransom quickly changed the subject. "Imagine. She took the time to look up our address and come miles out of her way, just to bring us something for Christmas."

"Hey," Rooster said from across the room, "who the hell was that, anyway?"

Ransom turned to him, several glib answers forming on his tongue. But when he met Rooster's eyes, he knew he couldn't lie. The man had seen too much of what Ransom had seen to be treated in so cavalier a manner.

"Just another loony tune, Rooster," he said. "Another person who goes south when the moon is full."

Rooster grunted. "She didn't look like much of a heavyweight. What could some little old lady like *her* do?"

"It's a pretty long story."

"Hell," Rooster said, pulling another can out of his ice chest. "I've got the time and I've got the beer, as they say on TV. Besides, it's halftime."

Ransom squeezed Marla's shoulder and left her. He sat down next to Rooster.

"Well, pal," he began, "it's like this."

Ransom, exactly one dollar poorer than he had been before the conclusion of the football game, stood at the window as the van pulled up outside. Behind it, three cycles roared in slowly.

"Is that them?" Marla called from the kitchen.

"Yeah," Ransom answered. He turned to Rooster. "Looks like they picked up a stray somewhere along the line."

"Stand aside. Lemme see." Rooster studied the entourage for a moment. "I ain't never seen him before." His voice lowered. "I've seen that big mother bike, though, or its twin brother."

When Ransom glanced back at him, Rooster's hand had gone under the blanket he always kept on his lap.

Freedom came through the door first. "Brrrr," she said. "It may *look* sunny out there, but don't you believe it's warm."

"Who's the new dude?" Rooster asked, menace hovering in his voice.

"Friend of Randy and Joseph's, lover. He was living next door to 'em under the bridge." Freedom spied Marla then and went to her. "Hey, Marla, I hope you don't mind. There's this guy that's been hangin' out with Randy and Joseph and—well, he doesn't have a family or a place to go or anything, and I thought . . ."

"Sure. There's plenty."

Freedom's face creased in a smile. "Okay with you, then?" she asked Ransom. He nodded. "Good." Going to the door, she opened it a crack and shouted, "C'mon in, guys."

Ransom stood beside the door. He recognized the first two and nodded to them, returning their greetings of "Hi, Prof."

The third man was small, his sandy, oily hair combed up into a failed pompadour. The thin face was sallow, with large, luminous, almost overstated eyes that reminded Ransom of those dime-store prints of puppies and children. Although the man was dressed in de rigueur motorcycle clothes—frayed jeans, black jacket—his size and demeanor made him look like a little boy playing grown-up.

"Hello," Ransom said cordially. "I'm—"

"Oh, I know who you are, man. I wrote you once."

The reedy voice seemed unreal. Behind Ransom, Rooster fidgeted.

"Wrote me?" Ransom asked slowly.

"Yeah. You might not remember, though." He stuck out a small hand. "Thanks for asking me over to your feed. I'm Charles McNutt, and I think this is just top of the line."

CHAPTER TWENTY

And the moon rose. . . .

Moonlight chilled the bathroom window. It showed in a rectangular gap between the blue flowers of the window curtains, as if the light itself had pushed the curtains aside.

Ransom knew there was no shutting it out. A glance toward the window showed him something else that he would have known without looking—the glass was crawling with tendrils of frost.

He checked again to make sure the door was locked. Sometimes it seemed locked but still needed a sharp pull to make the lock catch. Not this time, though.

His hand withdrew, trembling, from the knob that had been clear glass only a moment before. Now it blurred to white, and a crack split the center of it with a sound like a pencil snapping.

Turning on the hot tap, he let the water run until it steamed, and then jammed in the rubber drain plug. The water stung his fingers. Warm, he thought. It's supposed to be no more than warm.

Scalding, though, seemed better.

He listened at the door. The sound of the television downstairs played dimly through the wood, difficult to separate from the churning of water as the sink ran full.

The scene downstairs was clear to him, as clear as if he were there: Marla sitting on the sofa with the big green pillow propped behind her, a bowl of popcorn on the end table. It was *Masterpiece Theatre* night, and she was ready for the evening's entertainment, but she wasn't really comfortable and wouldn't be until *he* got there.

Sorry. I'm sorry, Marla. I'm—

Water was spilling over the sink's edge, spattering onto the floor, hissing against the ice that never melted.

He shut off the tap and reached into the medicine cabinet, withdrawing the package of razor blades.

This *wasn't* the way to do it. He knew that. Wasn't the way that he wanted—

Wanted!

He *wanted* to sit there beside her. Put his arm around her. Just one more time, to put his arm around her. Why not? *Why not?*

His mind gave him the answer. It showed him what he would do to her; and then it showed him the only way out.

The way out. Oh, yes. So carefully planned. So easily planned. Write the note, load the gun, and that takes care of that. Very easily done, keeping in mind that the world is really a sane place, all in all; and, some time later, you will take out that note again, laugh at the idiocy of it, and put the gun back in the closet with the other collector's items, back behind the boxes of comic books and movie posters and baseball cards, just something more to be forgotten. And never mind the dreams. And never mind the black-outs, the dizziness, the cut on your wrist pulling open again, sometimes bleeding, sometimes looking like splintered glass. Just try to ignore it. *Believe* it away, *Professor* Ransom. Don't let it happen. Until too late, too late, so damn far too late. That's right. Wait until all you can think of is how wonderful it would be to let the *thing* in you have its way; how *fine* it would be to find that warm, soft place of her throat, just below the chin, and to tear it away, to lift her with fingers pierced into the eye sockets. . . .

Wait for *that*, Ransom. And run then. Get away from her. Run for the gun. But it *knows* about the gun. It *knows*. And it's stronger now, a living, screaming force inside you, coming at you in waves of madness.

So you do what you can. That's the hell of it. You wait for the wave that will crush you, and you do what you can.

Lock the door.

Run the water.

And the blade. The blade. At least give *it* something it wasn't expecting, and you might still—

Cut it out. Hear that? *Cut it out*. Don't tell it to quit; say, "Cut it out."

Ransom knew that he shouldn't be laughing. It was insane to be laughing now, but he was, even as he crinkled off the paper that read "Gillette."

He pressed the blade tightly between the thumb and forefinger of his right hand to keep from dropping it, resting his left hand, wrist up, on the sink's edge.

Cut toward the elbow.

Pretty soon she would call to him. Maybe he could answer, and that would buy him a few more minutes. But when he didn't answer, then she would come looking for him, to see if something was wrong.

Do it.

He pressed the blade into his arm, just hard enough to make the skin go white against the metal. Fear held the razor in place. It wasn't even trembling now; it wasn't moving at all. Fear held it, and something more.

Ransom found the word for it. Amazement.

It was amazing that he could be as calm as he was, could accept—

Suicide. There's another word. Just a word, and a word can't hurt you. Do it.

—accept the necessity of it. He could stand there, alone, with a razor to his arm, knowing full well, full damn well, what he was doing, the consequences of the act. That Marla would find what was left of him . . .

Press. Down and back. Both arms.

Amazement. To know that he was going to die. Here. Now. Right in this room. Here in the company of the old pedestal-legged bathtub, with an orange washcloth draped wetly over the faucet; the fuzzy yellow rug under his feet; the stool making the same soft gurgling sound that it always made; the copy of *Reader's Digest* on top of the tank, its pages crinkled and curled from a month of hot showers in a small room, a room now suddenly vivid to the smallest detail. The cracks in the worn-thin pink bar of soap on the sink's edge, beside his arm . . .

Cut. Make it deep.

This wasn't the way. Not like this. Not with Marla so close that he could *feel* her like she was part of the air. Marla— thinking, maybe, daring to think she could trust him again.

Now! While you can, make it now.

Should have planned. Should have left or never come back. Last chance, last move. Should have done it right. Or not at all. Such a simple thought: *I don't want to die.*

Please.

I don't want . . .

Ransom forced his head up, looked into the mirror on the medicine cabinet. Already his eyes were gone, transformed into slits of ice. They were the eyes of the moon-thing inside him.

He pressed, and the blade bit in.

Evil, twisting thing, behind those eyes. It sought him out, set him up. Came to him like a nightmare on a dark road. Played him like a lover. Got into the heart of him.

Used up and gone

But here, right here, right now— *here*, he was stopping it. A dead stop.

but the silence lives on

He drew the embedded blade up his arm. The flesh split open and blood spurted.

in the heart

The water swirled red. Ransom jammed the razor into the numbing fingers of his left hand, using it to cut open his other arm in a series of slashes.

in the heart

He saw blood running down the sides of the sink, blood on the soap, on the toothpaste.

The blood meant he'd won.

No matter the sick fear of feeling the moon-thing take hold of him again, the mindless hopes, right to the end, that maybe it would go away, that it wasn't real—that it wouldn't *let* him die.

He was killing it.

He was watching it throb from his veins.

He was top of the line.

And the moon rose. . . .

Marla sat, knees drawn up against her, feeling more alone

than she would have allowed herself to feel not so long ago. She tried not to fight with her feelings now; she just let them come and go, like wasps that might not sting—not so much, anyway—if she didn't move, just didn't move at all.

Because if she fought her feelings, they would lead to questions, and then she would have to wonder what had become of Keith.

Keith, she told herself, was in the bathroom. Feeling "a little upset." That's what he had said. No big deal; be out soon. Nothing to worry about.

If she fought, she would have to wonder if she and Keith would ever get back to a state of normalcy. If that happened, then he could be out of the room and she wouldn't think something awful had happened to him. He could be sitting beside her without making her want to keep looking at him for signs of something *wrong*. Then he could be . . .

Just Keith. Just Keith again. Without *the book*.

The book.

She'd come to think of it as an object, a physical thing in her life, even though it wasn't. *The book* was a jumble of papers and notes and other books propped open, pages underlined or folded over. *The book* was Keith staring blankly at nothing, sometimes not even pretending to listen to her. *The book* was a closed door, typewriter chattering from behind it. *The book* was a secret—a confidence shared between her husband and the old Olivetti, its voice the hard, hollow striking of metal against paper, talking to him, talking with him. It knew him much better than she did.

"When it's finished, Marla," he would say. "That's when I want you to read it. It's like . . . you wouldn't want to show me a half-finished painting, would you?" She couldn't argue with that.

The difference was, she loved to paint. But he didn't love writing *the book*, not that she could tell. It didn't make him happy; it was more like he was pulling demons out of himself and forcing them onto the paper, where they couldn't hurt him anymore. Relief, perhaps, but not happiness.

Maybe she ought to be grateful for that, anyway. Keith did seem to be loosening up as *the book* went along. He had, after all, made the trip to her father's house, taking along a gift-wrapped copy of an old *Batman* comic from his collection (appraised at $250) and a limerick he'd written about counting bed sheets. And he had promised to "redeem" the Christmas coupon when she handed it back to him, even though she had scratched out the part that read, "valid after the book is complete."

On the back of the card she had written: "I hereby redeem this coupon for one free trip to the living room, with husband, to watch television—or whatever—all night long. All night long, especially in case of whatever."

That was the deal. That was what she wanted. But now he was gone again.

Maybe he was using the excuse of feeling "a little upset" to sneak back into the room upstairs and deal with *the book* again. If that was the case, she would feel hurt, angry, betrayed—but not surprised.

At first she had wanted to help him with it, or at least encourage him to keep going. (As if it made any difference whether she helped him or not; he *was* going to write the damn thing, and she knew him well enough to know that no one would be able to stop him, anyway.) It was an apology for Keith. Something for him to do, something for her to say. *Keith is working on the book.*

But he was losing weight. He wasn't looking right.

She wondered what would happen if she gathered up *the book* and got rid of it, sometime when he wasn't there. The consequences of that action would be horrible, she knew—but increasingly she found herself thinking about just that.

She knew she couldn't, though, and that was the worst thing of all about *the book*. She was sickly afraid that it was the only thing holding him together. He was doing his best to fool her into thinking everything was all right—and it was a good act, a very good show, with just the right number of funny lines and moments of affection. As if she hadn't known all the times that he'd gotten out of bed at night to work on *the book*, when he thought she was asleep. As if she'd never wondered what happened to him while he was gone. As if she hadn't done some getting up at night herself, just to stand over him, looking at him, wishing that sleep would bring some semblance of peace to his face, his knotted-up body. Not daring to wake him, not daring, ever, to startle him, to doubt him, to question, because he was fragile; he was glass, and the smallest thing might break him.

She was losing weight, too, thanks to the miracle diet of aching, ever-present worry.

She sat on the sofa, listening for the hard, muffled clacking of the typewriter, the way it would seem to whisper to her, *He's mine now, mine now,* in mocking staccato.

All she heard was the sound of the television as a British flag unfurled in streamers of red and white on the screen in front of her. *Masterpiece Theatre.* The encore presentation of the venerable PBS drama series was coming on at the same time as one of Keith's indefensibly favorite old snoozers, *Attack of the Crab Monsters,* and he knew it, and she wanted him to make a big deal about switching over.

That was the scenario. Then they would sit beside each other, watching *Crab Monsters* probably, just long enough to collect the elusive warm feeling of being together, simply home together, nobody else there, nobody else expected.

Something else not to question: the whereabouts of Rooster and Elizabeth and the other two, Randy and Joseph. Crazy as it was, she'd almost come to think of them as family, especially since Christmas Eve.

(Strange, *strange* night, but somehow just as it should have been—except for the arrival of the little guy, McNutt. For such a seeming nonentity he had had a profound effect on both Rooster and Keith. Rooster, surlier than usual, sitting in the corner and glowering at McNutt, his hand never leaving his blanket-covered lap, the gun underneath. And Keith, trying to talk to McNutt, and McNutt not saying much of anything, just staring at Keith.

Things had been uncomfortable with him there. Then, without warning, he had just gotten up and left without a word. With Joseph calling after him, "*Ho-ho* and a friggin' *ho* to you, too, Charlie," followed by Rooster's growl: "Didn't you see his *bike*, you son of a bitch?"

It had taken them a while to calm Rooster down. Keith had seemed to help, talking to Rooster in low tones not meant for anyone else to hear. Marla never had figured out exactly what all that was about.)

Then, New Year's Day—Freedom/Elizabeth getting up to

make pancakes for everybody, slices of Spam cooked in the middle of each one. She'd called it "Hotcake Surprise."

Elizabeth, Marla thought now, was just about the only friend she had anymore, the only person she could really talk with, here in what the rest of the world—meaning Staci and Brenda—seemed to regard as the House on Haunted Hill. The sharing of chores, the little confidences shared over coffee—Elizabeth was the next best thing to having a dorm sister.

She was a preacher's kid whose folks had died young, and most of what she remembered of growing up had to do with straight-backed Southern Baptist pews and straight-backed Southern Baptist ministers in an endless parade of revivals and potluck suppers. Mostly she talked about Rooster.

("He was—I wish you could have seen him, Marla. All that red hair. He looked like a lion, and acted like one too. And he could go anywhere, and nobody would give him any trouble, just because of who he was. But he wasn't all mean, you know? I think he's got every bit the sense of good, deep down, that my father had. You just won't catch him preaching it.")

Marla remembered her saying that, and her own feeling of bewilderment at those words. She tried to equate Rooster with the word *good*, but she simply couldn't think of him in that way. Randy always looked at her like he was trying to melt off her clothes, and Joseph was a mountain of good intentions covering a core of cold, hard meanness. But Rooster—he was the scary one. Even though he had lived in her house for weeks, had talked with her, and, in his own way, shared things with her, she still couldn't look at him without feeling the skin prickle at the back of her neck.

Many times she had tried to analyze that feeling. Perhaps, she thought, it was her knowledge of how much he was hurting—so much that the air hurt around him. Yet she felt sure that he could inflict pain as well as receive it, and that frightened her. There was doom as well as rebellion in Rooster's reddened eyes, and when Marla looked at him, sometimes a line from a poem would come into her head: "Do not go gentle into that good night. . . ." It seemed to describe him, his attitude, the revolver he carried under the blanket on his lap. She had been afraid he was going to use it on Charles McNutt.

And then, his talk about the Moon Rider. Even though the talk was never meant for her, it had her almost to the point of believing in ghosts and demons sometimes.

She knew such a bad injury was bound to have done bad things to his head. She had to make allowances. . . .

It was the night of the full moon. So, *of course*, the way things were going, people would have to start acting screwy around the Ransom estate. A convenient enough reason for all of the bikers to clear out for the night, she supposed.

In time, Marla told herself, she would come to think of all the strangeness and fear of the past weeks as a bad dream, like the hazy remembrance of one of Keith's old movies that she had mostly slept through. Nothing left but a few bits of grainy black-and-white that might drift through her mind now and then.

But now the images were three-dimensional. She allowed herself to unreel them in her mind once again, as if repetition could blunt them, take away their sting. Coming home to find Keith gone . . . the death of Ben Taylor (that *sound*, that awful *sound* outside) . . . the moment that Rooster's wheelchair came rolling through her door . . .

Perhaps it all would fade someday. But of all of the scenes, she was afraid the one she would never forget was the one that had happened only an hour ago—the look on Rooster's face, just before Elizabeth had slid shut the side door of the van. Keith and her standing there, like they were bidding good-bye to some visiting uncle, and Rooster looking . . .

Haunted.

That was it. There was a time she might have laughed at the expression, but it fit. There were ghosts in his eyes— phantoms of sadness and pain that all but obscured the defiance, the rebellion.

Rooster had looked at the moon. First at the full moon, the light of it fractured by tree limbs surrounding the house. Then at Keith. And at the moon again.

He had nodded slowly. "It all goes down tonight, man. You feel it?"

Keith hadn't answered. But something in the silence had made her suddenly certain that Keith and the crippled biker understood each other in ways that would always be kept secret from her.

"Watch out for your lady," Rooster had said, as if Marla hadn't been there. "She's solid gold."

"I will."

"Well, then, my man, we'll have some mindblowers to tell, come morning. Or somebody will."

Rooster had lifted his arm then. His *right* arm, the one that wasn't supposed to work, the hand clenching in a thumbs-up gesture.

And Elizabeth, sobbing as she slid the door of the van shut, looking away from them, and the hollow clang of metal.

Marla heard that sound again now; she felt again the impact of it in the well of her stomach. Looking around, her eyes focused on the arm of the sofa, where the night's newspaper lay folded open to the comics. Juliet Jones was advising her sister, Eve, not to be hasty about marriage.

Great advice, Marla thought, and got up, scarcely noticing the rectangle of newsprint torn from the facing page.

"Keith," she called.

On the television, Alistair Cooke was talking about English music halls. He seemed immensely pleased with the subject. The show was starting.

Marla didn't want much. Just for Keith to *be there*, to make a little fuss over changing to *Attack of the Crab Monsters*. To make a little fuss over her. Just her, for a change.

And she wouldn't say a thing to him about how much she wanted out of this house, how desperately much she wanted to sell it, *burn* it, to get out and go away and start over. Later for all of that. Tonight . . .

"Keith?"

She started up the stairway.

I love you, Keith. I wish I didn't.

At the landing, she heard water dripping from behind the closed bathroom door.

"Keith? You okay?"

No answer. She pressed her ear to the door, feeling the crawling of fear like a cold, slimy thing, trying to take hold of her, trying to make her think, *No, of course he's not okay. He'll* never *be okay.*

You saw *him, didn't you? The way his eyes had gone blank like ice—just for a second, but you saw it, you didn't imagine it. Something changed deep inside him, like that night on the roadside. You didn't imagine it* then, *either. Something got him. Something evil and strong, and you know it.*

She told herself she didn't know any such thing. She knew the show was starting, and Keith was going to miss it, and they were going to lose the best chance for a good night together in what seemed like a hundred years.

"Keith!" She rapped at the door, then tried the knob. Locked.

Looking down, she saw water pooling at her feet from under the edge of the door.

The water was tinged red.

And she was screaming now. She was throwing herself against the door, and the old wood was cracking. She was wrenching at the knob, her fingers slipping and tightening, clawing for a hold against the glass that felt so cold, so bitterly cold. And something in the lock broke loose.

The door slammed open.

Freedom did just what he told her. She drove to the end of the block, just around the corner from the Ransom place, parked the van, and killed the engine.

Right up until the motor died, Rooster had been afraid she was going to play mama on him—going to drive him away to the hospital, like she was always talking about doing, or just away, someplace safe, and he couldn't have done a damn thing about it.

But she did what he told her. Maybe she knew that to treat him like anything less than a man would have ruined what was left of him. Or maybe she never had thought of it that way at all; maybe she just never thought she had a choice.

Rooster realized suddenly that he'd never questioned or understood (or cared?) about her. He was John Wayne of the Satyrs, and it was a given that he should have a full-time lady; no shortage of applicants for *that* position. Could it be that he'd chosen her only because she looked the part: slender and blond and eyes like clear blue marbles and pointed breasts of exactly the right size to fit the cup of his hand. Maybe so. Maybe it was nothing but that.

But then, why was *she* still with *him*? Why was she ever there at all?

He jammed shut his eyes a moment to blank out the weight

of too many uncertainties, doubts that had swarmed in from nowhere on him. As his mind cleared, he felt the one certainty he couldn't shake. He was going to miss her. All to hell, he was going to miss her.

She sat now, facing ahead, lost in thoughts of her own, and he wished he could talk to her. They never had talked much, though, and talking might make it worse.

The van was parked under a streetlight that spilled a blue light through the windshield, making a silhouette of her, hazy blue on the edges. The street beyond was dark and glistening wet, cleared of snow, although there were still slushy mounds along the curb line. The sky was a piercing, vivid black, with the full moon like a circle of burning white neon.

Rooster thought of Charmaine Chambers, his brother Tony's girlfriend for a while. She belonged to a prayer group (which pretty much spelled the end of going with Tony) that would meet every night of the full moon to pray for peace. They believed that a prayer had more wallop under the full moon, for all sorts of cosmic-sounding reasons, and he hoped they were right. Rooster knew what he was going to pray for that night, even though it wasn't peace.

He fumbled in his shirt pocket for the clipping he'd torn out of the morning's *World*:

> Muskogee, OK—The death of an Illinois man whose car swerved off the Muskogee Turnpike into a concrete bridge abutment shortly after midnight this morning is being investigated as a "possible homicide."
>
> State police said William Freesboro, 57, of Decatur, Illinois, told them he was forced off the eastbound highway by a motorcyclist. The cyclist overtook him, then turned and came directly at him, he said. Police reported Freesboro died less than an hour later of massive internal injuries.
>
> A search is on for the . . .

Eastbound. That was the big word, the word Rooster was looking for. Eastbound. Headed for Tulsa, *back* to Tulsa.

There was some deep connection between Ransom and the Moon Rider that Rooster knew he might never get straight,

except that they both went psycho on nights of the full moon.
They both—
   Try it. See how it sounds.
   They weren't human.
   The difference was, Ransom was trying to fight it. Rooster
could see that just as surely as he knew the Moon Goon *loved*
whatever change it was that the moon worked on him.

   Tonight Rooster had seen the prof's eyes go moon-blank,
flickering to dead a couple of times—but he'd also seen Ransom call up some strength to fight the thing off. He'd seen
the pain-sweat beads on Ransom's temples. And Ransom, his
head rolling, chin grinding against his chest. Like a spasm,
and so fast that maybe nobody else even noticed.

   Like nobody else knew about Ransom coming home that
night, eyes lit with moonfire, almost as bad as the Rider.

   Rooster was betting the prof could hold out. He was betting
the life of Marla Ransom, among others.

   Wadding the clipping into a tight ball, he dropped it, wishing for Randy and Joseph to show up. He didn't want to think
anymore, he just wanted to wait—and listen. Still, there was
one more question that wouldn't let go of him.

   What about that little shrimp-ass, McNutt?

   McNutt had the Moon Rider's machine. Rooster was sure
of it. There couldn't be two like that—Harley, but custom-
rebuilt, with a back tire that looked like it came off an airplane. And the engine sound; it was more like an animal's
scream.

   Take your choice, Rooster thought: He found it. Bought it.
Stole it (like hell).

   Or . . . McNutt was like Ransom. The moon made him
change, turned him psycho—and worse.

   And that's why the little piss-ant had shown up on Christmas Eve, Rooster thought. It was like saying, "Look at me,
crip. I did that to you. Killed your friends, too. And you
can't do a damn thing about it. You don't drop the hammer
on some poor little wimp under the twinkle lights. Right,
crip?"

   Rooster knew that he sure as hell would, given the chance
again. He could be wild-hair wrong about Charles McNutt
and still not mind pulling the trigger.

   All he knew for sure was that Randy and Joseph had gone

out looking for McNutt afterward and found nothing. He'd been gone, like a ghost.

What Rooster had figured was only a guess, but he seemed to be on a roll with guesses. He figured McNutt *was* the Moon Rider. And now the Rider was coming for Ransom.

Why? He could more than guess at that one: Survival of the strongest. The Rider might have thought it was a joke, a real elbow jabber, to have the ragtag leftovers of the Satyrs barking after him, but it was *Ransom* he wanted. The old challenge, top dog, fastest gun in the West.

Only Rooster was taking first claim on the Moon Goon.

His mind flashed to Randy and Joseph. They should have been with him by now—hell, they should have been with him and *ready*. Unless they'd hit trouble, and the only kind of trouble that would have stopped them was . . . the kind that had stopped Tony. And Busted Tom, Stoney, Shovelhead, Slug. That kind.

The Rider.

The sound of the engine kicking on startled him, and he lurched forward, as if to yank Freedom aside from the wheel. The brace sent a rock of pain down his spine.

She turned, smiling a hospital smile. "Just thought we should have some heat in here," she said.

"Yeah. Okay."

She didn't know what he was planning. Nobody did, except Randy and Joseph. He was counting on them to get her out of the way, but it wouldn't be easy.

Rooster thought of himself telling the prof, "We'll have some mindblowers to tell, come morning." As if there was going to be another morning for him to talk to Ransom.

But if there was—and he let himself trip out on the thought of it—if there was, what he would do would be this: He'd go back into the stinking hospital, and they'd make him right, no matter how long it took. He'd walk out of the place. And Freedom would be there with him. And they would go *home*, a place that looked a lot like Ransom's house in his thoughts, not so cluttered up with junk, maybe, but a real house, because it wouldn't be half bad to have a real house. And he would tell her—

"I love you, lady."

She turned toward him, her face showing sudden, almost

unbearable love in return, and it was only then that Rooster knew the words had come out of him, right out loud.

"I always thought so," she said.

She came to him there in the van, kneeling beside him, reaching to touch his face. He smiled, and her fingers played then along his lips, as if to trace and remember the moment.

Leaning toward him, she kissed him, a long kiss with anything but pity in it. Rooster felt like they were inventing a new kind of kiss, one that could have lasted forever. ·

"I think we just broke some kind of law," he said.

"Let's break it again."

The rush of her breath *touched* him. It was like everything else that he'd ever done was a waste and a joke, like he didn't need muscle and machine to hold his own, just the warmth of her breath and the *feel* of her next to him. Sappy, man, he thought. Break out the roses. But it was true.

He thought of her . . . at Christmas, the colored lights, red and gold, blue and glitter . . .

Rooster almost didn't hear the bikes come rumbling up. He almost didn't care.

But when the front door of the van clicked open, Rooster's hand was on the revolver.

Joseph's head thrust into the doorway. "We got it all," he said.

Rooster took a deep breath that hurt. He told Freedom, almost in a whisper, "Go with Joseph."

"Go where?"

"Just do it. Now."

"Bullshit!" No more cuddle-kitten. Rooster felt proud of her, but he couldn't let it show. "You think I don't know what tonight *is*?" she said. "You think I'm going to leave you?" Her hands fluttered, then balled to tiny, hard fists as she stood looking down on him.

"Don't even ask it," she finished.

Rooster nodded to Joseph.

Joseph hoisted his bulk through the doorway, making the van list sideways to the sound of rattling beer cans. Freedom turned, just in time to be caught on the jaw by a quick, short, almost silly-looking jab. There was nothing funny about the crack that went with it. She spun and fell at Rooster's feet as Joseph stood above her, his arm still outstretched. He looked half guilty and half pleased, like a kid caught breaking a church window.

"Get her out of here," Rooster said. "And tell Randy to keep his hands off her."

Joseph grunted, bending the van's seat backward as he reached to catch her by one arm. He pulled her up, grabbing her at the waist, and lifted her over the seat and out the door. The van rocked again, and a cold wind came to take away even the shampooed scent of her hair.

The last Rooster saw, Freedom's mouth was open and frothy with blood, and she looked like a baby in Joseph's arms. He was carrying her, cradling her, as he crossed in front of the van, taking her into the shelter of a wooded yard across the street. He'd even thought to bring along a blanket.

Not exactly the usual goings-on for a nice, quiet, keep-up-the-lawn kind of neighborhood, Rooster thought. He had wanted the van and the bikers to be seen around until people quit gawking at them just for being there, but he knew one of the neighbors was bound to call the cops on them before long, anyway. That would screw everything up, but it couldn't be helped. All he could do was hope—

"Get on with it," Rooster yelled. His voice made hollow echoes.

Randy clambered in then, bringing the gas can and a bucket. The bucket was shiny-new, straight from True Value.

"I don't like this, man," Randy said.

"It's not your party."

Randy tried to lock eyes with him and couldn't. He went to work, doing what Rooster told him.

Then he asked, "What now?"

"There's a bottle of Jack Daniel's in here someplace. Get that for me, and some good sound on the radio. And split, brother. Be ready."

Randy clanked and rattled around in the back of the van. He came back, finally, with the bottle and unscrewed the cap.

"Have one yourself," Rooster said.

Randy turned up the bottle. Amber drops beaded his bramble of a beard. "Had some mean times," he said, handing over the Black Jack.

"Gonna have some meaner ones," Rooster said, and tipped it back. "Here's to those."

Randy backed toward the door. "It won't be for nothing," he said. "Promise you that."

Rooster grinned. "You forgot the music, you dumb fugger."

Randy pulled at the droop of his mustache, teeth showing as if in response to a bad joke. He snapped on the van's radio, caught Lynyrd Skynyrd in the middle of "Free Bird."

"See you, man," Rooster said, and then he was alone, just him and the radio and the bottle between his legs.

So many ways he could be wrong.

He could be parked on the wrong end of the block. He didn't think so, because this end was closest to the Interstate, and the other way led into a rambling puzzle of residential curves. But he could be wrong. In which case he would be hearing the gut-wham of Joseph's shotgun from down the street.

The music wasn't such a great idea, either. Coupled with the rattling of the van's engine—too much noise. Cold and quiet; should've had it cold and quiet. He didn't think he could move enough to reach the dashboard.

Some hero. Couldn't even kill the music.

And then, even if the Rider showed, he might not give a shit about the van, might not even see it, might just wheel on past.

Rooster didn't think so. But he could be wrong. All he could do now was wait.

He'd been looking forward to this part of it—the wait. Somehow he'd been expecting all sorts of answers to come to him there, alone and waiting. Like his mind should have known the clock was running, should have sharpened up before the buzzer sounded and time ran out.

Now it was AC/DC on the radio, the beat of the music sending sharp, tinny vibrations through the van. "We sa-*lute* you."

No answers to Ransom. To Freedom.

"We sa-*lute* you."

No answers to that big, round, yellow-white monster in the night sky.

Rooster joined the chorus the next time around, his voice rasping as he lifted the bottle of Black Jack, his eyes rolling upward toward the place overhead where he thought the moon would be—hell, he *knew* where it was. He could *feel* its cold breath.

"To you," he said. "Damn you," and he drank.

The song cut off. He could hear the liquor swishing in his mouth. Could hear—

The roar of a bike.

It was a thundering sound, swelling and trailing away but coming back again—louder. And louder still.

Rooster dropped the bottle. His hand found the revolver jammed between his leg and the chair, then it slapped at his shirt pocket, feeling for the cigarettes and matches, as if some kind of magic might have stolen things away from him.

And now, down the street, he saw the headlight coming toward him. A blind white eye, never wavering, coming straight on. Just like before.

Dead voices came to him, out of the night air of the desert. *That* night.

Slug: "What's wrong with 'im, man?"

Busted Tom: "Rooster, maybe we got the wrong man here. You think of that? Rooster?"

And his own voice, but so different then, so very different, so god-awful sure of himself: "The son of a bitch could be the devil for all I care. . . ."

Now he cared a lot.

Tony, why'd you have to get me into this? he thought. *Are you watching, brother? Are you with me?*

No, it wasn't a great night for answers.

The light came straight on, closer and brighter. Rooster tried to see through the glare, his eyes burning. Then, suddenly, the light swerved, cutting toward the curb line in front of him, and the windshield flashed blinding white. Outside, a motor drummed at idle, more machine than should have been possible. The van shook in time with the noise. Behind the engine's scream there was something else. Something like breathing.

The motor cut off. Silence fell, a silence made of metal.

Rooster supposed the radio was playing, but he could no longer hear it.

What he heard was the crunch of heavy boots against the street paving. Heard—

The click of the door.

It was all he could do to leave the gun alone.

The door wrenched open, and Rooster thought madly of Freedom tying her orange-and-white tube top onto the bars of his bike, only this time he didn't have any good-luck charms going for him.

And the Rider was there.

He was a black-leathered arm reaching in, black glove on the swivel seat nearest the door. The arm tightened, pulled, and the seat gave way with a whining and shearing of bolts. The van seesawed, throwing Rooster from side to side in the wheelchair. Bursts of pure silver pain sparked at the base of his neck.

The bucket slid and sloshed. Out of reach! he thought through the pain, but the van moved again, and it thumped against the wheel. Gas fumes choked the air.

The next thing Rooster saw, the van seat was gone, and he was held transfixed by the white, shimmering eyes of the black shape that loomed in its place.

His hand closed on the revolver like it was a small, fast animal trying to get away from him. The barrel lifted, pointed, rock-heavy and shaking. He squeezed the trigger.

The shot sounded like a bomb going off. Whites and oranges flashed, and Rooster's hand felt like it had been struck with a hammer.

The Rider slammed backward, doubled over. When he fell, Rooster saw a section of the windshield blown out behind him, the remaining glass spattered with bits of pink and black, streaming blood.

So easy. So easy, after all.

Rooster felt suddenly bone-weary, as if his spine might collapse like a piece of string.

He'd taken a chance with the gun. Hadn't meant to. But then, what the hell? It'd *worked*, didn't it?

"Rooster, maybe we got the wrong man here. You think of that? Rooster?"

No way, Tom, he thought. *The right man. And we got him.* Got *the bastard. Didn't we, Stoney?*

Right, man.

He thought he could see them all—Busted Tom with that idiot grin of his, and Stoney holding out a beer to him. Slug whining in that nasty way he had. And Tony . . . Tony . . . ?

Got him. We got him, Tony. Didn't we? Didn't we, man? You saw that dude—

But then: a stirring. The rustling of leather. The thud of a knee against the floor of the van.

Rooster's heart was an engine trying to tear out of its mountings. He leveled the gun again, not sure that he still had the strength to use it.

The shape rose before him.

Again the gun slammed, echoing color and noise. But this time Rooster's aim was off. He'd meant to put another one into the chest; instead he saw fragments of leather explode in a bloody mist from the Rider's left shoulder.

The Rider stood, showing a crescent of teeth against a face that seemed made of dull white light, impossible to make out as flesh and bone.

Stronger. So much stronger now. A monster before, but now . . . now . . .

The Rider reached with liquid grace toward the glistening wreckage of his shoulder. Black-gloved fingers plunged into the hole, withdrawing a white sliver of bone.

Stronger every time the moon came full, Rooster thought.

Blackness filled in around him, and he fought it, thinking of Randy and Joseph. They'd be coming to help him now, no matter what he'd told them before. And just like him, they were going to die. Unless—

Rooster tried for a deep breath, coughed out a lungful of smoke from the .357. He rested the gun between his legs, feeling with distant amusement that the denim was warmly soaked. You bet. Some hero.

The Rider came forward, crouching under the van's roof, arms outstretched, filling the whole damn inside like a spreading shadow.

Rooster fumbled for the pack of Camels in his shirt pocket, shook a cigarette out, stuck it in his mouth.

"Smoke?" he asked, tossing the crumpled pack at the Rider's face. "Think I will."

He got hold of the matches then, using his right hand to light one.

The Rider's arm stretched out to him. Rooster felt the cold slickness of the black-leathered hand against his throat. But the hand wasn't tightening, not this time. It was lifting straight up.

Rooster groped with his left arm, swinging wildly, striking nothing but air.

Then—metal. The rim of the bucket. He grabbed it, threw it forward, spilling and splattering gas. His right hand held the match, but he couldn't be sure it was still lit.

Something cracked in his neck, like a small stick snapping, and the Rider's face smeared to a white glow that flooded him, smothered him. He was drowning in the light.

Rooster dropped the match.

There was a mad *whoosh*! sound, a rush of heat. The *clung*! of the van's door slamming shut—Randy out there, taking care of business, just the way Rooster had told him. The van's insides flared like a furnace.

The Moon Rider's hand pulled back.

Rooster forced his eyes open, feeling like his eyelids were on fire. And before long, he thought, they would be, but not yet, not yet, not before—

The Rider stood. He seemed to be watching the fire crawl at his legs, up his legs, flickering and dancing. And still that lifeless grin.

Rooster felt the dance begin on him too. But pain was an old companion to him, and he was a willing partner.

And now, as it turned out, the Rider *did* have a face. He could do more than grin. He could show dumb bewilderment at being hurt unexpectedly, and hurt more and more as the flames rose to swallow him.

The Rider stumbled backward, clumsily, like his feet were too big for him. He fell, flaming, staggered up again, and now the black coils of his hair and beard were snapping and streaming fire.

The Moon Rider's hands flew to his face. One of his gloves was whipped off, and Rooster saw the hand beneath it, thin and banty-wristed. The black jacket draped now like a stiff blanket thrown over the narrowing shoulders—and underneath, curling and blackening under the fire, the T-shirt read, MCNUTT'S CYCLE REPAIR.

Shrinking. The dude was *shrinking*, Rooster thought, but he was long past amazement.

The Rider dropped to his knees, arms wrapped over his

head, smoke and fire closing in around him. And he had a
voice now, or something like a voice. It was a *nuh-nuh* sound,
like a *no*! that couldn't get out past the strangling noise, and
he took a dead drop to his knees.

Rooster knew that he must have been inches away, but he
couldn't see him anymore through the smoke and ash. There
was nothing left to see, nothing left to breathe. The air was
death.

Rooster's hand closed on the grip of the revolver. His arm
came up, trailing fire from the sleeve.

The smoke swirled heavily, breaking just a moment, long
enough to show Rooster that the Rider had eyes, too, big and
wild, pleading toward him. Eyes that could only smile when
the body was being cruel, beating the shit out of somebody
who couldn't hurt back. "Candy punk," Tony would have
called him.

"Well, now, Charlie," Rooster said, hearing his voice rasp
against the insane crackle of the fire that now threaded through
his hair, redder against the red. "Let's try it again."

The revolver whammed, shooting a bolt of white flame.

The eyes in the smoke split apart, a red burst between
them, and the smoke swirled in and covered the rest of it.
Blood dripped from the barrel of the revolver and Rooster's
hand, steaming and spattering and hissing.

In a way, Rooster thought, he was being kind.

The van lurched then with the dull, angry thud of the gas
tank exploding, and Rooster felt himself lift into the air,
thrown to his feet.

And he felt himself walking in sudden, blind silence, alone,
reaching out. Until a strong, familiar hand was there, clasping his own.

Hey, man, Rooster said.

Hey, Tony.

CHAPTER TWENTY-ONE

Slowly Ransom understood that he'd killed her. The beast gave back his eyes so he could see. It gave back his voice, and he was crying.

And it gave him something else—the death of her, over and over, in perfect detail. Not as a memory. As a happening. It could do that; it could bend time. It could make him go through it again. Again.

Again . . .

The blade in his hand. He drew it along the length of his arm and watched it, wanting to scream. But the beast wouldn't let him.

Just watch, it said.

The razor cut into the pale underside of his arm, trailing a thin, bubbling wake of blood, but the skin was smooth, unbroken, untouched. The edge cut through his flesh with no more effect than a knife drawn through water, skin healing as fast as the blood ran.

And the other cuts: healed, every one of them. Even the one across his throat. .

"Keith!"

Marla's voice reached to him through the locked door of the bathroom, and his hand tightened, still gripping the razor.

Want to see magic, Marla?

There was a pounding against the door, coupled with a shrieking cry. The knob rattled.

He reached to snap open the lock.

Make you magic.

The door was hit, hard. She must have thrown herself into it, he thought, forcing it to bow inward, splintering.

Ransom glanced toward the red-spattered mirror over the sink. His face now held a whiter cast than the whites of his eyes. It blurred, made of crystal and frost.

The door jolted again, giving way even more.

He could feel the thing seizing hold of the last part of him, the last struggling portion of his mind, the last vestige of the person named Keith Ransom. It tore at him. He couldn't stop it.

The window . . . !

He yanked loose the blue-flowered curtains and thrust himself forward, headlong into the glass. His left eye flared to crimson, then went dark, but only for a moment.

He was halfway out, hands slapping red prints against the wood siding, when he heard the bathroom door slam open behind him. Then he shoved, and he was surrounded by cold air, the night's darkness, under the Devil's eye.

Now—run!

He could do that. It would let him do that. It wanted the movement, the flexing of muscle, the rhythm and the terror.

At first his ankle buckled beneath him, broken by the fall, but it mended and straightened in the middle of his first stride, bones grinding. He ran with no sense of weight, as if he had no more substance than the moon shadows that dappled the ground, dancing ahead of him and around him. But the air drummed in his ears, and his hair whipped as if blown by a storm wind. He felt like he was moving on air, but his feet, clad in shredded gray socks, struck sudden depressions into the winter-hard ground, making clacking sounds when he hit the sidewalk and street pavement.

His senses felt electric, supercharged.

Down the block he saw the biker, Joseph, posted with a shotgun by one of the elm trees that lined the street. The man was trying to crouch behind it, but his bulk made the tree look almost small.

And there, in a parked car in mid-block, Ransom saw the heavy, watching face of Lieutenant Larry Donaldson. He could *feel* the man's heartbeat quicken.

You want me? Come on, then. Follow me.

Ransom thought of the Moon Rider's glove. What had seemed a mad act—leaving the glove—now became a gesture Ransom could understand. The purpose was clear: It was the old challenge, the *dare-you* of throwing down the gauntlet.

You can't stop me, Larry. But come on and try.

The police car's headlights flashed on, catching a white skitter of motion that crossed in front of Ransom. It was Marla's cat, Strawberry, Ransom saw, just Strawberry out for a night prowl, looking for small things to fit small white teeth.

But then he saw the cat straighten, stand erect, and grin at him. The grin grew wide, wider, splitting open the animal face and lifting up the top of the head, eyes all the while dancing and glittering.

Ransom, then, knew he had stopped fighting, and he let in the final compulsion, allowed the final madness to enter him and take him over.

He became the beast.

Out for a night prowl.

Marla dropped to her knees on the cold ground and lost everything with a quickness she wouldn't have thought possible. When she looked up, nothing had changed. The window was still there, the glinting edges of broken glass, the dark streaks and smears and handprints around the white, peeling frame. More blood trailed down the side of the house, splotched and dripping. The winter-dried grass beneath the window lay crushed flat and shining dull red, reflecting the moon from a thousand small points of light.

"Keith . . . ?"

He couldn't have moved, couldn't have gone far.

She was long past crying, as if her body had simply found that it didn't help and would no longer allow it. But her eyes still burned, from the same fire that crept from the sides of her stomach and into her throat. She seemed to hurt all over, from pain felt and pain hidden.

Patches of bloodied ground led her away from the house, into the narrow front yard, to the old sidewalk, the street—

To nothing.

She looked toward the far end of the block, saw only the silent, shadowed tree-shapes, the cars parked along the curb,

houses with curtained windows that were mostly dark now.
Dimly, from somewhere down the street, came the sound of
a radio playing. Just another night on—

The gunshot wrenched a cry from her.

Marla jerked toward the sound. She wanted to think she
had imagined it, but the chorus of dog's howls told her she
hadn't.

Then a second shot, chasing the mind-echoes of the first.

She ran toward the sound, slippered feet scuffing the rough
pavement. Blue metal and checkered grip—she thought of
that. A huge, horrid gun, and the big hand that held it.
Rooster!

Close to the corner now, she could see the van, only something was . . . wrong. Something flickered inside. A mad
light playing through the side window, spilling out reds and
oranges.

The gun echoed again from inside the van. Marla was close
enough to *feel* the sound, close enough to be knocked back
by a wall of searing heat as flame licked up from under the
van. A roiling ball of fire lifted up from the buckled roof,
raining ribbons of flame onto the street. She was scarcely
aware of big arms lifting her, shaking her, carrying her on
the run.

She looked up to see Joseph. The night air cut coldly around
her, but his face shone with rivulets of sweat. Curls of long
hair stuck to his forehead and the sides of his face. They were
moving, and he was a great, thudding ball around her.

She could have drowned in dizziness. Some part of her
wanted to sink into the swirling darkness, never to come up
again. Another part of her wanted to break.

People break, she thought. They take all they can, and they
try all they can, but they reach a limit. Then they break, and
they don't have to take any more. Nothing matters anymore.

Isn't that right, Keith? People reach their limit, like a line
marked in red to make it easy. And they break if they want
to, just break, want to break, want—

Marla's head snapped at the stinging impact to the side of
her face. The second time she knew the pain came from a
slap, and she blocked the hand that would have struck her
again.

Then she heard the voice.

"—need you. *Please*, lady."

She was looking toward Joseph again. The wet curls framed an almost childlike, openmouthed nod of intended encouragement.

"Need you. Okay? You can do it. Okay, lady?"

"I think—"

"You got it."

The scene came into focus. She was back at the house, in front of it, leaning against Keith's old Datsun—and now the car's hood slammed shut. The engine was running. The other biker, Randy, moved like a shadow from the front of the car.

"You drive," Joseph said, practically shoving her behind the wheel. He ended the motion by patting her awkwardly on the shoulder.

The door slammed and he was gone. She sat there, coming awake to the rattling of the cold, balking motor, watching the surreal play of colors at the end of the block.

It was almost pretty, Marla thought. It could be pretty if you just thought of the colors and not the smell of burning. Of death.

Lights were coming on in houses. Front doors opened along the street.

Beside her, outside the open car window, Randy watched along with her. "Ol' Rooster, he would have *loved* this," he said, glancing toward her. "Damn, can't you hear 'im? Laughin' his balls off. What a circus."

"Rooster . . . ?" Marla said, knowing the answer.

Randy swung onto his bike with a creaking of leather, kicked the starter, gunned a roar from the engine. Lifting his arm in a closed-fist salute, he said, "Ride with the wind, brother."

Marla felt tears starting. She tried to give them names—for Keith, for Rooster, for me—but the names and the tears ran together, and the colors blurred, pretty colors.

It was Joseph she saw coming out of the fire-painting, a load in his arms that took shape as a body—

Keith!

The figure broke loose and began struggling with Joseph, right in the middle of Rockford Street. It was Elizabeth—Marla could see that now—screaming at Joseph, fighting, trying to force her way past his bulk back to the blazing van.

As Marla watched, Joseph got a headlock on Elizabeth and began dragging her with lumbering steps toward the car, past the neighbors who now lined the streets. Not a soul tried to stop him.

They fell with a rocking thud against the Datsun, and Randy, on his bike, was laughing. "Rooster was the only one ever could handle that one," he said.

Elizabeth's eyes flashed violence. Randy shut up, and Joseph let go of her.

"The man was dead a long time ago," Randy said over the idling rumble of the bike. "You know that. He knew it. We've said our good-byes, and we'll pay our respects in the way that he wanted. And that is to get the hell out of here."

Elizabeth looked toward Marla, and Marla saw for the first time the bloodied angry bruise that spread across the side of her face, the hollowed cast of her eyes, funereal eyes that tried for a look of surprise.

"You don't belong here," Elizabeth said.

Joseph pursed his lips and shrugged. "We thought you'd want to ride in a car . . . after . . ."

Elizabeth's hands quivered, as if they were trying to get hold of some small thing in the air, and then knotted to fists. She struck at Joseph's face again and again. He stood there and took it.

"I don't need help. You *hear* me?" she said, punctuating her words with blows. "I am still Rooster's lady. And that means I . . . don't . . . need . . . help—not ever."

Marla heard the sirens coming closer.

"I do," she said. "I do . . . need . . ."

Down the street, past lighted windows, the sound of a guitar, the sight of toys and a backyard sandbox in the dark; across the Reinholdt practice field, the campus oval, Mc-Kendrick Hall, the humming red neon of the Keg 'n' Pizza, and *high*! over the hedge wall.

Ransom dropped to a crouch in the safety-lit parking lot of the sprawling Aspen Meadows Apartments. Rich-kid city. He stripped off the bloody remnants of his shirt as a baby-blue Datsun Z wheeled past, wafting the voice of Billy Joel into the night air.

The car made a neat turn into a neatly striped parking space; the taillights winked out.

The doors clicked open.

Driver's side first, and the girl who stepped out wore a creamy-beige cape-coat that swirled as she reached for her notebook and purse. Toby Harris was with her. Ransom knew Toby from the film class; he had plans of being a screenwriter. He didn't know the girl. But he could taste the red warmth of her.

He watched from the shadows, between a sports car and Brat pickup, while the couple stood across the lot whispering. As if he couldn't hear them.

Toby's arm was around her now, as they walked toward the complex. Ransom wanted to laugh then. He couldn't, but he wanted to—at himself, and so many, so damn many shadow-fears; at himself and the way that he'd fought it. The change.

He'd been so afraid. Afraid of giving in to it, afraid that his mind would be lost, that he would go raving and drooling over the countryside like the monster in *Curse of the Were-wolf*. Or like a zombie, powerless, forced to stumble around blindly doing whatever its master bid.

But it was nothing like that. He felt like himself, only better. Sharper. That was the word for it—*sharper*, like a knife's edge.

Top of the line.

He could remember . . . freckle-faced Toby. The film class. Everything . . . and why not? The difference was that he knew the secret now. Dr. Bergman had said that compulsion meant weakness, but only the voice of the moon told the truth.

It told him now. What to do.

Ransom crossed the lot as softly as moonlight toward the walking couple. They might have heard the whispering scrape of the nails on his feet against the paved ground, had they been listening for it. But they hadn't; they never turned.

They almost could have felt his breath against them.

The moon told him now, as it always had, every time it came full. Grab the card, buy the car, sell the song, get the job. And Marla, sweet Marla . . . the wine of obsession . . .

The compulsion that held him now was nothing so different, this night of the full moon. It was an ache, a void, a

burning, something invisible and just beyond his touch, like
always, and, especially like the past few months, stronger
with each full moon.

The voice told him, *Give in.*

He reached, twining the girl's honey hair lightly into his
fingers, so lightly that his hand would have felt to her like
nothing but the night wind. She was talking about changing
majors, worried that she would never be good at math but
would lose a year in changing to education or maybe psy-
chology. She had to decide in the next week.

They were close to the curb now, and the curving walk that
led into the cluster of redbrick apartments.

The moon told him, *Give in.* But giving in wasn't a weakness—Ransom knew that now. Giving in made you strong.
Strength was having what you wanted to have. And strength
was—

Ransom tightened his hold. The girl's head jerked back,
and she let out a squeal of surprise.

Strength was the twist of one hand—just the flex of his
wrist that in another second would have ended for her the
trouble of deciding majors.

But, no. Not her. He could have what he wanted, exactly.
She wasn't the one that he'd come for. He had to remember
his purpose, of course; he was much too sharp just to move
randomly.

The girl swung around, swatting at the cold air in the place
where Ransom's hand had been, striking only the glitters of
ice.

"What is it?" Toby asked.

"I don't—" She looked at him dumbly a moment, then
caught herself and gave a small shrug. She laughed, just a
little too loudly. "I don't know," she said.

Ransom peered from the darkness at the side of the apartment house, just beyond the reach of the light mounted to the
wall overhead. He noticed that the light splayed across a series of wood-scripted letters that read ASPEN MEADOWS, and
down, making each of the bricks seem to stand out in shadowed perfection.

The voice screamed in rage at him. It tried to hurt him,
but he couldn't be hurt. He wasn't some pathetic fool to be
driven mad, like McGivern.

His thoughts were in place like the bricks, perfect and bright. He knew what he wanted.

Marla had never ridden on the back of a motorcycle before. It felt like a carnival ride, only out of control, and it felt like being on top of something alive, some kind of wild thing that roared into the night.

She bent forward, pressing against Joseph, trying to reach far enough to lock one hand on to the other. *Buckle up for safety.* But he was too big around, and every time they took a corner, Marla jammed her eyes shut and held her breath and tried not to think of herself being thrown, rolling, onto the street.

She couldn't see a thing ahead—just the cold black leather that stretched across the wall of Joseph's back. The wind made his long hair stream and snap. It stung the side of her face. Houses, lighted signs, passing cars, all smeared together.

But she *had* to keep watch.

She could have missed him already. She could have been looking the wrong way, and never be allowed another chance.

It wasn't much of a plan. Marla corrected herself—it was *no* plan. They didn't have a single goddamn plan that made sense. *Forgive me, God, forgive me*, she thought. But how could there be any *plan*?

You don't plan for madness. You don't see it coming, or don't want to see it, or can't stop it, anyway. You don't have a plan that reads, What to Do When Keith Goes Mad. *And the world along with him.*

But the blood led to the street, so—

They would crisscross the neighborhood in a widening pattern toward the Reinholdt campus, because Joseph had seen a kind of movement on the street that might have been Keith going in that direction.

"Shit, no, it didn't look like him. It was . . . like a shadow, real quick. And I wasn't out watching for shadows. Right? But there it went."

One shadow. And a car, pulling out from the curb at the same time, forcing Joseph to hunker out of sight behind the hedgerow, shotgun squeezed into the fold of his belly.

It might have been Keith, that shadow.

Marla shot a look behind her, into the glaring eye of the
headlamp on Randy's bike, the figure of Elizabeth behind
him. To the side, the yellow blur of a Winchell's Donut Shop.

Might have been—

Her stomach lurched sideways as Joseph cut a turn onto
another residential street, an old one, with double rows of
decaying brick houses, porch swings here and there, hanging
plants silhouetted inside the warm, lighted windows.

Might have—

And what did she expect? That she would look to just the
right place and Keith would be there, giving a wave?

God, no, she thought. *Forgive me.*

Keith was dead.

He shouldn't have been able to get up at all, should have
been dead on the ground outside the window, God help him.
But he was dead now, and they would never find him, not
searching like this.

No more the quick wit, the soft looks, no more the touch
of him, his voice speaking her name. No more the comics,
the movies, the Christmas tree. No more the nightmares.

No more.

From ahead came the red neon sign of the Keg 'n' Pizza,
flashing from side to side. Keg . . . Pizza . . . Keg . . .

She had a plan now.

Marla risked letting go with one hand to slap Joseph on the
shoulder, pointing toward the off-campus restaurant with its
scattering of cars parked outside.

She would go in and call the police.

It wouldn't have to sound so crazy. Maybe she could talk
to Lieutenant Donaldson; he seemed to know a lot about
Keith, and he would get things done, even if he didn't do
them in a kindly way. Even if he didn't once believe her.

Joseph and Randy . . . Elizabeth . . . could be gone in the
meantime. They should be gone already, anyway.

There. A plan.

Any better ideas, Keith? she thought.

Marla felt a coolness, a calmness, as the bike slowed to a
rumble, pulling toward the restaurant. She could hear the
jukebox playing from inside, and the air smelled warm and
spicy.

• • •

The courtyard blurred past him. He wasn't aware of his
body in motion, only the blanking of space between him and
Wendy Layton's apartment, and he thought of red mittens.

He stopped, looking around. The apartments surrounded
the courtyard and a swimming pool, rimmed with bare trees
that stirred with a brittle creaking. It was a toy-sized pool,
made for showing off suntans in small suits that never got
wet. But the lounge chairs were put away now, the umbrellas
taken down. A dangling row of lanterns swayed over the
memory of summer, glinting moonlight.

Something moved at the far end of the walkway, coming
toward him. Fast. Running.

Ransom knew the figure. He could make out the bulky-
coated shape of Larry Donaldson, and Donaldson's face,
etched in frost-white lines. Under his glasses the cop's eyes
were narrowed and darting—he couldn't see through the night,
beyond the yellowed haze of the nearest yard light.

Donaldson's breath came in hard gasps that gave way to
coughing. He bent, hands braced on his knees, and Ransom
saw the blue-metal gleam of a revolver clasped in the detective's right hand.

Donaldson straightened, wiping at his mouth with the back
of his gun hand. He craned to the side, where another hedge-
lined walkway led to a different block of apartments. Hesi-
tating, he looked past the courtyard and directly toward
Ransom but blindly; when he moved again, it was with a
lurching run that took him out of sight between the buildings.

Ransom turned, and his foot struck the base of a Hasty
Bake grill, with a clank and crunching of dried leaves that he
thought would surely bring Donaldson back. But he didn't
wait to see; he didn't care. That game was over.

He took the leap easily, catching hold of the ledge that
projected from the second floor, pulling himself over the or-
namented iron fencework and onto the balcony patio. Standing there a moment, he heard the faraway, singsong wailings
of an assembly of sirens—fire, police maybe, and the banshee
cry of an ambulance—converging at a point that seemed to
be near his own house. Ransom thought of going home then.
He wanted that too.

Marla, stop me. Make it stop. Can't you?

A dim light played through the curtains and the glass of the patio door, but no sound came from inside. Ransom tried the door. It was locked, and he saw that it was also braced with a length of wood inside to bar it from moving. Still, he didn't have to break the glass. The impact of his hand against the door's handle tore loose the metal track at the top, ripping the lock, and the door fell with a soft thud onto the orange shag carpeting, taking the curtains with it.

Neatness counts. You will be graded ten percent for neatness.

Inside, he saw an end table lamp switched on, the only light in the room. The sofa, with big, crazy-patterned pillows scattered around it; schoolbooks and a briefcase on the coffee table; stereo turntable spinning but the records played out. The air was drunk with incense.

A shuffling sound came from the hallway that led to the bedroom.

He would have called to her, but the sound of her name turned to a rasping deep in his throat, and came spattering out of his mouth in a white, bubbling froth.

And it wasn't Wendy standing there in front of him.

Morris Thurman seemed carved from pale stone, hands frozen in the act of knotting the belt of a brown velvet bathrobe. The silver-haired Thurman—a study in frenzied, changing expressions. There was the tight-mouthed fright of a man caught in what Thurman himself might have termed "compromising circumstances," changing to a drop-jawed look of disbelief, and then . . . the warping of his face to something not really human, made worse by the raking of his hands against the slack skin under his eyes.

And Ransom was on him.

Thurman tried to scream once—a jabbering not quite up to the standards of *The Lyric Echo*, Ransom thought—before his lips were stitched shut by a webbing of white threads. His mouth opened only enough to show the squirming of pearl-white legs from within.

It was finished too quickly, Ransom thought. A good, last lesson from his department chairman. *Take your time—savor the next one.*

Ransom withdrew his hand from under the heavy, wet bathrobe, pulled it free with a sucking sound. Stepping over the body, he confronted the closed door of the bedroom. The door was covered with a poster showing a unicorn in a garden of roses. The colors were nice.

"What the hell is going on out there?"

Wendy's voice carried through to him with an odd shrillness, a slapstick attempt to sound threatening. She must have known something was wrong, he thought, must have heard the rasping of his breath.

"Answer me!"

Ransom forced a burst of air out of his throat, shaping it to the name she trusted.

"It's Keith."

A long, mindless pause. "Keith . . . ?" She was close to the door, he thought—inches away. Maybe she had nothing on. He wanted the sight of her then; his blood surged at the thought.

"Keith, how did you—I mean, did you break in, or what? It's not funny."

He tapped a little rhythm on the unicorn's eye.

"It's not funny, Keith."

His nails drew clean cuts through the paper.

"Get out of here. Right now. Just get your ass out of here and leave us . . . leave . . . *dammit!*" The door whammed with the sound of a hard kick. "What about *him*? What became of him?"

Ransom forced the word. "Gone."

"You didn't . . . hurt him, did you? Not like . . ."

"Gone."

Her voice became whisperlike, laced with the hint of a shared amusement. "Gone off in his bathrobe," she said from behind the door. "You know, Keith, he brought along, like, an overnight case, and he put all his clothes up on hangers. That's all he got done."

Ransom heard steps in her room, and the rustle of clothing. When she spoke again, the voice seemed farther away.

"You wouldn't get rid of him that way . . . *would* you, Keith?"

More steps, and the click of the lock opening. He wouldn't have thought she would have had a locking door. A revolving one, maybe.

"Keith, just to have it said . . . about Morris Thurman. It was like Bozo the Clown time in here. He was a joke—hell, *you* know that. But he was the joke that could get me the Bellem scholarship for grad school.''

The door edged open. Ransom glimpsed red satin.

''So much for *that* idea, thanks to you. I think you might owe me something, *Mr.* Ransom. Some consolation, let's say, for—''

The door swung wide, and he gave her a second to look at him. Her eyes, huge and bright, cast back the ice-white of his own face.

A downward, ripping motion, and the satin hung in tatters from his hand.

She was on the floor, unmoving, looking up at him. Ransom thought she must have felt like she was in a nightmare, one of those where you can't move, or you move with a terrible slowness, and something big and fast and murderous is coming to get you. She was probably telling herself that's what it was, and that it couldn't really hurt. She probably thought she would wake up, feeling angry at herself for having lost control, for being scared. She would snap on the light at her bedside, let a cigarette burn to the filter, leaving a small black wedge on the side of the bed table; and she would think about things that she wanted, and how to have those things, every one of them.

Ransom knew the feeling. Better than she did.

Sometimes when it was him awake at night, Ransom had thought about Wendy, wanting her. Wendy . . . and Marla. Two parts of the whole. But it wasn't like wanting them both at once, both in bed with him—that didn't work even as dark-of-the-night, midnight make-believe. Marla was everything good to him, and Wendy was . . . everything wrong with him. But you had to have both, had to collect the matched set. That's what made a collection; you didn't have to like every part of it, but you couldn't leave anything out, or the voice deep inside would keep telling you, tellingyoutelling-you, keeping you up at night, telling you, burning inside of you, telling you, *Got to have, got to have, gotta.*

Want you, Wendy. Gotta, Wendy.

GOTTA!

She fought him, and it wasn't cute. She meant to kill him. Wendy knew the voice, too, he thought, maybe not as a scream but as a whisper. She was too much the same as him not to have known, and she must have had some of the strength. Wendy's hands glistened red, the fingers hooked like scythes, tearing at him.

There was a delicate blue vein that ran up the side of her left breast, and he traced it with the point of a clawed finger. The hand sunk into her. Bone cracked; muscle split. His hand gripped the hammering motor of Wendy's heart, and crushed it.

The orange shag darkened around her. She was still now, and white, so white, like the color of moonlight, with sparkles of ice on her face, and tears that ran softly, even in death. Then the tears stopped.

Slowly he understood that he'd killed her. He could see that. The beast let him see; it let him cry.

And again, *again*—!

"RANSOM!"

He jerked toward the sound of the voice. It was behind him, down the short hallway, past the twisted remains of Morris Thurman. Donaldson stood there, both hands clenching the revolver, the barrel of it pointed toward Ransom like a small, gray finger. The barrel shook, like Donaldson was fighting with some force that wanted to yank it away from him.

"*Stand up*, you—get away from her, you son of a—"

Donaldson's face blanched at the sight of Wendy, his mouth screwing up in a tightened mass of lines like he might drop to his knees and throw his guts up. But he didn't. He seemed to get hold of himself with the suddenness of a cord drawn tight to the breaking point.

The revolver leveled at Ransom's chest. "Gimme a reason," Donaldson said. "Damn you! *Try* for me."

Ransom wiped his hands across his bare chest. The skin was hot, slick with blood and perspiration. He could feel the blood rushing, pounding through him.

"Do it," he said. "Do it now, or get out of here. You don't know—"

"I *know*, God help me. Too late for them. But not for you, Ransom." Donaldson cleared the sweat from his face with a snapping shake of his head, his glasses foggy. He looked like a tired old dog, out for one last hunt.

"Got a call from some of your neighbors, Ransom . . . said your biker pals were out squirreling around, and the fat one had a shotgun. Otherwise I might not have been out there, checking things out, when you came through the window. But I might have been, anyway. I've been out there a lot. Watching. Waiting for you. You never did throw me off, Ransom—I want you to know that. I want you to scream in hell knowing that."

Ransom felt a cold throbbing inside his eyes, coupled with a sudden rush of strength. He seemed to be lifting off the floor—but it wasn't that. Something inside him— *pressing,* trying to get out.

Donaldson's head tilted back, and he staggered, like some monster-sized jack-in-the-box had sprung up in front of him.

The revolver cracked. Ransom felt the bullet strike him in the neck, the impact knocking him backward. A terrible, dull weight of pain smashed his throat, but the pain gave way to a new rush of breath.

The second shot whined past his face. Third—

Caught him square in the mouth. Ransom heard more than felt the sharp sound of his skull splintering open from the back, and he welcomed the darkness.

The coming of night.

The night of no sky.

Still, the voice screamed inside of him, screamed from the darkness. Screamed, changing pitch as his blind, groping hands caught the fabric of Donaldson's coat, tearing.

Her name. Again and again and again.

Marla!

MARLA!

As Joseph's bike slowed for the Keg 'n' Pizza parking lot, Marla glanced back to see if Randy and Elizabeth were following. At that same instant a white shape struck the side of Randy's bike, lifting the wheels sideways and smashing the bike onto the pavement. It thrashed like a shark out of water, throwing sparks and metal. As Randy toppled, the back wheel caught his hair, and he jerked like a doll, his face slamming into the howling tread. The motor halted with a *whumpf*! sound, caught again, sending blood spraying into the air.

Paralyzed, Marla watched as Elizabeth rolled over the pavement and onto her feet, but not before the white shape was on her. A ghost shape. A thing of smoke and ice. Hands locked around Elizabeth's throat, lifting her.

"Keith, *no*!" The words exploded from Marla, ringing in her mind.

And he turned toward her, a scant few feet away.

"Keith . . . ?"

He moved like a shifting of light. It was as if Marla were looking at him through frosted glass, his face there, but dim, distorted. The face was Keith's, but the eyes were glinting ice. The voice belonged to someone—something—else.

"Run," it said.

The word seemed to echo from nowhere and everywhere, like the rolling of thunder on a summer's night.

"Like friggin *hell*!"

The answer was Joseph's. With a shove he knocked Marla from the rear of the bike and wheeled in a circle. The engine screamed; blue smoke churned the air. Joseph barreled straight ahead, with a bellow that carried over the bike, ramming Keith head-on.

Marla saw Elizabeth thrown free to the side, the bike lurching nose-down, Joseph falling like a boulder onto the pavement. There were shouts and cries from the front of the restaurant, people swarming the sidewalk—an explosion of images and sounds that Marla's numbed senses froze to a single moment of horror.

The bike struck Keith's left hand at full speed, and the hand splintered off. His wrist broke with a hard crack! that she heard over everything else. But when the hand came loose, there was no blood, not at first, just a burst of white glitter, like crystals of ice.

Then, blood. Tracing circles of red as the hand fell, writhing, grasping at the air. It clawed and curled against the street, dying finally with a spasm, like the final death twitch of an animal.

Keith stood, pointing the severed wrist toward Marla as if it were nothing.

The welling of blood stopped. The wrist crusted to black, and a pale, trembling thing broke the crust, twisting outward like a tendril, taking shape as palm and fingers.

It pointed toward her.

''*Run!*'' he said.

He let her go, let her run, gagging and crying, until she thought she might get away, and then he bore down on her. Out of the moon shadows he came for her . . .

It was what the moon promised—a nightmare come true to the smallest detail, to the frost of his breath, and the surge of her screams, and the cold light around them.

. . . giving her time to turn, to know him . . .

He knew what came next.

He knew, and he couldn't stop it.

. . . and he was on her—

He let her run as far as the campus oval, just past the stilled fountain, where the ground declined softly into a manicured, circular walkway called the Rose Path. There weren't any roses now. Bare branches and thorns lined the walkway, tearing at skin and clothing, as he lunged toward her and brought her down.

When her eyes went wide, they gleamed of moonlight . . .

Ransom clung to the hope that he might be insane.

. . . his teeth sank into her throat . . .

That what he would do to her

. . . softness giving way . . .

might be real just to him. Not to her. Might be only the ravings of a lunatic, locked away, and there never was a Marla.

Or there was, and he'd killed her, but not like this. He'd killed her and gone mad, turning loose the monster inside him that could bend time—that could make him go through it all again.

And again.

Or the ultimate lunacy: that it was real every time.

. . . softness giving way . . .

Not a vision, that night on the Arkansas roadside, not a

flash of cruel madness. The ultimate lunacy: Marla had died then, just as she would now, again.

And it might never stop.

The voice. *Marla, do you hear the voice? I don't want to do what it tells me, Marla, but it hurts. It always did. I can't make it stop.*

Don't you hear it?

Give in.

Hear it?

GIVE IN!

He rolled back his head. The moon hung, immense, like a mad face above him—a face of frost eyes and white, murdering teeth, telling him, telling him . . .

The way.

The strength of madness.

The answer at last. It came pounding through him. There was no escape from the twisting terror of lunacy. Not for him. No exit. But the way *in* was open, always open, as deep and black as the night sky, and he was still fighting back, poised on the edge of it, pulling back from the rim of the black, sucking pit that beckoned him.

It was so easy. He simply let himself fall.

With a scream toward the moon he fell, tumbling. With the strength of his madness he would blind the Devil's eye. He would fall to the bottom of the void where the beast lived, where the beast might be killed.

He let her go, let her run, gagging and crying . . .

But they weren't on the oval now; they were at McIntosh Elementary, out by the bike rack. All he wanted to do was show her . . .

See, Marla?

He crinkled off the bright, waxy paper from the package of baseball cards. He could see—and his heart tripped—the signature across the bottom of the first card. Wayne Terwilliger.

But as he peeled the rest of the paper back, he saw that the face wasn't Terwilliger's. It belonged to Dr. Bergman.

"Got to learn to fit in, boy," Dr. Bergman said. The doctor's head was framed by hanging ivy; plants were supposed to be soothing. "Fit in, not *give in*. Now, I'll say a word, and you tell me if you know what it means."

Something small, like a bead of white, dropped from the ivy.

"*Compulsion*," the doctor said.

The bead was a spider. It leapt onto the doctor's shoulder and began climbing up his neck, leaving a series of red welts. Just below a neatly clipped sideburn, the spider stopped a moment, legs twitching, and then crawled into Dr. Bergman's ear.

"The word is *compulsion*."

More beads, dropping like slow rain. Dr. Bergman brushed at them, until they webbed his arms to the chair; he looked coldly toward Ransom, even as the spiders wrapped him white, the biggest one of all settling on him.

"*Compulsion*," the doctor said.

And a second voice. "Keith!" Marla clasped him. "Keith, look what I've done." She drew back the cloth covering from the easel, stirring the sharp scent of oil paints.

The canvas beneath was a portrait of him. The eyes were like frost, crystalline and glittering.

"I finally got it finished. Do you like it?" she asked.

"It needs something," Randy said to him. He stood beside Ransom, his voice making bubbles of blood. His face was a red smear, broken by the scraped white of his forehead and cheekbones.

Randy spoke again. "Needs a li'l something, man." A blade flicked open from his hand, and he slashed at the throat of the painting. Ransom felt the cold slicing, the blood that spilled from between his fingers, as he tried to hold the wound closed.

"Much better," Morris Thurman said. But the voice came from the moving mouth of a silvery Persian cat, cradled in the arms of Ida Milburn.

Setting the cat down, she said, "He likes a treat, this one does."

The cat began lapping at Ransom's blood. A pool of it on the floor, shimmering at the touch of the animal's tongue. It danced with ripples of light, and then it was all light; it was round and white and suspended above him.

. . . softness giving way . . .

The night air bore a stinging chill, and there were voices all around him, coming from a circle of school desks. The students were shadowed silhouettes, but he knew them all—Toby Harris, John Walkingdeer, Diana Kendall; the whole class watching him. Toby's hand was up.

"Wendy's not here, Mr. Ransom," he said.

Another hand waved in the darkness, another voice. "Want to know why?"

Ben Taylor stepped forward, moonlight illuminating his grin. "Want to know why?" he asked. His square jaw dropped open at a broken angle; his tongue reached out, stretching to touch the lower teeth and dripping red.

Taylor pointed to the ground beneath Ransom.

"Don't look, Keith," Marla said. But she was too late—he couldn't stop now.

"Don't look—"

He clicked the door open. The bottom of it swished lightly against the orange shag and opened to show him the face of a monster.

Himself.

"Run," it said, eyes gleaming.

They were standing by the fountain in the campus oval. The moon swelled as if to crush them.

"Run."

Marla pulled at him, desperate hands clutching. "Keith, you can't fight it. Got to run, Keith. Both of us. *Run!* Or we don't have a chance, Keith!"

Out of the moon shadows—it came for her, ripping at her. But Ransom was there with claws of his own, tearing into the moon-beast.

The final compuslion—to see it dead, to strangle the life from it, crush the force of it. *Gotta!*

He slashed, and the beast screamed in rage. A burst of light caught the grounds like a lightning flash.

GOTTA!

The beast tried to throw him off, but it couldn't be done. Ransom knew what he wanted. He clung as the beast straightened. He tore at the scaled wings that split the surface of the wide, muscled back; he ripped at the neck as it lengthened, snaking the head toward him.

The dragon's jaws gaped open above him, even as it lifted from the ground with a blast of wind from the great, glittering wings.

Ransom allowed himself the small sanity of a last look toward Marla.

He couldn't see her, not really. But he knew she was there, by the fountain, as the campus fell beneath him, the rooftops of Reinholdt giving way to the light-dots of the city, the blue, curving line of the horizon, the night stars, the full moon. He knew she was there, looking up toward him. She might never again feel safe from the grasp of madness.

But she *was* safe.

He would make sure of it.

And he went for the heart of the dragon.

CHAPTER TWENTY-TWO

Tulsa, OK—State and federal officers have joined the search for a Tulsa man charged in a Thursday night murder rampage that claimed at least four lives.

Police named Keith E. Ransom, 34, former Reinholdt University faculty member, as wanted under warrant for the killings of Morris Thurman, 57, chairman of the Reinholdt English Department; Wendy Diane Layton, 22, a Reinholdt senior and editor of the campus newspaper; and Lieutenant Larry Donaldson, 45, a ten-year veteran of the Tulsa Police Department.

All three bodies were found in Layton's apartment in the Aspen Meadows complex near the university.

Investigators termed the murder scene a "massacre," describing the bodies as "torn and dismembered."

Ransom is also charged in the death of a California motorcyclist, Randall Wycoff, accused of having caused the fatal collision of Wycoff's motorcycle.

Wycoff was one of at least a dozen people allegedly attacked by Ransom in front of the Keg 'n' Pizza restaurant in what police called a "bloodbath."

Some of those injured were hurt in trying to subdue the suspect, police said; some were attacked in what seemed to be "sheer madness."

Also, Ransom is sought in connection with the explosion of a Dodge van less than a block from Ransom's address, 6717 South Rockford Street.

Police said two bodies were found in the van, burned beyond recognition. Neither has been identified, but they are believed to have been members, along with Wycoff, of a California motorcycle gang called the Satyrs.

A third member of the Satyrs, and a female companion, were among those injured in the struggle with Ransom, police said. Both disappeared from the emergency room of . . .

• • •

Thursday night's sudden "bloody red" coloring of the full moon was due to a dust layer in the atmosphere, Reinholdt University meteorology instructor David Holstrom explained.

Police, the National Weather Service, and other agencies reported answering dozens of calls about the moon's appearance.

The "red effect" is common when the moon is seen close to the horizon, because of the density of the atmosphere, Holstrom said.

"I have never seen the effect take place before in center sky, or so quickly," he said. "The only explanation . . ."

• • •

. . . confirmed that the New York publisher has negotiated a "six-figure" advance for the book, to be completed by Marla Ransom, wife of the escaped mass slaying suspect.

Mrs. Ransom has repeatedly told reporters that she believes Ransom is dead. But she refused to be interviewed about the still unsolved "full-moon" killings.

The publishing house spokesman said Mrs. Ransom would be working from notes and a partially completed manuscript that Ransom assembled shortly before the night of violence.

He said she also intends writing a "personal section," describing Ransom "as she knew him—a man of torment, compulsion, intelligence, kindness, and great courage."

The money will be given to research on the "mental

stress factor of the full moon'' through the Chester A. McGivern Foundation, a charitable . . .

• • •

Fire-breathing dragons are terrorizing the night skies of America!!! *The Midnight Enquirer* has learned exclusively . . .